Price of Innocence

Price of Innocence

Book One of Sonder's Song

Michelle Piper

Lorist House Media

Price of Innocence (Sonder's Song, Book One)
Published by Lorist Media House Second Edition, August 2022
Denver, CO

ISBN: 979-8-9866761-2-8
E-ISBN: 979-8-9866761-0-4

Cover illustration by Caleb Goessens and Michelle Piper. Cover formatting by Dragan Bilic. Edited by Dylan Garity. Internal maps by Dewi Hargreaves. Internal design and illustrations done by
Michelle Piper

Because like you, this book is many beginnings.
You were my new beginning.

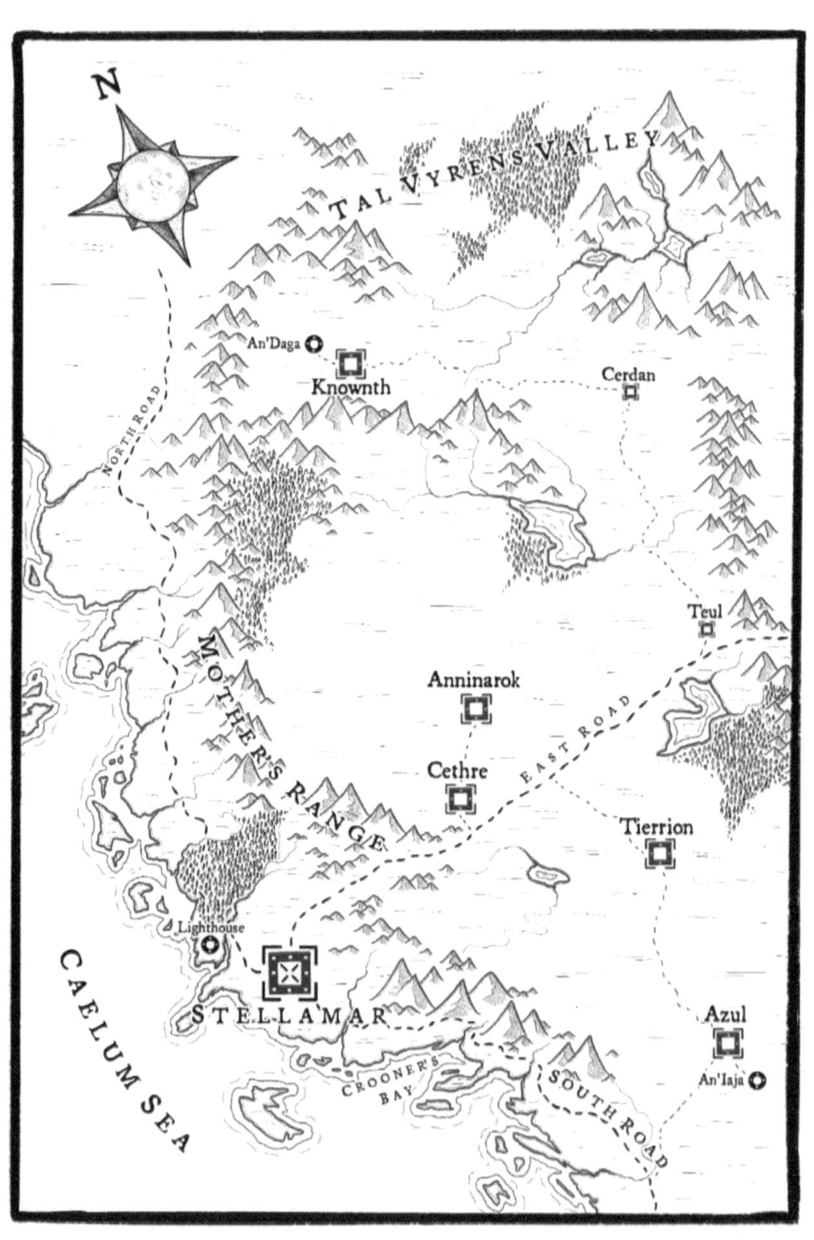

N
TAL VYREN'S VALLEY
NORTH ROAD
An'Daga
Knownth
Cerdan
MOTHER'S RANGE
Teul
Anninarok
Cethre
EAST ROAD
Tierrion
Lighthouse
STELLAMAR
Azul
An'Iaja
CAELUM SEA
CROONER'S BAY
SOUTH ROAD

Bran's personal map

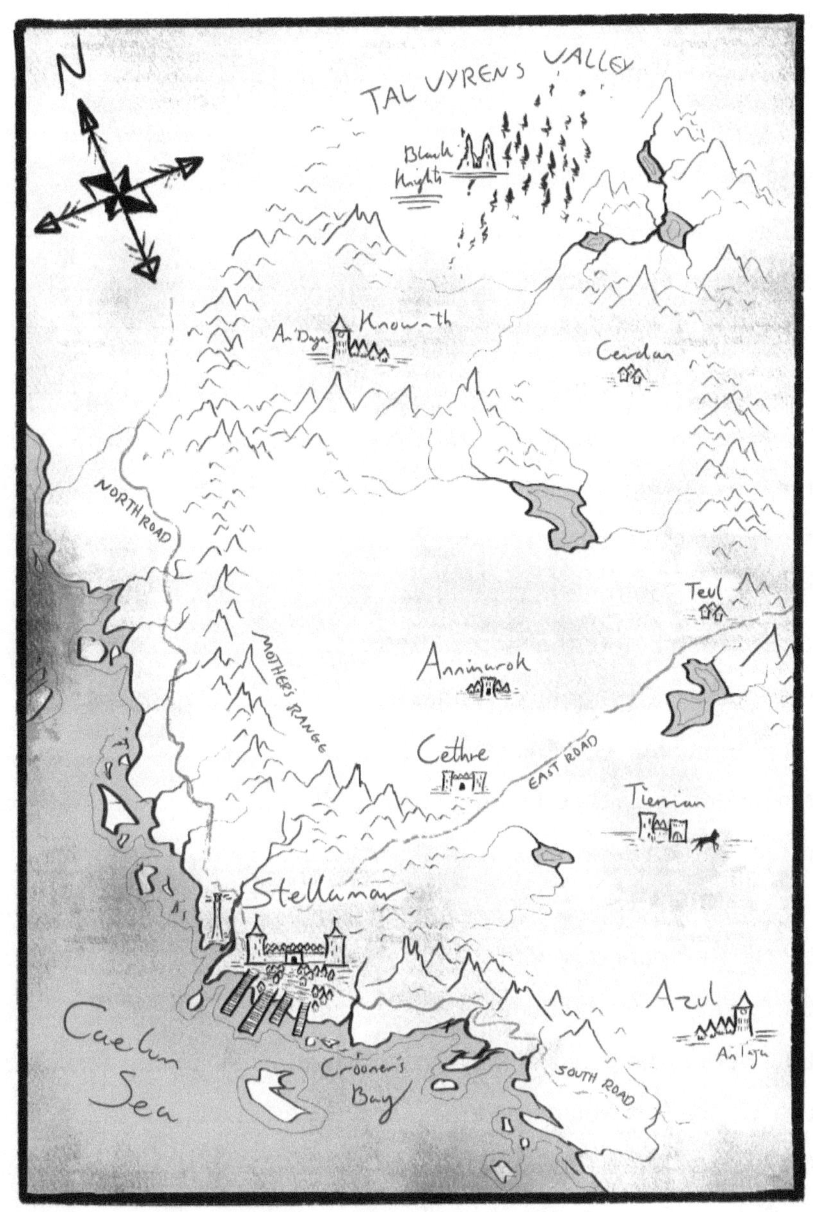

Contents

Chapter Zero
And the Last Stars Fell

A man walked through the castle, and the shadows watched.

Unlit torches filled the long corridor leading to the queen's chambers. Ribbons of sunlight filtered through the barred windows. Between each pane of glass, dusk stretched across the bare stone floor, leaving plenty of space for the creatures of stillness to gather. They lurked throughout the castle, but here they were supercharged, like the gathering of a thunderstorm in the desert. They crawled along the walls and whispered eagerly, waiting for the bolt of lightning to open the skies.

Raolin rounded the corner and headed toward the heavy wood doors. His boots echoed ahead and behind, sounding like guards flanking him, though he walked alone. The shadow-creatures parted around him, then filled the space in his wake.

He wore a quilted tunic. At his hip was a sword in a worn scabbard. The blade was what the walls watched. It had been made especially for his order, magically wrought to hold its edge better than most. The wink of black steel gave it away—as if his all-black clothing wasn't enough, or the Black Knight sigil stitched onto his left breast.

It was not by chance that one wore that seal. Sosten's sea dragon twined around a halberd, and Phyrias, the North Star, stitched over his heart, meant far less.

His face was aged and weathered, with gray beginning to pepper the brunette of his beard. Every fiber of his body spoke confidence, yet his hazel eyes betrayed his hesitance.

At the end of the corridor was a single guard. The setting sun made his standard steel armor appear gilded. Delicate details etched into the breastplate marked him as a castle guard. The half helm concealed most of his face, leaving only his nose and mouth visible, set in a firm line. He held a double-handed sword loosely, with the point resting on the stone floor. Raolin cringed as he approached. Although he knew the sword was imbued similarly to his, it was poor practice and a crude display of Aspera's power.

Finally, his path ended with them standing face-to-face.

Ordinarily, the guard would have raised his sword and barred the path of anyone approaching. Instead, neither moved as the stillness reclaimed the space. Long seconds crept by. The more that passed, the more the face of the black knight began to age, his weariness breaking through. Finally, just before the sound of the silence became stifling, the guard's rigidity caved.

Armor joints creaked as his body shifted like a plant leaning toward the sun. His gaze fell to the black sword. "Why are you here, Sir Raolin?"

For another long moment, Raolin remained silent. "She said it was about my brother." Despite his visible exhaustion, he still carried himself resolutely.

The guard looked up with admiration, but a deep concern darkened his face. He spoke quietly but firmly. "You should leave."

Raolin's jaw set, the muscles clenching and releasing. Given the current political climate, it would be impossible to flee the capital without help. The lines of who to trust were rapidly deteriorating.

"I shouldn't have come, Tristian, but I must know what happened to Lucrid. He is my brother despite all he has done as the Black Daemon," he said, finally meeting the guard's gaze.

Anxiety wrenched Tristian's face. "Please, sir. You can still leave the city and find a haven. My father has always been friends with yours."

Raolin smiled, but his mood remained tired and unchanged. For every family willing to help him, more would be quick to report him for the queen's favor. He laid a heavy hand on the young man's shoulder. "I have to know." His hand fell away, and his face hardened again. "Compose yourself. You're a soldier in the royal guard—you should act like it. Be glad these doors permit no sound."

The guard straightened. He turned toward the door and lifted a heavy knocker with militant crispness. Three times he let it fall with a rhythmic boom. A small rap responded. Tristian turned to stand at attention, and his eyes met the older man's once more.

Another brief, reassuring hand fell on the boy's shoulder—boy to him, anyway. Raolin took a second to settle his nerves before pushing the heavy doors open. Then, with confident strides, he entered the room and passed the two guards flanking the doors on the inside. Unlike Tristian, this pair was unwavering. They stood like stone and radiated the same unforgiving chill.

Heavy curtains were drawn halfway over the windows, shrouding the room in a hazy dimness against the brightness he came from. Raolin's eyes refused to adjust, only seeing a short distance past the foyer. A subtle sweetness hung in the air, mingling with musky wood. He could hear the swish of silk in the hush. The sensation of his skin crawling was heightened here. The conversation with Tristian had chafed him, but with hands clasped, he waited.

Time crept by. It gave Raolin time to remind himself of every precaution he knew to take with the queen and how woefully inadequate he felt.

Finally, the padding of bare feet advanced toward him. A shadow materialized, wearing a smile that reflected the light spilling into the room.

"Ah, Raolin, thank you for joining me."

Raolin bowed deeply. "Your Highness. I hope I didn't keep you waiting."

Her fingers were nimbly tying off a thick braid. The musky-sweet smell grew stronger as she approached. "Oh, not at all. You have perfect timing. I've just finished my bath." She stopped in the column of light, and her eyes flickered to the guards, face and voice turning stern. "Leave us."

Their armor rattled with life as they came to attention and bowed wordlessly. With disciplined strides, they left the room, dragging the doors closed. Raolin thought he heard a gasp from Tristian, but he couldn't be sure it wasn't a play of layered sounds.

His eyes finally adjusted to the filtered light. To his dismay, he saw that the queen wore only a floor-length robe, with lace paneling revealing a creamy hint of bare skin.

She opened an arm. "Please, come in."

As she turned, he hesitated long enough to take a steadying breath before following her through the foyer doors.

A seating area with an overstuffed couch and chairs greeted him, arranged around a small table with wine. But the space was dominated by a large bed. Four posts reached toward the high ceiling. The silk curtains were tied back, revealing a mattress half-covered in bolsters and pillows. A heavy wall hanging embroidered with the sea dragon surrounded by flowering embellishment with winking beads hung above the head.

Every piece of art and furniture spoke of her wealth.

Raolin waited to be offered a seat. As the queen casually floated about the room to tug open the window drapes, he found a fixed point on the wall, avoiding further glimpses into her personal life. Sweat was beginning to moisten his armpits. He knew she was using a deliberate slowness to get into his head, and he silently cursed at how easily she could.

The last lamp was lit, and the queen puffed the lighting stick out. "That's better." She turned to face him, reclining on the edge of the bed. "Please, make yourself comfortable," she said.

The only piece of furniture that would allow him to sit facing her was the couch. However, he felt too restless to sit. "Thank you, Your Grace. However, I would prefer to continue standing if it pleases you?"

"Oh, come now, Raolin, drop the formality. We aren't in court, so there is no need for it. Please. Sit." It wasn't a request.

Reluctantly, he obeyed. As the soft couch engulfed him, he was overcome with the sense that this was not somewhere he belonged.

Her smile returned. "Would you like some wine?" she asked.

He dipped his chin. "Thank you, my lady, but I will decline. With the current situation, and my father ill, I find it best to keep a clear head to stand in on his behalf as your advisor."

"What a shame. By all accounts, you were the entertaining brother. Equally as competent as Lucrid." The splash of her pouring wine seemed too loud. "But, the brother everyone wanted to be with when off duty." Glass clinked. "I suppose that's because you were the youngest. No duties were immediately yours, so you could afford to have fun." She brought the wine to her lips and paused, an eyebrow arching prettily. "I had hoped to get the fun one." Tossing her head back, she downed the wine all at once. She placed the back of her hand against her lips as she swallowed. "I certainly know what being the second-born is like."

Raolin's body flushed as he watched her. Until then, he had done his best to look past her attire. Yet as the tops of her breasts peeked out of the deep-cut neckline, he couldn't help but acknowledge her beauty. The way her loose hair tumbled around her face and how she brushed her lips—he kicked himself, and the muscles around her lips tugged up once more. She could see what he was thinking.

It was one thing to have Lucrid tell him how to navigate the queen's erratic behavior or to receive a lesson on avoiding being manipulated by the very magic sanctioned by her laws. But if the rumors about her were half true, she was a better second-born than him, and he was a fool to have thought he could come here.

She looked at him. "We had business, didn't we?"

Raolin sat up straighter. "Yes, m'lady. I received—"

"Please, Raolin, no formalities. You're boring me. Our families are no strangers. You know my name."

"Lady Aspera, then." He steadied himself. "I received the message from your carrier. There was news from my brother's garrison. Have they found those responsible for your family's deaths?"

She swirled the remnants in her glass with a satisfied hum. "Yes. The news is good."

He waited for her to continue until the silence became uncomfortable. "M'lady—the news?"

Her face twisted, the façade of a sweet young woman melting. She set her glass down sharply and stood. "You are terribly trying, Raolin. The news was good!"

He showed his palms to placate her. "Lady Aspera, forgive me. I'm just eager to hear news of him, so I can send word to his wife and our father."

Aspera rubbed her temple. Slowly, her face settled back into her charm, though anger wavered beneath her olive skin. Her honey-brown eyes fixed on him after a final ragged breath. The ferocity of her mood felt suddenly intimate.

The change caused Raolin's adrenaline to spike. A sharp pain seared through his chest, and in response, he sucked in a small breath. The silence betrayed him, making it sound like he'd been stabbed. Like a cat toying with an injured bird, the queen uncoiled toward him.

"I understand," she said softly. "My family's death has put me ill at ease. I would normally be more sympathetic to your fears about your family. How narrow-minded of me. The last several months have been trying, haven't they? I want answers just as badly as you. Can you forgive me?" She walked toward him with slow, lilting grace, her hips swaying with the hypnotic draw of a dancing flame, her eyes bright with mischief.

"No, my lady. It was discourteous of me to press the matter. We are all threadbare. Forgive my insolence," he said, feeling his body pull away from her, but his gaze could not. The queen was beautiful and had a way that forced the eye.

"We're both at our wit's end, it seems." She swept her robe aside and sat next to him, the warmth from her body embracing his.

The room's edges lightened as if he had just come out of a tunnel. "Ah, forgive me. Yes, it has been hard, m-managing all of this," he said too honestly. It was a physical struggle to drag his mind back from the quicksand that seemed to surround his thoughts. "The news? Has Lucrid found them?" He felt akin to a drunk who finds himself asleep on the streets come morning, listening to his voice. Then, without realizing he had moved, he faced her.

Aspera tenderly brushed a strand of his hair back. "It has been so lonely since I took the throne. Not knowing who I can trust. Constantly having to listen to the prattle of old men telling me how I should use my army and resources." Her eyes ravaged him as a fingertip idly traced his chest. "How is your marriage, Sir Raolin?"

He grew rigid. "My lady, I mourn their loss and your plight. But, as your loyal subject, I feel obliged to tell you this is inappropriate." She was not only his sovereign but half his age, merely twenty years old.

The queen pouted. "Why are you so tense?"

Raolin's temper began to ignite, and his hands clenched. Her treachery ran deep, and he felt himself fighting to climb out of the spell she had started to weave. "Aspera, please. Your letter said that we had business to attend. We need to focus so we—"

Her cool finger touched his lips, her face darkening. "You're starting to sound like those prattling old men."

The couch protested, and the smell of her warm body and breath engulfed him. Long fingers cradled his neck, and the softness of her lips on his felt like slipping into a warm spring. He cried out in the corner of his mind, cursing her cunning, but it was a thread torn to shreds in her clutches.

The weight that pressed him down soothed him, held him in a downy embrace. A deep weariness gripped his mind and limbs. The intoxicating smell of clean sweat filled his lungs as his vision swam. Heightened sensitivity crawled across his skin—something blared for his attention.

His chest constricted in agony for the second time with the knife twist of adrenaline. The room snapped into focus.

Bedposts loomed over him. A second exhale overlapped his own. The high note over his gravelly chest tone drew his attention to the queen beside him. Her eyes were heavy with the sultry look of release, and her hair was mussed. Repulsion pushed Raolin away. Silky linen brushed his bare skin, and his stomach knotted.

"There is nothing more soothing than the release from sex. I feel like I can finally discuss the matters of the war with you." Her head rested in her hand as she watched him.

"What did you do to me?" Raolin choked on the words, fighting not to be sick.

She almost looked hurt. "Was I not satisfying?"

"What did you do to me!" he raged.

"Have you never been hypnotized by a woman's beauty?" she taunted. She had glamoured him, and they both knew it. "It's just for appearances."

She had framed him.

"You snake." Formality be thrown into Tulyra's storm.

Her teeth flashed white. "And I love it." She crossed her legs with no regard for being naked. "Let's discuss your brother and the wonderful news I've received, shall we?"

Raolin's stomach continued to twist as he glowered at her, hiding his nakedness with the sheets. He saw his sword cast aside along with his clothes. Despite his silence, Aspera continued cheerily, thoroughly relishing her control of the situation.

"The letter came in yesterday from Lucrid's second-in-command. They made it to their destination. Your brother was stabbed in the back while they marched, which caused some brief fighting to break out. Any men loyal to Lucrid were detained and killed. A few of my men were injured, but they had the element of surprise, so none were lost." The fingers idly twirling her braid stilled. "Any man who obstructs my will is being dealt with."

Listening to her, Raolin slipped into a pit of black rage. The bite of his nails into his palms kept him from falling completely. The muscles along his jaw clenched so hard his throat constricted, making his breaths ragged. "You are as evil as they say."

"Come now. Despite all the promises your pathetic father feeds me, or your brother's gallantry chasing my family's murderers, you know as well as I that there are too many people who look to your order as their beacon of morality. All your father, your rotting brother, or even you, despite your flippant reputation, would have to do is denounce me, and half the kingdom would rally behind your banner. Killing you all off is me ending something before it even starts."

Raolin just stared at her.

The queen smiled almost tenderly. "You underestimated me?" she asked. "All those years of training feeling empty because none of you knew how powerful I am?"

Raolin's voice was brittle as glass. "You will never be able to extinguish my family's legacy. Killing us won't stop the people from turning against you."

The walls echoed with her laughter, and the sound grated against his ears. Aspera gasped and wiped tears from her eyes. His heart was a stone falling into a lake containing no bottom, all his composure gone.

"It brings me joy that you truly have no idea how boundless my desire is to be rid of your filthy legacy. A garrison should be sitting down at your family's castle. The pretext of their visit is to check in on your father, buried to his nose in furs and illness. No doubt your family welcomed them and broke bread. Your wife, your children—your mother, father, cousins, and servants—will burn in thanks." Her face darkened. "There will be no home left to escape to and no army to raise."

"No." His heart found its bottom.

"Oh yes. Men are positioned to stifle any uprisings. Spiders have already started spreading the word that your brother killed my family. Any books mentioning you will be burned. Your family name just became the cause of this war. Because of your legacy, villages will be wiped out, families destroyed, and crops poisoned. The black armor you wear will become a symbol of fear."

"You're insane," Raolin breathed. "You will never succeed." It was a living nightmare. In one sweeping motion, Aspera had stolen everything.

"Before you jump to that conclusion, you haven't heard the best part. Your brother had a son, am I right?" His face bled all color, and she feigned shock. "Oh, you thought I didn't know? There are no secrets kept from me. Especially such wonderful news as one of my most loyal knights having a boy."

Raolin saw his little girl's face leaning over her new cousin's. He could still hear her laughter. Both their wives had fawned over the boy; their husbands were too busy being royal servants to give them all the children they wanted. It had been years since he had seen Lucrid truly smile. He finally recognized his big brother as he radiated joy. It had given Raolin hope that Lucrid would untangle himself from the queen.

Now, his anger hyper-focused on his nephew's fate. "What are you going to do to him?"

"Oh, don't worry, I'll not harm a hair on his head. He's going to be my ward, and knighted. For far too long, your family has been the kingdom's peacemakers, keeping a dying system alive. Your nephew will help finish the work Lucrid started. Become the next Black Daemon."

Tears blurred his vision, and his voice dripped malice. "How dare you steal his family from him? Lucrid was more than your pet, and to make him believe that's all his father was is asinine."

"The future he will be building will be greater than the one I took away. All that knowledge your wretched family has kept locked away and stifled will be mine."

Raolin's entire body thrummed with potential energy. "The deep-rooted respect for us won't allow you to do that. No matter how hard you try, there will always be someone who will protect our legacy."

"Do you mean the small tribes and villages scattered throughout the countryside? I can address that. If you're thinking about the men who plague my guard and army, that will be a nuisance. However, I believe in using example to keep people in line. I have eyes and ears everywhere, and I've got nothing but time."

A muffled cry and the sound of armor striking stone came from outside. Even distorted by thick wood, there was no mistaking the clanking of a kicked sword. Raolin looked at the doors, confused. In his mind, he couldn't understand what he was hearing. It took a split second to look away and just as long for him to realize what it meant and look back at her.

"The doors are only soundproof when I want them to be. Tristian will be dealt with accordingly for his treason."

Blood pulsed in his ears. "You used him as a plant."

"I did. Unfortunately, I must call our meeting to an end and see that you and Tristian end up in the appropriate places. I'm glad that even though you knew better, you came. It cleaned out an infected pox wound from my guard and got you taken care of without a manhunt. Even though I hate you all, your family has always been good to the crown." Her eyes swept the suggestion of his body one more time. "Plus, it's refreshing to seduce someone who isn't constantly vying for me."

The coils in his muscles finally released, and he scrambled across the bed toward his sword. Aspera pulled the sheets against her body and let out a piercing scream. Raolin fumbled with the twisting fabric despite the purpose coursing through his body. Finally, his feet hit the ground solidly. He crossed the room to his sword in two strides, dropped down, and wrapped his hand around the hilt. He drew it and turned, only to feel a metal fist slam into his jaw.

He crumpled like a sack. His ears rang. A flurry of activity swirled around his head, but the cold stone against his cheek was all that mattered. The sound of sobbing fought for his attention. His eyes bounced back and forth as he tried to understand where it came from, but he didn't have the energy to hold them still.

Heavy metal boots stepped into his vision. Sharp gauntlets cut into his scalp and dragged him to his feet. A snarling face, obscured by a half helm, dominated his attention.

"What should I do with this filth, Queen Aspera? I could kill him here if you wish?" Raolin recognized Elio's voice.

"Hush, dear," a maid cooed while she smoothed Aspera's hair. Then, an intense, protective fury lit her eyes. "No, don't kill him here. It would be a terrible mess."

Aspera sniffled, rubbing tears on the maid's dress. She resembled a frightened child. The sheet she clutched to her chest barely hid her nakedness. "Lidia is right. Now that we know the truth, let the people see justice."

Elio bowed his head. "Your will, m'lady."

Raolin grunted in pain as his legs scrambled to relieve the pulling on his scalp. The knight grabbed his already-swollen face. A metal thumb ground into the broken bones, and Raolin's throat went raw from the agonized cry that tore out of him.

Elio pulled Raolin's face closer to his, his teeth bared. "You're going to rot, and I will make sure you suffer, you self-righteous filth."

Raolin's eyes rolled back, and his body collapsed to the floor.

Elio hauled Raolin by the arm. Once he reached the open doors, he barked at another knight in the corridor for help.

A pool of blood was smeared and tracked down the corridor as they left. The sound of metal boot falls and the hiss of Raolin's limp body faded, and the silence refilled the space. The shadows grew, and their whispers started back up with a renewed vigor. By morning, there would be no evidence of the mess.

Jail

Everything bled together. The only markers of time were the glaring sun making Raolin's head pound and the respite of the night's darkness. It was hard to grasp who he was, let alone where and why. He was given thin broths with stale bread, but it took three days before his stomach settled enough for food to look appetizing.

When the spinning began to slow, and the hunger gnawed unbearably, only then could he swim through the fog enough to know he was chained in the dungeon, high above the city. He could finally name Lucrid in the vague memories of a man dying and know his family's castle as it burned. But he couldn't be sure if they were real or just dreams. It was agony to drink the broth and impossible to chew the bread. One of his eyes was blinded, and the lack of depth perception made his nausea worse.

To pass the time, he tried to pace the room. It took a defiant, morbid determination to push through the discomfort. After just a couple of laps, exhaustion forced him to sit down. The movement helped with the aching in his joints but made his head and face throb. The energy didn't last, and he begged for extra food. Only a handful of the guards would give it to him with sympathetic looks.

One day, Raolin mustered the energy to walk to the door before he had to sit down, sucking in rattling breaths. "Tell me, brother, what happened?"

There was a long silence through the barred window on the door. His heart sank until a whisper came, so low he wasn't sure if it was the nightly breeze playing tricks.

"Excuse me?" Raolin croaked.

"I'm sorry," the guard repeated.

They were the first words he had heard since waking up in this place.

Raolin willed his aching body to bring his face to the bars. "What's going on?"

"You should have fled. I hate to see you this way, my brother." The guard's voice changed. "The city is in upheaval because of your family. You should have just fled when you decided to betray the crown."

Raolin peered at the guard through the gloom. He felt he knew this man. But more pressing in his mind was the switch of his tone, from accusation to pity. It felt wrong.

Before he could decide if he trusted his observation, a door opened. There were two garbled voices. The guard snapped to attention and responded, "Yes, sir!"

A softer female voice grew louder, and Raolin's body went numb. "You have been relieved, sir. Thank you for your service tonight. Report to the Magisterium."

"The Magisterium, Your Highness?"

A man responded in her stead. "Her Majesty gave you an order!"

It was Sir Elio.

"We're in the process of assessing the suitability of our soldiers. Given the current situation," Aspera added kindly.

"Yes, my lady. I'll go at once." The quick departure betrayed the guard's nervousness.

Raolin wondered if he'd been left alone until the jangle of keys broke the silence. Tumblers fell, and the hinges swung open with a dry screech. Fear ignited his body, giving him the strength to scuttle away from the door.

She ducked into the room, and their eyes met. The memories came back spitefully. The skirmish involving Tristian. Her greed as she admired his nakedness—the twinkle in her eye as she got away with the lie. Aspera had glamoured him, and now his body broke out in a cold sweat remembering the magic. She hadn't bothered to replace the memories. It had all been a test of her power. It had only increased, and he was powerless to stop it.

"I see your memories are back. Good. That concussion of yours was rather worrisome." Her brow wrinkled with mock concern. Her eyes swept over him, and she gloated anew. "You look horrible."

Raolin knew it was true without seeing himself. The stench of stale waste clung to him, and he could tell that his muscles had already weakened. There was no need to know the motley of bruises and swelling that distorted his face, nor see his sunken eyes. The hole in his heart was enough.

"Why have you done this?"

"Because I can. I want the power my father wouldn't allow me to pursue. The power your family protected. Let it finally end. I've grown tired of gentler methods." Her hand waved dismissively. "I've told you this."

Raolin stared at the shackles on his wrists.

"It's amazing, isn't it, Elio? How quickly a spirit breaks when you know its weaknesses."

"Yes, Your Highness." The man's tone was flat.

"Why not just kill me?" Raolin asked.

"We're waiting for your nephew to arrive so he can watch the last of his family die. Should be any day now," Aspera responded. "He may be just an infant, but I like the sentiment."

Agony seized his heart. "Why not just kill him, too?"

"He'll be the last Auza-Bendith, if the legends are true. Besides, the legacy his father left behind is still useful to me. The Black Daemon is a powerful symbol. I've arranged for Bran to see to his upbringing."

Raolin flinched at the name. His brother's best friend. The man who brushed shoulders with her. Bran had spearheaded many arguments against their order on Aspera's behalf. He had set Lucrid down his path, all while arguing that it was best for the order.

The queen knew it would hurt, so she paused before going on. "The second most talented man I know besides Lucrid. He'll be like his father if the child is worth anything. Leading armies. My armies. Eradicating his heritage while I unlock all the secrets you Verndari kept from me." She shrugged dismissively. "If he proves too difficult, I can kill him too."

Raolin still had no idea what she was talking about each time she spoke of secrets. He knew of none. "You're insane. You can't rewrite history."

Aspera stepped aside, and Elio covered an uncanny amount of ground in just a few movements to stand in front of him. Raolin curled up and whimpered, sure that a blow would fall. But instead, the queen's skirts brushed him as she knelt.

"You're wrong, Raolin. I've rewritten yours already, haven't I? You're here."

He met her eyes, tears streaming down his face. If only he had been a better son and brother instead of gallivanting around Stellamar.

"If it gives you any comfort to tell yourself that I cannot do this while you wait to die, torture yourself for me. It's my favorite pleasure, watching someone else tear themselves down. It reveals so much."

Just then, a man dressed in all black appeared in the doorway. "Your Majesty." He held a sealed note out to her.

Raolin's body flushed with cold anger as Aspera crossed the cell to take the news from Bran's hand. The only sound was the wax seal breaking and the unfolding of parchment. Bran's eyes locked on his.

"Ah, the criminals with your nephew were spotted. They're a day early. They arrive tonight." She turned, beaming at Elio. "I did well in my choice of them."

"You did, my queen," Elio said.

Aspera floated back across the room. "Criminals backed into a corner can be so reliable. Especially when they have bigger plans for themselves." She crumpled the page, and ash and smoke rose when she opened her hand. She knelt in front of Raolin again, and he flinched away. Gently, she lifted his chin, pushing his hair out of his face. "Be sure to continue to rip your heart out. If you had been less noble and fled, you may have saved several lives."

The gesture of her tenderness reminded him of the look she had given him when she framed him, and he pulled his head away.

She stood up with a triumphant smirk. "Elio, send word through the city that the criminal who defiled the queen and conspired to usurp will be put to death tomorrow evening."

"Yes, Your Majesty."

"I'll ensure the last face you see is your nephew's," she said, looking down at Raolin. "Bran, you'll join me in welcoming your recruits."

Angry tears rolled slowly down Raolin's cheeks. A dark hunger contorted Aspera's face, and she knelt once more. Where before there was tenderness, now she roughly wiped a tear away. Greedily, she sucked it from her fingertips. Her eyes fluttered. "The taste of despair, and hope, leaving the body. There's no torture sweeter." She stood. "You have your tasks."

Once Aspera turned, Bran had eyes only for her. "I'll remain until the guard returns."

There was a tense moment where Aspera pursed her lips and scrutinized Bran. Finally, she nodded and dropped the keys into his gloved hand.

Raolin's anger grew as the rustle of their footsteps receded down the stairwell. His chest heaved with it. It was he who finally broke their standoff when the silence enveloped them.

"A lot of nerve you have showing your face here," he rasped. His voice was exhausted from disuse.

"They say you raped her. That you tried to kill her." Bran spoke down to him as if chastising a little brother.

"I didn't," Raolin snapped. "She summoned me about Lucrid. Ask Tristian. He was there. He'll speak on my behalf—"

"Tristian is dead," Bran said flatly.

Raolin's shoulders slumped. "Dead?"

"He attacked when the alarm went out. Trying to help you escape."

Tears filled Raolin's eyes once more. The last of his denial died as his death dawned on him. His lips cracked, and he clenched his jaw, turning his glare toward Bran.

"This is your fault. Is this what you wanted, to be the last living Black Knight? You've betrayed your order. Lucrid trusted you."

"I've done nothing but protect this realm," Bran retorted.

"My entire family is dead," Raolin said with venom. "Lucrid is dead, and it's your fault."

Bran's brow furrowed. "He's not dead."

It was Raolin's turn to look confused. Before either could say anything, the distinct sound of armor broke their reflection. Bran glanced at the door, then stepped into the cell.

The smell of warm grass and metal wafted over Raolin as Bran knelt. "Why did you go to her? Did you not get my warning about the rumors?"

Tristian's warning came back in a flood, and Raolin felt breathless in its wake. "No."

"Fuck," Bran said through his teeth. "Goddess's wrath, Raolin. Tell me you were drunk or having your bed warmed."

Raolin reached out to Bran. The supple leather glove clasping his hand was soothing, and Raolin wished his armor were on his shoulders to signal normalcy.

"I'll find out what has happened. I'll protect the boy. But pray to the Goddess, because only she can help you now."

• • ——————— • • • ——————— • •

Execution

Four travel-weary criminals stood off to the side of the raised platform. It was an elevated position. They no longer lurked in the shadows or among the commoners—an honor for viewing such a public execution.

Bran knew not one of them appreciated it. Even if they hadn't been wanted, with their likeness posted on every message board, they would never have been in the assize square before. If only the gathered knew that the queen had employed criminals to commit crimes while she condemned an innocent man. Where was the line? Who were they to stand righteously, watching an execution, when they themselves were just one decision away from falling from the queen's grace?

Áki shifted. He was a hulking man with flaming red hair wearing a cut-off vest that showed a body no stranger to heavy use. Everything about the man was loud. Merrick, meanwhile, was the opposite. A man packed into a body nearly a head shorter, though no less built, with only his striking blue eyes standing out.

The slender woman with her arms folded across her chest was Drisil. She had bright almond eyes and an undertone in her skin, which, if it saw the sun more, would darken to a rich brown. She wore a ruby and topaz scarf around her hair, and her painted red lips and kohl-lined eyes made her stand out against the subdued wools that blended with the gray sky and clay cobbles. A tilt to her hips drew the looks of a few men around her, and she seemed to relish their stares, though she kept her hood tugged low.

The only one who appeared comfortable was Randal. He looked like he belonged, with his dark, refined features and regal posture. But unlike Drisil, he didn't hide his magical prowess, either.

Not one of them would call the others friend, but they were bound as partners for however long their quest continued, whether they liked it or not.

People crammed together, a motley of faces straining to see the solemn gathering of officials. Children perched up the walls, or on lamp posts, or had their fists full of their parents' hair as they balanced on shoulders to view the queen in her black veil and velvet gown.

Compared to most executions, this was a huge turnout. This was a usurper who had raped the queen. A Black Knight, to sweeten the spectacle. The conversations wove together into a din, with filaments drawing through clearly.

"Filthy Black Knights. I swore they kept us oppressed," a man said.

"There's no way it's true. They were kind and loyal," a woman whispered.

"She's a liar. I'm only here for solidarity. We're leaving for the country tomorrow," another man spat.

There was a sea of unknown faces to witness whatever it was they wished to see. It left a bad taste in Bran's mouth, but he kept his anger in check. His eyes drifted toward the four again, catching Merrick's gaze. Clearly, the man felt the same.

Bran watched the justice sent by the church mount the stage, marked by the firebird stitched into his chest. His gray wool robes were richly lined with bright white silk. The intent was to look plain, but there was no hiding the quality of the material. His presence marked this as a momentous ruling. Standing before the crowd, he unrolled a parchment. Calm and collected, he projected his voice like a man accustomed to drawing a crowd into himself. The hush that fell over the people was abrupt.

"We are gathered here to witness the execution of Raolin Uland, a descendant of the Auza-Verndari, leaders of the Black Knights. The charges are presented." He paused for dramatic effect, his eyes sweeping the crowd. "Attempted murder of Our Lady, Queen Aspera Aurbornet, usurping the royal crown and defiling Her Majesty." There was a collective gasp, and he let the crowd's murmurs lap at his feet before continuing. "Today, we bring witnesses before you for these charges." He stepped aside so that the center stage was available for witness testimony.

Lidia, Aspera's chambermaid, bustled onto the stage. She wore a simple maroon-dyed dress, and her hair was neatly tucked into a white scarf. Her voice carried well, and her stern look made it evident she ran an efficient house. However, once she began to recount what she had seen that night, she became tearful.

The queen had been lured by Raolin, then bound and gagged. "It's fortunate that he's an egotistical man, taken to gloating once he had spent himself. It gave Her Majesty time to free herself and call for help." Her voice grew distant. "It keeps me up at night, thinking if Sir Elio and I weren't close." Her voice cracked at the end, and she was offered a kerchief from the justice to dab her eyes.

"Mistress Lidia, as you know, it is customary for the Priesthood to ask questions when the Church is asked to bear witness." She nodded, clutching the square to her lips. "Why was Raolin in the royal bedchambers?"

Lidia's voice was strong and steady over the mutters. "She trusted him. He and Lucrid were like uncles to her, Your Priestship. Until that day, she often met with them in her private chambers."

It didn't seem to convince the crowd entirely, and their chatter grew. It was uncouth for the queen to entertain men alone.

"Why were you not present in the room with them to chaperone?"

Lidia looked affronted. "Are you trying to imply that Her Highness asked for this, my lord?" She straightened up before the man could respond, looking twice her size with fury. "She sent me to fetch Raolin something to eat and drink because he had ridden all day to meet with her. None of us heard her scream because he had choked the air from her." She pointed her finger at the crowd. "I'll have you know that I've held that poor girl every night because of the terrors. That man defiled your queen and tried to kill her!"

The words struck a chord, and the queen turned her head and choked back a sob, looking like the girl of twenty. Lidia gave a final, withering glare toward the crowd, daring them to blame Aspera. She gathered her skirts, hurried over to the queen, and gently dabbed her eyes to preserve her makeup. Bran caught glimpses of the painted bruises beneath the high collar.

It was a convincing account. Unsure faces wavered.

The royal physician, Galen, stood up and confirmed evidence of the queen being incapacitated and restrained. "We also scraped beneath her nails and found that it reacted with a heima tincture, which means there was blood. So it is likely she fought before help could arrive."

When the Priest-Justice asked whether the I'aja mages had been summoned, Galen said the college could not send anyone to confirm the findings, thus leaving the ruling up to Stellamar's erudites. When dismissed, Galen bowed and returned to his seat on the dais.

Sir Elio was last. He was an imposing figure, and as his angry gaze swept over the crowd, the murmurs died down into an unnerving silence. His armor was ornate, a quality steel plate so well made it was tinged with an iridescent blue.

Sir Elio didn't wait for permission to begin. "The queen dismissed me to guard her chambers, as is customary with my position." His head turned slowly toward the Priest-Justice and fixed him with a brief, cold glance as if threatening the man to question him. "When I heard the scream, I entered her chambers and saw Raolin in a state of undress, going for his sword. There was no remorse for his actions. He fought me and the other two guards present. It is good he is a lesser swordsman than Lucrid because we were hard-pressed to stop him. Sir Tristian was injured and later succumbed to his wounds."

Bran's mind perked at the change in story as some in the crowd began to express their shock.

After the strategic pause, Elio let his voice ring out, "It was the queen's grace that stopped me from striking him down so that you all could witness the demise of this coward and receive the justice you are equally due."

The crowd stirred. Not only was Sir Elio trusted, but the mention of Tristian's death all but sealed Raolin's fate. Tristian had been a well-loved man in Stellamar. He had been decidedly average in the festival games. What he lacked in skill, he made up for in charisma. He and his family had been friendly with the order, and Raolin had mentored him. It was a betrayal deeply felt.

There was no kindness left for the condemned.

Elio looked at the Priest-Justice, who indicated he had no questions. The knight bowed and returned to Aspera's side, gently placing his hand on her shoulder before facing the crowd. She smiled up at him.

The Priest-Justice returned to center stage and projected his voice. "You have heard witnesses' accounts of Raolin's crimes against the crown." Jeers rose at the name. "In addition to shattering his oath, it was discovered the Verndari were responsible for the deaths of the royal family." He paused again, letting the collective gasp ripple out to those not close enough to hear.

Bran's grip tightened on the pommel of his sword.

For months, the rumors about the royal family had run rampant through the streets. This was the first time any official had publicly addressed it.

"Bear witness to the man who betrayed you all. Feast your eyes on he who would lay waste to our salvation." The Priest-Justice had to yell over the crescendo of stamping feet and shouts. Stepping back, he swept his arms open, sleeves dangling.

Two armored guards with their visors drawn dragged Raolin out. He was hollowed, dirty, and had an empty look in his eye. Bran felt an instant pity. One of the guards shoved Raolin, and he stumbled but kept his feet. The crowd was nearly rabid, getting swept up in the energy. Rotten food arched through the air, most missing and splattering across the platform. Only the strongest-willed wore faces of sadness.

Movement caught Bran's eye, and he looked toward the front just as an older woman slipped through the wall of people. He felt a ripple in his instincts that drew his gaze back to the criminals.

Confusion wrinkled Merrick's brow. The newcomer held Sonder, whom they had brought to the city just last night. Bran heard Raolin forced to his knees, head roughly positioned onto the block. Bran followed Merrick's gaze as Raolin looked up at the crowd.

Life filled the man's eyes where none had been before. Raolin knew the child with nothing but fondness.

Bran looked at the queen, and her treacherous smirk sickened him. The crowd was too transfixed by the spectacle to see. Another glance confirmed that his feelings were mirrored on Merrick's face.

The criminal understood their position. They were prisoners, whether in a cell or not, and their life was no longer theirs.

Only a fraction of the noise dulled when the Priest-Justice resumed speaking. "After extensive investigation, it was discovered that the royal family's advisor and ambassador, Lucrid Uland, was directly responsible for the deaths of King Drynard Leofric, Queen Abril Aurbornet, and the royal Prince Jamil Leofric-Aurbornet. The betrayal of the Uland family and the Black Knights runs deep, and the people have been right to grow wary. Lucrid found death in a battle against our army. Today, the execution of Raolin Uland not only punishes his crimes but symbolizes justice brought for the disgusting—"

Suddenly, a woman thrashed through the crowd, throwing a handful of what smelled like manure at the priest. "Lies! You speak the queen's poison!" she wailed.

An arrow whistled overhead and pierced the woman's throat. Her eyes grew wide as a terrible wet gasp gurgled from her lips. Someone screamed, and the front of the crowd began to stumble backward. Those at the rear were oblivious.

A keen rose from the back, and heads began to bob and sway as the people started to realize something had gone wrong. There were angry curses as people were shoved. From their higher vantage point, the guards could see more than those on the ground. They drew their bows.

"Halt!"

Bran steeled himself as he drew his blade. He sent a prayer to the Goddess of Stars.

Fear gripped the masses from all sides. Men at arms rushed forward and met a tangle of limbs clawing to be free. They were forced to wade through the chaos, leading with shields and spears.

The queen rose and amplified her voice with magic. "Elio, kill him!"

The giant knight drew his sword and closed the distance. Those not being immediately shoved aside looked up and watched the mighty arc of the weapon.

Raolin gazed at Sonder with a deep longing. Bran again looked at Merrick and saw heartache. Elio's weapon began its descent, and Raolin's eyes closed.

There was a sudden bright burst off of the blade. Everyone lifted their hands to shield their eyes. A soft thud echoed in the eerie silence. Bran blinked through the blinding light toward the dais. There was a body, but Elio held his sword oddly while he cast around, as if expecting someone to attack him.

A soft pop sounded, and a deafening uproar of panic ensued. Weapons rang as a small group of people threw themselves at the capital's soldiers. The sudden confusion was all-encompassing.

Arrows crisscrossed over the square from the surrounding walls. Answering arrows sailed from the rooftops, some bouncing across the stage. The queen had been swept away, followed by Elio, who still blinked as if seeing spots.

The crowd dispersed quickly, despite how many spectators had attended. Pockets of people who fought were cut down quickly once the royal guard distinguished the rebels.

Bran struck down a man who mounted the dais to follow the queen. Turning, he saw that Raolin's remains had already been dragged away, without even an official presentation of the head.

Chapter One
The Watcher

Hearth's Inn, beginning

"We're glad we stopped here." Merrick handed the man enough money to cover the rooms, stable, and half the supplies.

Tomas looked surprised. "Grace did tell you it was on the house, did she not?"

"She did, but I'd be remiss to not repay your kindness. As she said, we all ought to do what any good citizen should in these times. A place like yours needs to be cared for."

Tomas met Merrick's eyes, and it was apparent he admired what he saw. With a nod of assent, he placed the money in his pocket. "Thank you. Your words are high praise. You all are always welcome here. Come back when the babe gets older. Grace would love to see her well-timed handiwork pay off." Tomas left them with a bow to return to his numbers.

Grace met Merrick's eye knowingly before sweeping them all with her smile. "I'll see that the children have gotten everything ready."

Present, age three

It was nigh impossible to keep track of time properly. Between months of travel and the constant barrage of duties, it became easier to hold a moment rather than place it. It was the folly of youth to think that every date written above a memory would not smear into monotony. Events stood clear as day until one looked down and realized the years had slipped through the leather gloves of justice. Add whatever magic the queen exerted on the world and all that remained was to hold the significant events dear while everything else burned.

Bran looked up from his worn black glove to the tavern and blinked the thought away. Through a window, he saw a familiar silhouette stuffing a bag. The morning was gray, with fog rolling through the village. He had sat outside most of the night watching that window. He had been there when the candle winked out long past the turning of the torches—long enough for the cold to seep through his heavy layers. He flexed his hand with an impatient sigh, try-ing to will the clumsiness from his bones.

None of the other houses displayed any movement. The smell of baking bread was the only indication that the town was stirring. The man's thumb drummed the saddle as he scanned the streets once more, although he had done so only a minute earlier. A horse whickered in the distance.

"Come on," he growled. He looked up, and the window stood empty.

Several more minutes passed. Finally, Merrick rounded the corner from the back, leading a chestnut pony. To anyone else, he would have looked like a simple traveler—unless they knew the steel glinting angrily at his hip.

Merrick caught sight of Bran. They had been playing this game for years now. The slight pause of being caught was unmistakable. The mare tossed its head when redirected toward Bran's midnight destrier.

"Are you here to kill me?" Merrick asked when they stood face-to-face.

"If I were here for that, I would have done it already." It was true.

"How long have you been here?"

"All night."

"Why?" Merrick asked a half beat after.

Bran reached into his cloak and presented a parchment with the queen's wax seal. Scrawled across its face in her lacy hand read, *Merrick.* "To give you orders."

Merrick looked from the presented note to Bran's face before taking it. "How did you find me?"

"Is it not my job to know?" Bran asked.

It had been nearly three years since they'd passed through Grace and To-mas's tavern with a wailing bundle of an infant, their merry band of criminals vying for a pardon. The four of them were ordered by the very man who now towered over Merrick on a beast reserved for the queen's elite—a universal symbol of death to a village like this. The wailing babe was now a toddler if Merrick's memory served.

No . . . Sonder was older than that.

"Are you here for them?" Merrick dropped his hand to a throwing knife tucked into his belt.

"If I were, I would have started with you."

"Then why not give me this sooner?" Merrick asked.

Bran's face softened. "Why interrupt?"

Merrick felt exposed. Bran had never shown himself to be a liar. "Who else knows?"

"Your secrets are safe. Now, get on your horse before someone sees us." Bran's steed tossed its head in response to his impatience.

As the man turned to leave, Merrick briefly looked over his shoulder to en-sure that no one had seen them. Grace and her family lived in a back apartment, so there was no chance of them eavesdropping. But his gut still knotted at the thought. He wanted to be sure there was no young Paul or poised Rosein sent by Grace to fetch him while she stoked the ovens.

All he saw was the inn still asleep and silent. Reassured, he pulled himself into the saddle and followed.

His farewell was left on the kitchen counter, his gratitude written on a note weighted by a small bag of coins. Tomas was unwell, so the money was meant to help pay for medical expenses. Merrick had had no business returning here. Bran's spectral appearance confirmed that. Yet here he was once more.

As they passed into the trees, it was as if the man Merrick pretended to be snagged on the branches and remained hanging there, like a skin he could slip into next time. Or perhaps he was returning to the costume. It was hard to tell.

"Should I not leave?" Merrick asked after the village was well behind them and no more had been discussed.

"It's not pressing. You can leave tomorrow morning," Bran said. He turned his head so his voice was clearer. "Ride with me."

Merrick inhaled sharply. Bran's purpose was merely disguised by the sealed letter now stuffed in a bag.

They followed a game trail away from Teul. Odds were the ground was as worn as it was because of him. The idea made him feel ashamed now that someone traveled with him. This path would eventually dump them on the road toward Cethre, the next and last major city outpost before Stellamar. Merrick knew this route well. It was the one they had traveled when they'd stolen Sonder. The memory burned bright here, and he used it as a beacon to remind himself.

"Where is your horse?" Bran asked after nearly an hour more of silence.

"In the Cethre barns with its chit."

A subtle eyebrow lift preceded a glance at his attire. "Whose horse is that, then?"

Merrick remained tall in the saddle. "I bought her from a farmer." The little chestnut was nearly four hands shorter but was sure-footed and well-mannered.

Bran made a thoughtful sound, then suddenly turned his horse from the trail and led them through the oak and birch trees. Merrick inhaled the smell of the forest as their horses stirred the soil and shrubs. He eventually urged his mare forward to lead the way without being prompted. If Bran wanted privacy, who better to show them to a place to camp than him?

When the sun had passed its zenith, Merrick halted at a spot blanketed in the soft grass The lay of the land created a natural screen with an outcropping of rocks wrapping around them. There was evidence of a campfire long gone cold tucked up into the stones, and foliage was reclaiming the cleared ground.

"I have none of my gear," Merrick said as he took in the familiarity of this place, a little slice of refuge painted with a sliver of his essence.

Bran dropped down from his saddle. Within seconds, the man had a tarpaulin untied. As he pulled it free from the saddle, he revealed a primitive camp pack and two bedrolls. Merrick caught sight of an unstrung bow and breathed through the wash of emotion.

"I've heard you can use these," Bran said as he walked over, offering up the bow and quiver. The man held the pony steady while Merrick dismounted.

Merrick soon returned with two fat rabbits slung over his shoulder. As he approached, he paused to watch Bran through the trees. The ground around the gaily burning fire was cleared once more. Bran had made a simple tent using the rock.

A loud crack echoed through the trees, and two halves of a log fell to the ground. The woodpile was more than enough for the night, yet Bran grabbed another piece to split.

Merrick's loneliness was a crude beast that plagued him even as his heart filled with gratitude for the company. He had a deep fondness for camping on the road.

As the sun sank, the two men sat beside the fire. Bran slumped against his saddle with a fur-trimmed coat draped over his shoulders and his chin buried in his chest. Merrick crouched near the flames. A small box in his hand snapped shut, and Bran's keen brown eyes watched as Merrick crumbled herbs into the stew.

Bran took a drink of his mug of lukewarm honey water as Merrick settled beside him to watch the fire.

"It'll be done soon," Merrick said.

"I've missed your trail cooking." Bran offered Merrick his own cup of water.

Merrick accepted it. "How did you know where to find me?"

"It's my job to know everything," he said flatly. Then, when Merrick didn't respond, Bran glanced at him. "That, and Drisil told me."

Merrick stopped running through any potential missteps. Instead, he met Bran's eye and saw the twinkle there. The man was bantering.

Bran lifted his cup. "Master of secrets."

Finally, the feeling in his stomach loosened. The two men had ridden in near silence the entire day, and the whole time Merrick had followed his thoughts through scenarios, each worse than the previous. He had even wondered if the man he rode beside had somehow lost a hold on himself. It wasn't impossible.

As if he could read Merrick's thoughts, Bran piped up, "I am still myself, Merrick. Peace."

He tried to relax, leaning back against his saddle. But the action only reminded him about the orders stuffed into his bag. The tension between them now was uncharacteristic. They were confidants. What usually came easily was now stuck and fearful. Not even the most urgent orders would cause Bran to seek him out intimately.

Merrick turned to fish the letter out. The wax seal broke, and so did the shackles that bound their voices.

"The girls have finally been found," Bran said as Merrick's eyes scanned the page.

"I hoped we never would find them." Merrick lowered the parchment into his lap. "So, we're to go get them?"

"Only Drisil and Áki. They're waiting for you in Cethre." Bran took another drink of water.

"Randal?" Merrick continued.

"To remain in Stellamar with the books from Knownth."

They had been to the city many times since they first bent the knee. It was not a happy place for any of them. The last college outside of Stellamar stood there, and their weapons had left it a shell of itself. "Do we trust him to the task? I'd wager that he speaks nothing but praise for Aspera more often than not. The stacks of pages to save grow shorter."

Bran heaved a sigh. "We'll keep faith until we can't. Drisil swears he's still with us."

The stew bubbled, and the herbs had grown aromatic. There was still something neither of them was saying.

Merrick lifted the page from his lap. "So, what's to happen after this?"

"It'll likely take you six months between retrieval and deliverance. After that, it will be the same as it was with Sonder," Bran droned.

"Both girls?" Merrick asked.

"If you can." Bran threw a piece of kindling into the fire. "Aspera has expressed qualms about dealing with the older one. So long as the youngest ends up in your care, she'll consider it a success. Both would not garner additional favor."

Merrick grunted. This was the aspect of his work he loathed. Taking children as hostages was the lowest act of this war, yet Aspera demanded it. There was no point taking the girls as wards. The Lorist resistance had dwindled significantly since Aspera had begun to employ their expertise. They'd found the head of the serpent and cut it off.

"They'll come to no harm?" Merrick finally asked.

"No. They're the daughters of Lorist chieftains. They'll likely have some prowess in the magical arts like their mother. Aspera's vanity will keep them safe if they show promise."

Merrick read over the note once more to let the new weight settle on his shoulders. It meant another child he would feel responsible for. He looked up to the fire after the last words. He sucked his teeth, and anger seeped unintentionally into his words. "You said 'you,' not 'we.'"

"I am not coming," Bran said.

Merrick tossed the page into the fire. The edges began to curl. "I don't want to do it."

"You will," the man said firmly.

Merrick's jaw clenched, but he didn't argue. Of course he was going to. "Where will you go?"

This question was the crux of Bran's solicitude. He was a reserved man, but Merrick could feel whenever his mind was heavy. Bran opened his mouth twice to speak before he finally found the words. "Do you remember the abandoned keep?"

Merrick's eyes moved back and forth as he searched his memories. "Which one?"

Merrick saw the flash of disappointment twist Bran's face, even though the man's tone revealed he'd regained himself. "It doesn't matter. There's a place I want to search one more time. I hope it'll be the last."

Merrick's breathing grew shallow. "I'm struggling, Bran. It gets harder to keep my memories from slipping."

"I know." The man looked at his own hand again as he had that morning.

"How do you remember so much?"

Iterations of this conversation had plagued them, and Bran always remained resigned to it. "It's a matter of constitution. You have to decide who you are and hold on to that. To what matters most. Do everything with intention."

The answer always upset Merrick. To this day, he still hadn't told Bran who he was before attempting the assassination of a royal army officer. There were no records of his joining that garrison, nor tax ledgers. Once, Merrick had told Bran he had the most to lose out of their four, yet never explained why. Now he struggled to remember.

"That's why I return to their tavern. I know it's dangerous, but it's one of the few places I don't feel at war with myself." Merrick felt protective of Grace and her family. The worry that Bran might know his secret returned. "Are you going to tell me to stop?"

"I'll do no such thing. You know the risks you take."

"I plan every visit deliberately."

"I know." Bran let out a mirthless laugh. "Your visits are the same as my searching. I know the level of care you take because it's the same as my own. They're good for you. Have your peace."

Merrick searched the man's face with grim gratitude. His pony let out a snort that broke his reverie. Then, reminded of the stew, he stiffly pushed himself up. The liquid had thickened, letting off a rich smell, bitter and sweet. After filling their bowls and settling back in, Merrick pulled a bundle out of his pack, tore a loaf, and offered Bran half.

"Drisil was probably hoping you'd tell me to stop," Merrick said as they both sat blowing on their food.

"Her demands fall on deaf ears," Bran responded gruffly.

"How would she feel knowing you're sharing your secrets with me?" Merrick couldn't help the twitch of a grin when Bran looked at him.

"Now you jest?" Bran said with a raised eyebrow before he grew serious again. "She did demand I stop you. She knows how our affair ends, and instead of admitting she's afraid, she gets angry."

"Would you want any less from our sorceress?" Merrick asked more seriously. The gravity of their situation would always plague their humor.

"Of course not."

The whimsical look on the man's face didn't escape Merrick. "You love her."

"Doing so makes me all the more determined to stop Aspera. A tragic dilemma."

Merrick scoffed at the irony. "The very one we all seem to struggle with."

"It brings me a measure of happiness to let her have her own." Bran took the bite of stew on his spoon, which had gone cold in the night air. His face lit up with surprise. "This is very good."

Warmth spread across Merrick's face. "It's Grace's recipe." He had already eaten half of his.

"This Grace . . . is she a lover?"

A bark of laughter escaped him. "What? No." When he saw the stern look on Bran's face, his brow furrowed. "Did Drisil not tell you? We owe Sonder's life to her. Had she not opened her home to us and cared for him, things would have gone differently. Most innkeepers would have thrown the lot of us out on sight." He laughed darkly and then drained his honey water. "No. Grace has a husband and two children and is probably ten years older than me. She is no lover. Just a woman who reminds me of home." He took another bite as an excuse to stop talking.

Bran tapped his foot with a pensive look toward the surrounding trees. "That seasoning—" Bran paused thoughtfully. "It's curry, isn't it?"

Merrick stopped chewing, and they met each other's eyes. He swallowed what he could to speak. "Yes."

"The flavor is as it should be." Bran looked away and took another bite. It was a simple thing to say but meant he knew a great deal more. "When you return with the girls, it will be nearly time to claim Sonder from his caregiver. I suspect, however, you'll make some excuse to revisit Grace. Correct?"

Merrick remained quiet. Bran wore a sly smirk as he looked back at him, and added, "Give Grace my compliments."

26

Chapter Two
Reclaimed

Queen Aspera's apartment, four years ago

"Your Highness, if I may ask your intentions with the boy?"

"Well, the vast majority of it doesn't pertain to you. But, since you asked, my goal is to train him to be one of our top knights. Given his family's history, I'd like to use that to my advantage in this war." Her tone darkened. "Why do you ask, Merrick?"

"I'd like to volunteer to be his mentor."

Aspera's eyes crinkled, and her head tilted with genuine interest. "Why? By all accounts, you took no interest in him. Now you want to be responsible for his care?"

"I've proven myself to be your best swordsman."

"Arguable. What of Áki?"

"Lacks the mental capacity. What he has in brute strength and skill, he lacks in foresight."

"Why not one of my current advisors?" Her lips betrayed her enjoyment. "I've heard talk Bran bested you once. Before you truly submitted to me."

Merrick kept his face devoid of emotion. "They have an investment in his history. I have none. I have no idea, and I couldn't care less."

Aspera leaned back in her throne. "Well, I suppose I can't argue with that." Her well-kept nails drummed wood stained from many hands. Finally, she shrugged one shoulder and looked away. "Stay alive, and keep me happy. I'll consider it then."

Present, age five

A small boy squatted in the yard, pushing a wooden horse through the dirt, his butt nearly touching the ground. Birds sang in the surrounding trees, flitting between branches. A few brave ones ventured to investigate the yard; their heads turned to ensure that the boy hadn't moved.

Spring was in full bloom. Shades of vibrant green contrasted with the clinging browns of winter. Pops of purple, yellow, and white bobbed behind the curtains of tall grass, straining to be seen. There was a bite in the breeze, but the day promised to be warm when it settled.

On mornings like these, Sonder imagined the weather was like a grouchy adult that needed tea to be nice.

Over the noise of life, he quietly hummed a random string of riffs from festival songs. He had fashioned a dowel wrapped in black cloth to resemble a rider. He drew incoherent lines through a forest of collected sticks, pretending a knight was fighting battles for a beautiful queen. When he let out a shrill whinny, the horses in the paddock looked up from their hay, tails flicking like laughter.

It should have been a happy scene, with the world shedding winter and a carefree little boy playing. Except Sonder was alone.

No other children came bursting through the door, nor caretakers bustling about their chores to briefly watch the joy of a child at play. All he had for company was the animals, going about their daily routine, paying him no mind.

The yard backed up to a modest cottage. The windows were empty and watchful, the door a dark slit on its face. In his haste to be outside, he hadn't closed it all the way. Each time the wind blew, it edged open like a gaping maw trying to suck him back.

Some window frames sagged, and the daub crumbled in places, but wealth seeped out of the corners and the barrels. It was in the smell of fresh-cut wood to replace supports that had gone soft; in the yard's maintained look, down to the plump horses and animals grazed in tilled fields. The cellars were still well-stocked for the end of winter, too. But, most of all, it could be seen in the threads holding Sonder's clothes together.

Not even the first glance of a lonely cottage, miles outside of the capital, could completely mask the stench of royal money dripping off of everything.

Down the road, a solitary rider left fresh hoofprints in the soft ground recently smoothed by the road tenders. It was a grueling task of shoveling gravel to fill in wheel ruts and gouges from runoff water.

Winter had followed after the last bout of battles six months prior, so few people traveled. Many were holed up in their homes or else scurried quickly to and from the market. The skirmish had been against the last remnants of the mages' college, one hundred miles away in D'alma. The repercussions were felt far beyond their lands.

Books had been burned by the thousands. Heads had rolled in similar numbers. Queen Aspera had decreed to have any magic users who harbored a school of thought connected to the gods and their colleges eliminated. But, until she and her council settled on a replacement system and established the new laws, few wanted to be perceived as sympathizers. Or worse, part of the Lorists ferrying traitors out of the cities.

Magic was rapidly dying as a consequence, and the land reeled from its loss.

The resulting quiet and cool air carried the distinct jingle of the horse's reigns. It was a sound that struck fear in many hearts as it echoed over the fields and into homes through open windows. The sound of the queen's elite Justices and the new order of Black Knights.

When the noise finally cut through Sonder's play, he looked up. His eyes were wide with hope. As the rider crested the hill, a smile broke across his face. The horse was a hulking beast of midnight bearing a man with a familiar build. Sonder jumped up with the athleticism only a child or a drunk could possess.

"Merrick!" His boyish voice caused the birds nearby to flutter up and onto the fence posts, looking indignant. His little legs brought him to the gate just before Merrick. The excitement caused the horse to flatten its ears and snort.

In a fluid motion, Merrick dismounted. His boots dug deep divots into the mud. He wore all black, from the hardened leather armor with flowing details to the cloak that hung from his shoulders. Dark splotches and stains marred the details. But his fearsome appearance and stern expression did not deter the young boy, nor did the stench of many miles traveled and brutal battles fought tinged with tree-oil soap.

Bouncing on his toes, Sonder held himself back until Merrick faced him. Then he let out a squeal and ran to the man, opening his arms out wide.

The horse grew more agitated and tossed its head. Merrick remained rooted, and just before they met, he backhanded Sonder across the face.

Sonder sprawled backward on the ground with a wheeze as the air was forced from his lungs. It was a slow process for him to turn onto his side. His small hand came up to his cheek. The severe lines on Sonder's face were a harsh contrast to the joy he wore moments before.

Merrick's jaw worked as Sonder looked up at him.

Saying nothing, the man stepped around him, and his horse followed the tug on its lead. The beast let out a protest as it delicately sidestepped around the tiny human and gladly saw itself to the hay scattered through the yard.

Sonder continued to hold his swelling cheek as he watched Merrick's receding back. The mud soaked through his clothes, chilling his body. His chin trembled with sadness and confusion at what had transpired. Merrick had never struck him before.

Guilt gripped Merrick, and he felt bile threatening to rise as he left Sonder on the ground.

There was no accusation in Sonder's boyish gaze, nor anger. Instead, it was more akin to the slow death of trust and a growing perverse reverence. It made Merrick loath how Aspera forced his hand.

An older woman appeared in the doorway with a dirty apron tied around her plump waist. Her frame spoke of only recently growing soft, muscles built through labor still shaping her limbs. Even if she went through the trouble of covering her sunspots and brushing her graying auburn hair, there was no way to hide a lifetime of work before her newly acquired wealth.

She had fierce blue eyes and a mouth stuck in a permanent scowl. Flour powdered her cheeks. Merrick could smell what she was cooking wafting off her clothing as he neared.

"I expected you nearly a week ago, lad." Her voice was as stern as her look.

"I got held up." His tone matched hers, the uneasy feeling still churning his stomach.

"Well, yee've come to take the boy as promised? I was told no more'n five, and it's been six." Her accent marked her peasant roots.

Merrick's look darkened. "It has only been five, Merna." He stopped shy of entering the house. He hadn't been invited, and he knew he wasn't welcomed. "You also owe your newfound comfort to the boy. You ought to show a bit more gratitude."

A wicked sneer revealed her browning teeth, her voice pitching lower. "Says a man who just laid him out. Have yee not benefited as much as I?"

Merrick chose to ignore her last remark. "To answer your question, yes, I am here to take him to the palace. Your services are no longer needed."

Merna wiped her hands on her apron again and smiled. "Very good. Has Her Majesty arranged for my final payment?"

Watching the older woman wring her hands and smile greedily always disgusted Merrick. Several times a year since Sonder was a baby, he would check on the boy, bearing all manner of compensation. Now, Merna's pale tongue poked out and moistened the corner of her mouth. He entertained the thought that she was salivating, imagining stuffing her greedy mouth with fatty meats and sweet candies.

"I have not come to speak on her behalf. My orders were to collect the boy upon finishing my duties as a Royal Justice." He emphasized his title, which gave him the freedom to act on the queen's behalf as he saw fit. He couldn't help himself from insulting her further. "Not to entertain your greed."

She didn't miss the blackness of his mood and the implications of his explanation. "How very like yee to come to my home and threaten me. Her Majesty promised me compensation for tending to the boy. I want to be done with it."

Merrick made a face, which made her scoff. He wanted to laugh in her face and tell her that the queen never relinquished those who did her bidding. There was no being done with it. More likely than not, some armored men would eventually sweep her from her home and ransack the place. Better yet, he'd be the one to come knocking with a scroll intended for her, bearing the Royal Justice's mark.

The words bubbled up in him, morphing into something just as poisonous. "I'm sure you do. No widow as low as you could have maintained so much wealth without selling your soul to the crown. Best your neighbors don't finish the work before I do."

Merna glared at him before yelling at Sonder, "Oy! Boy. Get in here and pack your things, you hear me? You'll not be coming back here. Get it all out." She again wrung her hands on her apron, the movement angrier. "And I don't want to see you around here unless you got payment, *sir*." She spat at Merrick's feet.

He bowed while holding eye contact. "You and what guard, milkmaid?"

Sonder tentatively slipped past Merrick with a soft apology. Merna huffed and followed the boy inside to help him pack, smacking him on the back of the head.

As he stood outside, Merrick's thoughts were scattered. More than anything, he wanted to grab a drink to slow them down. Standing alone on the stoop, he could almost imagine that it was a happy place, with the warm scent of breakfast loaves. It certainly had been when the hag would go to town and leave the two of them alone together.

A soft jingling of bells drew his eyes to the hill he had crested earlier. A black charger with flowing feathers at its feet and chin bore Drisil. Only she would line her black cloak with flashy maroon silk. Merrick's anxiety increased as he became too aware of how much time he had lost.

Drisil stopped just outside the gate and watched him. Soon, Sonder and Merna reappeared.

Merna hissed, "Great, she's here too?" She raised her voice to be heard across the yard. "Do you have my payment, Mistress?"

"No, I don't, Keeper," Drisil called back. "Her Majesty sends her apologies. I'm here for the boy, but it seems Justice Merrick indeed has arrived."

Merna turned a narrowed gaze on him. "At least she has the decency to address me with the respect I'm owed."

Merrick couldn't help himself and laughed. "If imagining you deserve anything helps you sleep at night." Tenderly, he placed a hand behind Sonder's head to guide him through the door. "Come, boy, you're to ride with me."

Sonder looked relieved at the kind touch as he clutched his meager bag of belongings. "Where are we going, Merrick?"

"You're to become a royal page. Then, if you do well, you'll become my squire." He smiled, trying to be reassuring, which came easier now.

"You mean it? I'm going to become a knight?" Sonder had not yet learned to see the sadness in his mentor's eyes. He broke out into a grin.

"If you work hard and do well, yes." Merrick patted him on the back and urged him on. "Now, get on." His mood changed as he looked at Merna. "Have one of your horses saddled for him."

Merna sputtered in protest, "Those are my horses!"

"Given to you by Lady Aspera to serve the crown's needs. So have it done, whether by your hands or one of the enslaved allotted to you."

Merna glowered and called to one of her hands before she disappeared back inside and slammed the door on them. A boy of about fifteen came trotting from the back to do as Merna demanded. Just as the boy reached the horses, Merna yelled through a window for him to give them the weaker of the beasts before shutting it loudly.

The hand looked nervously at Merrick to see if he'd protest. Merrick relished the confirmation of his authority, knowing Merna no doubt continued to watch. With a nod, the smaller of the two was saddled. Although it would have given him satisfaction to gouge Merna, the feeling would have been short-lived, and he itched to be done with it as much as she.

"Is the horse really mine?" Sonder asked.

Merrick chuckled and led him to the paddock. "You will have many horses." He lifted the boy. When he was satisfied that Sonder could guide the horse, he swung back up onto his own. "Now, follow me."

Like all of the royal horses, the smaller beast was well trained, though to be safe, Merrick held the lead rope in case the little chestnut decided to take advantage of the boy.

Drisil had watched wordlessly like a regal shadow. Merrick led Sonder's horse through the gate past her. She turned her horse to fall in beside him.

Sonder called out a shy greeting to her. She responded warmly before turning her attention back to Merrick. "You know, it's rather unbecoming of you to pester the old woman."

Merrick scowled. "She did the bare minimum caring for the boy. All she cared about was getting paid and growing fat."

"Says the man who hit him." Merrick's jaw clenched. "I see the bruise on his cheek. At least the old has-been never hit him."

"If he's to survive at the palace, he can't see me as a friend," Merrick grumbled.

Drisil smiled, her voice teasing. "I still can't place the soft spot you have for the boy."

They kept their voices low so Sonder wouldn't overhear them, although there was little need to. The boy looked around with awe as they rode, craning eagerly as they neared the capital. He had never traveled so far from the cottage. Not even for festivals or to go with Merna to the markets. Instead, he had been kept with the servants or with Merrick if he had returned from the queen's campaigns.

First, the blue haze of the sea came into view, peeping through the trees; the moisture that hung in the air obscured the horizon. Next, the trees fell away and revealed fields of crops and grazing animals, neatly organized and separated by fences. The walls that surrounded the city materialized the closer they got. That was when Sonder's questions began to boil out of him. Merrick and Drisil answered them patiently as the buildings grew out of the murk. The pointed towers of the castle were the most striking of all.

It was the second time Merrick and Drisil had carried the boy into Aspera's clutches. Five years might have elapsed, but somehow nothing had changed, except the notice boards no longer had their faces under the words "WANTED" and "REWARD."

They approached the gate, the stone towers looming. Sonder's jaw dropped as he took in the bands of reinforcement, the sharp metal grates, and the tunnel lined with murder holes. They were met on the other side by an armored mass to oversee the boy to the castle. So very like the first time, except then Drisil had clutched a baby to her chest. The same boy who now sat on a docile chestnut.

Four criminals, banded together by no more than their proximity to death and naivety.

Initially, Sonder protested, his eyes and face pale with fright. Merrick let promises tumble from his mouth as he ushered him forward to be engulfed by the gleaming plates and sharp weapons. Part of Merrick recoiled. It had taken five years of mental games to justify being involved with the queen's business, explaining to himself how this was his duty.

Merrick refused to meet Sonder's backward gaze as the rattling guard led the boy away. This gate was near the tavern he liked to frequent. His skin was hot and crawling by now. Instead of seeing their choice through, he turned his horse and rode to the Jaded Whisper, where the bite of the ale would cool his guilt.

Chapter Three
The Queen's Criminals

Alleys of Stellamar, five years ago

Bran threw the last of his scrolls on the ground. He roared a single word of power, and Áki was met in his advance by a wall that threw him backward. The parchment went up in rose-gold smoke, and Bran felt a pang of remorse. The last of an old magic, wasted on these four.

"Would you idiots just stop?" His voice was still raised, and his sides heaved. "I'm on your side, by the Goddess's wrath!"

"You're the queen's shadow! Every time she gives us an order, you're the one delivering it," Áki bellowed back, not alarmed in the least by the fact he had just seen war magic.

Merrick held his bleeding arm, a throwing knife buried in his shoulder, and the two casters paused at the display. At least they showed caution.

Bran still held his sword at the ready, glad they were finally listening. "Yet I've not told her your secrets, have I? About your hideout, or the gambling rings. How you've tried to undermine her orders every step of the way?"

"Why should we trust you?" Drisil interjected. "You're the one who killed those rebels she sent us after. That Druid woman tried to tell us something, and that knight knew you. If you're our ally, why do that? Maybe we should reveal her right hand is actually a rebel himself if you really are on our side?"

Bran's face twisted into a snarl. "You are insufferable, thinking you can have your way with a bat of an eyelash." Her smirk of challenge grated into his rage. "I serve the realm first, and I'm the only thing keeping you four alive."

"Let's hear what he has to say," Merrick said. Bran glanced at him, and their eyes met on the vast field of unspoken understanding.

Present, age five

The vantage over the city from the Queen's Tower had yet to grow old. Every time he stood in her presence, Randal wondered if it ever would. The view of Stellamar's entirety was unbroken. The light glittered over the sea to the west at sunset, painting the rooftops red and orange. Ships drifted like giant golden birds on the sound, their sails bearing the mark of their home-lands. The canvases wafted with each gentle breeze like wings while gulls winked in and out of the view, using the air currents generated by the galleys.

Randal could observe their delight as they made sudden maneuvers with seemingly no effort. To the east, mountains swathed in green reared up and curled protectively around the ripe fields. Those peaks caught the clouds that helped the crops thrive and offered rich soil, keeping the city fed. The mountains were aptly named the Mother's Range—angry and jagged but the nurturer of these lands.

Other sensations reached through the open windows. The constant buzz of the castle grounds teeming with movement and the jangle of harnesses. Endless smells of food and the scent of the sea. These wonders filled the tower while Queen Aspera bent over her life's work, oblivious to it.

Hers was a room of wonder in every aspect that it could be.

Randal was almost sure he'd never grow tired of this room as he watched her finish her notes, her full lips silently forming words.

The soft whisk of the tip of her pen stilled. Her honey eyes traced the page. Finally, she set her pen down with a satisfied nod. Randal rolled his shoulders back and stood up taller.

"There. That ought to do it," she said, doing one final check. "Right." She picked up the heavy parchment and handed it to him for inspection.

Randal quickly stepped forward to take it. He read the official document in her neat writing, naming him her Overseer of Magic. Pride swelled in his chest, and he had to fight down the smile that trembled on his lips.

"Well? Do you like it?" she asked softly, her long fingers spread over the block she wrote on to keep the ink from seeping.

"Yes, my lady. It's perfect," Randal breathed. He felt a little silly that tears began to brim his eyes.

"Good. I'm delighted you accepted. Now that the colleges have finally collapsed, I need someone I can trust to oversee the void they left. I trust you won't let me down?"

Randal met her gaze, still holding the parchment in front of him. "Of course not, my queen. It is my greatest honor to serve. Your will be done, my life for yours."

A warm smile softened her face. "I look forward to all the things we shall accomplish together." She looked down just slightly to show her appreciation. "Your services are no longer needed on the front lines. Instead, I require your presence here, with me. There are many things to be learned that those old mages kept hidden." Her excitement was barely contained. "Your knowledge and skill complement my own. I'll leave it to you to coordinate with your *comrades* to see any other matters requiring a justice." The word rolled off her tongue as if it tasted bitter.

Randal bowed low. "Of course, my lady. I will see it done." The way she had referred to Merrick and the others, emphasizing the word, made him feel superior to them.

The others still tried to push back against Her Majesty, whereas he leaned fully into his role. He had been a court member long before his face was plastered all over the kingdom.

When Bran had presented the opportunity to clear his name by stealing the child, he was eager to try to be the Queen's Mage once more. It was all he had wanted. His defiance against her resulted from the advisors who expelled him. Now they were long gone, some by his hand. His crimes were water under the bridge, and this day had finally come.

Randal doubted Merrick would ever fully come around, at least not with the boy so close, but maybe he could convince Drisil and Áki to see the idiocy in defying Aspera.

Aspera switched the subject to another matter she had summoned him for, as if she could read his mind. "You brought news of the boy, correct? Has he settled into the castle?"

"Indeed, my lady. The staff says he is struggling to adjust, but the eldest caretaker—Melody Merriweather, I believe it was? She thinks he is doing well."

"Is he ready to begin lessons? I'd like to start regaining some of my investment. It has proven a more difficult and expensive task than I previously thought. Merna has become more trouble than she was worth." Aspera rubbed her forehead and rolled her eyes.

Randal listened patiently to her rant before he continued. "Yes, Lady Aspera. Merriweather believes that starting his training will be the solution to his sulking."

"See to it, then. And the girl?" She began to pace the large room, playing with her fingernails.

"Well behaved as ever. The gardener, Master Wilkin, has nothing but glowing things to say and believes she will indeed become a very capable herbologist and healer. Gwenyvir thinks the same." He continued to look ahead, fighting the urge to watch her stroll around the room.

"Splendid. Is there anything else you had for me, Master Randal?" She stopped beside the chair and leaned over it. Now and then, she would be informal with him. The way she looked at him during these moments, and the easy tone of her voice, made him feel like he was necessary, and she cared what he had to say.

"There was one thing, if I may, Queen Aspera?" His heart quickened, and his voice was somewhat halting. He was still learning how to gauge her in these moments—whether or not he would displease her by being candid.

"Please, Master Randal. I'd like to be sure your concerns are addressed. I need you clear-headed as my advisor." She encouraged him with a smile and a sweep of her open palm.

"I would just like to confirm that the boy will be safe and treated well?" The second the words left his mouth, he felt like a fool. His face flushed, and there was no hiding it.

Aspera's face darkened, and a wicked smile replaced the soft, girlish appearance. "Let me guess—Merrick put you up to asking that, didn't he?"

He was confident he got a shade darker. "Y-yes, My Lady."

"Have I given him reason to believe I am an unkind sovereign?"

Randal began to stammer. He neither wanted to throw Merrick into the fire nor did he want to offend Aspera, whom he adored and admired regardless of some of her methods.

She stood straight once more and walked toward him. "That was unkind of me to put you on the spot." She stopped directly in front of him. She was only just shorter than him. "But let me remind you, Randal, that your loyalty is to me, not him or the others. I know you have a fondness for the boy. So, I will tell you now that I mean him no harm, so long as he serves his purpose. Just like you."

Her face was so close he could smell sweet mint on her breath and her musk beneath the perfumes. His body flushed with desire while he panted his hot, terrified breath in her face. He could still taste the garlic on his tongue from lunch.

"Of course, my queen. I meant no offense; I know you to be kind and giving. You are right about my fondness. I'd like to see him succeed."

"It appears that you and I want the same thing." She tilted her chin up. "Next time, I would encourage you to tell Sir Merrick to ask me himself rather than convince you to speak on his behalf. My advice would be not to get caught up with him if you want to continue as my confidant."

His Adam's apple bobbed.

"Now, if there is nothing else, you are dismissed," she said with pursed lips.

Randal took a step back and bowed deeply before hurrying out. The size of the room proved unfortunate in this case, giving him too much time to burn in embarrassment with her watching.

Sir Elio, who followed her everywhere, scowled from beneath his helmet as he pushed the doors open.

There were thankfully no other guards up here. Aspera demanded they stay farther down the tower to allow her privacy. Randal drew on that now as he stood with his hands trembling on the closed doors. With no prying eyes, he let his heart steady itself.

Curse Merrick and that wretched child—ran through his head over and over as he descended the stairs.

All he had ever wanted was within reach. Before him was a vast space, empty and ready for him to fill. Aspera's power and knowledge had always been tantalizing, and now she was entrusting secrets to him.

He was bitter when he fell from grace. Admittedly, he'd resented Aspera when she refused his counsel the first time. He had offered his services to lesser lords as retaliation, the ones who sought to control or assassinate her.

After years of running, the desire to undermine her had remained when they were ordered to steal Sonder and then kill the archmage of An-Dagda in Knownth. They had continued to risk their lives to hide her involvement with the fall of Sosten's institutions keeping her in check. The exchange was a pardon. It was easy to want to overthrow her when Bran suggested it. Randal's task was to get close to her and discover her true intentions.

Once they had proven their worth, and she'd elevated them as promised, his rebellion died. As cruel as she could be, Randal admired her.

He cared for them all, of course. They were his friends, and Sonder had stolen their hearts. Still, he could see it from Aspera's perspective. She wanted what they each had to offer to bring peace and prosperity. The queen was itching to give them their desires for nothing but their loyalty. If only he could convince them. They could reap the rewards as he did.

His opinions and insights mattered to her, and he could become a voice to soothe her rages. To tame her didn't feel quite right, because she shouldn't be diminished. But maybe he could stand beside her as an equal and guide her ambitions.

Randal took one final deep breath. His nerves no longer hummed with adrenaline.

That was the solution. He had to convince the others to abandon Bran's folly. He wouldn't show uncertainty in Aspera's presence again. The only men who had something to fear were those unaware of their power and who had something to hide. His power was Aspera's trust, and he gave everything.

How lucky that he should have concluded this when he was supposed to be on his way to meet the others for their weekly gathering. Áki called them "family dinners" to elicit eye rolls from their quartet, but they had been aptly named.

Randal stood up tall and straightened his new robe with as much dignity as possible. It was just one more reminder that he had climbed higher. It was no longer just an inky void with the Knight stitched into the chest, but full length and trimmed, distinguishing him as a faithful cabinet member. He ran his hands over the sides of his head to push back any hair that had fallen free.

Then, rolling his shoulders, he walked down the stairwell to meet his comrades.

The "family dinners" only worked because the majority of the time, only one of them left in a huff, and they seemed to take turns. Those odds allowed them to forget how trying it was for them all to be in the same room. Add alcohol, and it was a wonder no one had ended up being stitched up by the madame healer in town.

Randal dismounted in front of the Gilded Harpy. It was nestled comfortably in the mid-wealth district. When they'd first cleared their names, Aspera had put them up in one of the wealthiest inns in Stellamar, complete with the softest beds, three-course or more meals, and swarms of nobles and castle guards. No amount of the finest wines made the curious gazes worth it. After many months spent networking with the degenerates and plebs, they'd found this place instead. By then, they had a steady stream of income from gambling rings to subsidize their royal coin, so it was no issue buying out the owner to create a haven.

They'd also acquired an abandoned manor, but their newfound wealth meant they no longer wanted to cook for themselves. After years of scraping by to varying degrees, the weight in their pockets made them too good for scrubbing dishes and holes in the wall. They still traveled down the hill to meet here five years later, even if the finer wines had become their daily norm.

A girl greeted Randal at the door and offered to take his cloak. He blinked at her. There had never been someone to greet them before. Drisil caught the corner of his eye with a wave. There was a mocking raise to her eyebrow—she seemed to enjoy his confusion.

Once he was freed from his cloak, Randal pushed his hair back once more. He tugged at the collar of his tunic as he wove through the tables, having to adjust his seat several times to get his pants from binding. He missed his robes whenever he had to dress inconspicuously.

"Someone is feeling rather elevated tonight, aren't they?" Drisil teased. She accepted another glass of wine from the barkeep with a gracious smile.

Randal scoffed. Drisil always had a way of reading him like a book. This was expected—she was the queen's charlatan and arguably the most gifted sorceress behind Aspera herself. He just wished she would focus her talents on her marks instead of him.

"Of course he is. Look at that little flush in his cheeks. He's just come from talking to her," Áki taunted. He sat on the other side of Drisil.

The large, burly redhead was as dense as an ass. Suitable for heavy lifting, cutting down people, and satisfied to accept food as payment. He spoke too loud and delighted in heckling one to their wit's end. Randal was positive

Áki's only desire in life was to see everyone turn beet-red and look a fool. The mission was attainable because there wasn't enough substance in the man's skull for anyone to get an equivalent rise.

Drisil smoothed over Áki's taunting with poise. "Well? Do we have something to toast tonight or not? Have your efforts paid off?"

Randal's excitement became renewed, but before he could respond, Áki cut in again. "You mean kissing her feet?"

Drisil clenched her jaw and set her glass down. "Please, Áki."

Ordinarily, their conflict made Randal laugh, so long as he wasn't the one under fire. After today, however, he refused to let them perturb him. He was a man of the queen's cabinet, and if he was to fulfill his duties, he needed to rise above the drivel.

"The way he pines after the woman, I'd watch he doesn't try to convince you all to hop on board." Áki met Randal's eyes and lifted his half-empty mug in a toast before sucking it dry.

Drisil lost her temper then and rounded on him. Since the beginning, Áki had been the only person who ruffled her so. While she called him all manner of foul names and he reveled in her fury, Randal couldn't help but marvel at the idiot's clairvoyance. He never failed to hit the nail on the head. That was the man's true gift.

As they went on, Randal realized one dynamic was missing. Drisil huffed and turned away from the futile battle. But, before she spoke, Randal cut her off. "Where is Merrick?"

Randal often thought of him as the old man, but they were all roughly the same age. Merrick had a short fuse and a gruff way of handling most things. He usually lost his temper first and could stop their fighting with just a few words. He had become their leader in many ways.

It was alright that he wasn't there. Randal wasn't ready to deal with that conflict yet. Those blue eyes would have turned on him when Áki called him out for his closeness to Aspera. Better to whittle the other two down and let them win the hard-head over. If it was even possible to have him turn against Bran.

Drisil rolled her eyes. "Where do you think?"

Randal latched on to her annoyance to begin swaying them. "He is likely to get us all in trouble if he keeps it up."

"Or you ought to be careful. He may gut you himself when he finds out you sold your soul to get your little worm wet," Áki said.

Drisil stood up and rounded on Áki, slapping him across the face. "Get out." The room grew quiet.

The man sneered and stood up, unfazed. He was a whole head taller than Drisil, but she didn't back down. She grabbed the fabric of his tunic and pushed him toward the door. "Go take a piss or something," she snapped.

Áki walked out laughing, swiping a mug from one of the other tables as he passed by and downing it as the patron shouted after him. There was the unmistakable shatter of pottery against the cobble before the door closed.

Drisil watched him leave, shaking her head. "I swear. It would be nice to gut that imbecile myself." She gave Randal an apologetic look. The owner came up then, and Drisil apologized to him, offering to pay for a round of drinks for everyone.

"A little edgy tonight?" Randal asked gently once she had smoothed everything over. It was rare that she lost control of the spells keeping them shielded from prying eyes.

She gave him a tight-lipped smile. "He was being unkind. We should be celebrating your success."

"Is there more to it?" he pressed.

Her cool fingers took his, and she squeezed his hand. "It's about you tonight. Never mind me."

He didn't buy it for a second, but he relented. Five years revealed a lot about a person, even if they were masters of disguise.

They steered their conversation into safer territory while they ate and sipped the house wine, talking about the markets and gossip amongst the nobles and merchants. Áki soon rejoined them but remained quiet. Sophistication was not his strong suit, but sometimes he was self-aware enough to stay silent.

The drone around them remained even. People came and went, voices rose and fell, and sometimes there was a punch of laughter, but nothing distinguished itself as unique. So, when Drisil looked suddenly at the door, Randal looked too.

A stern-faced man entered the tavern and waved away the girl who stepped forward to greet him. He was easily a decade the quartet's senior, with grays at the temples. He still wore his black riding leathers, so every patron knew what he was. His cloak brushed people's chairs as he wove through the tables toward them. Randal couldn't help looking at Drisil's face, which had softened and grown hungry and concerned all at once.

The man stood behind her, placing his hands on the back of her chair.

She sucked in a slow breath and turned away, a coy smile tugging at her lips. "My. . . what a surprise. What brings you here, sir? Business or pleasure?" Drisil was a master of her craft. The way she let her sleeve slip, revealing a creamy wrist, and tilted her glass so her lips just grazed the rim. She could soak every fiber of her person with sex.

Most of the things she did were not inherently promiscuous. It was a switch with her. Randal had decided it was a type of litmus test. It seemed to be the men who were unmoved by her flirting that she latched on to.

The man's knuckles tightened. "Everything I do pertains to royal business, Mistress."

"Well, then, get on with it, so we can continue to the pleasure part of our night," Drisil purred.

The man flushed. "Do you take nothing seriously?"

"Only your threats to make me behave." She turned her smoky, kohl-lined eyes back on him. In the same movement, she arched her back against his hands.

The man stood his ground, but his blush deepened. Instead of engaging with her, he nodded at both Áki and Randal. Drisil took another sip and giggled into her glass. It was a girlish sound. The man was the stoic sort, and she clearly relished how she unnerved him. It had taken several years, thousands of miles, and many nights of camaraderie for her to steal a kiss from him.

Bran was the queen's head practitioner, jack-of-all-trades, head of all the justices, and traveling right-hand man. Elio was the protector by Aspera's side, and Bran was her sword. Although they all knew of the fraternization and familiarity Bran and Drisil shared, he tried to hide it. There was supposed to be no room for such frivolous things in their line of work.

Those knuckles must have been bone-white beneath his gloves with how hard he squeezed her chair. Had she not been into her cups, more than likely, she would have been more ill at ease.

Bran addressed Randal directly. "What news of Sonder?"

He stammered. He had been so caught up in his thoughts, watching the tension between Bran and Drisil, he had to gather them all together again. "I—I asked after him as you and Merrick asked. Nothing changed. There's no indication she has any plans other than raising and knighting him."

Bran's jaw was so clenched it looked like it physically hurt to nod.

Áki raised yet another half-empty mug to Bran. "Ya know, lad, if you'd have a drink and just admit you and the lady of the night are having an affair, I'd bet ye'd find ye'self less pent up."

The look Bran gave Áki was layered with spite and pretend surprise he had learned from decades of working with Aspera. "It still amazes me how successful the queen's experiment with you has been. Who would have guessed how quickly a criminal could bow to the sovereign who condemned him? How the servant forgets he will always be a servant given enough coin." Bran's gaze could have cut stone.

Áki's nostrils flared as he set his cup down, but he remained quiet. It wasn't often he was cowed without rage.

The statement was fraught with accusations, or threats, depending on who was listening. To a loyalist, it was draped in threats on behalf of the queen. To Randal, Drisil, and Áki, it cut to the core of who they were. Drisil instantly sobered and turned to take in her lover.

"What is it?" she whispered.

Bran lowered his voice, glancing between Áki and Randal. "Where is Merrick?"

"Not here, as you can see," she said, the sauciness in her voice returning. "I'm not his keeper."

Bran slipped into the space between Randal and Drisil, taking her arm. He brought his lips to her ear and spoke in a grave whisper, "How is his drinking?"

Drisil stiffened, and her lips formed a hard line. "The same, I suppose."

There was a brief moment where Bran leaned closer, and his anger softened into yearning. Drisil's lips parted, and she turned her head a breath toward Bran's. The electricity between them! Randal felt his body flush. It was a brief moment of desire, broken when Bran caught him looking.

Randal looked away, embarrassed—until his eyes inevitably were drawn back. He envied what they had.

Gently, Bran pulled Drisil to her feet, a suggestion that she obeyed. More surfaces of their bodies touched now. "May I speak to you in private, please?"

Another double-edged statement. Randal didn't see any indication of his meaning from Bran, but Drisil met Randal's eye. He felt like the world's biggest idiot for not looking away when Bran caught him the first time. But the gesture was even worse than a simple, *We have company*. No, it implied that he was not trusted enough to hear what Bran had to say. Nor was Áki, surely. But it was Randal they worried about.

Drisil let Bran lead her out by the hand.

For good reason, Randal thought, still hot with longing, embarrassment, and shame. He turned back to the bar and held his mug between his hands.

Áki set his mug down with a loud crack. Randal jumped. "What an ass," he growled. "Implying that I'm a moralless brute! That I just goes where the money is. Have I not been clear about that from the start?" He fixed Randal with a bleary-eyed scowl.

Randal sighed. "Immoral is a better word. But you have indeed been rather clear about it, yes."

"So, what's he getting at, pointing out the obvious?" Áki always spoke too loudly. Some heads turned their way.

"Well, he got under your skin, didn't he?" Randal said. Usually, he would take the higher ground. It rarely worked, but he tried to defuse the situation, turning a positive leaf. Tonight, he didn't care.

Áki's eyebrow arched so high it nearly sat in the middle of his forehead. "Wow, I like this new fire of yours, Randal. I'm looking forward to seeing how deep your assholery goes."

Before Randal could again correct the man, Áki stood up noisily. It was always alarming how hulking he was. It only took a step in his direction for the long, thick-as-a-tree arm to bridge the distance and clap Randal roughly on the back. The thumping of his boots made Randal's teeth rattle.

"Hey! Where are you going?" Randal turned and called out.

Áki raised a hand in farewell. "I'm not getting stuck alone with your boring ass. Tab's yours!" he hollered before the door shut.

Randal grumbled a string of curses under his breath. A classic family dinner. For several minutes he stared into his mug, seething. He was far too restless to sit with his indignity.

He stood, letting the coins clatter noisily onto the bar. It was a sum far higher than the cost of their drinks and food: the price they paid to have a place with the illusion of privacy. Return to the same watering hole enough, though, and the hunter would come. Silence and a blind eye only meant so much. Were they not a perfect example of what becomes of criminals given a warm bed? They'd turned complacent and fat.

Randal tugged his cloak back on and mounted his horse. Instead of heading back to his quarters, he led the horse farther up the hill toward their collective manor. They rarely used it anymore, now that they had private accommodations at the castle. Soon, he would be given an estate all his own, with staff to fit his new position. Its emptiness was why Randal knew it was where the two lovers went. Drisil had glamoured it, so it was the safest place for them within Stellamar's walls.

Complacent and fat.

Randal had taken up a post at a neighboring abandoned home so as not to disturb them. It was nearing midnight when Drisil finally emerged. She straightened her dress and hair, then began down the street.

Randal leaned against a wall, and he got the satisfaction of a little gasp. "You really ought to be careful, Drisil."

She glared at him. Her cheeks were still flushed, her lips dark from countless kisses. "What are you doing here, Randal? Were you spying, you creep?" She intended for her words to sting—such a difference from earlier.

Randal's nerves had settled, however, and he was unmoved. "I'm here to warn you. Aspera was clear about getting mixed up with Merrick. You should rethink your loyalties."

Her eyes narrowed. "So, you're on a first-name basis now? Getting a little too familiar, don't you think?"

Randal's heart quickened, but he kept himself steady. Her insults cut differently. "I now outrank Bran."

Drisil moved with frightening speed. Her slender fingers grabbed the collar of his tunic, and she brought her face close to his. He could smell the sweet wine still on her breath, mixed with mint. "Are you threatening me?"

He fought the sudden urge to kiss her. "No, Sila, I'm warning you. I want to protect you."

It was an alarming thing to see tears fill her eyes. "Only me?"

Randal stood up taller. He felt ashamed again. "Do you really think Bran and Merrick want your protection? What have you said already to try and convince them otherwise? Have your efforts worked? If they don't want your protection, I can promise you that they don't want mine."

It broke his heart to see her lip quiver. She must know something he didn't. Angrily, she shoved him against the wall and released him. "Fuck you, Randal. How quickly you've let the power go to your head."

"How quickly you've let your love of a man box you out of your full potential."

"At least my love isn't wasted." Her lips were pressed together so tightly the color had gone. It made him glad to see the traces of Bran fade.

"At least I'm aware that I'm below my love's ambition. Even though it's returned, I'm always second," Drisil said darkly.

Randal knew nothing that had transpired between them that night. Maybe he would have offered a friendly face instead of cutting into a wound if he had.

Drisil's chest heaved, and a single tear slid down her face. "It's Sil, and don't you ever call me it again. Only a real man will ever get to be so familiar." She dug right back into his wounds.

It hurt. It was a reminder that he would never have her that way, either—as a friend or a lover.

She continued down the road, regal and strong like the princess she once had been, not looking back. It hadn't gone as planned, but Randal still felt confident it had gone well. Drisil was smart. She would see the truth in his words and eventually turn away from her folly. She would see that loyalty was the only way. Given enough time, their friendship would heal. They were too similarly broken by misguided love not to be drawn together to find comfort.

Chapter Four
Another Child

Queen's study, two years ago

Aspera looked up as Merrick entered the room wearing a stern expression. After a solid fortnight of riding, he was still covered in the dust from the road. Heavy bags lay under his eyes, and the valleys of his wrinkles were filled with filth.

Aspera rose from her seat. "My, you never displease with your haste, Merrick."

Merrick dropped to one knee and bowed deeply. "Your Highness."

"Were you successful?" She gave a small gesture for him to rise.

Merrick stood with some effort, bracing his hand on his knee. "Yes, Your Highness. We were able to locate the child. By all accounts, she is the daughter of Aoife we've been looking for."

Aspera steepled her fingertips to hide her wicked smile behind them. "Splendid. She is being cared for?" Merrick simply dipped his head in acknowledgment. "Then you may go."

He turned to leave but paused halfway to the door.

"Is there something else, Merrick?"

"If I may, my lady?" He looked over his shoulder just enough so his voice would reach her. She didn't respond, so he pressed on. "This is the last child I'll deliver to you."

He didn't need to see her face to know that she gave him a mocking smile. "If you say so."

He left without looking back.

Present, age five

Sonder had been at the castle for over a month, and he was still struggling with getting settled. He didn't miss Merna; she hadn't been very kind to him. Nor had he loved his life at the cottage. There had been no other children to play with, so he had no friends to miss. When he cried himself to sleep, he thought about the horses and the chickens he had cared for every day.

It was the daily routine he missed—and playing unmolested by Merna's hollers, which had taken years to accomplish.

Every part of the castle was foreign. The bed was too soft, with too many pillows, instead of the warm smell of hay. He often woke tangled in blankets, breathless and sweaty, feeling like someone was stealing him away. There were foods of every color and taste under the sun. Merna's cooking hadn't been good, but at least it was familiar. After something that looked like a traditional stew fooled him, he trusted only the breads and pastries. There was a constant battle between him and the cook, who scolded him to eat every time she passed.

Even looking out the windows was different. The city moved below him, with vibrant fabrics and noises and people. He was too young to appreciate the irony that all he wanted was to see the trees that kept the world out when he had pestered Merna endlessly to see the city.

By all accounts, his life was enviable, and most children would have balked at his sulking.

As awful as it had been at Merna's, at least there he knew what to expect. He knew when she was happiest and meanest, and when he could get away with something. Everything felt off-limits now. No one spoke to him unless it was a porter telling him to stop being disruptive or a maid instructing him where to be. He'd get turned around partway between places when he tried to obey. He wouldn't mind having the old lady berate him. Here, the servants just kept their heads down and hurried about their duties, seeming to avoid him.

The worst was that Merrick hadn't come back. Sonder wanted to ask after the man, but he didn't for fear his caretakers would be offended. They were the nicest people to him, and the only recognizable faces. Instead, when someone wearing the queen's black walked by, he stole little peeks to see if he knew the person. It was never Merrick. It made him feel foolish and lonelier every time.

Another day dawned. It was still spring, which usually meant rain. He rolled over in bed, letting his final dreams drift through another dreary day. As he stirred, the bright light through his eyelids registered. The sun seemed out— it couldn't be.

Sonder shot out of bed in a flurry of blankets and crossed the little room that was his. The chill that saturated his nightclothes served to wake him further. Then, in a giant leap, he jumped onto the window seat to look. The window faced the courtyard.

It was confirmed. He thrust his fists into the air with a loud whoop and jumped off, doing a complete turn with an innocent giggle. All of his previous worries were forgotten.

The previous day had been relatively dry, with an off-and-on drizzle. Now that the sun was out, the mud was sure to solidify. It meant he would be allowed to go outside. It was a cause for celebration, which included a little dance.

He didn't hear the knock at the door in his revelry. "Master Sonder, what on this good earth do you think you're doing?"

He yelped and whirled around, immediately putting his hands behind his back. "Nothing." She gave him a skeptical look. "Sorry, Missus Merriweather. It's a nice day today. The sun is out."

She tried to remain serious, but Sonder saw a smile tugging at her mouth. "Well, I suppose 'tis a nice day, isn't it?"

He smiled shyly, glad that she agreed. "That means I can go outside, right?"

Merriweather had been his caretaker in the mornings and evenings for the past week, and she was the nicest of them all. "'Tis an unfortunate lot you're to start your lessons today." She gave him a knowing look as he became crestfallen. "There's no going outside until you've finished thems and your chores."

"Lessons? What kind of lessons?" His voice went from a whine to curiosity as he realized there would finally be a change in his aimless days.

"Don't become downcast on me. You're a ward of the queen. It's decided you've had enough time to get adjusted. You'll have to see to your chores and duties as a page. Did you really think you were brought here just to play outside?"

Sonder gave a dramatic sigh and slumped his shoulders. "Can't I play first? It won't make my chores worse if I do."

Surprise flitted across her face, but she quickly regained her composure. "Absolutely not. Come now; breakfast is waiting. I shouldn't've let you sleep in had I known you'd argue with me." She picked up a dirty stocking from the floor. "We ought to start working on your manners. You'll never do as a royal page."

Merriweather busied herself picking up his dirty laundry, but he saw the twinkle in her eye. Even though she scolded him, there was always an upturn to her lips. He hadn't been assigned a primary yet, but he hoped she would get the position because she was the kindest.

Sonder stayed standing in the sliver of sunlight. It warmed his back, and the sensation kept the unhappiness at bay. He watched her contemplate which color shirt to dress him in. She picked the indigo one with a decisive nod, then inspected the brown trousers from the day before. They were still clean enough since he had been kept indoors.

When she turned to look at him, he must have seemed as dejected as he felt. "What's the matter now, young master?"

He lifted his arms over his head so she could take his nightclothes off. "When can I go home?"

"This is your home," she said. Her cold hands brushed his skin as she pulled his clean shirt on. "Oh, dear. Sorry me hands are cold, love." Deftly she set on the neck lacing.

Tears welled in his eyes. When she looked up, her eyebrows knit together. "Why the tears?"

"I miss the chickens, I guess." He didn't have any other way to describe the homesickness he felt. His concept of home was perverted.

Merriweather glanced around as if to ensure no one was looking in on them, then knelt in front of him, wiping a tear away just as it spilled down his cheek. She smiled and pushed his hair off his face. "Come now. That old Merna couldn't possibly have been that good, was she?"

He looked at her with a measure of surprise. None of the adults had been quite so direct with him, especially at the expense of another. He sniffled, then shook his head. "No, I guess not."

She tilted her head and squeezed his shoulders. "No, she wasn't." Then she lowered her voice further. "Mean old bat, that one." Sonder drew in a laugh and wiped more tears from his eyes. "There's it. No tears, alright? So long as you focus on your duties and do well, you'll see, things'll get better once you get taken on as squire. Soon you'll be so busy you won't have time to think about it, and you'll not look back, neither."

Sonder listened intently, then nodded. Being a knight and spending more time with Merrick thrilled him.

Merriweather winked and put her hand on his cheek for encouragement. "Here now, put these on." She picked up the trousers and pressed them into his hands.

Together they put his stockings on, and she helped him lace the soft leather shoes he wore inside the castle. This was his second pair. The first he had worn outside and wholly ruined. He'd spent a day scrubbing the mud out of the carpets as punishment.

Breakfast was his favorite meal. It was the only one where he could make requests, making it the safest. So every day, he had porridge with fresh milk and a slice of warm bread smeared with fruit jam.

He ate every bite, happily swinging his feet at the table in a kitchen alcove, giggling while the head cook barked orders at the rest of the kitchen staff. There were always stately visitors to impress, and the old cook was a master at her craft, making her hard to please.

As much fun as the people watching was, the best part was being on the front lines to sneak pastries. The baker was a creature of habit. She placed the plate piled near toppling on the counter beside him. No matter how full he was, he'd grab as many as possible and stuff them into his mouth or pockets until he was caught. Today, he made it to a fourth before the sharp crack of a wooden spoon made him jump out of his seat.

"Boy, you must be the densest child, or you've sheep's wool in your ears. No more'n one! You'll thank me when you see other men going soft, and you stay nice and trim." She wagged her spoon at him.

Wordlessly, Sonder offered it back. He fought to hide his smile, attempting a remorseful look.

She looked confused at the offering before it registered. "Oh, keep it! You've already touched the thing!" she huffed with an exasperated wave of her hand before she hurried off with the rest for the notable diners.

He took a bite and looked toward the back door with a triumphant grin. There was a small window where he could watch the gardener readying the little kitchen plot for spring. The castle had the resources to use magic to keep all manner of herbs and leafy vegetables flourishing through the winter.

An escaped chicken roamed behind the man, picking through the plants. It wasn't until the bird passed the man's hand that he noticed. The gardener tried to shoo it away with a shout, but it flapped and clucked, forcing him to stand up and try to catch it. A laugh escaped past the flaky dough stuffed into Sonder's mouth as he watched them flail about.

Another caretaker rounded the corner and saw him. "There you are!" The woman lunged at him and grabbed him roughly by the wrist. "You're in big trouble, young man. You were due at your lesson half an hour ago."

He stumbled to his feet, tripping on the table as she dragged him along. "I'm sorry, I didn't know I was supposed to be—"

"I don't want to hear it. Sir Merrick'll hear about it. I'm sure he'll give you a-talkin' about being punctual."

"Is he here?" Sonder couldn't keep the excitement out of his voice. He wouldn't mind seeing the older man, even if it meant getting a few lashes to his bottom.

"No, and be glad. It's a good list of things about you."

It was awkward for the woman to walk holding him. He stepped on the back of her heels, and she dropped his hand. "Keep up," she hissed, then doubled her speed.

He managed to move his legs fast enough to stay close. This hallway was unfamiliar to him. Flashes of green caught the corner of his eye. He couldn't resist stealing a glance. And then another.

It was the castle garden.

One of the first things he was told when he arrived was to avoid it because some plants could kill him with one touch. The warning had been more than enough to keep him away. He had stolen many looks from afar but never from above.

His eyes followed the green puffs of the treetops and drank it all in. Some trees had bright spring blooms on them. Then, the green fell away abruptly, and a brown yard opened in its place. Several knights sparred in the center while others watched. Arrows whizzed through the air and buried themselves in leather dummies off to one corner. Without realizing it, Sonder was walking slower.

Two men stood off by themselves. They swung actual blades at each other, full tilt, with the entire force of their strength behind each blow. One sword came sweeping up from below, and the other man blocked it with a ring so loud it carried through the thick, wavy glass-paned windows. There were several other arching blows, each one deflected with impressive speed. Sonder let out a little gasp as one man made a daring move, a quick turn from his non-dominant side.

It, too, was deflected. Both men were bright red with the exertion, but they hardly seemed tired, not slowing a bit.

Sonder had fully stopped, and the caretaker came stomping back.

"Queen's mercy, child! You're hopeless." She grabbed his arm again and dragged him the rest of the way.

She opened the door and thrust him into a room when they arrived. A string of muttered curses barraged his back before it closed again.

A tall, thin man at the head of the room looked up at the commotion. His lips formed a hard line, a scowl shadowing his dark eyes. "You're late."

Sonder pressed himself against the closed door. "Forgive me, sir—"

"Master," the man cut in. "Master Fallen. You're to begin your etiquette lessons." The man turned and muttered, "Which you obviously need. Not knowing how to address people properly."

Sonder stayed frozen, feeling more exposed.

Master Fallen looked back at him. "Sit," he ordered. "I've heard rumors, but I see we've a long way to get you to where you need to be." Sonder continued to give him a blank stare. Fallen grumbled and swiped his hand impatiently as if willing the air to guide him to his seat. "Over there, boy."

Sonder looked and saw an armchair where the old man had gestured. He had been so focused on the man he didn't expect to see another child.

The girl had wavy brown hair that fell loose around her face, and her bright green eyes were fixed on him. She looked just as surprised to see him as he was to see her.

With one more nervous glance at Fallen, Sonder crossed toward the empty chair. The whole way, the girl's eyes stayed glued on him. He tried to be sly and watch her from the corner of his eye.

Sonder took his seat at the small table. After a few more seconds of scrutiny, the girl finally looked back toward Fallen, waiting for the lesson to begin.

She was the first child he had seen in a year, and she looked to be his age.

Sonder didn't learn very much from that first lesson. It had started overwhelmingly, with him being thrust unapologetically into the limelight. As Master Fallen droned on, his thoughts returned to the sword fight in the training yard.

For as long as he could remember, becoming a warrior had intrigued him. Merna hadn't told him stories, but occasionally they went into town during festivals where there were storytellers. He would squeeze through the press of bodies until he could lay eyes on them. Not every teller traveled with a troupe, but if they did, they called themselves word-weavers, and they never displeased. He'd watch the reenactments of battles until Merna yelled into the crowd, and he'd wiggle his way out.

Witnessing combat firsthand gave it a reality that he wasn't sure how to parse. It was nothing like the dances of the performers. He was too young and naïve to reconcile the thrill and trepidation of what it truly meant to wield a weapon against another man.

More distracting still was how his lesson-mate kept staring. She knew how to tilt her head just right, so her hair screened her from Master Fallen. Sonder sat ramrod straight, determined to ignore her. But he couldn't help but glance to see if his ploy was working. Despite his efforts, each time he checked, she was still looking.

By the time the sun was at its zenith, Sonder had to cross his legs and clench his hands to keep from squirming. It felt as though his stomach was turning on him, and his mouth was so dry it was difficult to swallow. The girl had her cheek resting in the palm of her hand, gazing off wistfully.

She blinked, and for the thousandth time, their eyes met.

It took all his self-control not to shout his pent-up frustrations.

"Now, before you two are dismissed." Sonder perked up to listen. "Name one thing each of you learned today. And do sit right, young lady," Master Fallen chided.

The girl obliged, straightening and folding her hands in her lap. Fallen continued to give her a scolding look before turning his attention to Sonder. "Well?"

Sonder wasn't sure what the man was expecting. The shock of being addressed made him cast out for an answer, trying to remember anything. Countless titles for the ladies and men of the court blended in his mind. His speech was halting as he settled on what he hoped was correct. "Sir is a title for a knight?"

Master Fallen eyed him. "Simple, but correct. And you're not to be asking the questions, understood?"

Sonder didn't understand what he meant. Master Fallen continued to stare at him for so long that Sonder began to think a response was expected. Thankfully, with an arch of his eyebrow, Fallen turned to the girl.

She offered her response with no prompting. "That it's appropriate to address any woman you're uncertain of as Lady, but it is not as appropriate with a man. It's best to address him by his title, and only as Lord if you've nothing better to work with."

Sonder was dumbstruck by how formal she sounded. It made him feel like a dimwit.

"Correct." Master Fallen clapped his hands loudly. Sonder jumped. "That concludes our lesson for today, children. My, it seems we've gone past the proper meal. No matter. There should be food held over for you."

Sonder stood up. His legs felt like jelly. He hoped his chores were simple because he wanted nothing more than to run through the courtyard to spend his bottled energy. He was nearly bursting from it.

As Sonder made to leave, Fallen called out to him, "Boy, before you go, I have a correspondence intended for the High Justice. If you'd see to its delivery."

Sonder's face flushed as he stuttered, "I'm not sure where he is, sir. I-I mean, Master Fallen."

Fallen's eyes narrowed slightly. The girl spoke up before he could launch into his reprimand. "I can show him, Master Fallen."

The man's brow remained knit as he considered it, tapping the wax-sealed letter on his desk. Had it been earlier in the day, he would have no doubt still scolded Sonder. "Alright. See to it."

Sonder hesitated, neither the girl nor the man saying anything. Fallen cleared his throat loudly and looked at the letter with his eyes nearly popping out. He hurried forward to take it, managing to bark his shin on the table leg. Fallen was unmoved as Sonder sucked in a pained breath and hopped the rest of the way.

"Be sure it gets there undamaged. Have you not had a proper tour of the castle?" Fallen asked.

"No, sir," Sonder said, clutching the letter.

The master brought his hand up to rub his face. The loose skin around his chin pulled and stretched, making his features droopy. "I'll have to have a word with your caretakers. But, for now, follow the young mistress. I'll let your next engagement know you won't be attending." He gathered up the papers on the table and tapped them lightly to straighten them before putting them in a drawer. "Please get him up to speed."

The girl gave a little curtsy. "Of course, Master Fallen."

Sonder wasn't sure if he had been dismissed. Before Fallen scolded them more, the girl snatched his hand and led him from the room.

Once they reached the main hallway, she dropped his hand. Not knowing where he was or how to find the kitchens, he hurried after her. The only part about this wing that stood out was the color of the carpets. The branch of the castle he lived in had red carpets styled with white flowers. Here they were predominately blue with shapes that reminded him of sunbursts.

When his strides matched hers, she broke the silence. "You're really shy, aren't you?"

Sonder's face flushed. "Am not." The little girl giggled. He kept looking at her out of the corner of his eye. Surprisingly, she didn't look back at him. "What's your name?"

"Rhianwyn. What's yours?" They came to a branching corridor, and she stopped abruptly. Her green eyes met his.

Sonder took her face in. He thought she was beautiful. She looked like wilderness glimmered just beneath her almond-toned skin with freckles dusting her nose. But he scrunched his nose up as if smelling something foul. "That's a weird name."

"Not as weird as how timid you are," she shot back. She remained stone-faced. "What's your name?"

He scowled. "Sonder."

Rhianwyn smiled so brightly her eyes squinted closed. Her curtsy was punctuated with a shoulder bob. "It's nice to meet you, Sonder." She grew serious again, and her nose crinkled a touch. "That's how you meet new people. Now, we're supposed to go that way."

She pointed over his shoulder and then brushed by him. He had to turn and hurry to catch her. "Why haven't I seen you before?"

Rhianwyn continued not to look at him, walking with a bounce in her step as she emphasized rolling to the balls of her feet. "Because I didn't want you to."

He went slack-jawed. "Huh?"

Her smile was warm and genuine, with little dimples appearing on her cheeks. "I've been watching you since you got here. I was too busy in the garden to go to you, but I also didn't want to introduce myself if you turned out to be mean."

Sonder leaned forward a little to get a better look at her expression. Now he wished she would look at him so he could tell if she was joking. "How do you know I'm not mean?"

She stopped again and made him take a step back to face her. "Anyone who talks that much to the animals has to be nice. They wouldn't listen to you jabber away if you weren't. They don't like to listen to mean people."

He felt his face growing hot again. She had been watching him making playmates out of the animals. The whole time, he hadn't considered that anyone might hear him. Now he knew how silly that was. Even the staff could have listened. They all must be laughing at him while he wasn't around.

"Well, are you going to knock so we can go?" He couldn't decide yet if he liked how her eyes twinkled, as if she was constantly partaking in some joke. "He's probably not here, but his attendant will be."

Sonder turned and saw that they were in front of a dark door with a knocker too high for him to reach. He rapped the heavy wood with his knuckles and stepped back to wait. Rhianwyn let out a restless sigh and used the heel of her hand to bang on it. She gave him a sidelong look, then stepped aside so she wouldn't be seen.

A woman in black robes lined with sky-blue silk looked out. Her dark hair was tied in a tight bun, and the silks made her eyes look all the more intense. They showed a moment of surprise until she looked down and saw him. "Can I help you?"

"I'm a page. This letter is from Master Fallen, for the justice." His voice tremored, but he felt a sense of pride in getting the details right. He sought Rhianwyn's approval.

The look did not get past the woman. She leaned farther out of the doorway to look, and her face went emotionless. "Rhianwyn." Her tone was curt.

Rhianwyn merely bobbed another curtsy and said nothing, which left Sonder bewildered.

The attendant looked back at him. "You must be Merrick's boy, then?"

Sonder perked up at the name. "Is he here?"

"No. There's work he needed to see to. But a bird a week ago said we should expect you." The letter slipped into her sleeve, and she shooed them away. "Go on, I have work to get done."

The door closed, leaving them in the gloomy hallway.

Rhianwyn began back down the way they had come, leaving Sonder behind. He soon caught up to her. "Does she not like you?"

The girl didn't look at him. "It's usually her that catches me breaking the rules. They never listen because they think she has it out for me." She looked pleased with herself. "Who's Merrick?"

It was all he could do to keep up with her. "I don't really know what to call him, but he's been checking in on me since I was a baby."

"That's weird." They walked in silence until they rounded a corner. "Do you have any parents?"

"I never knew them." Sonder did his best to look around at what part of the castle they were in.

"Me neither." She said it so evenly Sonder turned to her, examining her profile.

When she didn't say anything further, Sonder decided to offer more himself. "I had a caretaker until Merrick brought me here a month ago." She still didn't say anything. "How long have you lived here?" he tried.

"I was brought here about two years ago. When I was four. I don't remember why. There was a fire, and then a man brought me. I haven't seen him since." She looked at Sonder then. "How old are you?"

"I'm five," he said. He was too nervous to admit he wasn't sure.

Her face lit up. She turned toward him. "Hey, me too! When is your birthday? I was born in April."

Sonder hesitated. He had never been around other kids, so her sudden excitement caught him off guard. "I don't know. No one has ever told me." Merna had counted down the springs until he would be taken away. He wasn't sure what a birthday was.

She looked at him as if he were sprouting a third eye. "You don't know? How can you not know?" He shrugged again, beginning to feel hurt. Rhianwyn thought for a moment, one side of her mouth tucking in and her eyes looking up. Then her face brightened, and she grabbed both his hands and squeezed them. "We'll say it's in autumn. That makes me older." She stood a bit taller, puffing her chest up.

"Why should you get to be older?" He pulled his hands out of hers and gave her the satisfaction of looking indignant. Sonder knew enough to know that being older meant more privileges.

She lifted her chin a little higher and preened. "Well, for starters, I am helping you, right? So, I know more. Now, come on, I'm ravenous." She began to walk again, making him catch up once more.

For several minutes they walked in silence, with Rhianwyn leading and Sonder struggling to remember where they were going. After a while, she spoke again. "So, are we going to be friends?"

He glanced at her, but she had her gaze fixed forward. He again thought it odd how she had stared at him throughout the lecture yet seemed satisfied not to look at all now. He couldn't gauge her. When he didn't answer, she stopped and fixed him with a stern look, lips pursed and eyes big. "Well?" she pressed

"Uh, sure. I guess we can be friends."

Rhianwyn gave a satisfied nod. Then she took his hand in hers, looking away once more. It was the easiest their friendship would ever be.

Chapter Five
First Year

Merrick took the mug of spiced cider offered to him, even though his joints ached for something stronger. He was unwilling to let his demons mar this home, filled with the laughter of children and tender kisses between husband and wife. He was just Uncle Merrick here. Let the shadows stay wrapped in his saddlebags.

"Feels like just yesterday we saw you, lad." Grace smirked at him as he took a sip.

"My work brought me this way," Merrick responded.

"You still have yet to tell me what manner of work that is." The older woman lowered herself into a stuffed armchair beside the fire. Merrick drummed the ceramic and fixed her with an uncomfortable look. Finally, she took a drink of her own cider and let out a contented sigh. "I suppose it doesn't matter, does it? You can keep your secrets here if you'd like. How's that sweet boy doing?"

Merrick's face softened. He looked down and let himself remember the last time he had seen Sonder, the feeling of the boy tumbling into his outstretched hands and their shared laughter.

He had been lucky to catch his first steps. The memory made his heart feel brittle. Someday his arms would have to stop being a place of refuge.

Grace responded to his silence with a laugh. "Well, that's good to hear." The mischief on her face turned whimsical. "When will we have the pleasure of seeing him again?"

Merrick fought to keep the pain from his smile. "My road is no place for a child." It ached more than usual tonight.

"I suppose not." She let him nurse his wounds, changing the subject. "I've renounced the Lorist way, but let's have a story, hm? It's a fine night for it." She let her words linger before she hollered for the family to join them.

Two girls and a young boy came running. It was a cacophony of jostling and joy for somewhere to sit. Paul had no regard for the steaming liquid in Merrick's hands as he clamored into his lap. The girls protested, and Merrick couldn't help but laugh. Before Grace began, he met her eye and smiled with gratitude, her son's head resting against his shoulder.

Present, age six

It took another month for Sonder to adjust to his new routine, but Merriweather had been right: the rigorous schedule kept him constantly on the move and too busy to look back at his old life.

Mornings were for lectures until lunch. Rhianwyn was a near-constant companion for those. The lessons taught them how to hold a fork and make their bows look smart. Once they were deemed presentable, the lectures included reading and writing, and basic arithmetic. For a while, they played games, like seeing who could make the other laugh during their dance lessons, until it earned Sonder a bright-red lash. Afterward, they kept their fun less obvious, only letting out their suppressed giggles in their free time.

They were taught like noble children but were treated very differently. Since Merrick was a justice and an advisor to the queen, Sonder's education would be more profound than the average knight's. Rhianwyn was the better student and helped him often, which he outwardly begrudged but was secretly grateful for.

Afternoons were for chores. Rhianwyn helped the healers or in the gardens while Sonder was assigned to the Knights-Justices. He did everything from running messages, cleaning their offices, helping them into formal clothes for events, and any odd errands. He only had to offer afternoon sweet biscuits and tea to his teachers on the best days. Many people were trying to fill the void of Merrick's continued absence.

One month, Sonder was assigned to Áki, whom he had vague memories of. He was scrubbing the man's leathers the first day, and the water turned a rusty brown. He wondered at it but never asked because of a foreboding feeling. The reek was impossible to get out, too. It was far more unpleasant than how Merrick smelled from traveling.

Áki had Sonder polishing his weapons every day. He would go on and on about caring for them, techniques for each, and how they were crafted. He accentuated his words with sweets in hand and lounged across every piece of furniture he could.

That went on until Merriweather happened by and saw. The fit the woman threw on Sonder's behalf was impressive, punctuated by colorful insults about the contents of the man's skull, or lack thereof. The following day, while Sonder was tidying the man's study, which was a never-ending process, the brute of a man spoke about the "old bat" fondly.

Although he was the rudest, most disgusting person Sonder had ever met, the boy enjoyed working for him. The brazen attitude was refreshing, and he spent lots of time stifling his laughter with shy smiles. Best of all, Áki slipped him pastries as he worked with a wink.

It was a sad day when Áki left on royal business. Before he went, he laid a heavy hand on Sonder's shoulder, and the warmth in Áki's regard left Sonder starry-eyed.

Drisil took over occasionally, too. She helped him with reading and asked him questions that made him think, like how eating his favorite food made him feel or how he would describe smells. She told him it would help develop his magical abilities—if he had any. Despite her kind smiles, Sonder always felt uneasy around her. The woman's stare felt like she could see into his thoughts. He hoped she liked what she saw.

She often left, too.

Twice, a man named Bran came to him. Sonder thought it was Merrick the first time because of how he moved, but then saw that this man was shorter and older. An old scar marred his eyebrow down to his clean-shaven jaw. Sonder froze under that intense brown gaze—it looked like it knew everything.

The second time, Sonder handed Bran a letter. A justice had asked him to deliver it that morning. Sonder recognized the feather stamped into the wax and knew it was from Merrick, who still hadn't come to see him.

"Goddess's wrath," Bran cursed, crumpling the note.

"What does that mean?" Sonder tilted his head.

Bran looked at him as if surprised to see him there. "Don't repeat it."

"Why?" Sonder asked.

"Because it'll get you whipped," Bran snapped, and began to walk away.

"Why?" Sonder repeated.

Bran rounded on him. Despite how Sonder's heart hammered, he didn't feel unsafe. He could see the man's fury cool before he answered. "It's a curse of the old ways. The queen has made mention of the gods punishable by death. Repeating it will cause you far worse."

"Why?" Sonder was enraptured. His brow furrowed. He had no idea what could be worse than death.

Bran hesitated. "Because Aspera is greedy and doesn't want to share power with the gods. You, most of all, must never invoke them."

Tears brimmed Sonder's eyes as he looked up at Bran. "Why?"

Bran knelt in front of the young ward with a conflicted look, one that Sonder didn't understand. "Because you're part of the gods' legacy." Bran placed a hand on Sonder's cheek. The gentleness the man responded with made the boy ache for something he did not know. "So do as you're told." He stood up. "And don't repeat this to anyone, or I'll whip you. Then have Merrick do it."

Sonder nodded rapidly with saucer eyes. "Yes, sir."

"Good. If only Merrick listened as well as you," Bran growled. "The cursed fool forgets himself and got too sick for your first weapons lesson, so I'll be your teacher today."

Sonder noted Bran's disappointment in Merrick's non-presence. When the man turned to leave Merrick's study, Sonder hurried after him, excited he was finally learning how to fight, even if it was swinging a wooden sword against a wooden beam.

The only reliable marker of time was Sundays.

There were no lectures on Sundays. Of course, Sonder was still expected to be available for any odd tasks that cropped up, but he didn't mind, especially as the weather got nicer and he was sent to the stables to help with the horses. Once everything was finished, he and Rhianwyn were given time to just be kids.

They played hide-and-find in the yard or fought with sticks until they got underfoot and shooed away. They would sneak into the kitchens and steal sweets until the baker caught them and flung her spoons after them as they burst into delighted squeals. The staff did their best to hide their delight while scolding the two.

For five months, they found plenty of trouble without much consequence. It was a freedom they took for granted.

Somewhere along the way, Sonder had stopped thinking about his mentor. Then, one day, as he was changing out of formal wear from an etiquette lesson into something more suitable for chores, he turned and saw Merrick standing in the doorway.

Sonder's heart leapt. He stood stock-still, his tunic left untied.

Once, Sonder had imagined all sorts of scenarios for how this would go. A soft reunion, where Merrick offered a hug like old times, the incident of being struck forgotten. Other days, he wanted to rage at the man for abandoning him.

Instead, he was struck dumb in his underwear. Merrick looked worn, with shadows under his eyes, and his hands nervously rolling his horse crop.

Merrick broke the silence. "Are you well?"

That gruff voice caused a slew of emotions. "Yes, sir," Sonder replied. He wanted the man to open his arms to him. His lip trembled.

Instead, Merrick asked, "You've begun your studies?"

Sonder tightened his composure as he had learned. "Yes, sir."

"The masters will speak well of you, then?" Sonder hadn't noticed Merrick's lack of eye contact until those blue eyes cleared, and he came back from his distant thoughts. The man was looking at him now.

"Yes, sir." Sonder felt like he may be lying. He had no idea if they would speak well of him. Telling a lie worried him because he could be punished, and he could almost remember the sting from Merrick's hand.

Merrick nodded, satisfied. "You're comfortable, then?" Before Sonder could answer, he asked, "Who is your caretaker?" His brow furrowed as if realizing this was more important.

Sonder raised his shoulder. "I don't know, sir. It's always changing. Mistress Merriweather is my favorite, though."

Merrick's brow deepened. "No primary has been assigned?"

Sonder shook his head, nervous at the man's sudden displeasure.

"I'll see to it. Merriweather, you say?"

Sonder could only interpret Merrick's frustration as a result of something he had done, so he opted for even more formality. "Yes, Sir Merrick."

Sonder could not read his expression. The man closed the distance between them. Sonder flinched and shut his eyes, expecting the worst. Instead, Merrick knelt.

He still wore his riding leathers. They were always pungent from stale sweat, mingled with the dust from the road and the warm smell of horses, the peppery sting of tree soap layered under it. It was a harsh scent that Sonder loved.

Merrick laid a heavy hand on the boy's shoulder, and after several seconds, Sonder looked his mentor in the eye.

There was a play of emotions on Merrick's face as he struggled to settle on what to say. After the pause, he finally muttered, "You're going to be alright here."

Merrick's words brought a flood of relief. Sonder's lip trembled anew as he nodded.

Tenderly, Merrick put his gloved hand on the cheek he had hit. The worn leather felt soft as the thumb traced along his skin. It was as much of an apology as he could muster.

Merrick dropped his hand with a heavy sigh, and the moment was over. He stood up with a fluidity that spoke to his fitness. "I've other matters to see to. I'll try to join you for dinner this evening."

He didn't come for dinner. But as promised, Merriweather announced that evening that she would be his head caregiver. It lessened the disappointment when she said Merrick had left for several more months.

The next day, after the chores were done, Rhianwyn met Sonder near the stables as planned. She leaned against the building with her hands behind her back while drawing in the dirt with her foot.

She looked up as he approached and smiled; her purple wool dress made her green eyes sparkle. "Do you want to go explore the gardens today?"

Sonder's mind had been on Merrick, so her question jarred him. "You go to the gardens? Aren't there poisonous plants?" he asked with alarm.

She laughed at him. "Who in the world told you that?" She answered with more consideration when he looked indignant. "Well, I guess some are. But I help Master Wilkin tend the grounds. Most of them are harmless, and I know where the dangerous ones are." A sly smile crossed her face.

Sonder thought for a second. It had been a nameless face in the sea of servants who had told him it was forbidden for him to go into the gardens. Since then, he had learned that some of them used empty threats to avoid the work of watching them. The curious tug toward the place returned, same as when he had seen it from the window.

Rhianwyn's eyes sparkled, and he didn't want to say no and have her tease him endlessly until he relented anyway. "Okay."

"Come on then!" She grabbed his hands and led him through the archway with its wrought-iron gate open for the day.

The central paths all led to different themed areas. Off of those, many ended in quiet places, obscured by the canopy and fans of leaves. Flowers of all shapes and colors grew in each bed, and sweet smells drifted through the air. Neat tags adorned the most useful foliage with blurbs for their application. Sonder looked in amazement as they walked through the overgrown trellises with bright blooms. The shade was a welcome relief from the late-summer sun. It had been so long since Sonder had been surrounded by plants, he hadn't realized how much he missed them. He had never seen something so frivolous.

"Lots of flora here are nearly impossible to find within a hundred miles of Stellamar," Rhianwyn said. Her fingers were still wrapped around his even though he followed of his own will. Her expression had grown wistful with the joy of showing him her favorite place.

"How did they get here?" he asked. The canopy of vines gave way to a tunnel of trees. The wonder of it left him breathless.

"I don't know. I ask about a hundred questions a day so that Master Wilkin won't answer them anymore. I think it's because he doesn't know. It's too bad you can't work here with me, because it's a lot of fun. Not nearly as strict as working for the justices, that's for sure." Rhianwyn swung their arms.

"Why do you get to work in here?" Sonder asked.

She shrugged. "Something about the queen wanting me to be medicant, whatever that means. The Master of the Gardens says a lot of crazy things." She rolled her eyes, but she sounded fond of the man. "Wilkin says I'm good at it, but I just enjoy getting to be outside. He and Mistress Gwenyvir have been giving me lots of easy quizzes on plants and healing." She shrugged again. "They leave me alone a lot."

Sonder's shoulders slumped. "I wish I was as smart as you."

Rhianwyn made a comforting noise. "Don't say that. I get left alone so that I can focus on learning." When she saw he looked disappointed, she bumped her shoulder into his arm. "It's fine. I'll show you some of the best places to hide. We can spy on all sorts of people here, and there's less staff to watch over us and make demands."

Sonder grinned when she bumped him again. "Okay." A place for him to get away from all the pressure.

She smiled, then tugged him suddenly onto a faint trail of trampled grass that looked like only animals used it. They had to skirt around branches threatening to snag their clothes. Soon, the narrow path opened up into a hidden clearing blanketed in soft grass, where a tree stood heavy with fruit.

Rhianwyn dropped his hand and ran to it. She snagged two of the fuzzy fruits from the lower branches. He walked up, and she tossed one at him, which he caught cleanly.

"What is this?" he asked, looking down at it. The skin was velvety to the touch and a soft orange-red.

She balked. "You've never had a peach before?" Juice ran down her chin as she took a bite out of hers.

"This is what they look like? I've had them, but never off of the tree." He looked concerned. "Are we allowed to eat them if they're in the queen's private garden?"

Rhianwyn rolled her eyes and opened her palm up to the tree. "Do you see how many there are? She won't miss two of them. Plus, if they aren't picked soon, they will go bad. We're making sure they aren't wasted." Quick as a cat, she snagged his hand and tugged him down. "Come on, sit down and eat it already. They're the last of the season."

Sonder obliged. It was one of the best peaches he had ever had. The skin was thin, and the flesh so tender that each bite meant he had to slurp up the juices. They giggled at each other, wiping their mouths on their sleeves. When the pits were picked clean, they stood up to see how far they could throw them. That, at least, was something that Sonder was better at, although just barely. They both sat back down. He grew serious again once their laughter died.

Rhianwyn noticed the lull and tipped her head. "What's wrong?"

Sonder picked at the grass. "Merrick came to see me yesterday."

"He did? What did he say?" He just shrugged. "He didn't say anything?"

"He asked how everything was going. He didn't show up for dinner like he said he would, but Merriweather was named my head caretaker." He still pulled at the delicate green stalks.

"Well, I guess there's that. Did you see him today?"

Sonder shook his head. "When I reported for the day, he had already left. Merriweather said he would leave, but I didn't think so soon."

Rhianwyn whistled. "Sheesh. He sounds scary if he's that busy all the time for the queen."

"He isn't really. I mean, he *is* scary, but he's also nice. I don't know how to explain it." Sonder paused, and she let him gather his thoughts. "I wish he were here more." A tinge of frustration laced through him. "I was just getting used to everything, and now I feel on edge again, looking for him in the yard." Sonder sighed. "I don't know."

"Well, he did one good thing. Merriweather is the best of all the caregivers. Lucky duck." Rhianwyn nudged him and tried to reassure him with a smile.

Sonder smiled back. "Thanks, Wyn."

She wrinkled her freckled nose and gave him a goofy smile. "Anytime, Mister Serious."

Sonder nudged her, and she pushed back. Within seconds, they were wrestling in the grass. Sonder took a big handful and sprinkled it over her. She wiggled free with a squeal and, in one motion, jumped up to run away.

"Can't catch me!" she shouted over her shoulder.

Sonder got up and ran after her. Rhianwyn disappeared into the mass of foliage. He crashed through but quickly slowed as he didn't immediately see her in the shade. She was faster than him, and had a clear advantage of knowing the garden better. Suddenly, every plant looked dangerous, and he wondered if they were poisonous.

"Rhianwyn?" he called out.

She materialized from behind a bush and shushed him. "Quiet!" she scolded. Her warm fingers wrapped around his. "There are other people here!"

Rhianwyn wore the wicked grin that she got when she was up to no good. Movement caught his eye through the leaves. A man dressed like a noble was leading a woman of the castle staff.

"Let's follow them and spy on them!" Rhianwyn whispered.

With no real reason to object, Sonder followed. They trailed the pair quietly. Occasionally, the woman would look over her shoulder to see if they were followed. Rhianwyn noted that the winding path the couple was taking was backtracking, her excitement growing.

"Why are you so good at this?" Sonder whispered as they slowly crept forward to listen better.

Rhianwyn put her fingers to her lips. "There's a girl who visits me here in the garden. She asked me to keep my eyes peeled for anything suspicious, so I follow people around."

"A girl?" Sonder asked.

"Shhhh, keep your voice down. Another girl, yes. A little older than us." Rhianwyn pulled some branches aside to let him pass.

"The other kids talk to you?" He felt a slight pang of jealousy. They weren't allowed to play with the other children.

"No. I don't think she's from the castle. I only see her here, but she's never there when Master Wilkin gives us our tasks. I don't know who she is."

"Doesn't that make you nervous?"

Rhianwyn shook her head with a bit of a grin, then again pressed her finger to her lips. The rustle of the couple moving through the underbrush stopped.

They were in a nook with a bench, surrounded by tall bushes that obscured them but also the children.

"I don't think we've been followed. Do you?" the man asked.

The woman shook her head, tugging her shawl tighter around her shoulders. "I was meticulous when I snuck out."

"As was I. What news have you?" the man asked.

The answer made little sense to the children. The woman murmured of a man named Randal and some order he had given to the justices. Rhianwyn looked at Sonder and silently asked if he understood what they were talking about, but he shook his head.

The man looked grave while he listened, and once the woman finished, he nodded. "Thank you." He placed both hands on her cheeks. "We need to try and warn them in the slums that a raid is coming. To hide whatever books they have left. I am so sorry to ask this of you. After this, we'll leave and get to safety."

The woman stood up on her tip-toes and pressed her lips to his. It was passionate, with both of them clinging to each other, savoring it as if it would be their last. The children let out little gasps, though they couldn't be heard over the life in the garden. "I love you," she breathed when she pulled away.

"I love you." The man's hands still lingered on her face. "Once we do this, meet me by the gate in three days. I'll send word to Cerdan, and hopefully, he can pass it on to Mother Eissie. She'll know what to do." He kissed her once more, briefly, then pulled her forehead to his lips.

The woman held the man's hand before the distance forced them to part ways.

When they were good and gone, Rhianwyn whispered, "What do you think that was all about?"

Sonder's nose wrinkled with disgust. "I don't know. Why was she sucking the man's face?"

Rhianwyn gaped. "I don't know!"

A week later, they sat outside studying, enjoying a particularly gorgeous day. Sonder looked up and saw the same woman being led roughly by the castle guards. It was hard to tell initially, but he gently nudged Rhianwyn with his elbow once he was sure.

"Hey, Wyn, isn't that the woman we saw talking to that man last week?" he asked.

Her nose rose from her book, and she looked around as if reentering their dimension. Sonder had to point her in the right direction.

Rhianwyn squinted. "That does look like her. How strange." Her face grew severe the more she looked. "That looks like the same dress she was wearing. It's just filthy now. I wonder what she's done that the guards have her?"

Sonder shook his head, and they returned to their studies.

The next day, he sat in on a trial. Drisil escorted him because Merrick still hadn't returned. It was the first trial Sonder had ever seen, and his insides buzzed with anticipation.

They sat near the back. As each member entered the room, Drisil told him their name and position in the court. A little thrill went through him when Queen Aspera was announced.

Sonder did his best to pay attention to everything Drisil whispered to him, but he found his eye drawn to a giant slab of wood behind the throne. It was polished to a shine, its color deep red and comforting, and even from the back of the room, he felt as though each grain held a story. The urge to let his fingers follow their grooves was overwhelming until an itch drew his eye to the queen. Her eyes felt like they were burrowing into his soul, and he quickly looked away.

The morning began with citizens' complaints against their neighbors. It was a slow process. To Drisil's credit, she tried to make the process more entertaining, but Sonder found his diversion in the people. His favorite was the man bent over a tablet, taking notes. His knuckles were so knobby that they looked like they'd be stuck in the shape of a claw. A few other children older than him would catch him staring, but they all averted their gazes quickly. Sonder even saw someone picking at their nose in the sea of grim-faced officials. When he made a noise, Drisil's hand had rested on his lap, and her look silenced him. He was glad the queen wasn't watching him right then.

After a short break for lunch, the proceedings moved into the trails. There were so many people considered enemies of the crown.

Some shouted it was lies, claiming they were framed. Others fell to their knees and begged for mercy, pleading to reveal their secrets. The process left Sonder awestruck, and Drisil didn't have to keep him enraptured.

Near the end, the man he and Rhianwyn had seen in the garden was thrust into the room. Drisil leaned over and explained his crimes, as she had done all day. The man was being tried for treason and espionage. Sonder drank in every detail, including the sad resignation the man wore like a badge.

Sonder wanted to tell Rhianwyn everything. He knew the answer to why the woman had been captured. But the following day was Equinox Eve, and the castle erupted in a flurry of activity, so he didn't get the chance.

For weeks, the cumulation of their lectures had pertained to the etiquette for the event. On the day of, their only obligation was a breakfast with the queen, where they sat at the very end of the table, prim, proper, and silent. All they had to do was be sure to use the right glass, stand when they were supposed to, and utter the correct script with the other diners. Sonder watched Rhianwyn as she continually stole looks at Aspera. Although there was an odd tension among the staff, the queen was as demure and generous with her smiles as any sovereign.

Once Aspera rose and dismissed them, the rest of their day was theirs to do as they pleased.

They weren't allowed to attend any of the gatherings in the city or the ball because they had no chaperons, but there were plenty of wonders still. Rhianwyn had seen two festivals already, so she took Sonder by the hand and ensured the day wasn't squandered.

The castle teemed with vendors laden with exquisite jeweled masks, lacy fans, and decorative swords. Costumed performers danced and tumbled in the courtyards. At the same time, nobles from all over the country dressed in their finest strolled through the corridors. The children wove through all of it on the hunt for tables covered in plates of food. They tasted from every single one, and the servants were too busy to scold them.

All of the gaiety was intoxicating. As the sun began to set, Rhianwyn convinced Sonder to climb up the curtain wall to watch the revelers in the streets while more nobles streamed through the castle gates in their decorated carriages.

Just as the children got settled, tiny torches strung across the walkways winked to life, one by one. Servants lit paper lanterns and cast them to drift in the fountains. It looked like the night sky beneath them as the streets blazed with life just a few blocks away. Even people not invited into the castle wore their most expensive silks and furs.

"Wow," Sonder breathed.

"Told you." Rhianwyn let out a self-satisfied giggle. It was well earned.

As they watched, she pulled out some slices of smoked sausage and a variety of roasted vegetables and fruits freshly harvested for the festival. As they ate the bounty, Sonder finally mentioned the trial to her.

"Did you hear his sentence?" she asked, talking with her mouth full.

"Hanging. The nobles are required to go to it tomorrow. Something about him being part of a group of traitors. Lorists, I think?"

She toyed with the last blackberry on the napkin. "What about the woman?"

Sonder didn't understand the change in her mood. "I'm not sure, and I'd be afraid to ask. I don't think I should recognize them." He popped another slice of sausage into his mouth and sucked the grease off his fingers.

"True," she whispered.

"Why?" he asked, finally picking up that she was upset. He remembered the girl Rhianwyn had mentioned when they spied on the two traitors, and he knew then she was hiding something.

"Nothing. Here." She pulled out two small cakes wrapped in a cloth. She handled them delicately, even though they had been roughed up in her skirt pocket, and offered him one.

"What's this for?" he asked, cupping the cake.

"It's your birthday today, remember?" Her tone still hadn't regained its brightness.

"You changed the subject," he pressed. He watched her hand wrap around his and hold it out.

Rhianwyn held him steady while the second cake balanced precariously in her lap. "It's just, they looked like friends. I'd be sad if something happened to you and I didn't know what." She stuck a slender candle into his cake and lit it with a match. When the wick caught, she smiled up at him. "You're supposed to make a wish and blow it out. Don't tell anyone your wish, or it won't come true," she blurted as he opened his mouth to speak.

The warm candlelight illuminated her face from beneath. She knew so much more about castle life than he did. He returned her smile because he had no idea how to comfort her, nor how to press her to reveal what she was hiding.

I wish we can both be happy.

He blew the little flame out as a giant, glittering sky-burst exploded over the rooftops.

Chapter Six
Garden of Secrets

A fringe village near the border, four years ago

Merrick walked up to Áki, who was silhouetted against the blazing house. The sound of singing swords and screams still rang in his ears. It was no surprise things had gotten away from them. He had been here earlier that day, demanding the two girls be given over. He had tried to avoid this. At least, that was what he'd told himself as the hulking man grinned when Merrick relinquished his control.

"Where is the other one?" Merrick demanded now. Only one girl, the youngest, sat cowering in the grass.

"Wasn't here," Áki drawled.

"You're positive?" Merrick snapped.

"Left no table or pillow unturned." Áki's grin revealed that he enjoyed this sort of thing too much.

"You're sure this is Aoife's daughter?" Merrick's tone spoke the rest for him: What if you've left an unnecessary mess again?

Áki grinned. "You know as well as I that this is the one." He bent down and plucked a soiled dress from the ground and used it to wipe the blood from his blade. "If you want, I can burn the rest of it down looking for the other one."

"No," Merrick growled, "you've done plenty."

He turned away from the jeering man. The grass whispered as he trod through it. The fire was really taking off, a loud roar as it consumed all the air around them and spat its angry breath against his back. It was hard to hear the girl's sniffling, but he knew the sound well, for better or worse.

He knelt in front of her. She looked up like a frightened rabbit. He offered his hand out to her, palm up.

"Come here, girl. I promise I'll keep you safe."

Merrick decided he was imagining the sound of another small voice calling out for the girl, and that the fleeing shadow was his own, dancing with the fire.

Bran said only the youngest was needed.

Present, age six

The festival season began with the Equinox Ball and continued until the Hallowed tournaments. The season's magic was more thrilling now that Rhianwyn had someone to experience it with. The two previous years dulled in comparison. There were small parties nearly every week somewhere in Stellamar. Once one set of decorations came down, another went up, celebrating the phases of autumn. With her knowledge of how to enjoy it, she could tell Sonder had fallen in love with this time of year, too.

Every morning, she woke looking forward to their time together. With the shortened days, colder weather, and constant preparation for the next celebration, their lessons were short and their chores sparse. The games and giggles continued in full force. The only thing she looked forward to more was seeing the girl in the garden.

Rhianwyn always knew when she was coming because a small warbler would come. It sang outside her window in the morning or found her while she worked on the flower and herb beds. The sweet tune would chip and buzz in her ears, and her heart would take off. It might be that day or a few if something kept the girl away, but she would come.

The air was heavy with the sea mist cradled against the Mother's Range when Rhianwyn heard the song. It pulled her from sleep with a start. Her bare feet pattered to the window, and she peered into the branches outside. Unlike Sonder's room, hers looked out over the garden. Sure enough, distorted by the water droplets and wavy glass, there was a little shock of subdued orange-brown standing against the muted colors of the season. A squeal escaped her before she glanced around her empty room and composed herself.

By the time Mistress Olive opened the door, Rhianwyn had dressed. She looked up from pulling on her stockings, and she flashed her best polite smile, complete with a shy bat of her eyelashes.

"You're ready early, Miss." Olive eyed her suspiciously.

"Master Wilkin said today we're pruning back the winter herbs for experiments later." Rhianwyn squeezed her hands between her knees to keep from fidgeting. She let the excitement at the day's possibilities light her voice.

"Well, tha' is excitin', innit?" Olive's accent was heavy with the Southern Inlands, full of soft *t*'s in unusual places and many letters pronounced similarly.

The staff called her Olive because of her complexion. Rhianwyn loved her dark, shiny hair and warm brown eyes with green around the edges.

"Yes, Mum." Rhianwyn looked up through her eyelashes once more.

A smile broke across Olive's face at the term of endearment familiar to her home. "Go on. Join Sonder for breakfast 'fore he's gone." Rhianwyn jumped up and scurried out. Olive hit her on the bottom with the towel in her hands. "An' stay outta trouble, Trouble."

She barreled through the hallways and rounded the corner into their kitchen nook, gasping for breath. Sonder looked up from his plate with a raised eyebrow. "What's gotten you?"

Rhianwyn held her side. "Nothing." Her joy broke across her face, and she snagged his piece of warm bread smeared with butter and jam. The crust crunched and flaked down her dress as she bit into the soft center. "Mmmm!"

"Hey!" he protested. "Wyn, what gives?"

She spoke around her full mouth. "I'm late," she lied. "I'll see you for chores tonight!" She took off toward the door. On second thought, she stopped, ran back, and snagged the bacon slice on his plate.

"Hey!" Sonder rounded in his chair to holler after her.

"Take mine! See you." Before she closed the door, she faced him with another toothy grin before shoving the bread in her mouth and running off.

Master Wilkin was a kindly older man who had only just begun to stoop, although his hair was hardly gray. Every day he wore the same colors. Sometimes it was a pair of brown trousers with a green tunic, others vice versa, all covered up by his cloak, which was the shade of pine needles. Ever since she'd been brought to the castle, Rhianwyn had spent several days a week under his watchful eye, which actually moseyed. He leaned against his gnarled staff and walked up and down the line of help he had each day. When she had asked about the walking stick, Wilkin had said it was an old injury. The wood was hawthorn, with lots of knobby eyes all over it. To watch her better, he said, which made her giggle endlessly.

Already, people were lined up. One was another girl who'd started her apprenticeship just a few weeks prior. Her name was Alessia, and as Rhianwyn took her place at the end of the line, she glanced at the other girl and waved from the hip. There was a gap in Alessia's returned grin.

Wilkin walked down the line with his thunk-shuffle-shuffle gait. Rhianwyn looked down and folded her hands neatly in front of her.

"Don't try to play as if you've no energy this morning, young lady. Your cheeks are already windburned from running around. Finish the pruning you didn't yesterday."

"Yessir!" she said, so fast the words blended.

Before he could respond, Rhianwyn bolted to the shed and grabbed the bucket she'd left ready. Wilkin was watching for her when she shouldered back outside.

"You find me when you're done, you hear?" he shouted from the line of people still waiting.

Rhianwyn bowed. "Yes, Master Wilken." Rhianwyn saw Alessia looking at her, and she smiled again at the girl before running off through the foliage.

The first warbler came earlier that week, and she wanted to be sure she had something to keep her hidden should the second show up. So, all week, she left tasks half-finished in secluded areas, with the unfinished pruning tucked well out of sight.

Rhianwyn had spent lots of time in the gardens, combing for the most hidden spots where people rarely went because they didn't appreciate the plants. Sometimes she wanted to tell them they were missing out on the most exciting things, like the tiny flowers that opened and closed with the sun and rolled up their leaves at night. But today, she was glad they knew none of those delights.

She pushed her two pinkies into her lips and whistled a song into the crisp air as she threaded through the trees and bushes. Her eyes watched the branches overhead. The moist morning air stung her cheeks as she caught sight of the little bird from her window. It flitted between the trees with Rhianwyn until she reached the clearing.

"Go get her," she whispered, and shooed the bird away as it took to the sky.

A half hour later, a rustle behind her drew her attention. A girl with long red hair and blue eyes visible beneath her hood stood by a tree. Both girls broke into ear-to-ear smiles. Rhianwyn jumped up from her half-hearted work and flew into the other girl's arms.

The girl smelled much like the first rain, full of loam and sun-warmed stones. She was five years older than Rhianwyn. Mid-embrace, she dropped to her knees and wrapped Rhianwyn even tighter. The silky texture of the cloak warmed Rhianwyn's exposed skin.

"It's so good to see you, little one," she whispered into Rhianwyn's hair.

"I missed you, Mae."

Maeveen broke the hug and held her at arms' length, eyes still crinkled. "My sweet summer child, you've grown!" Her hands played with the plait in Rhianwyn's hair while her eyes traced the lines of her face. "You grow more beautiful every day. You look so much like Mama."

"Then you must look like Papa, and he was the most beautiful."

Maeveen burst out laughing, which made Rhianwyn feel proud of herself. "He would have appreciated that. Here, I brought you something special."

The girls sat down on the damp ground with no regard for the cold seeping into their skin. Maeveen took a sack from underneath the billows of fabric and presented a puffed pastry packed with baked apples. Rhianwyn lit up, snatching it from her sister. She chewed the doughy treat with a satisfied hum, notes of cinnamon pricking her tongue. A stoppered flask was also offered.

"Just be careful. It's likely still quite hot."

It was liquid chocolate, so rich Rhianwyn's eyes fluttered. Her whole body thrummed with pleasure. "I could die happy," she sighed.

Maeveen snorted. "Don't get ahead of yourself. You're only six, dummy."

"But it's so good," she cooed.

Maeveen rolled her eyes and grabbed the flask back. "Mmm. . . You're right. That was a good batch. I could die too."

Rhianwyn giggled as she offered the final bite of the apple puff. Maeveen grinned and snatched it right out of her fingers with her mouth and sucked her fingers clean. Rhianwyn shrieked with equal parts disgust and delight.

Maeveen laughed initially but then put her fingers to her lips. "This cloak can't hide me from everything." She opened her arm so that Rhianwyn could burrow against her side. "Come."

Rhianwyn was all too happy to nestle up against the older girl. They sat quietly, passing the flask back and forth. Rhianwyn gathered the hem of Maeveen's cloak in her hands and ran the cloth through her fingers. It was beautiful, with colors like the forest, but pooling like silver. Maeveen played with her dark braid with motherly tenderness.

"You sure do like this old thing," Maeveen said warmly. She pushed stray hairs behind Rhianwyn's ear.

"It's gorgeous," she breathed. "How come I've never seen anything like it?" Rhianwyn turned her eyes up toward her sister.

"Because it's forbidden here in Sosten."

"Why?" she asked.

"Aspera hates our magic. Mama and Papa's magic. She can't control it, so she outlawed it."

"Aren't you afraid to be here?" Rhianwyn's eyes widened.

Maeveen exhaled a laugh. "No, I'm not." She gathered the material and moved it around so it caught the light. "See that? It's like a mirror of where ever I am. It makes me nearly invisible unless someone knows what to look for." Mischief returned to her eyes as she let the cloak go. "Lucky for me, not many people know what to look for. Anyone passing by will think you're talking to yourself like a loon." She tapped Rhianwyn's nose. "It lets me sneak in." Then she shrugged. "Not that it matters. There are so many servants here, no one will think twice about it. I bring it so I don't get you in trouble."

Rhianwyn held the hem, bending and twisting the incredible magic in her hands. She couldn't get enough of it, nor could she still her rapid heartbeat. "I wish I could have a cloak like this."

"Best not. It'd get you in trouble. There are things you can accomplish with less."

"How's it made?"

Maeveen was the best teller Rhianwyn had ever met. Her words seemed to spark with life. "There are people who have studied their whole lives to make these strands, spending years of trial and error spinning wool and harvesting silk. It's beautiful watching the Weavers. Their hands sparkle, and their skin is dyed like a field of flowers. Years ago, a woman named Zizu made this dye that mimics life's colors. It's her magic and writings we still make cloaks like this to blend in with the world around us."

Rhianwyn listened with awe. Maeveen always brought mystery and danger. It made Rhianwyn feel alive like no games with Sonder could. As if whatever she was up to, like sending warblers who sang unique songs to find her, was part of something bigger.

"Will you teach me?"

"Teach you what?" Maeveen coaxed.

"Magic. Like yours. Like Mama's, and Papa's." Rhianwyn felt breathless.

"It'll be dangerous. You'll have to keep us a secret. You can't tell anyone, and you'll have to do your best to hide it, so Aspera and her mages never find out." The playful luring left her, and she grew serious.

Rhianwyn was struck by guilt, and she hardly realized how her sister's face wavered. "I told him."

Maeveen's brows met. "Told who?"

"Sonder." Rhianwyn stopped worrying the cloth and picked at her dirty nails instead. "I told him about you. When we spied on the two adults in the garden, he asked why I was so good at sneaking around, and I told him." She looked up with teary eyes. "I was having so much fun I forgot."

Maeveen sighed with relief and took her little sister's hands in hers. "It's okay."

"You're not mad?"

"No. I'm here to help him, too. It's just too dangerous for me to meet him." She pushed a stray lock of hair behind Rhianwyn's ear. "What did he say?"

"Well, I lied and said I didn't know who you were. He asked if it made me nervous." She felt like she could get lost in the kindness and warmth on Mae's face. "He doesn't know you're my sister."

Maeveen's sweet laugh rang out in response. "Probably better that way. I'd be careful telling him too much. If I teach you magic, I also want to ask one more thing from you besides guarding the secret with your life."

"Anything." She meant it with her whole heart.

"Will you help me protect him?" Maeveen tilted her head.

Rhianwyn blurted out a laugh. The idea felt so absurd to her. "I already do!" She took a second to calm her fit. "I'm the one who shows him around the castle and helps him study to stay out of trouble with the masters. They're a lot harder on him than me." Images of his bright red skin from switches and slaps flashed in her mind, and she felt terrible for laughing. A fierce protectiveness came over her. "I'll help you." She looked her sister in the eye as she spoke the words.

Maeveen's took Rhianwyn's hands in hers. Her face was inches away, and the flame of rebellion that burned in her jumped the gap and lit Rhianwyn's chest. "Then I'll teach you everything I know."

The next day, when Rhianwyn saw Sonder, her heart was warm and light. He wrinkled his nose and asked why she was grinning like a jackal, but she said nothing.

At that moment, Rhianwyn knew there was no need for a promise to protect him. She would do it regardless. Maeveen had said if Sonder ever found out about what the two girls were up to, he would likely suffer. But if he didn't know the truth, he couldn't be hurt. That made it easy to keep the secret from him.

Another year began. Their occasional lows never dampened their happiness. Come summer, though, it dawned on Rhianwyn that they would have to work harder to cherish their friendship as they grew older.

It began with them no longer spending lessons together. As a future healer, she spent more time on herbology and medicine. Sonder, meanwhile, was to be Merrick's squire, so he learned about warfare on top of the kingdom's history and law. Many of his lectures included sitting in on trials. More and more expectations continued to mount on his shoulders, and he found less time to spend with her. Therefore, Rhianwyn was sure never to miss the opportunities when they came, even if it was sitting in the library studying numbers or playing strategy games.

She enjoyed offering a distraction as duty bound him tighter.

"Sonder loves stories," Rhianwyn said one sunny day while taking a break from her assigned chores. She and Maeveen sat in the shade with the discarded tools around their feet.

Rhianwyn wove a crown out of flowers and grass, an art from her childhood before being brought to the castle. It now sat unmoving in her lap. She gathered the courage to ask permission to tell Sonder more about the older girl.

Maeveen looked delighted, pulling her needle through the embroidery in her hands. "He does?" Rhianwyn nodded. "Are you asking if you can tell him mine?" The responding nod was shyer. Maeveen giggled in her chest. "Alright."

While they hid beneath their bedsheets, she told Sonder the forbidden stories—tales of valiant knights slaying corrupt kings and wise women who saved nations from misguided sorcerers. Some of their favorites were the creation stories with gods.

Regal Harina in her gowns of summer, and her sister, Astraía, deity of autumn and the stars. Wise Dagda and Tulyra of wind and sea. This went on until they had stayed up too late one night and been caught still asleep together in his bed.

It was Merriweather who caught them. Rhianwyn had launched herself from the bed and fallen to her knees, begging for her not to report it to Merrick.

"We were studying too late, Mistress Merriweather. Honest! He asked me to help him study for tests next week. I was foolish to keep on even though we were tired."

Merriweather looked as if she wanted to say Sonder could speak for himself, but she relented. "Mistress Olive was looking for you. Go to her."

Rhianwyn wiped the fat tears she shed as she left until the matron called her attention back.

"I ought to warn you, young miss. Master Sonder can't afford this type of trouble. Sir Merrick won't tolerate it. I'll not have you jeopardizing him."

Rhianwyn bowed and left, feeling like she understood Sonder's plight better.

The garden became the only place with any semblance of their previously enjoyed freedom. There, they could be kids playing games. Even those felt different, though—they felt more real.

Sure, there was the illusion of innocence. She and Sonder called themselves Spiderlings in training as they snuck around. In the spirit of pretend, Sonder personified Merrick, gruff and bold, despite not knowing what the man did when he was away. She adopted a persona like Drisil, regal and glamorous with depths of knowledge beneath her smoky kohl eyes. But the game ended there. Rhianwyn demanded that they not tell the adults anything they overheard.

"Why?" Sonder asked.

"I don't want anyone else hurt, especially not because of us." It was nonnegotiable for her. "I don't want any more friends separated."

"Okay, I won't. I promise," Sonder said soberly.

In contrast to what he experienced, her freedom continued to expand, and she didn't squander such liberty.

Her intended apprenticeship with the royal healers was announced when she turned seven. Not only that, but she would also learn true magic if she showed promise. This delighted and frightened her. Come Solstice, it would be official.

Maeveen taught different schools of thought, which improved every aspect of Rhianwyn's castle life. As a result, people were friendly with her, and she rarely found herself in trouble. The insight made her progress rapidly with the herbs and healing, giving her more time to herself as the masters struggled to keep her busy.

Many of Rhianwyn's formal lessons brought her into close contact with the other children sent to the capital to learn to be healers and physicians. Maeveen encouraged her to build a network of people to gather information. Within a few months, she counted many among her friends, and she enjoyed interacting with them.

Some were from wealthy families with a surplus of children vying for the family name. Many, however, were from outer cities and towns that no longer had access to the colleges since their fall—a younger generation sent to keep their communities alive and healthy.

Long before the war spurred by the Betrayal and the death of Aspera's family, the colleges had been failing. When the last one sided with the Black Knight usurpers, Aspera had made quick work of the final remnants of their legacy. Now Stellamar was the only city with sanctioned schools, which meant it held the guild headquarters. Other places tried to maintain the universities, but they all ran the risk of having their doors kicked in by the Royal Justices to ensure they followed the laws. Not many made it beyond a handful of years.

Rhianwyn learned all of this as she moved through her days, listening. She overheard the other students sigh about being homesick and repeat their parents' gripes about the system. She felt for them, but she was also glad for it.

After all, that was how she and Alessia became friends. She lived with her aunt and uncle and studied at the castle. Both were part of the Merchants Guild. She looked like her ancestors had come from the same region as Olive, with skin that tanned in the sun and dark hair. She and Rhianwyn were fast friends. It was a welcomed change from the otherwise-drab existence, and it gave her eyes to the world outside of the castle walls. Not even Maeveen gave her that.

Alessia knew the castle gossip, word on the street, and what the other children did. She filled Rhianwyn's ear, and Rhianwyn couldn't wait until she could join in.

Before she knew it, another festival season had come and gone. Then, as the world lay sleepily in the grips of winter, another warbler came, and she found herself sitting on ground dusted with snow beside Maeveen. It was a week until the Solstice. Gwenyvir had confirmed she would be formally recognized as a ward, and her apprenticeship announced.

"Mama would be proud. She was the most powerful healer our tribe knew," Maeveen said when Rhianwyn told her.

"What if they find out about my magic, though?" Rhianwyn asked. She watched Maeveen trim back the branches of the wild roses for her. "The magic you've taught me?"

Maeveen looked up with alarm. "Wyn," she began, "I didn't mean to make you afraid. Let your magic soar. Just be careful letting your mentors on to it. Don't show them you know more than them—or teach them anything." She crawled over and spoke firmly, her fingers squeezing Rhianwyn's shoulders. "If they question it, spew their lectures back at them. They'll get complacent about it. Eventually, they'll think it's a gift versus wondering at it. That's how anyone gifted with magic is. Sometimes it catches and takes like wildfire. Be afraid of them, but don't dare be afraid of your magic."

Rhianwyn thrummed with excitement. "Okay."

When the day finally came, she stood beside Sonder in the throne room. Both of them were dressed in their best. Rhianwyn wore a heavy blue gown with many layers, her hair wrapped up and hidden beneath a white scarf. Sonder wore an all-black ensemble, with a blouse ruffled beneath his chin. From behind Drisil and a man named Bran, Rhianwyn hid her smile at his dour expression. Mistress Gwenyvir caught her attention and silenced her with a fierce scowl. Drisil called her forward, and as she curtsied to the queen, her heart hammered. No one else was present except Sir Elio and Randal, who flanked the queen.

"Your Highness, I present to you the young Lady Rhianwyn. She lives by your grace and hearth."

When Aspera claimed her as a ward, a broad smile broke out across Rhianwyn's face. It felt like a new freedom.

"You've both done well."

The following Sunday, she sat with Alessia on a bench in the garden. They shared imbued berries after their morning chores, still summer-sweet from the market.

"So, what's it like, finally being unleashed on the world as a ward?" the other girl asked, swinging her feet just above the ground.

"Strange. But, Queen's mercy, it's wonderful. I can't wait until all the tests are done and things settle down."

"I hear you looked gorgeous in your dress." Alessia shrugged her shoulders close to her ears with a whimsical sigh. "I wish I could wear something like it."

"I suppose. The damn thing was so heavy." She ignored Alessia's conspiring grin at her curse. "Who told you that?"

"My uncle knows someone in the healer's guild who heard about it. They're very invested in you." Alessia knew all of the gossip. Rhianwyn just rolled her eyes, so the girl went on with a glimmer in her eye. "I hear Sonder looked dapper himself."

Rhianwyn blushed and hit the other girl in the arm. "Don't you dare!"

Alessia giggled. "What'd you think? Was he so handsome?"

Despite her best efforts, her face remained pink, and the apples of her cheeks ached from her smile. "He was." Rhianwyn covered her lips and snorted. "He looked so serious, though."

Alessia bumped her shoulder. "You like him, don't you?"

"He's my best boy friend. Obviously I do. I've known him forever, and we do everything together. But it's not like that." Rhianwyn crinkled her nose.

Alessia raised an eyebrow. "Mmm-hmm," she hummed. She turned forward again, put her hands between her legs, and shimmied happily. "So, if you don't fancy him, can I? I think him dashing, always looking so dour."

Rhianwyn hit her again with a protest, and the two of them fell into a fit of laughing. Their foreheads bent together as they shared in the joke. Neither one noticed the boy's approach.

"Wyn?" Sonder said quietly.

Both girls immediately sat up straighter.

"Sonder," Rhianwyn said breathlessly.

He looked uncomfortable standing in front of them. "Alessia," he said, his tone oddly formal. The smile he forced was small.

Alessia beamed at him. Rhianwyn kept herself from scowling at the girl as Sonder blushed in response.

"What's wrong?" Rhianwyn asked. Her voice still bubbled with glee.

"May I speak with you? If it's alright, Alessia. It can wait."

"Not at all. I need to be getting home anyway. My uncle is having guests over from the Merchants Guild." She rolled her eyes and then stood. "Drab, if you ask me." She kissed his cheek, then turned to Rhianwyn and took her hand as she stood. "I'll tell you all about it."

The girls kissed each other's cheeks. Then Rhianwyn took Sonder's hand with a smile and began to lead him to a private spot. When she turned to give Alessia a parting glance, the other girl was grinning from ear to ear in delight. Rhianwyn couldn't suppress her smile even as she mouthed for Alessia to stop teasing.

When they reached a less frequented part of the gardens, she pulled Sonder up a grassy knoll and pulled him down beside her. "What's wrong?"

"I have a bad feeling," he said quietly.

Her heart grew heavy for him. "Why? What's happened?"

"Merrick is due back any day now. He was supposed to present me to the queen, but Bran had to. I'm afraid of what happens when he comes back." He plucked at the grass as he spoke. "Bran said something to Drisil and Áki the other day. About how Merrick won't be pleased when he returns."

She slumped with disappointment. "Is he ever pleased?"

Sonder kept his gaze down, and his shoulders lifted in a shrug. "He says everything he does is because he cares about me. I'm worried about what the other masters will say, though. If they've told Bran, or the queen."

Rhianwyn thought for a moment. "Well," she drew the word out, "has the queen told you she's unhappy?" She used the tone she always did when she jumped into imaginary conversations about his mentors' failed reasoning.

Sonder shook his head, seeming too absorbed in his misery to stop her. "I've never spoken to her. You know that. She doesn't say anything at trials, and she's always on the other side of the room. Then there's the dinners, but you're there, you know how those go. But you see the way the staff acts like mice fleeing a cat. She seems kind, but the way she watches me sometimes . . ." Sonder shuddered. "I wish I knew what she wants with me, and why it makes Merrick angry with me."

"True," Rhianwyn sighed. Then, when he didn't offer anything else, she bumped against him. "Well, if I ever meet Merrick, I'll tell him what I think of him. All our tutors think you're doing fine. What else could he possibly want?"

Sonder let out a soft laugh. "I'd love to see you try."

"You don't think I will?" She sat up straighter and looked at him.

Sonder didn't look at her, but the sides of his mouth tugged up in a smirk. "No."

"I have so much good rapport. If I mouthed off, I'd get away with just a warning. If you want me to do it, I will." She wiggled her shoulders with an arched eyebrow.

Sonder laughed more genuinely. "Don't forget your reputation for being fiery. Make sure your rapport can offset that." The smile held but then wavered and fell. "Maybe it's nothing. I didn't hear all of what they said, and it didn't make much sense. I just don't know if I want to see him. I just want him to be pleased with me." His voice dropped. "I miss him."

Rhianwyn studied the side of his face and the play of his emotions. It was hard sometimes to help the boy stay positive. Especially since there was no way for her to bear some of the burden except by helping him study and offering distractions when she could.

An idea came to her, and she bumped Sonder's shoulder again. "Hey. Let's go sneak some food from the kitchen for a picnic. I'll tell you another story." She stood up and offered him her hand. "You can tell me about the other boys and what it's like swinging a sword around."

They walked hand in hand. She was happy to listen to him talk, even if it took some prompting. As they passed through the gates, her eyes drifted around in contentment until she caught sight of a man.

It seemed his eyes paused on them for just a moment, but then he turned and walked away from his horse.

She knew that face.

Rhianwyn grabbed Sonder's wrist with her other hand so hard he winced.

"Ouch! What gives?" he said, tugging his hand away.

"Who is that?" she breathed.

"Who?" He turned and followed her gaze. The man wore a long black cloak, followed by an attendant. "Oh. That's Merrick. He must've just gotten back."

Rhianwyn's eyes were wide as she glanced at him. "That's Merrick? That's your mentor?"

Sonder's brow knit in confusion. "Yeah. I'd know that gait anywhere. Why? What's wrong?" His eyes scanned her face.

Her forehead creased, eyes still wide. She spoke softly, without looking at him. "That's the man who brought me here." Then, trailing off, she looked him straight in the eye.

"Merrick brought you here?" Sonder asked, shocked.

Rhianwyn nodded, and her mouth worked as she tried to gather her words. "He showed up one day and told my caretakers that I was to go with him." Her eyes grew distant. "I remember the smell of smoke and feeling scared." Finally, she refocused on his face. "I haven't seen him since."

He was quiet for a while, and she knew he was fraught with his own emotions at seeing the man. "Maybe that girl you've mentioned knows something about it?"

She smiled tightly and dropped his wrist. "No, it's okay. I don't want to talk about it." Rhianwyn didn't blame him for not knowing how to help, but she was glad he didn't press her.

They stood awkwardly for a moment, neither one making eye contact. The rush of fear and memories, mingled with her excitement from earlier, made her feel suddenly lonely.

It felt like their world was closing in on them, and she felt his trepidation radiating alongside her own.

Chapter Seven
Dining with the Devil

Somewhere on the road, recurring

"You visited that Lorist woman again? What's her name? Grace?" Bran asked.

"I did, yes," Merrick responded reluctantly. "But she renounced that heritage."

"I am still myself, Merrick." Bran threw a shaving of kindling at the fire. "I'm glad. She's good for you." He sat close enough that his leg brushed against Merrick's, and neither of them pulled away.

"I don't understand how you do it. Do everything she asks of you but remain true to yourself," Merrick said.

Bran laughed sardonically. "I grew up a Black Knight. The old order. Before everything fell apart. I lost sight of what that meant, but never what we stood for. We served the realm first. Always. I can't undo what I've done, or the role Lucrid and I played in the fall. But I know what she did to bring us down." Those dark eyes met Merrick's, and the scar on Bran's face shone in the fire. "If serving her keeps me alive, so be it."

Present, age seven

Merrick had only just returned to Stellamar. The dust kicked up by his horse was still settling. Scurrying staff preceded him through the castle toward his study and its attached apartment. The door swung open, and dust motes swarmed angrily in the pools of mid-afternoon sunlight, dust so recently stirred that he heard the servants' entrance shut behind curtains still swaying.

Only just returned, he repeated to himself as he went to the cabinet where a decanter sat flanked by glasses.

He unstopped the bottle and poured himself a glass. The hideous wall hanging, depicting Black Knights mowing through enemies, chafed his foul mood. It was here before he occupied the space, and he had yet to personalize it years later.

The door to his office flew open again. The carpet on the floor muffled the heels, but that perfume was unmistakable.

"Well, you sure took your time, didn't you?" Drisil said once the door rebounded closed behind her.

Merrick sighed, setting the decanter down. "I've only just returned."

"You should have been back a week ago. Where were you?" she pressed. Her hand rested on her hip. One of her shaped eyebrows arched high over her smoky eyes. Her painted lips were pursed, forming a pretty curve with her cheekbones.

Merrick lifted his glass. "I tried not to dawdle on my way in."

Her nostrils flared. "Why in the world do you insist on visiting that damn barmaid? She helped us with the child. They showed us kindness and asked no questions. We paid a handsome sum. So what on earth calls you back? What risk is worth blowing your cover? By the gods' grace, she's married, so it's not like you're getting your member wet."

"His name is Sonder," Merrick said, merely to spite. He took a sip of the heady liquor and turned away. The burn caused him to suck in a breath to cool his throat.

It opened a wave of shame. He hadn't sent word of his impending arrival, and he notoriously failed to give direction regarding Sonder's training. He neglected his duties except hunting down people guilty of only their heritage.

Drisil appeared at his elbow. "I hope you have a good excuse." Her voice was sultry, but Merrick could hear her temper tarnishing it.

He braced his hands against the cabinet, and his leather gloves protested, gripping the wood. "I never fail to deliver. Whatever her majesty asks, she gets."

"You were supposed to present the wards at the Solstice." Her manicured nails tapped his glass. Scolding him for his drinking while she gouged with her words—she was never so cold about the children.

Merrick gritted his teeth and closed his eyes. "They have names, Drisil."

"We've been covering for you," she said softly, but her fist closed around the glass, and she upended it on the floor while holding him in her gaze.

"And I said I delivered!" Merrick slammed a fist. He rounded to face her. "More children for her experiments. More heads parted from their shoulders. Is she not satisfied?" Merrick spread his arms out and lowered himself into a condescending bow.

Drisil set the cup down and took a step closer to him. "Bran needed you. Randal has gotten cold feet—"

Merrick scoffed, "Of course he has. Bloody cur." He reached for the empty glass out of habit. The accusation on her face was enough to make his hand shrivel in on itself. He looked away.

"As you grovel at a heretic's feet, listening to stories," she said through her teeth. "We aren't the boy's mentors. You're the one who convinced the queen for that role. Act like it."

Merrick's jaw worked as he looked out the window.

He had purposely found ways to stay far from the capital. However, his absences made it challenging to maintain his promises and obligations. Everything he had committed himself to was at odds with itself. As his mind spiraled, his fingers drummed on the empty glass.

"Your drinking is getting worse, isn't it?" Drisil asked, softening. When he didn't respond, she went on. "You can ask for help, you know."

"Don't you use your magic on me, Sil, and don't you dare imply I let one of the queen's practitioners put their hands on me. I don't need help," Merrick ground out over his shoulder.

His words stung, but she closed the gap and grabbed his hand. "I don't mean that, Mer. You don't have to do this alone."

He breathed a laugh through his nose. "Of course I don't—if I choose to give in to her." He looked down at her slender fingers wrapped around his. "Tell me, Sil, now that you've won Bran over, do you still want to add me to your trophies?"

She squeezed his hand tighter. It was an unkind thing to ask. "One man of morals is exhausting enough." She brought her face closer to whisper in his ear. "Don't leave me too." She stepped back, though her fingers remained twined through his. Merrick looked at her and saw angry tears in her eyes. Drisil's grip tightened before she let go. "We dine with the queen tonight. Don't be late."

Merrick poured himself another glass. He raised it to her back, calling out, "I certainly wouldn't have chosen to start drinking here if I didn't have obligations." The door slammed. "I would have rather been at the Whisper, but I didn't dawdle. You're welcome," he said to himself before taking another sip. He opened the hand she had squeezed and saw one of the mint pellets that she used to hide the smell of alcohol. He was instantly sorry for having provoked her about her old desires for him. "Thanks, Sil," he whispered.

He searched the ceiling for the comfort he sought with a heavy sigh—to find the answers they needed before Bran inevitably crumbled and burned. The reason the queen kept Sonder and Wyn. A way to heal the ache in his soul. He blinked before the tears completely blurred his vision and swallowed the rest of the amber liquid before he went to wash the remnants of the road grit still on his skin.

Four hours later, Merrick rolled his shoulders as he straightened his jacket. As with his riding leathers and armor, everything was black. Each piece of his suit was the same bottomless color. Any variation was intentional to make details stand out. The Black Knight symbol was neatly stitched on the blouse, jacket, and cloak, in a shiny thread that caught the light. There would never be a question about his position. He had taken the time to trim his beard and hair, neatening the undercut properly. The man in the looking glass relieved him. It felt good to have the travel cleaned away.

Merrick wasn't a vain man. On the contrary, he took a militant satisfaction in it. It wasn't power that he sought, but he knew how to command it. That was what made him so successful as a representative of the queen.

A few hair strands were out of place, so he smoothed them back. The only thing he couldn't fix was the redness from the drinks he had already consumed. He had kept going in hopes of dulling the biting retorts sliding over each other, forming a slippery ball. But, looking at his bleary-eyed reflection, he mused that he'd had one too many. Every aspect of the queen's dinners irked him.

He grimaced and popped the mint into his mouth.

He thought back to how Drisil had barged into his office in a huff about his absence. Merrick did everything with the queen's blessing. Any detours he made to visit Grace were carefully crafted so that only the whispers of a privy snake would reveal them.

His sorceress friend harped on him endlessly to pick a side, yet he had. That was why he sat beside Grace's fire—and beside Bran's. Both helped him hold clarity.

He just happened to be good at doing all the queen asked.

Merrick bowed deeply to Aspera so she wouldn't see his heart, exposing his neck instead so she could take it whenever she wanted. Bran had taught him that—pretend there was nothing to hide.

His drunken brain finally realized he would see the man tonight. He had to turn away from his likeness to avoid getting ill. He wasn't ready.

Stumbling out of the apartment adjacent to the study, Merrick looked around. A pile of sealed letters had shifted and fallen to the floor, a cruel reminder of how he neglected aspects of his position. He walked to them with a sigh.

Bracing himself on the desk, he bent down to pick them up. As he reached to grab the first, his hand slipped, and his shoulder bashed the solid wood. Then, after a clip of curses, he looked up to see Merriweather looking down at him with concern. He had not heard her enter.

"Are you alright, Sir Merrick?" she asked softly.

Merrick brought his hand up to cover his eyes to stop the room from spinning. "Mistress Merriweather, forgive me. I did not hear you knock."

"I heard the crash first, actually. Here, sir, let me help you."

She must have done this before with someone else.

The older woman was surprisingly strong, as it seemed all strong-willed women were. He couldn't tell if his clumsy help did anything or if she hauled him up single-handedly. While he assessed his injuries, she pressed a glass of water into his hands and then bent to collate the fallen letters. She straightened the pages with a crisp series of taps, then laid them down. If she saw anything that upset her, she kept her face neutral.

"Thank you, Melody," he said, less formally. "To what do I owe this well-timed pleasure?" The glass of water was already serving him.

The fierce look on her face cowed him. "Should I inform Master Sonder of your return, sir?"

He couldn't look at her. The details in the woodgrain offered a distraction. "I'll let you know by night's end. It depends on how dinner with the queen goes. Which I'm late for." He never slurred, but his voice had a slower lilt to it.

Merriweather's brow furrowed with concern. Her worn fingers took the glass from Merrick's hand, and she refilled it, thrusting it back at him. "Forgive my mothering, but you ought to talk to someone rather than do this to yourself. Sir." She added the address as an afterthought, with a side-eyed look.

Merrick scoffed and drank half of the glass at once. "I'll be sure to do that." He placed it on his desk.

Clearing his throat, he re-straightened his jacket and moved his shoulder. It would ache for several days to remind him of his foolishness.

He was glad she'd caught him before he left. His head felt clearer. If he was sure to eat something and pace himself, he might survive the encounter unscathed. "Thank you, as always, for your service, Mistress Merriweather." He inclined his head, which brought his face closer to hers.

"Bran requested your presence after dinner." Her voice was barely audible over the buzzing in his ears. "Please be careful." Her lips barely moved.

Merrick took in a sharp breath but otherwise remained stone-faced. He had thought she was just here to pester about the boy and his drinking—as everyone seemed bent on doing. Instead, hearing Bran's name twice today filled him with many reservations.

He adjusted his jacket once more. "Thank you again, Melody. You may go." His tone had softened significantly. He felt sorry she had risked herself to deliver the message only to find him stumbling.

She inclined her head and curtsied.

As Merrick watched her leave, he wondered if all the corners he had backed himself into were a blessing or a curse.

The queen insisted on taking these dinners in intimate quarters. It was often just their merry band of ex-criminals, Bran, and Aspera, with the whole procession guarded by Elio. Occasionally, an advisor or noble was given an invitation as a morsel of celebration. Dining with Her Majesty and her cabinet granted the illusion of her pleasure. Afterward, bets about how long the fools would last followed. A cynical game for people similarly performing for their liege.

Guards flanked the double doors as Merrick approached. It was a modestly large room tucked into the wing of living quarters. Merrick had heard stories about these hallways. Some people heard whispers, while others saw shadows looking through the pillars. His skin crawled, but little else.

It always worried him that there wasn't more effect on him. The first time the four of them had discussed it, many years ago when they were still banded together, Áki had demanded that the rest of them stop trying to spook him. Áki claimed he felt nothing at all. At the time, it made Merrick worry that his head was nearly as empty as Áki's. Now, he thought it was because Áki's self-constitution was strong.

Merrick hoped he wasn't also an overconfident idiot if that was the case.

It was difficult to get deep into this area unmolested unless the queen gave permission. It kept anyone feeling particularity entitled to an audience at bay. Those who did barge through never lasted long, whether they were cut down along the way or suffered their demise later; perhaps for some, it happened by Merrick's blade.

The mask of stern indifference rested easily over his face. As he approached at a clipped pace, the guards bowed and pushed the doors open. The power had a bittersweet taste.

The gilded surfaces in the room glowed warmly. Every sconce on the wall, light in the chandelier, and candle on the table was lit, even though the waning sunlight still streamed through the windows, chasing nearly every shadow away. Red-violet hangings created an intimate atmosphere.

There was hardly anything in the room except the long table, with twenty plush seats nestled around it. Only six settings gleamed on the polished wood. A servant greeted him with a bow and offered to take his coat. Merrick didn't acknowledge the man; instead, his eyes locked ahead on the table, where three pairs stared back at him.

Praise whatever good was left in the world that Queen Aspera hadn't yet arrived. But Bran's face was still missing, making Merrick's empty stomach clench.

Drisil twisted around to glare at him. Her black hair was left long, with only a few simple pleats to keep the dark strands off of her face. She always found ways to add surprises of color, like her lips, a silk lining, or tonight, a jewel-toned ribbon woven through her braids. The emerald was a subtle touch. She chose to be subdued in Aspera's presence.

"Of course you're late," she said.

"How many sheets to the wind are ya, pal? Looking a bit hung out. I'll pour you a cup myself, so you don't get too dry," Áki sneered, twisting around to look at him.

Merrick ignored them both, instead becoming hyper-focused on Randal. The mage remained quiet, sipping his wine, smug and downcast, posture rigid.

With its deep-blue silk lining, the robe he wore gave him away. Merrick clenched his fist and fought back the urge to launch himself across the table.

A servant appeared at his elbow with a small tray and wineglass. "Drink, sir?"

Áki snapped his fingers. "Damn, they're too quick. Next one's on me ," he continued to wheedle.

"Bring me something to eat," Merrick growled, ignoring the wine. Randal finally met his eye with a smirk.

"Her Majesty should be here soon, sir, and we will serve the—"

"Something to eat," Merrick repeated, turning his gaze on the servant. "Anything you can manage."

The servant flushed and scrambled away.

Áki whistled softly. "The master of being scary as hell. Teach me your ways of veiled threats. I'm not subtle enough."

Merrick approached the table and stood behind Drisil and Áki. "I see you got the promotion."

Randal didn't flush, which only confirmed Merrick's suspicions. Instead, the man merely lifted his cup. "May we all find our place."

Merrick's lip curled. "I'll not sit next to him."

Áki rolled his eyes. "Gods, you are a man of such foul disposition."

Before Áki could go on, Merrick rounded on him. "Move," he snapped.

Drisil sighed and crossed her arms as she turned forward. Seeing that he would get no support from the woman, Áki stood. He looked down on Merrick with a hurt scowl before shoving through the chairs noisily. He made the long walk around to the other side, grumbling. Randal wore a self-satisfied smile, stifling a laugh.

Merrick sat next to Drisil right as the servant scurried in and set down a bread plate with a scoop of pork-fat butter on the side. Merrick tore the heel and used the little knife next to his plate to smear an impolite amount across the warm fare. "Tell me, how go the experiments?" Merrick spoke through a mouthful.

Drisil kicked him under the table.

"Tell me how the child-napping goes," Randal shot back.

The porcelain plate protested as the silver knife fell against it. Merrick placed his fists on the table and made to stand. Drisil grabbed his sleeve viper-fast and hissed at him to stop.

A man's voice cracked behind him before Merrick could stand to his full height. "Enough."

It was level and barely raised, but Merrick froze, then slowly sat back down. His fists remained balled beside his plate.

"If I were you, Sir Merrick, I'd keep eating that bread. Allow me to be embarrassed on your behalf. You lack the mental capacity to do so for yourself." The voice came from the right-hand side of the queen's seat.

"Forgive me, Sir Bran," Merrick muttered. He tore off another piece of bread and simply swiped it through the butter, propriety gone.

Bran stood behind his seat and inclined his head to Drisil, then to the two men on his side of the table. "Forgive me for being late. Her Majesty will follow shortly."

A different servant whisked into the room, bearing a tray with two wine glasses. Abiding by rank, the young boy went to Bran first. The older man accepted and took a long drink. Then, as the boy was walking to give the other glass to Merrick, Bran grunted with his mouth still full of wine, aggressively signaling the lad off. Áki snorted a laugh, which chastened Merrick further.

The redhead was nervous. As Merrick chewed his last bite, Drisil's warm hand rested briefly on his leg, and they met eyes.

"Peace," she breathed. She looked afraid, too.

Through the second set of doors near the head of the table, a royal herald, dressed in gold and purple, entered. The man bowed deeply, sweeping one arm wide. "Her Majesty, Queen Aspera, is on her way, gentlemen and lady."

The serving staff rushed to line up along the wall. The four of them joined Bran in standing. Bran finished his glass of wine, pulled the queen's seat out, then stood at relaxed attention. Merrick washed the last of the bread down with a sip from Drisil's wine, which won him a wide-eyed look challenging his audacity—and a smirk from Áki. As he finished wiping the crumbs off of his pants, Aspera entered the room, and they all lowered their heads.

Compared to how she would greet the public, she was casually dressed. Her hair hung loosely braided, and it appeared as if most of her makeup had been washed off, leaving only enough to accentuate her eyes. Her hand delicately rested on Elio's plated arm, and she gazed up at the knight as if he had just said something funny. Her smile turned on them when she arrived at her seat. Elio took his place behind her. A brief, uncomfortable look passed between him and Bran before the queen began speaking.

"Good evening, everyone." Their responses were a soft murmur. "Forgive me for being late. Please, have a seat."

Once she sat down, they followed. Bran pushed her chair in, took Aspera's offered hand, and kissed it before taking his own seat. She clapped her hands, and the staff came alive, bringing out a rich soup with hearty chunks of vegetables and ham.

"Sir Merrick, what a pleasure to have you here tonight. I worried you wouldn't make it." Aspera tilted her wine glass toward him before taking a sip. "We missed you at the Solstice Presentation."

He raised his cup of water in response. Her eyebrow twitched. So, even she wondered how he would behave tonight. "I made haste, my lady. I have been away too long. I saw naught to keep me away, and my other duties are pressing."

"It is good you did. While I am so lucky to have you to see to my affairs, it is said that if you want something done right, you ought to do it yourself."

Only the waitstaff were oblivious to the veiled jab spoken through a smile. His obligations were suffering, and he had yet to show why he'd asked to be Sonder's mentor.

The queen inclined her head, then smiled at Randal. "We have much to celebrate tonight. I can't recall the last time we were all together this past year. It's high time we drink to your advancement, Master Randal, my High Practitioner of Magic."

Randal inclined his head, looking as pompous as ever. "It has been an honor to serve you, Lady Aspera." She offered him her hand with a warm smile, and he took it and kissed it softly.

Merrick took a moment to glance at Áki, who was watching him. The look on the man's face made Merrick soften his own.

"Who would have guessed my little band of criminals would provide such high-quality service?" Aspera turned to Bran this time. Merrick couldn't be sure if he imagined a tighter look around her eyes. Bran was always a blank slate, offering no insight. He dropped his chin stiffly. Aspera's smile fell. She looked at one of the waiters standing against the wall. "I asked for a special toast, did I not?"

The serving woman snapped to attention and bolted through the servants' door. Aspera rolled her eyes before turning her smile back on them. Empty soup bowls were already being cleared away.

"Speaking of your services," Aspera said, looking toward Drisil. "Mistress Drisil, have you and Áki given any additional thought to my offer? Taking on an estate is a lot of work, but there are many very qualified members of my staff that I would be happy to loan while you get them up and running." Aspera acknowledged them both.

Merrick took a sip of his water to hide the twist of his mouth and noticed Áki do the same with his wine.

That explained part of Drisil's mood. She was being pressed on all sides if Aspera encouraged an estate, and Randal was pestering her between his sessions of kissing the queen's feet. She could only stand in for him for so long.

He saw it in the stiff way she set down her spoon and dabbed her lips before she spoke. "I have been engrossed in what you've entrusted me with. Those duties come first, Your Highness, and I haven't decided if it is an amount of energy I can sacrifice at the moment. Perhaps with Sir Merrick returned, I will find myself freed up enough to do so."

Drisil looked demure with her hands folded in her lap. She handled Merrick's shortcomings with so much grace, along with the pressures of the queen trying to ensnare them further with estates.

"I understand," Aspera said with an adoring glimmer in her eye. She was always careful not to push Drisil away. "What of you, Áki?"

Áki shrugged, crowding the table, so a waiter had to maneuver around him carefully. "I would hardly use it."

"That's no matter. Even in your absence, it could be well cared for." Aspera nodded to have her bowl taken.

"If you insist," the man responded, holding his empty wine glass out to be filled. He had only eaten half his soup.

The waitress ordered to bring the queen's special wine returned, bearing fresh glasses and a pitcher with the clear liquid inside.

"Ah, perfect timing! One more thing to toast, then." She swept them with a smile as her portion was poured. She looked at Merrick last. "Since we're on the topic, I cannot recall if I extended the offer to you, Sir Merrick, but let me tell you the same applies. You can have an estate if you want it." She swallowed the final sip of her regular wine.

Merrick inclined his head, his attention briefly grabbed by Drisil waving off her unfinished bowl of soup when a waiter offered to take it. "My lady, I am honored. However, at this time, I'll decline. While you generously promised the staff to establish it, I'd rather focus my energies on tending to my duties. There's no trouble with the current arrangements."

Aspera's slender fingers wrapped around the new glass of colorless wine. They followed her lead. "Now that you mention it, I agree it's not a good time." He kept his face blank at the remark, though it seemed like everyone else shifted. "There are many things that require your skills. Pardon me while I address this now before we toast.

"It has been brought to my attention that the boy severely lacked certain skills. It took extra time to bring him to an adequate level. The agreement with the woman in the hills was for his education to be satisfactory to fulfill her obligation. It was not. Once you have caught up with any correspondences requiring your attention, see that it's handled."

A blatant lie. While Merrick undoubtedly had been away, he'd made efforts to pass by to inquire after Sonder. The consensus had always been that the boy was doing exceptional in his studies, if not a bit slow upon each new concept. He recalled the time Merriweather had gushed about the boy's eloquence and ability to pose a compelling argument about his schedule. Sonder was a good child.

Merrick remembered the initial agreement with Merna. There had been little indicated for a tangible benchmark. Just an understanding that there was enough knowledge to make a solid foundation to build on. The old hag had done that.

It made his stomach sick. Not for any genuine sympathy for the woman; in all honesty, Merrick was eager to give her what she deserved. Instead, it was distressing because it was just another plastered facade to justify another death. Aspera's flimsy justice hollowed him.

Merrick lifted his glass of clear wine to Aspera. "I'll see to it, my lady. By the end of tonight, I expect to be caught up and will address it in the morning."

Her smile was too wide for his liking. "You continue to please me, Sir Merrick."

The waitstaff began to place the second course in front of them. Aspera lifted her glass anew. "You each have accomplished more than I could have ever hoped, and the rewards you all are given were hard-earned. I cannot think of any others more deserving among my counselors. A toast. To all of you."

"Your will be done," they echoed together.

Aspera brought the clear liquid to her lips and drank, and they mirrored the motion. A conniving smile tugged at her dark, painted lips. Too late, Merrick noticed that Bran had not been offered the special brew but instead sipped a plain glass. The red wine was thick by comparison, and Merrick saw the way Bran's mouth worked around it.

Merrick willed the man to look at him, but Bran remained a blank slate, staring ahead. Then, feeling eyes on him, Merrick looked up at Sir Elio and saw the knight glowering at him.

Merrick blinked and turned back to the conversation. The light liquor made the front of his face itch. Soon, the concern about Bran faded into merriment.

After the fourth course, his companions stopped their sideways glances whenever the wine pitcher passed him. He began to drink again, although at a much more moderate pace. The venom in his heart always ran hot after a campaign. However, it cooled with the abundant smiles, decadent food, and now-constant stream of pleasant banter and praise.

It didn't register until an hour after the dinner concluded how bitter the night was in his soul. It was too easy to forget everything when she smiled at them all the way she did. Smiled at Merrick as if he brought her nothing but pride. As if she didn't take joy in his misery or delight in pushing boundaries and hunting for fault and weakness.

As if every smile wasn't a double-edged sword.

After he donned a clean blouse and trousers, he remembered Merriweather's summons. The mood he'd been so eager to drink away returned. Even if there were parts of this work he enjoyed, it was tainted. If it were anyone else but Bran, he would have taken to the bottle once more. Instead, he let his insobriety dissipate until he saw to his obligations.

Merrick splashed cold water on his face to wake himself up before leaving his apartment. An exhausted servant stood by in the office, waiting to be dismissed for the night.

"You." The young boy perked up. "Before you retire for the evening, see that Mistress Merriweather receives word that I want Master Sonder to report to me the day after tomorrow."

"So, Monday, Sir Merrick?" the boy asked, the gears visibly turning in his head as he struggled to do the maths.

Merrick thought about it as he put on his black cloak. "No, Sunday. I suppose it's after midnight, so that means tomorrow. I have commitments in the morning." His mind was on Merna.

The boy nodded sleepily, then pushed the door open for him. "It will be done, Sir Merrick. Goodnight."

"Goodnight. Go rest."

Bran's estate was just outside of the castle walls. Only a handful of torches were lit once he passed unmolested through the gates and crossed into the streets. The benefits of his position made themselves known once more. Not even a lingering look from the officer in charge of the watch.

How things have changed, Merrick thought as he kept to the shadows. Even after seven years of passing through the portcullis, his skin still crawled as if he would be detained.

The home was one of the few single-story buildings this close to the castle. Modest, as well, considering the man's rank. Any manner of riches could have been his. Yet Bran chose to dedicate every breath to serving Queen Aspera. For the first two years, Merrick had been convinced the man never slept.

Every breath was given to the crown, but only after giving the first to the realm.

Only one window was lit, and dimly. Merrick didn't enter through the main gate but instead took the side entrance, allowing him to look through it. He wasn't an inquisitive man, or nosy. On the contrary, he was a master of filtering through details with no attachment—he used cold, rigid objectivity to carry out what was necessary. However, given his mood now, a morbid curiosity made him slow down and peer inside. An odd desire to see a man he admired in a moment of vulnerability with the woman who shared his bed.

Sitting on a cushioned stool with her back to him was Drisil. The room was the boudoir Bran had created for her, complete with a mirrored vanity where she now sat. Her creamy, almond skin was laid bare, with nothing but her long black hair obscuring her curves. Standing behind her was Bran, clad in a simple robe, hanging open and unbelted from his shoulders.

It was impossible to hear them, but Merrick knew Drisil well enough to see the anger on her shoulders. Knew Bran enough to see his exhaustion. Those hands, responsible for many deaths on behalf of Sosten, traced a line across her skin as he pressed his lips to her shoulder. Bran buried his nose in the hair that covered her ear, and the shiver that ran through her body made a long-suppressed memory stir in Merrick beneath the layers of alcohol.

She turned and kissed him. It was the type of kiss two people shared when each desperately sought to be healed by the other.

It was a moment not meant to be stolen by him, but Merrick took it anyway. He felt their heartbreak as his own, mingled with his misgivings. He had been summoned here for a reason. Bran had not drank with them. Merrick would give many things to undo what had gotten them to this point.

The long kiss finally ended, and Bran pressed his forehead against hers, holding her face. He looked as if he wanted to take more. Her hand grasped at his chest while she steadied herself.

Bran's eyes opened, and he caught sight of Merrick, standing in the shadows. It wasn't a discovery made by accident. Merrick knew no other person so aware of prying eyes and the environment around him.

Bran kissed Drisil again, a more absentminded gesture this time. Merrick saw their mouths move in a brief conversation as Bran dismissed himself. His hand lingered on her face before he disappeared from view.

Drisil's shoulder's slumped as she was left alone. For a brief moment, Merrick continued to watch her profile. It was too hard to tell, but he thought he saw her eyes settle on him before she looked back at the large mirror and returned to brushing her hair.

No, he thought, she was no idiot. She had seen him.

Bran appeared in the window and tugged the curtains closed on her, confirming Merrick's suspicion. A moment later, the man stepped outside into the warm evening air, tying off his robe.

"I'm glad Melody was able to get word to you. I was worried she hadn't. Or that you would decide not to come." Bran gave Merrick a critical look. Even in a dressing robe, he was intimidating.

"Of course I came. I've not abandoned you in this." Merrick felt ashamed. "Contrary to what's believed."

Bran exhaled softly through his nose and crossed his arms across his chest. "Drisil is angry that I haven't abandoned this." She had been asking him to stop trying to discover the secrets the queen was after for years. "And at you, for getting dragged along with me, among other things."

Merrick had nothing to say in response.

The drinking. The continued unexplained absences. The secrets he and Bran shared. His rebellion and loyalty walked side by side. Sonder sat in strange limbo while Merrick struggled to hold it together.

He heard his heartbeat in his ears. Perhaps it would beat loud enough to keep him from hearing what Bran had summoned him to say.

"Merrick." It was all that was needed to shatter the dissociation. "You're a good man. That will never change. Aspera cannot take that away from you. If I've asked too much, forgive me."

He had an uncanny knack for saying the right things, whether as a wake-up or a balm.

"I've made promises to more than just you," Merrick began. He thought of Grace.

Before he could find the words, Bran went on. He knew where Merrick's obligations were.

"The walls are caving in on me, Merrick. You deserve to know that before you say anything else."

Merrick's heart lurched. He had never seen Bran look so vulnerable, and it wasn't just because he was nearly naked, arms wrapped around himself against the ocean breeze.

"Don't say that," he choked. Curse the alcohol wearing off, making his emotions raw. "I'll not abandon this, but I need you. We can wait. Find a way to diffuse the situation."

Bran extended a hand and squeezed Merrick's shoulder. "None of you can stop me. Drisil has spent her rage. She has resigned herself to it. You're the only one left fighting it."

So that was why her temper had flashed earlier. She needed a new stone wall to focus her anger on. Merrick felt heartache for her and how she had kissed Bran with so much need. She could not handle loving the two of them so profoundly, but she did anyway.

One man of morals is enough.

He regretted gouging her earlier. She would need him if Bran was right about Aspera finally catching on.

Merrick crossed his arms, though his blood ran hot. He took in a ragged breath. "Bran, I feel my memories slipping." He was deflecting.

Bran let his hand fall away. He knew what Merrick was doing. "The drink doesn't help that," the man said. How many times had this conversation happened? He sounded disappointed this time.

"Sometimes, I enjoy it when I'm doing what she asks. It's the only thing I'm any good at. It's easy." Merrick held himself tighter. He had skirted saying as much for years. Knowing this may be his last chance made him blurt it out. "The smell of blood never goes away. My hands always smell like it. I drink because I hate myself. I hate everything about this—the killing. I know I need to remember, but I want to forget. Even if for a night." Angry tears filled his eyes.

Bran crushed him against his chest, and Merrick's breath caught in surprise. He kept his arms crossed, fighting to keep up the walls that separated him from everything.

"Merrick, you're part of Sonder's only hope. It's alright to protect yourself. Be good at everything Aspera asks of you. Don't fight it. But you can't forget." Bran said it gruffly.

Merrick took several more halting breaths before finally feeling a tear slide free. His arms came up and wrapped around Bran of their own accord. Bran held him long after the awkwardness dissipated. Merrick held tighter. The thing he most wanted to say burned in his throat.

The sound of footsteps approached. Bran loosened his hold, but he didn't let go until Merrick did. Then, a man branded as a Black Knight appeared out of the shadows. Bran showed neither alarm nor shame that they had embraced, so Merrick didn't either.

Áki didn't flinch as he bore Merrick's scrutiny. "Why is he here?" Bran's hand resting on his lower back held him still.

The man stopped a few paces away. He really was massive, especially when he returned Merrick's stare-down. But there was something else there. He looked subdued and nondescript in a way.

Whatever else Bran needed to say would wait. He stepped away from him and put a hand on Áki's shoulder. "Merrick, I've asked him to help. He's one of the few men I trust enough to."

"Since when?" The alcohol still filled his head, so he was quick to anger. It was an easier emotion to feel than everything else.

"Since I told him I wanted to," Áki said firmly. Even though he towered over Bran, he looked small in his submission.

"You took an estate. You've always been abrasive," Merrick snapped. "Why now?"

Áki looked at Bran, and Merrick realized the man wore respect on his sleeve. "Because I don't like this any more than you do." He looked at Merrick again. "I've always cared. You know that."

Chapter Eight
A Final Summer

"I won't!" Merrick bellowed, slamming his fist against the wall. Dust fell from the ceiling. His usually kept bun had gone array.

"I command you," Bran said evenly. His stern brown eyes were impassable, and his normally clean-shaven face was peppered with stubble. "When she names you her champion against me, you will do it."

"What has changed now? All these years, you've talked me through my qualms. Countless nights you've left Drisil's side to tell me your secrets instead. How you justify everything you've done. What has changed!"

Bran let Merrick's rage roll off of him, waiting patiently as he paced and let out one final yell before rounding on him. Only then did he speak.

"The night I slipped my blade into Lucrid's heart, he begged me to end his life. He couldn't live with what he had done. I thought it was because he had betrayed the crown. When I learned the truth, I justified it still because I was the last living Black Knight who knew the truth. It was my duty to see Sonder through." Bran's voice hardened. "You took an oath to me. I command you honor it." His voice quieted. "Don't do this to me."

For as long as Merrick had known him, he had never seen Bran look so broken. His rock had finally been battered and was crumbling in front of his eyes. The scar that marred Bran's face twisted with the turmoil.

"I know why Lucrid begged me to kill him. I can't carry the weight of all I've done anymore. She finally broke me." Bran's voice nearly cracked.

Merrick closed the distance between them. "You keep saying you've learned something. But you refuse to tell me what."

Bran took Merrick's hands and pressed a bundle of letters into them. "I've written it all down. Hide them where none will ever find them." Bran grabbed the back of Merrick's neck and brought their foreheads together. "When the time comes, and Aspera demands my death, I want you to do it." He took Merrick's face in his hands, and his calluses caught in Merrick's beard. Bran held him so he could see his eyes. "I'm sorry I couldn't find the answers you were looking for." Merrick could hear the man suck in a wet breath, and he listened to the pain as it traveled down his throat. "I've told you my secrets many times . . . I pray you find your answers."

Present, age nine (ten months later)

Summer gripped the land tightly, and autumn hadn't yet coaxed its fury down. The corridors were stuffy with the heat. It reminded Drisil of the burst of energy from the children at bedtime she often heard Olive and Merriweather lamenting. The image made her smile—both in the context of Rhianwyn and Sonder chattering away at night and the gods. It was so like the story of the seasons when regal Harina waited for her wizened sister of autumn to tell stories of Life and Death before their brother draped the land in frost.

The soft lines of Drisil's face fell as she remembered there was no longer a place for tales under Aspera's rule. It had been nearly a year since the last time she lay in Bran's bed, listening to stories rumble through his chest, his hands tracing the marks on her bare back. Her grief was still raw and in motion, like the waves that shaped the cliffs of Crooner's Bay.

With a deep breath, she let the sadness recede, feeling each reaching vine trickle out of the crevices of her heart.

Drisil would let it consume her behind closed doors, but she couldn't afford those emotions in the open. Servants lowered their faces to her as she passed.

She had finished Rhianwyn's lesson and was on her way to meet with the Council of Magic. They were still in the process of assessing the girl's skills. Today they had done voice amplification exercises. It had meant nothing to the girl until one of the masters brought up the mechanics of voice and breath. Within minutes, she managed to utter a few words. Drisil had to hide her smile at the girl's apparent boredom until that point.

Rhianwyn was a well of untapped potential. But it was evident her talents lay in medicine and not any other field.

Drisil passed by Master Fallen's study. There were glass panels on either side of the wooden door. She could see the distorted shape of Sonder peering up at the pacing man. Drisil paused to watch as the master waved his arm as if he were directing music.

A smile touched her lips. The glass was cool against her skin as she pressed her forehead to it. Then, she used her magic to focus her mind, and their muffled voices cleared.

Fallen was droning on about the Lorists and the famine that had struck during King Drynard's reign. History claimed that it resulted from the Lorists corrupting the twelve colleges. Using twisted magic, they poisoned the land and the people. When Aspera took the throne, she abolished the colleges. However, the corruption ran so deep, the war continued still.

Today Fallen specifically discussed Lucrid, Sonder's father, and how his family had contributed to Sosten's instability near the end.

Drisil's smile weakened. Listening to the lesson reminded her of her role. Sonder had never been told how four criminals had stolen him and murdered his family, nor that they trained him now, molding him into the man the queen demanded.

She had never cared to learn Lucrid's truth. But the name made her eyes flutter.

Bran had been the man's friend once. *Bran killed his best friend for Aspera, then turned around and made Merrick do the same.*

She instantly regretted the thought. The wound opened anew, and her prior efforts to calm herself washed away. Somewhere along the way, Bran had learned something that made him reevaluate his loyalty. She grit her teeth. *Yet he never told me.*

Sonder's voice cut through the droning.

"Excuse me, Master Fallen?"

So polite.

"If my family worked with the Lorists, and my father was responsible for the royal deaths, why did Queen Aspera let me live?"

"Because she believes that you can redeem the name of the Black Knights. That, and her endless grace, of course, young master." The way the man answered left no room for discussion, and he began to drone again.

Drisil lifted her forehead from the glass but left her hand. The spell ended. It was a stark reminder that whatever sense of happiness they had would not last. The boy never mentioned that his father was a subject matter.

Footsteps broke her introspection. Her lip curled.

"Mistress Drisil, what a pleasant surprise to find you here," Randal said.

"How convenient for you to find me now, *Randal.*" Drisil let her hand fall away, and she hid her hands in her sleeves. "I was on my way to the council. Am I late?" She didn't turn to look at him.

"No, you aren't. You know that. I just came from speaking with Her Majesty. Your services are requested." He stopped too close behind her. She could hear the glee in his voice.

Drisil continued to watch the jagged blob pace through the window. It was impossible not to inhale the thin, powdery film over his natural oily scent. "For you, or Her Majesty?"

His knuckles cracked as he flexed his hand. "For Her Majesty, of course." His voice dropped. "I still keep your secrets."

"Who is to see to the girl's and the boy's studies? Merrick won't allow it to be you." She finally turned to face him.

Randal sneered at the mention of Merrick's name. "Well, unless he can produce someone suitable to replace you while you're gone, it will be me." He reached out and took the pendant at her throat in his fingers.

She didn't give him the satisfaction of reacting to his touch. "When am I to meet with her for my assignment?"

"If you'd come with me, it's an urgent matter. You'll leave tonight, so let's make sure everything is in order." He tugged on her necklace before letting it fall to her skin.

Since the beginning of summer, things had felt lighter, with the children growing into themselves. They had provided a pleasant distraction. But their happiness felt like an apparition now.

Randal held the door for her into the Queen's Tower. Rooms lined the passage as she ascended the stairs, each dedicated to a different project. One had walls lined with diagrams of animals drawn on parchment. An illustration with the delicate lines of a bat wing jumped out at her. Then their climb startled a creature in a cage. She flinched as it thrashed inside its confines.

Randal's hand brushed her lower back, just above being immodest. "It's alright. It can't get out."

Drisil resented the way her body responded to his closeness. She wanted to stay angry. Saying nothing, she continued on.

They passed other rooms with wispy notes beneath drawings of plants, alcoves with bones, and rows of vials marked with strange runes. Before they reached the top, the urge to touch the knowledge overtook her, and she brushed the spine of a book. It was intoxicating being around so much curiosity.

In full view of Elio standing guard at the door, Randal took her hand and stopped her. He stepped in front of her and looked her in the eye. "You are so beautiful when you're around magic. You should be here with us."

"My duties lie where they are," she said slowly. How dare he address her so in front of the knight? His thumb brushed the corner of her tight-lipped smile, and it faltered.

Randal dipped his chin. "Of course."

The door swept open. The turret suite always stole her breath. The openness of the balconies and windows allowed the sunlight to stream in. The sea breeze cooled her damp skin, and she shivered. Randal's hand against her low back urged her into the room.

Aspera's face glowed with pleasure at their entrance. A man with his back to them looked over his shoulder with contempt.

The man turned back to the queen. "Your Majesty, we were in the middle of a conversation."

She raised her hand to silence him. "Thank you both for joining me." She acknowledged Randal with a look. "So punctual." Aspera swept past the man to greet them. As Drisil approached, the queen opened her arms, and they kissed each other's cheeks. She smelled like the summer blooms brightening her garden. "Your beauty brightens this room, Mistress." Her fingers brushed the orange and yellow silk of Drisil's undergown.

"You are too kind, Your Majesty." Drisil curtsied. "It is you who shines brightest, and I am only a reflection of your grace and light."

The apples of Aspera's cheeks tinged rose beneath the rouge. She held out her hand, and Drisil delicately placed her lips on the back. Drisil was a master of her craft, but she never dared believe she could seduce the queen. She had tried once, in a brazen attempt to free them from her clutches. Her body still remembered how the queen's magic had filled her mind and left her defenseless. That was why it was easy to side with Bran—until that crumbled around them.

"Your Majesty!" the man snapped.

Aspera's face became impassive as she turned her attention back to the man. "What, Counselor?" Drisil released her hand.

"We were having a discussion. Regardless of whether or not you want to put it off, it needs to be addressed." He looked at Randal and Drisil before meeting Aspera's anger without flinching. "You can send them away, or we can finish the discussion with them here."

Aspera lifted her chin. "I will not marry. You've pestered me for years about this, Counselor Rikard. What part is the one you don't understand?"

"Your Highness, with all due respect, our kingdom will only benefit from making an alliance and strengthening your claim to your throne."

"I will not share it." She emphasized each word.

"That is not how it works, Your Highness! It is through marriage that Sosten will grow."

"Then make me an empress." Her fury imposed on his space, though she did not raise her voice. "Either our neighbors bow to us, or our armies will destroy them. There is no marriage or treaty. Is that understood?"

Rikard stood up taller and swallowed. The muscles along his jaw clenched before he bowed deeply. "Your Highness."

"Good. Now, get out."

The three of them watched him leave. Before the doors closed, Drisil glanced at Aspera and felt the frustration radiating off her. She could sympathize with the sovereign, and she felt odd realizing it.

Aspera's warm eyes turned on her, and the heat of her anger still burned. "I want you to kill him. I'm tired of listening to him argue with me about how I should deal with our neighbors. He thinks he is on some self-righteous mission to save the world by undermining me. I will tolerate it no longer. Do you understand me?"

Drisil lowered her eyes. "Yes, Your Highness. I will begin spinning the webs."

"Good," Aspera said. She took a steady breath before she addressed why Drisil had been summoned. "If I have not mistaken my days, I believe you evaluated Sonder earlier this morning for any signs of magical prowess. That is correct?" The queen began to pace the room, wringing her hands. She thrummed with anticipation.

"That is correct." Drisil folded her hands into her sleeves and steeled herself.

Aspera's face grew hungry. "Tell me how it went. Did he show anything?"

"No, Your Highness, he did not. There is still no indication he has an ability for any of it."

Her anger returned, and the excitement on her face melted back into aggravation. "Damn it!" she hissed, looking at the ceiling to calm herself. "There's nothing?"

Drisil's felt as if the oxygen in her blood was being scoured as her heartbeat quickened. "Not yet. It may present itself with adolescence. If you suspect he ought to have some innate ability, it may be that his body needs to mature?"

Aspera lifted her hand for silence. "Has there truly been no sign of those documents that Bran discovered? You've both combed every hovel the fool could have used?"

Randal spoke to divert the queen's attention. "There has been nothing. He either hid them well or destroyed them."

"I want you to find something about it. Search the archives. Send somebody to the surrounding villages in Tal Vyrens. Something," she said through her teeth. "Find me anything about the Auza-Verndari Blessing. I want to know what it is!" Her fingers formed into claws with her ire.

Randal aimed to diffuse her temper. "Anything you ask, Your Majesty. I will send some of our best Spiders to see if there are any remaining texts in the Vale of Knights."

"I'll see what I can do, Your Majesty." Drisil averted her eyes when Aspera looked at her. Unassuming was safe.

That seemed to appease the queen. A trembling hand smoothed down the front of her dress and rested on her abdomen. "Right. I trust you two to rectify this. I believe you are correct, Drisil. It must require maturity." She looked between them while she caught the last of her breath. "What of the girl?"

A small smile crossed Drisil's lips before she composed herself. "Sharp as ever. It seems she inherited her mother's magic if the rumors were true. But, girls mature faster than boys, so her growth is expected," she added to appease further.

Aspera gave a single nod. "Good." She removed her hand and rubbed her hands together. Finally, she calmed herself. It was like shedding skin, and suddenly her demeanor was collected. "Drisil, I want you to bring the boy here. I want to test him myself. Randal, a moment?"

Drisil bowed, then strode from the room. It wasn't until she was well out of sight of Elio that she clutched her chest and leaned against the walls. It was the first time she had ever seen the queen have an outburst about Sonder. Aspera had seemed patient and unaffected until then if any part of his performance fell short. The boy always grasped the information. Some aspects he excelled in, like his weaponry and fitness. But the rage in Aspera's eye that he still showed no aptitude toward magic chilled her. Now the queen wanted to test him herself.

When her heart had slowed, Drisil continued down the stairs, her hand trailing the wall to keep herself from stumbling on weak legs. Dread soured her stomach. She prayed that Merrick would at least be half sober when she found him to deliver what had just happened. No one else would be willing to warn him.

Rhianwyn streaked through the corridors and nearly tackled Sonder as he came out of his room. It was another Equinox, which had become their only reliable time together. That summer, their lessons had increased, and their apprenticeships were in full force. As a result, any time they did find was sparse. Taking his hand, she dragged him toward the kitchens so they could taste all of the food for guests to eat throughout the day.

Come midday, they felt like stuffed chickens. They were close to bursting, but still, Rhianwyn nibbled at tiny candied balls painted like pearls. The fountain splashed at their backs, and their legs dangled over the edge. Rhianwyn had grown so much, her feet would brush the dirt if she didn't hold them just so. Sonder listened to her chatter about the other children who studied with her.

"Enough about my lessons. Tell me about yours. How are the other boys? Are they kind? What's it like finally crossing swords with someone instead of a post? Are you doing that yet?" The words rushed with her excitement. She hadn't seen him properly in nearly a month to just talk.

"They don't talk to me much. Only a boy named Tran," Sonder said. His hands were folded in his lap.

"I've heard of him! He's very well-liked by the other children. Alessia knows a boy who grew up with him. Is he as kind as they say?" Another finger-full of the candies rolled into her mouth. They bounced off her teeth with tiny ticks.

"He is."

"Are you friends, then? Have you finally made another besides me?" she taunted, nudging him.

"I think so," Sonder said after some thought.

She paused mid-grab and eyed him. "Alright, what's wrong? You've only eaten two pastries. You're very serious, even for yourself."

"Merrick got angry at me again," he said quietly.

Rhianwyn's heart fell. She turned her healer's eye and regarded him. It was only then that she noticed he was leaning oddly, as if supporting tender muscles. Her cool fingers took his chin and turned his face. The setting sunlight revealed the discoloration in his cheek that she had missed in her revelry.

She let him pull away. "Is he ever pleased with you?"

Sonder kept his gaze down, and his shoulders shrugged. "He says he's so hard on me to protect me. Before he hit me, I heard him shouting at Drisil about my magic lessons. Then he got angry with me. He's always going on about how dangerous the queen is."

Rhianwyn felt adrenaline spike in her blood. "Have you met her?"

Sonder nodded, too absorbed in his misery to hear the tinge of excitement. "Last week. Drisil interrupted Master Fallen's lecture about how my father was a brutal killer to take me to her."

Rhianwyn felt her blood go cold, and she felt breathless. She wanted to ask about the lesson because it was the first she had heard of it, but the idea of him finally meeting the queen was all she could focus on. "What happened?"

"She went on and on about magic. She conjured light in her hands and made herself look like a completely different person." His brow furrowed with terror. "I've never seen anything like it. I even heard her voice in my head. And Drisil and Randal just stood there and watched. Then she started asking me all sorts of questions. If I ever had dreams about the stars, or if there's a recurring theme, or someone in them."

"Why?" Rhianwyn whispered. Her mind raced with everything Maeveen had told her, yet she had never mentioned anything like Sonder described.

"Something about my family. She said I was born with some magic. She went over everything Drisil has done with me. The tests to see if they can detect anything."

"Did she?" Rhianwyn was awestruck.

"No," Sonder sighed. "It's the same as before. I'm not any good at it. Not even the best sorceress in the realm could find it in me."

"Was she angry?"

"No. At least, I don't think so."

"So she has never directly told you that she's unhappy with you?" Rhianwyn asked, letting her dislike of Merrick bleed back into her tone. "Not even last week?"

"No. Merrick and the other advisors are the closest I ever get to her words. But, even then, it's only Merrick who is upset. The others are indifferent. Not even Randal says anything, and he's the closest to the queen." Sonder sighed heavily.

Rhianwyn's nose crinkled. "I don't like Master Randal. I know he's the best mage besides the queen, but he scares me. He always watches me like he's looking for something. Like he's trying to figure out how to peer into my soul." She sat down again beside Sonder, so their shoulders were nearly touching.

Sonder just shrugged again.

They had gossiped enough about their instructors. There wasn't much to add, especially not now that he was so upset. Neither of them liked Randal. "What about Drisil? Has she said anything?"

"It's hard to describe how Drisil feels. She fights with Merrick about me, but I can't tell why. Sometimes she's angry because he's not doing what the queen wants, but then she's angry at him when he is. She's scary in her own way."

"True," she sighed.

"Ever since the fight with Bran, Merrick has been mean." Sonder took a shaky breath. "I don't know if I like him anymore. I miss how he used to be."

"Did you know him? Bran?"

"Sort of. Sometimes, he told me stories when Merrick wasn't here when he should've been. They reminded me of the stories you tell me." A smile flickered across his face.

Rhianwyn felt her heart grow warm at the mention of her stories. There had been something she wanted to ask him all day, and a glimmer of joy returned. She bumped his shoulder with hers. "Hey, cheer up? It's the Equinox. Let's not let grouchy men ruin it, okay?" He gave her a defiant look, even though he looked like he wanted to smile. She pushed on. "You know what'll fix it?"

Sonder bit. He could never deny her for long. "What?"

"Pastries," she said, as if they were wondrous.

Sonder barked a laugh.

"See? Already it's working. Besides"—she paused—"it's your ninth birthday, remember? So this is our last as children." She took his hand in hers and looked up at him through her eyelashes with a pout.

He swung his legs and swayed his body while he thought. Then his hand tightened around hers. "Alright."

"Happy birthday. We'll figure this out together."

She wondered when Maeveen would come again so that she could tell her about what Sonder had said.

Drisil found Áki outside Bran's manor like he'd said he would be. The man sat with his back pressed against the wall, knees drawn up and opened wide, with his elbows on his thighs. The yard was overgrown and unkept, and the little storage shed's door hung from its hinges.

Holding her cloak off the damp ground, she couldn't help looking into the window as she walked by. The vanity was still there, though the wood was dull and the mirror shattered. Clenching her jaw, Drisil looked back toward the hulking man. A place that had meant so much to her had become just another abandoned building in the city.

Now that Bran was gone, it was no longer a home.

Áki didn't look at her. Instead, he broke off some dead weeds and threw the stalks at the ground. As she stood over him, another piece flew.

"It's almost been a year," he said. His chin fell toward his chest as his shoulders slumped.

"I know," she said quietly. "Ten months and a day."

"So exact." His smirk stretched a scar on his face. Finally, he glanced up at her.

Drisil sucked her teeth. "I still don't understand why Bran chose you of all people."

Áki's face grew sad as he returned to his thoughts. First, he scoffed, seeming to search for what to say. Then, without looking at her, he offered his hand.

She hesitated, lifting her chin with a touch of disgust. His nails were dirty, and the coppery hair on his arms reflected the dim torchlight. But her curiosity piqued, and she let her soft hand take his.

The second his palm touched her fingertips, her eyes lit up. Her lips parted, and she sucked in a breath. "You have the Touch."

His answer was only a lift of his eyebrow as he turned his face further away. Another woody stalk of grass arched toward the dust.

"I don't understand. How've you kept it secret all this time?" She thought better, and her face screwed up. "How does someone so crass have the Touch?"

Áki laughed, a deep, throaty sound. "You've always been a bitch." He leaned his head back against the wall and met her eye. He patted the ground next to him. "Want to hear a story, Princess?"

Drisil felt her face soften. Sweeping the excess cloth out of the way, she sat down. Ever since Áki had started working beside Merrick, their relationship had improved. The loudmouth's fire had cooled somewhat, and the constant nonchalance eased her grief.

Drisil pulled her knees to her chest and wrapped her arms around them. "Tell me your story, Oh Flaming Asshole."

Áki's smile was surprisingly white and intact for someone so prone to brawls. Though his size intimidated, he had a genuine and kind face. It settled back into seriousness, which was growing more common. "Before all of this, I was a big brother. My da got called as a man-at-arms by some lord we've probably killed. His wages came through, for a while. But then they stopped. Things got lean. As the man of the house, I started taking care of me mam and sister doing odd jobs.

"Then, I discovered fightin'. I was good at it, so I went to the pits. We were finally doing okay. Weren't starving, at least. But one day, some men came. Told me I could make more if I fought for them. Gave me some papers. My dumbass couldn't read, so they told me what they said and how to sign my name." His laugh turned deprecating. "Turns out, the papers were forged certificates of sale. Said I was born into slavery. I'd no idea. I was seventeen when they took me."

His face enraptured Drisil as he sank into his memories.

"They didn't care if I died or not, so they put me in deathmatches. Luckily, the pits have some guidelines. There's a hierarchy in fighting. Gotta prove yourself. Even the underground won't take someone green; they need some reputation in the legal sphere first. Even other kingdoms and empires require a chit of caliber from other cities. Those are the highest paying. Spent some time in your homeland, Princess." He nodded to himself, and she knew he was omitting details. "Had to learn quick.

"I had to be abrasive to survive. Can you imagine what they'd do to a boy with the touch?" His eyes glistened when he looked at her. "They would've spit me out."

"That explains why you knew how to establish us among the criminal rings when we arrived. You knew them."

"Not only that. Eventually, I got fed up. Killed the bastards who *bought* me. I taught myself to read enough to gather documents. Prove the bill was forged. Got letters from the family saying they'd never owned slaves. Records of similar cases. Judges decided I had murdered in self-defense and let me go."

"If they let you go, how'd you end up a wanted man?" Drisil leaned closer. It had been nine years, and still, she had never sat down with Áki to hear his story.

Áki looked down at the stalk of grass he twirled in his hand, and his lip curled. "Went looking for my family. Turns out they'd been sold for their debts. Me mam went to a tavern to cook and change linens. My sister—" He paused to collect himself. "My sisters were sold to a brothel. Mam was too sick when I found her to come with me before I could reestablish myself. When I went looking for my sisters, turned out the city guards had brutalized them."

He pursed his lips and grinned, angry at the irony. "Hunted the bastards down and killed them. After that, I went after slavers who bought people's debts or lied about where their chattel came from." His smirk returned, and he again looked like the conniving man she knew. "Just didn't do it legally. Racked up a pretty penny for my head. But like I said, the underground has morals. I started coordinating with them to offset their losses. In exchange, they were happy to hide me until Aspera finally tracked me down."

"So that's how you could get us an in with the gambling rings in the beginning." She was impressed.

His smile was wolfish at the admiration on her face. "I ain't as dumb as I make out." Áki winked and tossed the stalk of grass to the ground. He seemed lighter. "That's why I'm alright culling the queen's shit. I'm alright killing the bastards she sends me. Do the bare minimum, which seems to be everyone's style. When I finally told Bran my story, he didn't distrust me anymore. Let him feel my intentions."

"That's why he asked you to look after Merrick."

Áki's face grew angrier than she had ever seen him. Not battle-hungry—that was mindless, to defend him from the horrors he committed. This was genuine dislike at hearing the man's name. "Can I tell you something, Sil, and you not get angry?" He looked at her.

"Of course," she said.

"If he doesn't stop drinking, I don't know if I can do it. I swore to Bran I would. I'll do anything for that boy. But I care about m'self first, and I'll do what's right in my heart, even if it means telling a dead man to fuck off. A good man, but dead. He ain't here to convince me none more, and that's his problem, not mine." Áki took a steadying breath. "If he hurts Sonder one more time, I may kill him. He's not the same man he used to be."

Just then, the sky-bursts began to explode and crackle. Both of their faces lit with different colors. Áki's hand reached over after a minute of the display and took Drisil's hand. Her dark eyes drifted down to his pale skin nestled against hers. When she glanced up at him, she saw the same longing for an amiable connection in his blue eyes. She smiled at him; then, they turned back to watch.

They sat that way for a long while in silence. The noise made it difficult to be heard, anyway. But when there was a lull as the performers scrambled to shift the canisters filled with powder, Áki spoke. "I hope we're doing the right thing."

Drisil looked at him but said nothing. The finale of the show saved her from having to.

Chapter Nine
Innocence's Kiss

Abandoned manor hideout, nine years ago

Merrick walked through the back door to their shared manor and was greeted by Áki leaning against the counter with a stein in his hands. The kitchen smelled of roast meat and vegetables.

"Ah, Master Always Serious, how are you? Hungry?" Beer sloshed over the rim as he swung his arm out to draw attention to the mess he had made.

Merrick's face knotted. "Are you ever not a bur?"

"I know your secret," Áki said with a jeer. Merrick fixed him with a dark stare, taking a rapid inventory of his armament and how drunk the man was. "I know you're not always serious."

Merrick visibly relaxed. "How drunk are you?"

"You tried to make us believe you hated the kid. The way you refused to touch him when we stole him. With that nasty scowl on your face, I almost thought you'd be the one to gut him with all his wailing. But then you swooped in, gentle as a poppy, to soothe him. Then today! I saw you actually playing and laughing with him. You got a real nice smile, you know. Makes those icy blues almost pleasant to look at." The man lifted his cup before siphoning off another mouthful.

Merrick hung his cloak on the wall-hook. "Why the hell were you anywhere near the milkmaid's?" He wondered how the man had managed to not be seen.

Áki lifted the bulk of his shoulders in a shrug. "Now that he's not screaming, he's grown on me. I stop in to play with him, too." He grew indignant with Merrick's incredulous bark of laughter. "You're not the only one who cares about him."

Merrick scoffed with a genuine grin as he grabbed his own mug and poured himself some of the amber liquid. "I suppose so."

Áki eyed his glass, then took a smaller, more tentative sip. "He ought to have more kids to play with." He raised his hand to cut off Merrick's retort. "I know he can't. So I stop by to play with him." It was a rare moment of seriousness for the man. "You'll make sure he makes friends when the time comes, won't you?"

"Why do you care?" Merrick leaned against the wall across from Áki, eyeing him over the rim of his mug.

Áki shifted. *"I had sisters growing up. The good memories get me through now that life is shit."* He scowled at his cup, realizing he had caught a buzz. *"That kid deserves to have something good to look back on."* Áki looked up at Merrick, who still wore a condescending smirk. *"Don't you have any good memories? A first love? Best friends?"*

Merrick kicked back the rest of the liquid and grimaced at the burn. *"No."* He turned to exit the room.

"Liar," Áki growled into his cup. Merrick heard but didn't turn around.

Present, age ten

Rhianwyn waited impatiently for any sign of Maeveen after the Ball. Then, as winter eased into spring, she worried that something had happened to the girl. Knowing she was considered a fugitive in Sosten, she feared her sister may have ended up in a cell to rot. Or put on trial. Sonder wouldn't have known to tell her. Or worse yet, she might've ended up part of the queen's experiments that Rhianwyn had heard whispers about.

When the warbler finally came, it blazed as orange as the blooming flowers. Its song was clipped, as if it didn't want to risk being noticed. It blended with the blossoms, and it took Rhianwyn a minute to see it.

It was midmorning when it came again, landing on a bush within arm's reach. It did not sing, merely regarded her with its beady black eyes.

"Wyn," the whisper came to her.

Heart racing like the chariot horses, Rhianwyn turned and was pulled into Maeveen's chest.

"I was so worried." Her cloak muffled her sob of relief.

"I am so sorry. I tried to come, but there were so many raids in the city that I couldn't stay. I had to seek refuge in the hills with a tavern owner's wife. I only just got word it was safe, and I came as quickly as possible." Maeveen held her by the shoulders and touched her face. "You grow more beautiful every day." Her warm lips pressed against her forehead.

"There's something I need to tell you," Rhianwyn said. "It's about Aspera. She's after Sonder."

"Quickly. I can't stay long."

Rhianwyn told her everything that Sonder had and more. About Aspera's outbursts with Drisil and Randal behind closed doors without Sonder there, overheard by servants who slunk around the room collecting dishes and cleaning. Or the snippets caught by pages standing in corners while their mentors had discussions of their own.

"She's after some magic of his," she finished.

"That's probably why she had so many raids in the towns," Maeveen breathed. Her mind was working fast.

"Do you know what it's about?" Rhianwyn pressed.

"No." Maeveen began to utter curses as she paced. "Shit!" She turned back toward Rhianwyn and gripped her shoulders again. "Wyn, I need to go. I've got to tell Mother Eissie about this. There may be a way to forge documents to hold Aspera off pressing him. That, or set her on the wrong trail entirely. What she's doing won't work, and it's likely only to make her angry."

"I've heard that name. The rebels that got killed years ago said that name. Who is Mother Eissie?" She wondered if Maeveen had said it before and it never struck her, or if it was the first time she was hearing it again.

"She is our Gwyn'Teilwyr, like a conduit to the Goddess Astraía. I need her guidance on this."

Rhianwyn's hands shot out and grasped Maeveen's hands. "Why can't you stay anymore? What changed?"

Maeveen's smile was almost sad. "I'm the War Chieftain Apparent, just like Papa, and Mother Eissie's heir, like Mama."

I should be with my people, Rhianwyn thought, knowing she was more like their mother, who was the heir, than Mae. Out loud, she said, "When will you return?" Maeveen began to shake her head. Before she could say something, Rhianwyn cut her off. "I need a way to write to you, then. Show me how to train a bird. Just like yours."

Maeveen began to retort but then paused. After a moment, she nodded. "I can't show you now, but I can at least get you one. We have animal whisperers who can help me. I'll imprint it to me. Any others you want can wait. I'll teach you later, I promise. What kind of bird would you like?"

"A blue jay," Rhianwyn said without hesitation.

"A blue jay?" Maeveen asked with an approving smirk. "They're clever and remember their home well."

"And the queen is trying to create blue ravens. I've heard it. So no one will think anything of a bluebird flying around the castle. I hear she's close, so it'll work."

Maeveen touched her cheek with a look of pride. In it was all her unspoken praise. "I'll see to it." The girls embraced once more, and Maeveen squeezed as hard as possible. She planted another rough kiss on Rhianwyn's forehead before she stepped back. "I must go now. Be safe, Little. Hopefully, when I send you your bird, I'll send it with news."

Rhianwyn just nodded, then watched the smooth edges of her sister bleed into the garden. The only giveaway was the ripple she knew to look for.

On her tenth birthday, Sonder met her in the garden like they did every year. Despite being his usual self, he wore a lopsided grin with his hair falling into his eyes. They had both had a tough go of things since the Equinox. Their apprenticeship grew busier, and his list of chores grew lengthier by the day with caring for people's armor and horses. But seeing his smile made her glad—it meant Merrick was gone and Áki was mentoring him.

He dropped down to the ground beside her and laid the sack he carried in his lap. "Sorry about the cakes. Catrine left them for me but didn't wrap them, so I had to."

They indeed were mangled. Rhianwyn laughed at the smushed icing sliding off the tops. She plucked up the one that had collected most of the buttery frosting. "It's alright. Means more for me."

He rolled his eyes. "You would take that one."

"Of course," she said, licking her fingers. "It is my birthday." Her grin turned wolfish as he stuck the candle into the melted mess. "Is this the year you'll finally sing to me?"

"Absolutely not," he shot back as he struck the lighting stick.

The flame danced as she giggled. He was too shy to sing for her, and she delighted in tormenting him when it was his turn to be sung to. Her smile softened as she gazed at the candle, awaiting her wish.

She wanted to wish for so many things, so she wished for a feeling. Her heart harbored hope and simple happiness at that moment, a sense that everything would eventually work out. She briefly glanced at him, and he still wore the contented look.

Sonder's hazel eyes met hers, and he blushed. "What?"

Rhianwyn shook her head as if nothing were amiss, then sent her wish off in a wisp of smoke. She offered him the candle, and he gladly sucked the frosting off without taking it.

Catrine's cakes were the best. The batter was fluffy and mildly sweet, letting the frosting accentuate its simplicity. While she savored each bite, Sonder pulled another wrapped package from his sack. She eyed it with her cheeks full, watching him clutch it nervously in his hands.

"I got you this," he finally said. He held on to it for a few more seconds before sheepishly offering it over.

"What is it?" she asked, not expecting an answer. Instead, she stuffed the remaining morsel into her mouth and wiped the crumbs on the grass before undoing the cloth. It was a pretty fabric, dyed blue with tiny gold and silver stars stitched in. There was enough of it there that it could easily be worn to tie her hair back.

"I asked Mistress Merriweather to make that," he offered. The suspense was making him squirm.

"It's charming," she said. Then, the last of the fabric fell away and revealed a book. She gave him a skeptical look before she examined it properly.

The cover was simple leather, scraps from a tanner versus the expensive cuts. The carving was sloppy, but her fingers ran over the grooves lovingly. "Did you make this?" He nodded, which she saw from the corner of her eye. She opened it, and his neatest scrawl greeted her on the parchment. The pages protested in their bindings, and some weren't cut straight.

"Do you like it?" Sonder whispered.

A smile broke across her face, and her vision blurred. She hadn't realized she'd gotten teary-eyed. "It's perfect." She loved it.

"It's my favorite story of yours. The one I made you tell me a thousand times."

"So you could write this?" She looked away from the words her eyes were tracing back to him. "The one about the star maiden who stayed behind when the gods were forced to leave."

He scratched the back of his head. "You swear you like it? I know it's a little messy."

Rhianwyn crawled on her hands and knees and planted a kiss on his cheek. "I love it. Thank you." She sat back down on her bottom and enjoyed how red his face burned.

She picked the book back up with a heavy sigh and gazed at the cover with its crude outline of a woman surrounded by stars. "Where am I going to hide this, though? If anyone found it, we'd be in so much trouble."

"We can bury it here, in the garden. I've brought oil skin to protect it. Then, when we finally leave the castle and can have our place, we'll take it and hide it somewhere better." The sack finally sat deflated of its surprises.

It broke her heart, but she nodded. "Let me read it, first?" She shook her head when she closed the back cover. "I'm impressed. How in the world did you manage to pull this off and not get caught?"

"I can be sneaky sometimes," Sonder said indignantly. "I asked Áki to get me the leather for the cover and stole the parchment from Fallen. Then, I'd crawl out of bed after dark and work on it."

"So you are teachable," she teased. A thought came to her that had been gnawing at her since the Equinox. She had wanted to ask him then, with their formal stockings and shoes scattered around them while the cold nipped at their toes and sky-bursts exploded around them. But she had been too shy. Now, she was overcome with fondness and appreciation.

She couldn't help the smile spreading across her face or the blush that made her heart beat faster. It was the moment she had waited for, and the excitement and fear mingled in her stomach until it felt like it would float away on bird wings. "Can I ask you something?"

"Sure," he said with a nonchalant shrug.

"When we're sixteen and come of age, will you promise we'll go to the ball together?"

Sonder's smile gradually grew as he gave it some thought. "Yeah, okay. That'll be fun. "

Rhianwyn's heart swelled with glee, and she beamed at him.

He offered his hand to her, and she stared at it. "Let's go bury it so it stays safe." His hand was warm when she took it.

All through the summer, there was no sign of Maeveen, nor did she see a blue jay waiting in the trees. What made it more difficult was that Sonder rarely could spend time with her anymore. The day he would be squired loomed, and there were many things that he needed to be competent at—understanding the ever-changing laws and the duty of upholding them, and how his family had nearly toppled the kingdom. That was on top of drills and tending to the needs of the other knights.

When he did get free time, he rarely smiled or laughed like before. Instead, whenever he caught himself enjoying himself, he'd grow serious. Rhianwyn couldn't help but feel forlorn about how mature he had become in the past year.

The only balm to the worry was her friendship with Alessia. Even if her concerns never stopped gnawing at her, she still found herself easygoing with the other girl. Some days, Rhianwyn wished she could confide everything to her, but she knew she couldn't tell Alessia about helping the Lorists or her true heritage.

As the days went on, however, she realized her fondness had grown for the castle's people. The more she got to know the world around her, the more she felt kindred to them, with a sense of duty to those she had known most of her life.

The Equinox Ball came again, and still, there was no sign of a cerulean bird. Finally, exasperated, Rhianwyn threw all her worries away and decided to enjoy the festivals until the celebration.

Alessia took her to the markets for the first time with a list from both Wilkin and Gwenyvir. Seeing the masks with silk ribbons hanging beside painted fans stole her breath. Had the vendors not leered at them as they passed, Rhianwyn would have touched every single one, even the giant spools of fabric displayed for the ladies who could afford a new dress to be made. She came back with her basket full of herbs and cleaned linens, but her heart full of wonder.

Tran and Alessia joined Rhianwyn and Sonder for the festivities on the day of. The two had never been inside the castle, so they showed them around. They were awed by the giant arching stained-glass images in the foyer, wavering with magic that pooled like curtains of falling mist. The windows stood open, yet the inside was chilled despite the sun beating down on the stone floor.

"The temperature is perfect here," Alessia breathed as she tilted her head back and spun to see the painted ceiling above them. "I heard she had this room specially built."

"She did. I learned about it in a history lesson," Tran offered.

Rhianwyn looked up and let herself take in the image of Stellamar's sea dragon coasting through a blanket of stars. The illustrations were in magical paint, and they could be changed.

Tran elbowed Sonder with a grin. "Can't wait till we're taken on as squires and can come. I'd love to see this place full of beautiful girls dressed in their best. I clean up nicely, you know. When I'm not wearing training leathers."

Sonder blushed at the mention of finely dressed girls. Rhianwyn and Alessia giggled at Tran, and their response made him question them indignantly.

Alessia's eyes began to wander again, and she pointed at the banners hanging from the balconies. "What are those?"

Both Sonder and Rhianwyn looked, and she quickly glanced at him as his face fell.

"Those are the coats-of-arms for the houses of Sosten," he said.

"Oh, yeah, you're right," Tran said. He named a few of them enthusiastically until he looked at the other side of the room. "I don't recognize some of them. The ones on that side."

"That's because they're enemies of the crown." The ones they talked about were damaged, some stained with rusty-brown splotches. There weren't many, but Sonder knew more were added periodically.

A servant came by then and shooed them away, and they continued the tour so they wouldn't be caught again.

Eventually, they ended up in the garden. Encouraged by Alessia's prodding, the boys agreed to put on a mock tournament to honor the day. While the girls called encouragement, the boys wrestled in the damp grass.

Tran was soon pinned, and Alessia let out an exasperated shout when he yielded. "Come on! You're supposed to be the best, Tran!" Rhianwyn sang her triumph behind her.

Sonder offered a hand to help Tran sit. The boys beamed at each other with cheeks flushed by exertion. "I was the best. But with all his extra training, it seems Sonder finally caught up. I'd wager that you'll be officially taken on as Sir Merrick's squire."

Rhianwyn's heart dropped as she heard the boys talk about the training yard, questioning who would squire Tran and the other boys. Before she could get too engrossed in their conversation, Alessia leaned over to whisper in her ear.

"They're adorable, aren't they? Talking about knighthood while they're still catching their breath?"

"You are so bad!" Rhianwyn laughed and nudged the other girl's shoulder.

"Have you kissed him yet?" Alessia glanced at the other two to ensure they were paying them no mind.

"Who?" Rhianwyn asked. It took a look, and she knew what the other girl was getting on about. "Ew, no! Why would I kiss Sonder?"

"All the other kids do it. They sneak off behind the shed during work." She grew incredulous. "You really haven't? You sneak to his room at night to tell him stories in bed, yet you haven't kissed him?"

"No." Rhianwyn felt her cheeks begin to tingle.

"What are you two talking about?" Tran called at them. "Which boy are you getting on about now, Alessia, huh?"

Alessia smiled at her before turning toward the boys and folding them back into the group. "Certainly neither of you, *if* that's what we were talking about. You both were all the talk two weeks ago before the other girls decided someone else had a nicer smile."

Rhianwyn laughed, then caught Sonder looking at her. She gave him her own knowing smile. They were trapped inside the castle walls, so the gossip the two bickered about meant less to them.

A week after the ball, she lay in bed. The blankets were tucked up to her chin to ward off the chill morning. The joy from the festival still warmed her heart when a jay appeared in the branches outside. She went to the window and opened it so it could hop inside.

"Hello, little one," she whispered. She offered a finger, and its little feet tickled. A note was tucked into a harness against its chest. Rhianwyn pulled it out, and the bird fluttered to the top of her wardrobe. It delighted her to see its bright color against the heavy, dark furniture.

I will come after the Hallowed Tournament. Watch for my bird.

"Well, at least you can bring me more information. I won't be guessing." She looked up at the jay, which turned its head to consider her. "You can't live in here, you know. You'd be seen in a heartbeat. Besides, it's too cramped."

Curious, she held her hand out. The bird immediately dropped to her finger.

"Look how beautiful you are," she whispered.

Gently, she touched its head, and when it let her, she began to scratch its neck, which made it fluff up. Rhianwyn beamed. "I have got to learn to whisper to animals. Hopefully, you'll be happy."

The bird looked up at her. The brown in its eye caught the morning light, and she smiled at it, feeling as if there was a connection buzzing in her mind.

She walked back to the window. "Well, go on then. I'll leave nuts in the garden for you! We'll figure out a special song for me to call you."

The bird took flight and was just out of sight when Olive knocked on the door and entered. "What are you doing, Miss? It's freezing in here. You've got the window open?" she exclaimed.

Rhianwyn smiled and stepped down from the window. "I wanted to smell the last of the warm soil before the cold sets in." The latch snapped shut. Before Olive could chide, she continued. "I know, I know, I have early lessons this morning. I'll get ready."

Two days after the Hallowed Tournament, Maeveen came, setting Rhianwyn's thoughts abuzz. The conversation was flurried. Talk of spying and rebels ferrying people across the land to the safety of Cerdan and the border. It was whimsical like their stories, yet terrifying in reality. But, most importantly, the information involving Sonder was successfully planted to keep Aspera at bay.

⁜

Sonder sat eating a late lunch in the kitchens. He traced the words of a book with one hand, and with the other, he periodically took bites of a pastry.

He couldn't stop himself, despite having stayed up late studying the same book with Rhianwyn. Even though Merrick and the others fell quiet when he entered the room, he knew they were agitated about his upcoming tests, so he exhausted himself trying to imagine the questions. After the tournaments two years earlier, his mentor was always on edge this time of year.

"Pssst," someone softly hissed from behind him, and he looked up.

"Rhianwyn? Why are you here?" he asked, setting down the pastry he had been eating and wiping his fingers on his napkin.

Her chest was heaving, and her face was bright red, making the freckles dusting her nose stand out. Sonder could tell by her belted skirts that she must have just run from the garden.

Rhianwyn looked around to be sure no one was taking mind of them. "I got out of my lessons this morning. There's something I want to tell you." She bit her lip and smiled, stepping out to grab his hand. "Do you have time?"

Sonder stood up. "I really should be studying—"

"It won't take long," she said, bouncing on her toes.

After a moment, he marked his page with a worn cloth and closed the cover. "Alright."

Rhianwyn squealed, then swiped his discarded pastry and popped the rest into her mouth. She snagged another one from a nearby tray with her mouth still full. Finally, she took his hand and pulled him out through the back door with a wink. He chuckled and shook his head—her joy always affected him.

She led him outside through the kitchen garden. They followed a narrow pathway that ran between two separate wings of the castle. Covered corridors bridged over their heads, upon which they saw people moving about their business.

"Where are we going? I didn't bring my coat," Sonder said.

Rhianwyn placed her hand on his chest to stop him and looked around the wall as another, smaller square opened in front of them. "Don't worry. It's just the back way. I saw Merriweather near the kitchens, and I didn't want her to follow us."

The news made his heart clench. But he couldn't think about it for long because nobody was there, and she darted across the path.

Most everyone was staying indoors today because of the cold. Nobody stopped to peer out the windows at the kids as they wove their way through the grounds, the dark gray stones looming around them.

Before long, they reached an entrance near the library. The warm air quickly chased the chill from their clothes, and they made sure to wipe their feet. There was no need to lead him anymore. A little nook lay around the corner, hard to see except from a certain angle. It was where they left notes to each other. No one had discovered it, as far as they could tell. It was unassuming and thus overlooked.

Sonder let her heard him into it.

"What is this about, Wyn?" He shifted aside as she squeezed in beside him.

The cold had pricked her cheeks red, and her hands were like ice in his.

"I have something to tell you that you can't tell anyone else."

Ever since she had dragged him out of the kitchens, his face had been softened by his smile. "Well, you've said that. What is it?" Sonder asked, feeding off her excitement.

Rhianwyn peeked around once more to be sure no one was around. She kept her voice low. "That girl I've told you about? She came today!"

Sonder's face fell, and he pulled his hands from hers. "I've told you to stop talking to her, Wyn. You're going to get in trouble."

"She knew my parents." Rhianwyn's mood remained bright, though a whine crept into her voice.

Sonder grew curious. Neither one of them had known their parents, and she didn't even know about hers at all, at least as far as he knew. He couldn't be mad at her for getting drawn into a conversation about them.

"Alright, I'll bite. What did she say? Who are they?" he said with a frustrated sigh.

Rhianwyn dropped her voice more, "She said I'm a princess!"

Sonder's nose crinkled. "A princess? No way."

"She said so!" Rhianwyn looked indignant.

"She probably just said that because you live in the castle." He shook his head, growing stern. "I mean it, Wyn. You shouldn't talk to her anymore. If you get caught, you'll probably be in trouble." He didn't need to say that he knew what it was like to always be in trouble. What he didn't express in words, his face gave away.

She pouted and crossed her arms. "No one ever sees us talking. I think she's the daughter of one of the servants or something. She helps me in the garden, so they probably don't think anything of it if anyone sees us. I'm allowed to have friends, you know."

"You know that's not true. If it was, you wouldn't be worried about if anyone has seen you or have an argument ready. Not to mention how you're looking around now. It's something. I'm not dumb." His frustration with how the adults treated him as if he didn't notice things mingled with his voice. Sonder was tired.

Rhianwyn's brows furrowed, and her lips puffed out. "So what? It's nice to talk to someone other than you on occasion." She crossed her arms. "You're just jealous."

He scoffed. "Jealous? Of what?"

"I have more friends than you. All you have is Tran and me." Her voice came out in a sing-song.

"That's not true." He crossed his arms uncomfortably, face flushing.

It was true. He always turned red when he was embarrassed or feeling shy. The fact Rhianwyn always seemed to know how he felt while he was left in the dark made him self-conscious

"Well, I believe her. If you don't want me to tell you about her, I won't anymore."

"That's not what I'm trying to say. I just think that she overhears us talking, and uses that to tell you what you want to hear, so you'll keep talking to her," he reasoned.

Sonder went on, trying to reiterate what he had told her many times. Most of his argument was based on what Merrick scolded him about. She hated how much the boy felt he needed to do everything on his own flawlessly. Her eyes drifted toward a silhouette walking by the window.

"Fine. I'll be more careful." She mirrored his incredulous look. "What? I'm not going to stop talking to her. Besides, she doesn't come around as often anymore."

"Why?" he asked, equally skeptical and genuinely curious.

"She has family she's helping to care for in another town. I can't remember the name of it. You probably would, with all your history lessons." She waved her hand dismissively, then pushed her hair behind her ears. "There was something else."

He could tell this wasn't how she'd wanted the conversation to go. "Oh?" he asked, leaning against the wall.

"The girl and I, we talk a lot about you." He grew stern again, and she flushed. "Nothing personal. She just knows you like her stories. That, and just—how our lessons are. She's like a big sister, almost." He didn't miss the twitch of a grimace across her face.

Sonder softened. "I'm sorry. I know you had a sister before Merrick brought you here. I just don't want you to get in trouble is all."

Her fingers tugged idly at her skirt. "Do you remember when we saw those two adults in the garden years ago?"

"Yeah, I do." He was skeptical, but he let her continue with the vein she had started.

"Well," she said haltingly, "do you remember how they put their lips together?" Rhianwyn's breathing quickened, and she didn't pause long enough to let him respond. "It's something adults do when they care about someone." She chewed the inside of her lip. "Do you want to try it?" She finally looked up.

Sonder was surprised. He hadn't expected the conversation to take this turn, and he grew thoughtful. They had been friends for a long time now, and they did everything they could together. He was too shy to say anything, but whenever she took his hand to hold it or teased him about how handsome he looked in his formal wear, he always blushed—as he did now.

While he thought about it, Rhianwyn gazed at him eagerly. She had never explicitly said that she cared about him.

"Okay, sure. But, do you know how we're supposed to do it?" he asked.

"Well, they just put their lips together, right?" she blurted, failing to hide her excitement.

Sonder paused to think. "Well—they used their tongues too, didn't they? I thought I saw them licking each other at one point." His nose scrunched at the strangeness.

Rhianwyn's shoulders lifted. "We can try it that way?"

Sonder idly picked at some dry skin on his lips before he nodded. His breath, still sweet from the pastry, puffed in her face as his heart hammered away too. She was slightly taller than him, and he had to tilt his head up. Then, as their faces drew together, they poked their tongues out with their eyes wide open.

Just before their tongues touched, she dissolved into a fit of giggles, and he pulled away.

"This is weird," he groaned. His face burned, and he wrapped his arms around himself.

"Your eyes were all crossed." She covered her mouth to stifle her laughs.

"I don't want to do this if you're just going to make fun of me," he complained.

Rhianwyn grabbed his hands. "No! I'm not making fun of you. It was just funny looking." She snorted and covered her mouth again. Though it was nice to see her happy again, he glared. She tilted her head. "Come on. Let's keep our eyes closed and just touch lips?"

Sonder thought about it, then said with reluctance, "Okay."

She squeezed his hands.

They both hesitated, listening to their nervous breaths mingle. Then, just before it turned awkward again, there was an unspoken agreement, and they both began to move together. Neither closed their eyes, each waiting to see if the other would. Sonder stopped as their noses brushed. They tilted their heads the same way at the same time. Her cold hands came up to hold his head steady. She glanced into his eyes and smiled shyly.

"Okay, now close your eyes," she whispered.

He did, and her hands fell away before she closed the gap.

Sonder's cheeks tingled where Rhianwyn's clammy palms were, and his heart pounded wildly. Her lips touched his in the darkness of his closed eyes.

He noticed most that she smelled and tasted like berries from the stolen pastry. The kiss was stiff and clumsy and felt strange. Yet there was something nice about it, too. He liked being this close to Rhianwyn.

He had seen adults kissing in passing, but he always had quickly averted his eyes because it was too embarrassing. There were rumors about the other kids kissing, but he had been too afraid to ask her if she wanted to try.

Sonder had no idea how long it should last, if he should do something with his hands, or even if she enjoyed it. His thoughts ran rampant. He began to pull away to ask, but at that exact moment, a woman gasped, and his heart clenched in fear.

Chapter Ten
Caught

Bran's manor, eight years ago

"It worked. She assigned me as his mentor. Just like you wanted." Merrick said, standing in the doorway to Bran's room.

"Good."

Merrick waited for the man to continue. Then, when he realized Bran wouldn't say anything else, he swallowed. "Why not you?"

Bran smiled with a faraway look. "Because, when I look at him, all I see is his father." Every time Bran looked at him that way, Merrick felt pinned. "There's a reason I knew how to coach you to plead your case to her." He looked away once more at the rain falling. "My heart can't bear looking at him."

"Why me?" Merrick didn't know why his own heart was hammering hard.

"When you look at him, I see the same ache that Lucrid had when he talked about his son."

Present, age ten

Sonder knew that hiss, and the angry voice that followed. "What on this good earth are you two doing?"

All their nervous energy shot them away from each other like a released arrow. Rhianwyn pushed Sonder, and he threw his hands up.

"Nothing!" they said in unison.

Merriweather glanced down the hallway as if to ensure no one had seen, then fixed her sharp eyes on him. "What have I told you?" She grabbed him with so much conviction it was nearly a lunge, her fingers digging in so intensely they'd leave bruises on his arm. Then, with her free hand, she struck him across the face.

Rhianwyn covered her mouth with both hands. Merriweather rounded on her, poking her in the chest.

"I've warned you both. Merrick won't allow this!" She glanced around once more and lowered her voice. "Nor would the queen. She'd make your lives more difficult one way or another. You've forgotten?"

Rhianwyn's shock cleared, and she clasped Merriweather's hand with her own. "Please, don't tell. It was my idea."

Merriweather yanked her hand free. "You're lucky t'was me come looking. Merrick's asked for you." She fumed at Sonder.

They both paled. Neither of them had known that Merrick had returned.

"You've heard me correctly," Merriweather snapped. She gave Sonder a little shake, her fingers gripping as if he were struggling. "Had it been him discovered you, you'd likely both be beaten!" Spittle flew from her lips as she swept her fierce eyes between them.

Sonder took the onslaught with his head hung. His whole body burned with embarrassment as tears slipped down his face. It was made worse because he could see Rhianwyn's concerned glances through the fall of his dark hair.

"Please don't tell," Rhianwyn begged. "It was my fault. We won't do it again." She implored with what sounded like her whole heart. Her resilience was always endearing.

Intrusive memories of getting caught in bed together came back to Sonder. They'd already been given their second chance.

Merriweather lowered her voice and jabbed Rhianwyn in the chest once more. "See that you don't, else it'll be more'n a beating the boy gets, girl." She turned toward Sonder and whacked him upside the head again before dragging him out of the little alcove.

Sonder stumbled after her. The angle she held his arm at twisted his body around. He looked up and saw Rhianwyn watching them go. He hated to see her cry for him.

Two staff members happened by as they came barreling out of the hiding spot. They watched, glancing between him and Rhianwyn, the laundry baskets balanced on their hips forgotten. Their heads bent together, and Sonder saw Rhianwyn's face grow angry at the gossip.

He stumbled through the threshold, and before they turned out of sight, Rhianwyn ran in the opposite direction.

Merriweather's look made the servants gasp and jump out of their way as they bowled through the corridors. The mistress was usually kind and even-tempered.

It was the most public punishment Sonder had ever received. Yet the whispers didn't make him angry like they did Rhianwyn. Instead, they added to how mortified he felt, stumbling behind his caregiver, with tears falling unbidden from his eyes.

Sonder entertained the idea that she would turn down a hall that led to an unkept part of the castle. He could be given an endless list of chores. He could be kept so busy he'd not see Rhianwyn, or the sun, for months. Or if she turned the other way, she could backtrack to his room and punish him herself. The public humiliation was enough. But each turn and step took them to where he knew they were going, and his anxiety grew.

They were heading toward the Justice Wing, where Merrick inevitably would be.

Merriweather entered Merrick's study without knocking, dragging Sonder and thrusting him into the room so hard he stumbled. Merrick looked up from the paperwork on his desk with raised eyebrows. It looked like he might laugh.

But that was the last of Sonder's hope. He realized his mentor's face was as stern as ever.

The door slammed behind them. Merriweather pointed at his surrendered back. "I caught this one and Rhianwyn kissing!" she shrilled, breathing heavily.

Sonder stared at the carpet, tears slipping down his cheeks. His fists were balled up by his sides.

He felt betrayed.

Merrick's chair scraped against the stone floor, and the sound made Sonder flinch. A soft jingle from the man's boots and armor preceded him as he crossed the room. He hadn't even taken off his cloak or unbuckled his sword yet.

Those black boots stopped just at the edge of Sonder's vision. Merrick spoke softly, "I'll see to this matter." There was little inflection to his voice. It was as glassy as the sea before a storm.

"See that you do," Merriweather insisted. "Had it been someone else who happened upon them—I dread the thought." Her voice cracked at the end.

"Thank you, Mistress Merriweather." Merrick lifted Sonder's chin. His cheek still smarted where his caretaker had struck him. Those blue eyes bore into him. "Call for a healer, please."

Sonder's brow furrowed ever so slightly, and he felt his lip quiver, betraying him. Then, gripped by fear, his eyes darted toward Merriweather as if there was still a chance she would whisk him away.

Merriweather inhaled. "Yes, sir." She curtsied, then gave Sonder a parting glance. Her brow was creased, and her eyes wide. She hiked her skirts and turned to leave. The door closed behind her with more control.

Merrick ran his callused thumb over Sonder's red cheek as he pinned the boy with a scowl. Dark circles marred his eyes, and the edges of his beard were more unruly than usual. The gray light streaming through the windows did him no favors, showing every exhausted line etched into his skin.

"At least you have the decency to look ashamed." There was a sour smell on his breath.

Sonder dropped his eyes. He hated that smell.

"No. Look at me," Merrick said.

Another warm tear slipped out of the corner of Sonder's eyes as he obeyed.

Merrick wiped it away. "I take no pleasure in this." His face was drawn as he searched the boy. "Go pick your switch."

Sonder hung his head as he turned and walked into the adjoining bedchamber. The walls were bare, the bed pristine, with a few pieces of furniture for storage. When he knew he was out of sight, he began to sob silently.

Then he heard a new voice, muffled. Drisil? Had she been hiding somewhere? "I think you do enjoy beating the boy on some level," she said. Her tone was mocking, as if she were making a dark joke.

"I'm keeping him alive," Merrick growled.

"Your sentiments contrast that job, don't you think?" she asked in the same tone.

"No one saw you?"

"No, neither the boy nor the matron could see me," Drisil responded, folding her hands into her sleeves.

Merrick sighed. "Reveal yourself to him. Let the gravity of it sink in. There is no place for love in his life. It's too great a liability."

"He is only ten, Merrick," Drisil responded. "When was your first kiss? It was probably an innocent thing. You're overreacting."

"Love has already destroyed us. I have time yet to keep him from the same fate. As you've told me many times before: there is no place for sentiments. Better he learns it now when it is innocent kissing." By Merrick's tone, Sonder knew the look he must be giving Drisil to silence her.

Sonder had never met his father, but at that moment he hated the man, blamed him for everything. If he hadn't been the Black Daemon, Sonder wouldn't be bound by duty to make amends for his crimes. Likewise, Merrick wouldn't be breaking because of the task of raising him.

Their muffled voices died, reminding Sonder that they were waiting. He scrubbed at his cheeks with his sleeve and looked up at the window. As he wiped snot from his nose, Sonder imagined slipping through. It was a short drop. He could run away to live with Rhianwyn's friend from the garden.

They both could if he waited for Rhianwyn to come looking for him. She knew where their favorite hiding spots were.

Sniffling, he took a deep breath, then turned toward the dresser where Merrick kept his belts and crop.

He'd never get away. Aspera wouldn't rest until she had what she wanted from him. Even if his other mentors believed he was sometimes too harsh, Sonder knew Merrick meant those things. As he ran his small hands over the leather he polished so often, he felt responsible for everything.

Sonder's hands closed around a belt, and he shuffled back toward the study. His eyes were drawn to Drisil and her grave look. Two of his mentors standing there, lit from behind so they looked like grim silhouettes, gave him pause. His heart quickened, and all his courage fled. It was such immense courage for one so small.

He froze in the doorway.

Merrick stepped toward him. Everything wilted inside of him, and he cowered. "Please, no," he begged. "I don't mean to disobey you."

Merrick took the belt and gently placed his hand on Sonder's back. He flinched like the belt had already bit into his skin. Drisil watched, swallowing audibly as Merrick guided him to a chair.

Sonder internalized the looks on their faces. He had failed them both by caring for Rhianwyn. Great warriors weren't supposed to love; their duty was to the crown first. He should have never forgotten that.

The man commanded him to kneel and remove his shirt. Sonder choked on a sob, and he saw Drisil clench her jaw and look away angrily.

The snap of leather was excessive, each one punctuated by a deep grunt and a boyish whimper. Five angry welts, two of them beaded with bright blood.

Sonder kept his face buried in his arms as he wept, his whole body shaking. Merrick walked away. The fear of what might come next made Sonder turn his head.

Merrick's back receded as he went to his desk. Drisil's hand shot out from her sleeves and grabbed his arm. Her painted nails bit into his skin. "You go too far, *sir*." Her eyes burned into him, as if willing him to look into her anger head-on.

Merrick set the belt down without looking at her. With his other hand, he picked up the decanter of wine. There was a subtle tremor in his fingers as he poured the red liquid into his glass. Some of the liquid splashed onto the wood.

He downed it in one gulp, and he finally looked at her. "Better me than the queen. At least I love the boy."

She got closer to him, her face inches from his. "You are mighty self-righteous for a man who will break the boy for her. You don't even know what side you've chosen. You're lost in the bottle." She looked close to tears.

Her words clearly struck a nerve, and Merrick yanked his arm away. Their anger seemed equally matched as they stared at each other, having a wordless conversation.

Merrick broke first, walking back to Sonder. He scooped him up slowly, as if trying to be careful, but Sonder let out a whimper as he was jostled.

Merrick held the boy to his chest and shushed him. "I'm sorry," he whispered into Sonder's hair.

The feeling made Sonder's stomach knot with mixed emotions. The man's voice was gruff as he repeated it before carrying him out of the room and away from Drisil's glare.

The cool air kissed his inflamed back, and Sonder felt ashamed without his shirt. As they passed through the corridors, servants and nobles watched them silently, as if they knew about the kiss and his punishment. Being carried like a baby made the embarrassment worse. Sonder buried his face in Merrick's chest to hide his face.

With his eyes hidden, he could imagine that all the prying stares had no idea who he was—just a strange child who could be anyone.

Every inhale was heavy with the smell of the man. But the scent he loved so much was tinged with anger, making it impossible to find the comfort he sought. The sour smell had gradually grown more overpowering.

When they reached his room, the door was cracked, and Merrick pushed it open.

Merriweather sat inside with her stitching in hand. As they entered, she stood. Wordlessly, she pulled Merrick to Sonder's bed. The man was unsteady as he set him down, and Sonder rolled to his stomach, defeated.

"Where is the healer?" Merrick asked.

An older woman pushed through the servant's door, breathing heavily. "Here. I came as quickly as I could." She was slightly plump, with a scarf wrapped around her cloud of graying hair. The smell of mixed herbs and soil filled the room as she slipped in. "Is there somewhere I can wash?" Merriweather pointed, and the woman hurried over to the basin. The tension in the room was palpable.

The woman was still patting her hands dry when she turned to take measure of the room. It was so quiet, Sonder's sniffles echoed. It drew her gaze to him.

"Thank you for coming, Gwen," Merrick said.

She glared. "Don't you thank me. I came for Sonder, not you." She set down the soft towel and then walked over to the bed. "Now, let me have a look at him." She waved him out of the way.

Shouldering around Merrick, she gazed upon the angry welts on Sonder's back. Mistress Gwenyvir bent over and gently began to prod his back. Despite the warm water, her fingers were cooler than the sore skin, which already burned and bruised as his immune system responded. Each touch made Sonder shudder.

The woman's face darkened further. "I'm getting tired of this, sir."

"Well, tell your apprentice—" Merrick began.

Gwenyvir rounded on him and jabbed her finger into his chest, though she was a whole head and a half shorter than him. "I'll tell my girl nothing you have to say. She's my ward, to tend as I see fit."

Merrick brought his face closer to hers. "Let me remind you they're both under my jurisdiction."

She didn't flinch. "Bran appointed me."

"Whose position is now mine," Merrick snarled.

"Are ye saying ye no longer trust his judgment?" Her voice grew lower.

Merrick's anger seemed to break, and he took a step back. "That's what I thought. Now, get off. Let me work."

The muscles in Merrick's jaw clenched, but he stepped farther away without saying anything. Gwenyvir set down her little satchel and dug through it, producing gauze and a collection of vials and jars.

Merrick came to Sonder's bedside and knelt as the woman shuffled and clinked noisily, so he was at eye level. Sonder looked up. The pillow was damp from tears and snot beneath his cheek. Merrick touched his face once more with a pained expression. "I do not relish this," he whispered, swallowing hard.

Drisil appeared in the doorway and coughed to make herself known. Sonder marveled at how Merrick could ignore three sets of angry eyes, regarding only him.

The healer sidled up and deliberately bumped the man's arm with her hip. "This will sting, young one," she said.

Merrick held Sonder's gaze as the dampened gauze was brought down to the sores. The boy let out a sob when he felt the cold bite lance through him. He turned his face away to hide his weakness.

Sonder could hear the frustration that punctuated the man's movement as he stood up.

"How much, sir?" Gwenyvir asked flatly, intent on her work.

"Only enough to help prevent infection." There was a collective scoff as he said it. "He needs to learn a lesson. Next time may see worse."

She shifted, and Sonder guessed she had turned to look at the man, because her hands paused.

"Let him suffer for them both." The words came out ugly and harsh. Merrick stalked away.

Sonder turned to watch him leave. Drisil blocked Merrick's exit, and Sonder was transfixed as her long fingers splayed across the man's chest. His momentum carried him until their bodies were nearly touching. He stared past her, even as he was stayed by her touch.

"You are too hard on both of you, Merrick," she said, just loud enough so her words reached Sonder's ear, though he doubted she meant for him to overhear.

Merrick looked at her. It seemed almost a tender moment. Drisil implored him to listen with her eyes.

For an instant, it looked like he may break, but his voice was steely when he responded. "Just see to his lessons when they begin. Teach him well. Yours are the most important."

Merrick dropped his shoulder and moved past her. Drisil took a deep breath and lingered, her hands tucked into her long sleeves as she observed in silence.

After a while, she bowed to Merriweather, causing the emerald jewels in her ears to catch the light. "You two can tend to this, Mistress?" she asked.

Merriweather was gathering up soiled linens. "Indeed, Lady Drisil. If I may be so bold, miss? Your energies would be better spent tending to Sir Merrick." Her nostrils flared as her face tightened. "Had I known, I would have seen to the punishment myself. We're all upset by the queen's decision this morning, but he went too far."

Drisil stood taller. "Mistress Merriweather, Sir Merrick has been charged to do the queen's bidding. As the boy's caregiver, you are responsible for bringing these things to his attention. I'll discuss it with him, but you'd be best to remember your place." Drisil looked at Gwenyvir, who had paused in the final touches to watch. "Both of you. Mistress Rhianwyn is also a ward of Her Majesty. See she understands her position as well, lest her rope shorten."

Drisil inclined her head, and both of the older women bowed back, tight-lipped. Then, with a final glance at Sonder, Drisil left the two to finish.

It was a blessing when Sonder was left alone. He had overheard more today than he could bargain for. For all the times he had tried to listen in on his overseers, the conversations buzzing noisily in his head made him realize he didn't want the knowledge.

Now he understood why everyone fell silent when he entered the room.

Something had happened to put Merrick on edge, and everyone seemed conflicted in going along with it. While he lay there, wincing with each throb of his back, he made a list of things he'd give up to go back to simpler days.

Even though he was spent and wanted nothing more than to sleep, he fought it. The pain and shivers from his fevered skin helped. If he stayed awake, then whatever was about to change couldn't come.

He must have started to doze because he woke with a start.

"It's okay, it's just me," came a whisper.

It was too dim to see clearly, but he knew that voice. "Go away, Rhianwyn," he said, turning his head to the other side. The movement pulled his skin, and he grimaced.

"I brought something to help with the pain," she said louder.

"I'm not supposed to. It's part of the punishment. I'll get in more trouble," he said, dejected.

There was a rustling under the bed as she crawled beneath it. Then a thump against his stomach and a whispered, "Ouch." Seconds later, her face popped up on the other side. "They won't know, I promise. It's just birch bark. It'll help with the pain and inflammation. So you can sleep."

He turned his head again. "Go away."

"But, you've been punished for us both. Let me help," she pled, resting her chin on the bed.

"I don't want to be friends anymore, Wyn. You should go." The pillow muffled his voice.

"Well, that's a little harsh, isn't it? I'm sorry you got in trouble, but—"

He spoke louder. "We aren't friends anymore."

Men who were bound to the queen only hurt the people they loved and cared about.

She huffed. Then he heard her crawl back over to his side. When she popped up again, he could see her narrowed eyes. "I think you're just saying that because they've gotten into your head. So, tell me why, at least. You owe me that much."

"Because I'm no good for you. You'll end up worse off if we stay friends," he said, his tone forced.

Rhianwyn pursed her lips and crossed her arms. "That's not fair."

"I'm not a good friend." He tried to look angry.

"That's not for you to decide," Rhianwyn pressed. "If you don't want to be my friend anymore, say so. Don't use your caring about me as an excuse. That makes you just like Merrick, Sonder."

His façade cracked, and his lip quivered. Then he sniffled, reliving every emotion from the day. Of course she could see through it. "At least that'll make the queen happy."

She hesitated. "You still want to be my friend, don't you?" she asked, sounding less sure of herself.

Sonder's brow furrowed. "Of course. But I'm not a good friend for you."

"Then we're still friends because I still do, too. I'm the one who asked you, remember? I wouldn't have if I thought you were a bad person." Her words came quickly, and she looked down. "I think you're a good friend."

It was rare for her to sound so vulnerable. Sonder heard it in her voice that he was hurting her feelings. But that only confirmed his fears, and his eyes grew wet again. "Everyone who is bound by duty hurts the people they love and care about. I don't want to hurt you." He thought of Bran then.

She shook her head. "Don't worry about me. You won't hurt me. It's my choice if you're a good friend or not. You don't get to decide that for me. You're worth it. Now, here." She pressed the bark into his hand, which he had just used to wipe his nose. "Just chew on it. It'll help with the pain and fever."

Obediently, he chewed. They sat in silence, which allowed his mind to run rampant again—thoughts of what it meant to love someone and how he had no idea what that looked like. Finally, everything began to leak from his eyes, and he tried to hide that he was crying. It worked until he sucked in a wet breath.

"Should I leave?" Rhianwyn sounded uncomfortable.

"Please stay," he sniffled, "just for a while?" He paused to strengthen his voice. "But this should be the last time."

In the dim light, her face softened. "Okay."

She placed her hand on the bed, and he took it. They stayed like that while he continued to cry, chewing the bark. A tear stalled on the tip of his nose, and Rhianwyn extended a finger to wipe it away. She laid her head down beside him, her cheek pressed against their clasped hands.

"Sonder?" she whispered. He said nothing, but he was listening. "Hurting someone is part of caring about them. But you're kind and thoughtful. Don't let them take that away from you. No matter who your dad was or how afraid Merrick is."

With the comfort of her presence, he began to drift. When she thought he was asleep, she carefully slid her hand out of his, paused, then slowly stood up. Her stomping woke him up.

Her cool fingers brushed a dark curl off his face, and his eyes fluttered open. "Rhianwyn?"

She smiled, but she looked sad and lonely, and close to tears herself. He wanted to fold her into his arms to chase her pain away.

Wordlessly, she pressed her lips to his forehead before she slipped out through the servants' door.

Chapter Eleven
Unwelcomed News

His Royal Highness Leofric,

Forgive me, sire, for writing you. However, I find myself in the position to once again implore you to take charge of Princess Aspera. She continues to ask about things that His Holy Excellency deems dangerous. Her curiosity into the gossamer substance of a man and how the gods have woven the world I do not believe are philosophical any longer. You may cry she is but a child, but when was the last time you listened to her speak about the world?

If she is not stopped, we will have to take matters into our own hands.

Forgive me, sire, but I must be frank as your advisor. This is the second time we've demanded you control her. His Holy Excellency has requested that the Auza-Verndari be contacted. I had to agree. Your fitness to rule has been brought to our attention, and the Black Knights now have the authority to step in and observe as they deem necessary. If you are incapable of maintaining your home, how can we trust you with the kingdom?

You have not seen her lack of regard for the sanctity of the gods' order. If you claim she is but a child, and this is a phase, then there is talk of examining the quality of your seed. What's to say that Prince Jamil may not end up being a mad king once you're gone and can no longer see to your children?

I do not write this to anger. I write as your friend. Please, Drynard, do not do this to Abril. Take heart that there is some turmoil amongst the Black Knights. Perhaps they won't take action. But regardless of their stance, the Colleges have gathered. They are a force to be reckoned with as much as Lord Uland-Baramore.

Take charge of your daughter before it is too late. Or I fear what is to become of Stellamar.

Yours, Hann

Letter from Holy Priest of An-Dagda to King Leofric, Third Reign

Present, age ten

R andal stood in the Queen's Tower, watching Aspera. Her back was to him, and she hummed a tune. If he turned in a full circle, the banks of windows would let him see toward every point of the compass. Instead, he just inhaled the salty air, tinged with the fresh flowers perched nearby.

Being in this turreted keep had yet to grow old.

These days, he found himself in the queen's company often, rather than sitting in his dingy office, with overgrown trees blocking the natural light. The studying they did together was far more interesting than reading the same pattern of correspondences about the front lines or small colleges creeping up only to be snuffed out by the queen's reach. Not even rewriting history compared. What they were accomplishing was rewriting the future. Lately, it felt like they were making leaps and bounds in everything they touched.

A smile touched Randal's lips as he let his thoughts drift to that morning. Their time together had started over breakfast, with the morning light bathing their newest notes. It was fitting that the pages involved Sonder's lineage, because Merrick shouldered his way into the room and interrupted them. Randal and Aspera had turned from each other and their stream of thoughts. It took only that one look for Randal to know the man had spent the night at the Jaded Whisper, drinking instead of tending to his duties.

Merrick had returned to Stellamar the night before, but he looked awful as he stood under their scrutiny. The neat lines of his beard were overgrown, and his disheveled hair looked grayer than Randal remembered. Sour sweat and ale mixed with a burnt smell rolled off of him like cologne. Randal had never seen the man so haggard.

The same smile that touched his face at that moment drew up the corners of Randal's mouth now, as the sun was beginning to set.

"Why are you grinning?" Aspera's voice broke his daydreaming.

"Nothing, my lady. It has just been a wonderful day. I'm glad it has finally come," Randal said, folding his hands into his sleeves.

Aspera smiled. It was one of her genuine smiles, where the faint lines of her face softened. "It has been, hasn't it?" She turned, and in her hands was a raven, fluffy and gray, with tufts of cerulean beginning to sprout. "Are they not beautiful?" she breathed, gently scratching at the feathers to help release them.

His heart wanted to say, *Not nearly so beautiful as you*, but he kept his desire still. "Stunning, my lady. Made more astonishing by the fact it was hard-fought. Combining two species of birds—the implications, Your Majesty. The potential—" He couldn't form his thoughts, so instead sighed whimsically.

She gazed at him through her thick eyelashes. "I think you've earned being able to drop the formalities, Randal. Don't you think?" She placed the bird back in its nest of wool fibers.

Randal's pulse quickened. "If you wish it, my lady."

That coy smile!

"I do."

"Aspera, then." The name was as sweet on his tongue as it was in his mind.

She giggled. Brushing the feather dust from her hands, she walked to the desk, touching the flowers from her garden. "If only I could put my trust in all my advisors as I can you. Then I could stay up here all day and night and never have to leave to fix their messes."

A soft knock echoed through the chamber.

"Enter," Aspera called out.

Drisil crossed the room with slow, deliberate movements, as if she were still working on steeling herself for something. Her eyes met Randal's, and his heart quickened anew.

She had washed most of the kohl from her eyes. He traced the foreign way her features blended. There was a puffiness to her eyes that the dewiness of her skin couldn't hide.

In no way did her power to command diminish. On the contrary, it was made more raw—primal, even. All the more so because her hair still hung damp with its natural texture. She wore a simple black dress with a high collar and an azure ribbon to hold her hair off her face. And yet, Randal had to take a breath in, because Drisil had stolen it.

She was not nearly as glad to see him, and her eyes passed over him with hardly a second to acknowledge him.

"Drisil," Aspera sighed. She opened her arms, and Drisil allowed herself to be folded into a polite embrace. "Yours is a face I am pleased to see." Aspera held her at length. "You were successful, then?"

Drisil bowed enough to bare the nape of her neck. "Your Majesty."

Aspera's fingertips came to her lips, and her eyes fluttered as she looked to a faraway place. A peculiar smile quivered there. "It's finally over."

Randal thought she looked like a child released from years of anguish.

Aspera's hands trembled as she opened the table drawer where the white flowers sat. Papers rustled, and something heavy moved aside before she pulled out a parchment that looked a hundred years old from being refolded and handled. When she set it down, Randal saw that the ink was so smudged it was a wonder it was still legible.

How often had she read it? Yet Randal had never seen the slip of paper before, addressed to Aspera's late father.

"Do you know how grateful I am for this, Lady Drisil?" The queen recovered herself. "You cannot imagine the agony of being surrounded by men all too happy to remind you that your father took his name from you. The constant shame of it. That man I sent you to kill reminded the entire kingdom of it when he sentenced my attacker. The day he sentenced Raolin on behalf of my family's murders." A twisted smile marred the innocent relief.

Randal rarely thought back to that day. He had listened to her lament over her frustrations many times, but she had never spoken of this before.

"To be reminded of how papa tore our family apart just to punish me because some old mage told him to." She ran her fingers over the already smeared ink. "My mother took her name away from poor Jamil as retaliation." Another tight smile couldn't hide the anger in her eyes. "The joke was on my father then. Mama had a stronger claim by birth and name than my father." Aspera smiled at Drisil, who stood stock-still. "How convenient the man who was happy to remind the kingdom I was no longer a Leofric forgot that when he named Jamil Aurbornet without mama's permission ten years ago."

Drisil said nothing.

Aspera's face softened again, and she looked once more like a young girl. She reached out, and her fingers wrapped around Drisil's. "I am sorry to have asked you to allow such a vile man to touch you." She turned Drisil's hand over and exposed the pale skin of her wrist. "Did you appear to him as you are?"

"No, my lady," Drisil said softly. "I came as he wanted me to appear. I got the secrets you asked for."

There was something very wrong with Drisil. Randal had never seen her so reserved, even in the queen's presence.

Aspera looked up from the lines on Drisil's hand, and their brown eyes met. "Extraordinary," she said. "You've never studied?"

"No, my lady. Aside from snippets of overhearing my brother's lessons on the human psyche, I learned purely by observation."

"I am even more sorry I asked this of you. I see you do know my pain." Aspera took the sides of Drisil's head and brought her lips to her forehead. "I'm ever more grateful." Her eyes sparkled as she looked into Drisil's once more. "You've ended a reign of turmoil for me."

Sir Elio stepped into the room. His appearance drew attention to the fact the sun had set. The city lights flickered, and the edges of the Caelum Sea began to fade into a dark void that stretched for hundreds of miles.

"Right," Aspera said, still holding Drisil's hands. "Bring dinner for three tonight, please. And send for Merrick." She seemed oblivious to how he and Drisil reacted to hearing that name.

Elio silently departed.

Aspera smiled at Drisil. "Come. Look at what we've accomplished while we drink and wait." She led her toward the baby raven.

They drank the finest wine and ate the most decadent food they had in months. It was a celebration of Drisil's success and all they had accomplished. They were beginning to manipulate life itself, not just harness it. To create it. Even if Drisil wasn't entirely privy to it all, it made no difference.

While Aspera was leaning toward Randal as he told a joke, Merrick entered the room for the second time that day. He delivered the punchline, and the queen let out her merriest laugh. Randal met Merrick's scowl.

Randal would never grow tired of the man's look when he saw the two of them together so intimately. Aspera's hand rested on his knee.

The queen turned her attention to the newcomer. "Ah, Merrick, thank you for coming." Her hand slid off of his leg.

Merrick's eyes caught the movement, but he bowed deeply. "Your Majesty." He had managed to clean himself up, looking militant and crisp again.

Randal saw his eyes shift briefly to Drisil, who sat ramrod straight with her eyes focused ahead. The tightness in her jaw revealed that she was angry with him. Randal took a sip of his wine to hide his pleasure.

"Upon further thought, I want you to be ready for the squiring ceremony tomorrow. I want Sonder to begin the next iteration of his training,"

Drisil looked down and away as Merrick paled. He swallowed and let his jaw work over the words as he tried to form them, focusing on the rafters. "I can't, my lady."

"Excuse me?" Her tone chilled. "Why ever not?" She feigned ignorance, making it evident with the tilt of her head.

Randal could see Merrick's shoulders rise and fall even from this distance. The look of his shame colored his cheeks. "I punished him for getting caught with the girl." His anger flared. "Is it not inappropriate to have him travel with me, burning estates and enslaving people? He's only ten."

Aspera rolled her neck, then steepled her fingertips with elbows on the table. The tension in the room could have been cut, and Randal and Drisil held their breath. "Tell me, Justice, what would you deem appropriate? I've left raising Sonder mostly in your hands. The only say I've had is in his lessons and the timeline. Even his training has largely been left to you. Are you unhappy with your methods?" She sounded like she genuinely would hear what he had to say.

It struck the intended wound, and Merrick looked away.

Her tone darkened. "That's what I thought. But I'll bite, sir. He won't be burning any villages or breaking down doors. The risk to him being harmed is too great, and I will have my investment repaid." She laid her hands flat on the table and drew a frustrated breath. "When, then, will he be ready?"

Merrick bowed his head and looked at the ground. "A week."

How prettily Aspera arched her eyebrow, though her lips grew thin. "Fine. Now, get out."

Drisil still refused to look at Merrick, leaving him standing there with no one to save him. It was a slow process, but Randal could see how the walls were beginning to close in on him. Finally, with a bow and no words, he left.

Soon after they finished dessert, Drisil stood up and dismissed herself, claiming exhaustion. She had returned that morning.

"A toast before you go," Aspera said, placing her hand on Drisil's back. Then, with her free hand, she commanded Randal to pour the clear wine she reserved for special occasions.

The liquid was almost iridescent with the way the sugars swirled inside their crystal glasses. He handed Aspera hers first. When Drisil took hers, their fingers touched, and she finally looked at him and saw him. He had never seen her look so furious.

"To you both. My two advisors who cause the least amount of stress." She led them in raising their glasses before they drank the subtly sweet but nearly flavorless liquid.

Randal found himself once again alone with Aspera, as he so often did long after the stars began to dance with the torches. His body was warm from food and wine. They waited to speak while the servants scuttled about collecting the dishes. They were careful not to look up for fear of seeing something they shouldn't. When the room settled, Randal stood in the middle to have a perfect view out each window.

Aspera was pensive, caressing the milky flower petals. Her fingers stilled. "Do you know who I miss?"

Randal kept his feet planted, though he wanted to go to her. "Who is that, Aspera?" He let the name roll off his tongue, tasting it. He had ached since Drisil had first arrived to say it once more.

She smiled at him knowingly. He waited as she put her nose to the big bloom, then sighed the name into the petals. "Bran."

Randal's cheer soured. "A traitor."

Aspera chuckled, trailing her fingers over the wood. "Of course. However, he was an incredibly efficient man—until he wasn't. If only he hadn't come across those letters." She touched a stack on her desk as if they were the letters she had spoken of. Those they had never been able to find. "He would have stayed loyal for a long time if he hadn't."

Randal couldn't wipe the disapproval from his tone. "Merrick was close to him." He was glad for the chance to plant a seed of doubt—anything to help the fool's demise.

"I know," she said, her voice still airy. She walked to him and took his arm, tugging him along. "Come. Drink with me." She poured their cups. As he took his, she asked, "Do you think he is capable of pulling this off?" She rested her cheek in her hand.

Randal couldn't stop his derisive laugh. "Perhaps if he doesn't stop drinking."

Her eyebrow arched as she took a sip. "Randal, you were there. We discussed with Drisil to get him to stop. As much as I enjoy his ill temper, it's liable to become a hindrance at the rate he's going. We don't want to break the boy entirely. Plus, Merrick has other duties."

Randal drank, eyeing her. The wine was smooth, with notes of summery fruits. The type of fare one savored rather than rushed—like earning his place to speak frankly where many men had fallen before. "Has he been successful to this point? Is what you desire even possible?"

There was a subtle twitch of her nose. Aspera didn't like being questioned. "Don't let your dislike of the man cloud your wits, Magister. He has been everything I could ask for in a man who so closely valued Lucrid's second-in-command. Merrick wears the mantle of the Black Knights well. He has sowed a field of fear, which Sonder will reap once he comes of age. It has taken too long to get to this point, but the legacy of the Verndari has finally fallen."

"He harbors sentiments for the people he has sworn to destroy, though." Randal hated how his voice betrayed his indignity.

Aspera smiled, seeing through everything he used to hide behind. "Your success is no less because he has done well. Remember, he's not the one here sharing my best wine to celebrate." The rim of her glass kissed his with a clear ring. She crossed her arms and swept her glass to emphasize her words. "Let him harbor those sentiments. The Lorists are hardly a concern anymore, now that Aoife and her ilk have been dealt with. All that's left is an old woman in the forest, barely managing to get them through the winters.

"Besides, it helps Merrick find the true rebels. If he'll eliminate them to protect his brood, fine. If I ever ask, he'll destroy them too." It was undeniably true, and it caused a chill to run down Randal's spine. Aspera shifted her weight, making her hips sway, then smirked and finished the last of her drink.

"But what if he fails with the boy?" Randal pressed again, unwilling to let the matter go.

"He's a trophy to mark my victory once we figure out how the Auza-Bendith works. It'd be a small thing to eliminate him if it came to it. He's a symbol of my power for now. Both children are, really. But let's hope they live up to their potential. The Black Daemon's son will become one of the greatest warriors this kingdom has ever known. Rhianwyn, daughter of a Lorist leader, the most talented healer. They'll usher in a golden age, and I tamed them." She looked up at the ceiling and reveled in the glory of it. "Truthfully, the girl is more useful. Speaking of her, how are her studies going, Magister?"

"Very well, Your Highness." His heart sank, returning to formalities. He had pushed too far, questioning her. "All reports say she is excelling. The other masters are struggling to keep up with her. She masters their lessons so quickly."

Aspera put her finger to her lips in thought, her empty glass still in her hand. "That could be useful. Put her in other subjects. Start introducing her to, well, anything. If she's as clever as you say, it will give her the chance to make connections." Her gaze became far away and tender. "Yes—" Aspera cleared her throat and looked at him. "See to that. I want to allow her to learn unhindered, unlike myself at that age."

"What if she learns too much?" Randal couldn't help himself tonight, it seemed.

The look she gave him signaled the end of their time together. A bit darker, a tilt to her head, and a tight line to her lips. His audacity had gone too far. "I control the knowledge that everyone has access to, Magister. You know that. You've rewritten the books and burned the others. She'll learn what I want her to. If you'd please excuse me, I believe I'd like to retire. The wine has made me weary."

Randal bowed. "Of course, my queen. Thank you for your company and grace this evening." The wine was far too good to waste, so he finished the glass and set it down on the table.

"Thank you for your continued loyalty. See that you use this night to remain focused on what I've kept you to do." She inclined her head a fraction.

Through the curtain of her smile, there were always those veiled words. It was Aspera's way. As the sole sovereign of the kingdom and a survivor of the attempt to usurp the throne, she needed to keep a tight hold on everyone. She was not unpredictable like everyone said, though. The queen was more like a wolf, giving warning before she struck.

Randal bowed once more, then turned to leave. His nerves fluttered with fear. It was an important thing, one he allowed himself always to feel. Handling Queen Aspera required healthy respect and a measurement of fear to survive.

Groveling was not what she wanted, nor needed. The ground blinded those men; they had no foresight and inevitably fell. Nor did she need to be questioned at every turn. She was brilliant, with an uncanny ability to adjust to any setback. She was ruthless about her pursuits, and if someone held her back, she had no shame in striking them from her skirts and leaving them behind.

Frankly, the only reason Aspera needed help ruling was because her ambitions were in learning.

So, Randal vowed to be the eyes at her back while she buried her nose in books. To be the gentle tug at her arm, pointing to the perils in front of them and offering up the hard questions. But never to grovel.

He refused to let himself fall to irrationality and carelessness like everyone else. To be valued, he needed to stand tall, burdened by his fear borne of respect, until she saw his devotion, even if he remained one step behind her. She could have the glory she deserved.

Randal found himself at his estate. It was a small place. When Aspera had gifted it to him and asked what he required, he had said just a place to lay his head. Grandeur was not his style with his personal effects. His joy came from working beside her—that and good food.

Constantly, his mind ruminated on his exchanges with Aspera and how he could have been better. He could hardly remember getting here.

Pushing the door open, the stillness he desperately craved greeted him. There was no clutter, only simple objects that brought him joy and enough furniture to fill the spaces. As Randal crossed the threshold, it was like walking through a portal. His mind quieted.

This was a simple oasis from the place he considered his home.

The hook next to the door was where his cloak went, dangling down beside the shelves he used to store books he needed at the time. Unlaced boots he placed in a box, so no dirt tracked inside. Another pair, delicate and black, were already there. The company was the last thing he wanted, but he shifted them aside and placed his own beside them.

The den contained the most comfortable couch and chair he had ever sat in. It was the only thing he dared keep that rivaled the queen's displays of wealth. And draped on the sofa was the only woman brave enough to do so.

Randal stood in the doorway. "Good evening again, Drisil."

"Someone is getting home late, isn't he?" She had taken the liberty of opening one of his best wines. The bottle sat already half gone.

"We all have duties to attend to."

"You're always so pompous." Drisil snorted, taking a sip. "That's an odd name for ambition chasing."

Randal kept his face even and his posture prim. The wheedling of his comrades had long since stopped stinging. "Did you speak to him, then?"

Her face fell, and Randal could see how much she had already drunk. There was a slight droop to her eyes and lips. "I don't want to see him."

Randal waited for her to go on as long as was genteel. "And?"

Her dark eyes met his. "You'll have what you want, *Master* Randal."

"What the queen wants, my lady. It's also what's best for Sonder. You forget your duties to him."

She downed the rest of her wine and stood up. "Not as much as you forget yourself."

Randal closed the distance between them with a look of concern. "Drisil, you have so much to gain. Your talent is unmatched, and Aspera values you." He took her hands in his and held them near his chest. She was tall, but he was taller. "When will you abandon the folly? Merrick will bring nothing but trouble to himself, despite everything. You know as well as I, she always finds out."

Drisil didn't pull away but instead met his gaze with defiance. Aye, she was the only woman who rivaled the queen with talent and beauty.

"She wouldn't know so much if your eyes and lips didn't tell."

He squeezed her hands tighter as he lowered them. "Why do you protect Merrick? He is the only thing holding you back from all the glory and power you deserve. I cannot protect you if he becomes too much."

"Oh, so you have no sway over her?" Drisil mocked him. "Tell me something, Randal. You've spent years building yourself into a man you think worthy, but at what cost?" She paused, her eyes sweeping over the lines of his face. "You'll never be king."

Randal's anger flared, more at himself than at her. "To what end, Drisil? You lower yourself for what will never be."

Her lips were nearly touching his, and she looked at him through her eyelashes. There wasn't any of the laughter she had looked at Bran with, nor the admiration that softened her face when she looked at Merrick—when they weren't fighting. How he longed, just once, to see what it would feel like if she looked at him the same way.

"Until the boy becomes a man." She couldn't look at him as she said it—clearly, it pained her.

"But why, Drisil?" Randal shook her hands. "You're so much more."

"Because I made a promise."

"To Bran?" He said it as a question, but he knew the answer. "A promise to a man that Merrick killed!" Randal took her face in his hands. At least with her, he could show how much he loved her.

"A man Merrick loved as much as I," she whispered. "Damn every other folly we had. Whatever she asks of me is hers. But not this. Not until we've seen the boy through. Then I cannot help him." Her lip quivered ever so slightly. "Bran was wrong thinking we could stop her. Especially since he kept his secrets."

The lack of emotion he wore as the queen's right hand crumbled. His smooth, ageless skin creased, and he searched her face—that look. The wine was thick on her breath, staining her lips and teeth. No doubt her drunkenness was the reason she lifted her face toward his.

"Tell me, Randal, are you lonely?" She swayed beneath his hands.

"As lonely as you," he said, his voice as husky as hers.

Again, Drisil tilted her chin toward him. "Name the price for your silence, then."

Her kisses still tasted sweet through his shame.

Chapter Twelve
Confronted

Private hospital, two years ago

Rhianwyn carried a tray with a medicinal tea that she and Mistress Gwenyvir had made. Her childish hands had ground the herbs and stirred the concoction while the older woman drew out the qualities she most needed from each. For once, Rhianwyn had kept her mouth shut, sensing the gravity from her mentor. Now, with Drisil's fingers pressed against her back, she hesitated in the doorway.

The man who had taken her from her burning home was lying in bed. Merrick, who stalked and loomed wherever he went, looked shriveled.

"Go on, little one," Drisil murmured.

Rhianwyn wanted to say she was scared, but she bit back her retort. Instead, she fortified herself and shuffled forward.

Those bloodshot and sunken sharp blue eyes opened and stilled her again. They stared at each other, and her eyes wandered over his face. She took inventory of his chapped lips and the pallor. The stench of sickness was thick, and she knew from caring for other patients what it meant.

"Scarlet," he rasped. "My little Rose." He clutched at his chest with one hand and reached toward her.

Rhianwyn tipped her head. "I'm not Scarlet, Sir Merrick. I'm Rhianwyn."

His vision cleared, and he came back from the edge of death. "Rhin?"

"Rhianwyn," she corrected.

Merrick swallowed what little his dehydrated body could muster. Sadness and resignation to whatever suicide he had chosen made his eyes flutter. "Why have you come"—his cheek fell against the pillow—"darling girl?"

"You're going to die if you don't take this." She lifted the tray with a frank look.

He drew further back into his ailing body. Briefly, his eyes shifted to look behind her. She didn't bother to look. The healer's mantle settled her mind and steeled her to the task at hand. Whatever business he had with Drisil was between them. When his gaze met hers again, she felt a chill run through her body. Just like that, life lit his eyes.

With a solemn nod, Merrick accepted her care. She didn't know why she knew to wait for permission. She set the tray down beside his bed, then turned toward, freezing as his hand grazed her cheek. His skin burned, and she smelled the infection on his fingertips. But the touch was tender.

"I'm sorry. I promised to keep you safe, and I haven't."

She couldn't help but press her cheek against him. Even in illness, she could smell the peppery pine of his skin through the stale sweat. He had held her when they shared a horse, comforting her. The smell was a memory of that. She opened her eyes. "Grief does that to a person," she said.

It was what he needed to hear, because he finally turned his back on Death.

Present, age ten

The buzz of conversation was a welcomed relief. Surrounded by the background noise of the Jaded Whisper, layered over the lightness of the alcohol, a space was created for Merrick to slip into where he let his mind be numb.

It had been days since he could let the blissful emptiness silence his thoughts. Letters, hearings, and audiences with Queen Aspera shrieked at him day in and day out. Punishing Sonder had left him in such a foul mood that he had broken a mirror in his office, imagining he could destroy the nightmare he was becoming. That was when the attendant had arrived, announcing a second audience with the queen.

Merrick's face twisted as the mist of thoughts solidified. He silenced them with another handy drink of his mead.

The images remained vivid.

The little streak he had left on Sonder's cheek, not knowing the tears on the boy's face would moisten the blood on his hands. The way Drisil refused to look at him as the queen announced Sonder was to be squired. Randal's delight as he turned ruddy with wine.

This was the place he sought to wipe his mind.

The memory of barreling through the Whisper's entrance. Patrons were already at his table but fled with his harsh command to leave. The bite from the candle flames as he snuffed them out with his fingers.

Merrick took another draught. His stomach knotted, and he pursed his lips against it.

A wall jutted out just enough to create a shadow for him to melt into. From this vantage, he could see the comings and goings and the sweep of the room.

The staff tolerated him. The barmaid, Tati, continued to give him sidelong looks each time she filled his cup. She was the only one willing. The others gave him a wide berth. The wages he contributed to the higher-end inn up the hill where the others insisted on frequenting had switched to here six months ago. The owner was happy to pocket the coin and remind his staff it was worth it.

Merrick liked Tati's spunk. It reminded him of Paul and April, Grace's children—and Rhianwyn.

The door flew open, bringing the spring air with it. Merrick's face screwed up as he exhaled the burn from another swallow. He had been waiting for that rattle of wood and bell. It was only a matter of time before his peace was shattered. He had been sure to drink enough to make it worthwhile.

His head throbbed in time to the clicks of Drisil's measured steps. That cadence divulged her fury. Several eyes traced the lines of her black cloak with the knight stitched into it. She narrowly dodged a woman who crossed her path, never breaking her gaze from Merrick.

He raised his mug when she was close enough to hear him over the din. "So, you found me."

Her hands splayed on the table, and she bent over into his face. As was her style, as a royal charlatan, her sapphire-trimmed dress was cut low. There was nothing suggestive about the way she moved now. "I should buy you out of your stake in this place so they'll throw you out."

He smirked and swayed. "You can't afford it. You've gone and got yourself an estate." Despite himself, his eyes drifted down to the swell of her breasts.

"Have you lost your senses, Merrick?" She had seen his wandering eyes. Typically, she would have teased him. But her voice was full of venom.

Her perfume wafted over him like it had when she confronted him in Sonder's doorway. It brought with it the memory of his anger and shame. It was always intimate. The scent made him want to crawl into her arms and feel small.

He lifted his mug once more, then brought it to his lips. "Trying to." The clay muffled his words.

Merrick had never seen such a spectacular display of rage play out across her face. Her lips curled in disgust, and her nostrils flared. She was just an uttered word away from burning the flesh from his face, even if magic didn't work that way. She reared to her full height like a cobra and struck him.

The mug flew from his hands, but not before its rim wrenched his face. The entire room fell silent and looked toward the sound of the shatter.

Merrick scrunched his nose and breathed through the stinging sensation of his cheek already swelling. There was a tickle on his lip, and when he licked it, he tasted salty iron. He touched it delicately, but the calluses caught on the split skin.

"Alright, I'm sober," he growled, looking at his bloodied fingers.

"Not enough." Drisil leaned back toward him. "When is this going to stop, Merrick?"

Tati began to walk over, but Merrick waved her off. Her concern surprised him.

"Was this necessary?" he asked, finally acknowledging Drisil. People started to talk again, but he still felt their curiosity. They'd been gawking since she walked in.

"Enough is enough. If you don't stop drinking of your own free will, I will glamour you to make it happen." Her lip curled, and she leaned closer.

His face darkened. "You wouldn't dare."

She spoke through her teeth, "I would. To hell with our friendship. I wouldn't want anything more to do with you if I have to magic you because you don't think it's a problem." He looked away, but she forced her face back into his. Her voice rose. "Well?"

Merrick looked away again. He bit his lip in irritation, hissed at the pain, then touched it once more. "How am I supposed to live with myself?"

"You figure it out," she snapped.

His tongue kept worrying the split. "She sends me on another raid, only to tell me when I return that Sonder is supposed to begin training in the atrocities of her ways." He looked at her. "She's unhappy with his progress. Says it's too slow. I can't get through to him. All he wants is to be a kid."

"It was just a kiss." She wrung the air as if it were his neck. "Griever's bane. He's only ten!" The curse was used amongst the poor who suffered the most from the black cloak raids. It was vulgar on her lips because they were the bane she spoke of. "You didn't have to beat him the way you did."

"No?" He raised his voice. "You want to sit here and tell me that if the wrong person caught him, it would've been less? That they're welcome to squander all she has invested because they thought the other alluring? That I won't be next if they fail?" He inhaled sharply. The memory of cutting into Merna's lung and her gaping, dead face assaulted him. He never talked about any of this, but it came out of him now, forbidden and dangerous. "Damn it if I wouldn't love to be the next one on the chopping block. But I don't dare so that Sonder has a chance!" He slammed his fist down on the table.

Drisil backed away, giving him more space. "You need to figure it out."

"I carved a man's chest, Drisil. If an infection doesn't take him, the scars will brand him a traitor and ruin him. I've tortured people for her. Stolen children despite telling her I won't. You want to tell me that's a place for a child?" His face twisted. "I killed the man I loved. All for her. Who is to say she won't do the same to control him as she does me?" He pounded his chest with his fist. "I drink to forget!"

"You don't need that kind of help! We forget enough as it is!"

"How do you live with yourself?" He felt wild and desperate. Already, his hands and head ached. The demons he drank to silence would break free of their prison if he stopped.

The question hurt her. He had asked her the same question before—asked all of them. He knew she struggled as much as he did. The brim of her eyes sparkled a little more. It took her a moment to compose herself.

When she did, she said quietly, "I remember what's important."

It was an equally low blow.

Neither of them took any pleasure in the tasks the queen gave them—him a murderer thinly veiled as a justice and her forced to use her charm to steal secrets. There was no honor or pride in taking children as hostages or planting false evidence whenever someone pushed back against the crown. Yet he wasn't able to live and let live like her.

His silence allowed her to lean in again. "What would Bran think if he saw you now, Merrick? You taint his memory by drinking. The last time I kissed him, I placed those false letters Aspera used to frame him in his hands so he could hide them himself. That was as far as I could go. I did it because you both asked me to. I framed the man I loved for this." She swept her hands, implying the figurative and literal. "To what end? So you can piss everything away? You insult me as much as him." Her voice dropped to a whisper. "You're cruel when you drink."

Merrick turned his face away, but she followed once more.

"Tell me now if you want to break the boy you claim to love like she wants you to. Tell me if you killed the man I loved in vain. Tell me now if the man I love in you is already dead, because I'll finish the job. Make me hate you for what you did to Bran." Her voice quivered. "Let me hate you."

Merrick's eyes closed, and the tears he fought so hard to keep locked away fell. He tried to swallow them, but they wouldn't go past the lump in his throat. She spoke everything he hated about himself.

The drinking made him move like the monster Aspera wanted him to be, creating a vicious cycle he could not break.

A sob choked out of him, and as he crumpled, her hands caught his face, and her warm lips pressed against his forehead.

"Stay with me, Merrick," she whispered into his dry skin and oily scalp.

"I hate myself," he moaned.

"You're going to hate yourself a whole lot more before this is over." She continued to hold his face while she looked into his eyes. "You've got to stop this," she begged. "Please? For everything we've already given."

"I can't do this without him." Tears pooled in the webs of her fingers.

"You have to." Her warm, dry lips pressed against his forehead once more, and a thrill of memories shot down his spine. "He poured himself into you. Gave all of himself to you."

Merrick couldn't help but wonder if the jealousy still haunted her. Bran had untangled himself from the bed they shared to seek Merrick's company. To join him by the fire and tell his secrets. She hadn't known all of him as Merrick had.

"You convinced us to listen to him," she whispered into his skin. "You who made us fall in love with both Bran and Sonder. That's why it hurts so much. We could have been free with all the money we had saved and the network we'd formed. Yet you convinced us to stay and fight. We looked to you first, and then to him when you said it was alright. And now Áki and I have to watch you spiral into everything she wants you to be."

She steeled herself. "That's why we demand you to pick a side. If you keep this up, you will become the monster she incites you to be. You'll break the boy. Áki and I cannot bear this any longer."

Merrick looked into her warm brown eyes. There was so much there that made him feel small. Finally, he nodded and buried his face in her shoulder as she wrapped her arms around his neck.

Since the day after Bran's pyre, he hadn't let her fold him into her arms. She had disguised a different body that dangled above the castle walls. He had crumpled as he had said the Goddess's rites over Bran. Then, she had gathered him into her arms, stoic.

Merrick still believed she had spent her tears over the entirety of their relationship, whereas Merrick had denied his until they grew too deep to contain.

He stayed in her arms now for as long as he had then. Until the fire burned through his heart, and he felt hollow and brittle.

His last fears drifted forward, and he expelled them from himself. "Randal would see me killed. Probably string me up in chains and torture me as they do to all those people in their dungeons."

She grew rigid and tightened her arms around him. "He won't."

Merrick expelled a grim laugh through his nose. "You're a fool if you don't see it."

"He still respects me, and I won't allow him to." Drisil's fingers began to rove through his hair. "He won't."

Merrick felt suddenly heavy as the tension he still held in his body melted. He was so starved of touch he had forgotten the pleasures of idly connecting with someone. The alcohol had burned off enough that his head was beginning to hurt, and he was tired. This was his chance. If he missed the window, he'd eventually find himself restless with another bout of energy.

"It's going to hurt," he whispered. His stomach clenched in anticipation of the nausea that awaited him when he stopped.

"The physicians and healers can help." She shifted. The awkward position of holding him across the table had finally gotten to her.

"I don't want them to touch me," he spat. He imagined what a physician in Randal's pocket would do to him if the sorcerer found out.

Drisil took his hand with a sad look and tugged him to his feet. She knew him well enough to know about the narrow window. She looked at his hands, covered in sunspots that made his skin nearly as dark as hers. "Then I'll help however I can." The pad of her thumb traced the edge of his beard, which was tender and swollen from her blow. She looked close to tears as she touched his split lip, then into his face.

"Come," she said, taking his hand once more.

Drisil led him to his room. The Jaded Whisper allotted him a space at the end of the hall, tucked away from the noise. Their specialty was filling people's bellies, getting them good and drunk, and lodging those who passed out in their spilled drink. They were not masters of comfort.

The cramped room spoke to that. But Merrick's investment accommodated him as well as it could. A worn chair sat in the corner, likely pilfered from an abandoned home, with his tunic folded neatly on its seat. His weapons lay on the small dresser, and his sword leaned against the wall beneath his leathers. The only other thing was a tiny, straw-stuffed bed.

Drisil insisted that he wash. She knew he would want to wake up clean. The staff couldn't draw a full bath, but the girl named Tati brought a basin of warm water, just enough to wash his pits and creases so they wouldn't stink and his hair wouldn't lie heavy on his scalp.

He began to disrobe to his undergarments. Drisil was no stranger to the injuries that crisscrossed his body. But before she could avert her gaze, she caught sight of the gnarled scar across his back. She hadn't seen him in a state of undress since he earned that one. A knot formed in her stomach, and she looked around the room while he wiped himself down.

He stayed there often enough that the room smelled like him. Yet it revealed nothing—the same way he moved through this life. It spoke to her because she knew him by observation alone; it was her job to know someone by what they presented, even if they tried to give nothing.

That scar spoke volumes. It had nearly taken his life.

Drisil stayed with him until he fell asleep. She cradled his head in her lap, sitting against the wall on that too-small bed. She slowly combed his damp hair through her fingers with a practiced touch, easing him to sleep.

It grew grayer by the year, which hurt her heart in ways she wondered if she'd ever tell him.

"You're going to have nightmares if you mean to stop." Her voice cracked, and she cleared her throat.

The ridge of his throat bobbed. "I know."

She stroked the soft fuzz of his cropped temples, then watched the longer strands curl around her fingers as she continued. Finally, she managed to gather the courage to speak her thoughts. "I can help."

His eyes remained closed. "Don't. I don't want your magic."

Just like Drisil knew him, he knew her. He saw the way people moved. He needed no magical bone to be aware of the desire to ease his suffering resting on her fingertips. Her body likely shimmered with it, and he didn't need to open his eyes to know. He felt her through their touch.

She swallowed the hurt. Randal exposed the wound, and Merrick's continued vehemence against her abilities only worked into it.

It always came back to how they'd likely speak more gently if any of them knew the depths of one another's pain. If only Merrick knew how the lance of his words opened a floodgate within her, making her instinctively draw closer to Randal. Even if it were perverse, the sorcerer was right. She imagined Merrick would be more thoughtful if he knew that.

He would have to be sober for that to happen, though.

When his breath grew heavy, she couldn't extricate herself fast enough.

The desire to wash away the old Priest-Justice's caresses consumed her. His ghost was still pawing her, and Randal's powdery smell was still in her hair. The peppery tree soap on her hands triggered the grossness of manipulating Merrick's pain. The magic was knowing him, but it still violated him somehow. Never mind that it felt good to let her anger out. She had been trying gentler methods for years.

She wanted to wash all of it away.

Merrick's hand reached up and took hers. Alcohol did strange things to his sleep. His thumb traced the shape of her knuckles, and the thrill of his mind's touch made her body warm.

"I'm sorry, Sil."

He meant it. Whether or not he meant it enough to survive the illness he was about to take on had yet to be seen. Doing it without magic to ease his suffering would mean hell twice over.

Taken by the swell of fondness, she once more kissed his forehead and let herself inhale the oiliness of his hair. It was Bran's thing. He had done it to her countless times, so she knew he had done the same for Merrick.

The sharp breath said as much.

She replayed the moment again, now that she was secluded in her own bath, and the knot of jealousy twisted again as she recalled the parting.

There had always been a seed of anger in her that she shared the only person she loved. Merrick knew it. She had thought she'd gotten over it until tonight when its tendrils leafed out. To this day, she didn't understand why Bran hadn't trusted her like he had Merrick.

Another shadow of thought encroached.

Drisil had been similarly jealous of Bran—he likely was drawn to Merrick because he knew the truth of the man. The two of them, complete mysteries to her, yet mirrors of each other's souls.

She opened her eyes and gazed up at the ceiling of her washroom. The image seared her mind and made her shiver despite the warm bath that reached up to her chin.

She swallowed the hurt anew, tracing the lines of the beams above her.

It was late. The sun would likely come up before she fell asleep. She was emotionally spent between visiting Randal and then seeking out Merrick.

The capacity for what she could take had grown since they started all of this ten years ago. Before, it would take days after an assassination before she felt like herself again. Now she could dredge through her demons while the ghosts of the newly dead still made her skin crawl.

Drisil sighed and ran her hands through the water. It was nearly cooled enough that she knew she should get out. Instead, she watched the remnant motes of soap swirl with the movement.

Tonight was the first time she had called Merrick by what he had done. She had alluded to it many times, but now she had voiced it in whole: Merrick killed Bran. It had been three years, yet tonight was the night she chose to say it. She couldn't be mad at him for gouging her so. They had both gone for the most harmful.

Her mind drifted to the scar that marred his back.

The horrible way it had healed spoke to how deeply Bran's death had cut him. It was the only time the royal healers had treated him. He had lost too much blood to protest. But not so much that he hadn't lied.

Lied wasn't right. He wasn't a liar.

He had still been able to bury the hurt so far down it was likely lost. All Merrick had to do was speak the truth while the surgeon treated him. Had he revealed even a sliver of it, the magic would have taken and made it heal clean.

She had stood by while he swayed from blood loss. Watched as the doctor imbued the needle and thread and was ready to listen as the ugly, curved tool pierced the splayed edges and drew them together.

Instead, Merrick had gazed at the floor, numb with shock, then repeated what had been declared. "The gods willed it."

The magic had failed to take, turning on him. The infection nearly killed him. Drisil had watched the wound fester, and the lacy red lines branch out, knowing why, and seethed.

Bran had made them take an oath to do whatever they could to oppose Aspera's power. No one knew what she was doing, how deep her knowledge went, and what her intention would be with it. They had sworn that they'd do all they could to find out, even in his death. Above all, they'd do it to protect Sonder, who was paramount to whatever the queen wanted.

Sometimes the lines of Drisil's loyalty got blurred, but she would never reveal all that she knew to the queen. So while Merrick refused help, she had kept her knowledge of Majick to herself to protect him first and then to keep it from Aspera—Drisil's innate understanding of this land's magic was why the queen was so careful around her.

Just as Merrick withheld the truth, she stilled her tongue from revealing how to save him, thus protecting his lie.

No one thought to question why the wound festered before the surgeon was blamed. He was no great practitioner, but how could he know that Bran had sacrificed himself to keep them safe or that Merrick had loved the man? Even with her paltry healing knowledge, the injuries Drisil had stitched healed better on him.

So Áki had killed the surgeon while he slept, and Merrick tried to die.

Drisil had manipulated him then, too. Sent the only person he would accept treatment from: Rhianwyn. Even as a ruthless killer, Merrick had a soft spot for pups. One of the yawning mysteries that nagged her—but she had refused to lose both men.

Although, she still ended up grieving both, even if one could still feel the ocean breeze.

Drisil sighed, lowering her lips into the water to blow tiny bubbles that popped against her nose. She'd done it as a child to soothe herself. She wanted to feel like that little girl again.

She'd grown up in a distant land, where the magic was a little wilder and coveted by the royal families. It was named Majick there. But, unlike Stellamar's gods, who were clear that everyone should have access to it, hers decreed otherwise. At least, that was what the priests and soothsayers said.

From her time in Sosten, though, she had learned her gods weren't so different, just called by another name, and she wondered if Jân Bāluvā had been wrong to rule by divine right. Especially knowing that soon after her family banished her, the kingdom fell, leaving her home broken into warring factions.

Her bubbles grew large enough that they splashed her frustration into her eyes. The prayers Merrick had said over Bran's body weren't so different from her homeland's death rites.

Drisil began to hum into the water a ballad about a man begging to be cleansed, sang in mourning, rejoicing, and prayer. The refrain in her mind, she sang for Merrick:

Maybe I've heard your voice
I know this feeling, hurt inside

Confronted

Peace if God wills it.

A knock on the doorframe drew her out of her reverie.

"I'm sure the water is tepid, Mistress. I prepared tea. Perhaps that will bring you the rest you desire?" The man's voice lilted with an accent from the faraway lands of her kingdom's southern neighbor. A scar arched beneath his eye—the brand of the slavers who captured him.

"You're right, Aadan. Privacy, please?" The water cascaded from her hair and skin as she lifted her body and accepted the towel he offered. "Thank you." She let their hands touch, so he knew the depth of her gratitude. She knew he wouldn't steal a look, and his eyes remained locked on hers to confirm this.

"Ma'am." His teeth shone white against his skin, reminding her of the wenge trees back home.

On paper, Aadan was merely a butler. However, he was more akin to her steward. He managed everything for her, from finances to the other staff of the house. All were rescued slaves or abused staff from different households. It had been the condition she imposed on Aspera for taking an estate. To the queen, it was merely charming that she should want to take in the downtrodden.

The reality of it was far more. Each of them earned a salary, which Aadan saw to—enough for them to eventually return to wherever they were from if they so desired. They were people here.

They adored Drisil. She explicitly paid some to masquerade as informants who would periodically meet with the queen's Spiders and lie on her behalf. Her estate was supposed to be a shackle, but instead, it chimed like an anklet as she found freedom within its walls—like Randal, who had foregone any staff. And Áki, who just used his for storage under constant watch.

Merrick could think what he wanted about her taking it, but she was not a caged bird. Not as caged as him.

She had made a promise she intended to keep as best she could. Maybe once Merrick sobered up, he'd understand that better.

Chapter Thirteen
Before the Storm

First time on the road, four years ago

Sonder edged closer to Áki, who spun slowly, looking for him. The boy watched his footwork from behind a screen of grass, because Áki was the best swordsman he knew. Merrick was supposedly better, but the boy rarely saw his mentor fight.

He let out a slow breath and listened to the world. He inched closer, careful to pace himself, so his noises blended with the earth's henaild. At least, that was how he imagined it. Rhianwyn's stories talked about the essence of everything, where magic came from. Sonder wasn't fool enough to think he could actually tap into it and become invisible like in those tales.

Áki was noisy, masking the outburst of Sonder's pounding feet until it was too late. He launched himself onto the man's back.

Áki roared, scrabbling at Sonder's hands before he toppled.

The boy giggled as he stood over Áki, whose head lolled to the side with his hands tangled in his cloak as if clutching a wound.

Merrick stepped into the clearing. "Good. Though that's a bit unnecessary, Áki."

Sonder looked up hopefully. Áki sat up and held out his hand for the boy to help him to his feet. Both grinned as he took it and tugged the man's arm.

Áki made another show as he stood up on his own. "Whew, boy, you're getting strong!" He thumped Sonder on the back. "You're good. I didn't think you'd get me on the first try."

Sonder averted his eyes. "Must be all the games of hide-and-find." He didn't mention the spying. He had promised he never would.

"You did well." Merrick reclaimed their training. "Let's see how much you practiced your drills."

Áki nudged Sonder. "You'll be unstoppable in the yard."

Merrick rounded on them. "Don't make enemies, Sonder. You cannot afford to."

Áki's brow furrowed. "Why should he be concerned about fragile egos?"

"Once they find out who he is, his enemies will look for any excuse to finish what was started the day his uncle was executed." Merrick's look made

Sonder's body go numb. "They fear you already. Don't give them a reason to think you're uncontrollable."

Present, age fifteen

A fresh breeze blew into Merrick's study through the open windows. It always felt as if one could lean out and brush the curtain wall—Sonder had tried as a child. It made the space feel closed in, yet not oppressively. Plenty of sunlight still streamed in, and the climbing roses gave it vibrancy. It was cozy with the shelves of leather-bound books, the musky wood polish, and a fire always lit with a teapot hung. A forgotten corner tucked away rather than a prison.

Sonder sat in the leather armchair near the fire. The stones of the castle walls always radiated cold. It didn't help that Merrick had finally torn down the tapestries with men and horses clashing in battle. The chill had been welcome when he was younger, coming inside after running around in the hot sun. Now, his body had acclimated to enduring the rays beating down on his black leathers and sleeping in stuffy tents.

He was just short enough to sit sideways in the chair with the armrests supporting his back. One leg threaded under the other, and a book lay open against his thigh. Warmed by the fire, he felt content as the gravel of Merrick's voice rumbled on.

"I may be the Battle Master, but the front lines are not my specialty. I've spent little time there. You'll have to speak to Áki. He'll point you to the right company."

"But sir, I was told to speak to you," another man protested.

"Which you have. My response is to talk to Áki. He is my second, and he oversees the front lines on my behalf. My specialty is the Black Knights." Merrick was growing impatient and seemed to realize that.

Sonder looked up from his reading to watch the two men at the remark of the Black Knights. Merrick reached for his tea to gather himself. The other man had looked over to the chair at the mention of the order. Alarm lit his face, and he looked back at Merrick.

Sonder was getting used to those reactions. Some days it still bothered him, but it got easier.

He shifted his attention to his mentor, and the two met eyes. Merrick sighed, then looked at the man again. "Look, I understand you want to know about your son. I can't keep track of every company. The information from your son is the same as mine. Áki knows those men. He'll know who to ask for the most accurate information."

The softer tone seemed to soothe the man. He nodded with renewed determination. "I understand. Thank you, sir."

"Tell Áki I sent you. He'll be less offensive that way." Merrick began to shift the papers around, signaling the end of it.

Sonder cracked a smile. The man chose that moment to turn to leave. They locked eyes once more, and the man bowed slightly. "Master Sonder."

Sonder dipped his chin and watched the man exit. The thought of the missing son made his heart feel heavy. He looked back down at the open book with his thoughts far away. The sound of porcelain coming together broke his attempt at concentration.

"He's dead, isn't he?"

"Lord Dusko's son was sent to the worst front." Merrick cleared his throat. "I understand the need, but it's a sorry lot."

"Will I end up there?" Sonder asked.

Merrick took a while to respond. "I don't know," he said. "I've spent a lot of time wondering what the queen has in store for you. I suspect you will. But likely not the worst." The man walked around the desk. "What are you reading?"

Sonder laid his hand on the page. "Studying for my tests. Master Fallen loaned me this book."

"What's it about?" Merrick poured more tea.

"The Battle of Daemon's Fell." Sonder grew far away. "The last great battle my father fought before they say he went mad." Sonder smiled, although he felt bitter. Reading about his sire allowed him to pretend he could glean who the man had been. Whenever he said it out loud, though, he had to face the reality that Lucrid was only a killer. "I think I've studied enough."

Merrick's tea filled Sonder's chest with its cloying, spicy scent as the man walked closer. "You have."

Sonder slowly closed the book, and Merrick took it from him as deliberately.

"Here," the man offered the cup, "I've never seen anyone look so cold in the worst of summer." Merrick tossed the book aside.

Sonder held it in both hands and smiled against the rim, savoring the smell. He wasn't sure why his mood had grown dour again.

"We'll be here long enough for your tests, and for me to catch up on things like that." He lifted a second cup toward the door to indicate the departed Lord Dusko. "Then there's the Naming of Wards Ceremony. After that, we'll likely leave again."

"Am I really to become an heir to the throne?"

Merrick took a sip. "That's what being her ward means."

"I don't want to be king." He regretted saying it, but he couldn't stop before the thought left him.

Merrick got that look he always had when he couldn't answer something. Sonder had learned over the years not to push. He was bound, and no other options existed. That was besides the fact it would only lead to trouble.

"Luckily, that won't happen tomorrow. It's a formality. It gives you and Rhianwyn the credibility to fulfill your roles."

He didn't need to say the rest. *An orphan girl and a son of a usurper require credibility.*

There was a knock on the door, and Merrick bade them enter. "Sir, you requested to know when the drills were starting." The page bowed.

"Thank you."

Sonder glanced up mid-sip.

"If I had it my way, I'd only have you drill. You're only useful if you're alive. Get out of here," Merrick said, and shook his head as Sonder leapt out of the chair. "Take Master Sonder to Áki."

"Yes, sir." The younger boy looked at Sonder nervously before leading the way.

When Sonder strode into the barracks where the other squires lived, he went for one bunk. Another young man was bent over a trunk at the foot of the bed. Despite the seriousness he'd maintained through the castle, seeing the familiar mop of black hair melted Sonder into a grin of relief.

"Back to the door?" Sonder called out. "Wait'll the Battle Masters hear about that."

Tran paused and slowly turned to look over his shoulder. "Well, well," he said. He stood up and faced Sonder. "If it isn't the lost boy returned from the road." They collided as Tran threw his arms open. Resounding thumps reverberated through their chests. "Does Merrick know how bad you smell?" the other boy asked.

Sonder laughed and broke their embrace. "Shut it. I've not had a proper bath yet."

"When did you get back?" Tran asked as he bent down to grab the rest of his training armor.

"Just this morning."

"Does that mean you'll get to train with us then?" Tran straightened with his hands full. He looked Sonder up and down, taking in his worn training leathers.

"For now, anyway." Sonder felt the familiar gratitude that Tran never seemed fazed by the black, unlike the other trainees.

He grunted as Tran thrust half of his gear into his hands, hoisting the rest over his shoulder. "Good. I've learned a few tricks. Maybe I'll best you for once. Come then, squire boy, let's go." Tran snagged his sword with his free hand and led the way out. Sonder grinned as he followed.

The sun was blinding as they stepped into the training yard. Most of the other boys were dressed. Some had even begun to cross swords as they moved through drills from previous days. There was a pleasant buzz as they all waited around. One group of boys erupted in laughter as a pair grappled, tumbling to the ground in a cloud of dust.

It had been so long since Sonder had been to the training field, he took it all in gladly. A few called out greetings to his tall, lanky friend, but they turned their heads and whispered when they caught sight of him. By the time they reached the wall, Sonder felt less excited about the prospect.

"Don't mind them," Tran said. Sonder wondered how obvious he had been about his disappointment. "For half of them, the black is the most exciting thing they've seen since the footman they thought was a knight last month."

Sonder snorted. Tran dumped his gear on the ground. Sonder was more ceremonious about the process, setting it down as neatly as possible.

"You always this late?" he asked as he looked around and realized Tran was the last one getting ready. When Tran gave him a sharp retort, fumbling with the armor, he shook his head. "Here, let me help you."

It was quick work for Sonder. He'd done up many buckles and ties by this point in his life.

"Such service," Tran teased, holding his arms out for bracers.

A petite boy with dusky blond hair jogged toward them. "Tran! Is this him? The boy you've told us about?"

"Aye, it is. Told you I wasn't lying." Tran flexed his arms to test the tightness.

The boy looked at Sonder with his mouth agape. "You're the Battle Master's squire? Really?"

Sonder felt suddenly shy, and he glanced at Tran before nodding. "That's right."

"What's it like being a squire?"

Sonder knelt and tugged the straps of Tran's greaves tight. "A lot like this. Helping uncoordinated men into their armor and stinking boots."

Tran knocked Sonder on the shoulder. "Hey!" he protested.

Sonder hadn't thought it a very clever statement, yet a burst of laughter rewarded him. "He's right, though, Tran; your feet do smell!"

"Don't come over here acting surprised I'm best friends with Merrick's squire, then turn around and laugh at his jokes, Gialan. You'll encourage his ego." Tran threw his arm around Sonder's shoulders when he stood and grinned. He had a way that folded people together.

Feeling better than he had just a few minutes ago, Sonder offered his hand. "I'm Sonder."

"Gialan." The boy took his hand and shook it. "Tran's little brother."

"Is that who I think it is?" a voice broke over them from behind. Several footsteps approached.

Gialan dropped Sonder's hand, and Sonder felt the boy's heart sink with it.

"Mikhail," Sonder said. The other boy's voice had changed since he'd last heard it, but he knew the discomfort on Gialan's face and the annoyance on Tran's.

"Wow. It seems the special training is paying off." Mikhail stopped a few paces away as Sonder turned to face him.

"You look fancy in those black leathers."

There were two other boys trailing along, likely sons of high lords. Their clothes weren't worn, and they were handsome and kept. Mikhail was Ealdric Vardulf's third son, a lord from the Northeast who had been satisfied to help overthrow Knownth when Queen Aspera had taken the throne.

Sonder had read about it in books, and gleaned that Mikhail's older brothers had grown ill over the years in court. The eldest had died, and the second was left crippled. It made Vardulf desperate to secure his family by more than just favor.

Sonder said nothing. He and Mikhail had gotten along well enough when they were just children swinging swords. They'd almost been friends, drawn together by strict father figures. A part of him still hoped the boy had forgiven what Sonder couldn't help.

"Shove off, Mikhail. No one asked for a peacock here. Go strut and caw somewhere else." Tran put his arm over Sonder's shoulders again. He didn't say it unkindly. Tran was too good-natured and diplomatic to be blatant. But his tone was colored by dislike, which told Sonder that Mikhail had soured into a bully.

Mikhail looked Tran up and down. "You look put together for once, Cathak." He used Tran's surname as if it were an insult, turning his sneer back on Sonder. "Did they finally realize an orphan makes a poor squire and send you to help him?"

Their conflict abruptly ended with the drill master's sharp whistle and orders to form up. Gialan looked relieved, and hurried off to retrieve his sword from another clump of boys with their heads bent together. Sonder's shoulders slumped when he saw eyes dart in his direction.

Tran's elbow drew him out of his thoughts. "Hey, ignore it. It's a bit shit that you have to wear that armor around." He kept his voice low as they walked. "But don't forget, they nearly wet themselves because of a footman. It'll be old news next week."

The drillmaster approached them, and Sonder looked up. "Sir Rodrick." Sonder bowed slightly.

The burly man had a wild brown beard with a patch of gray beneath his lip and wore his hair short on the sides and tied back on top like Merrick's. He thumped Sonder on the back so hard he took a step forward to catch himself. "Good to see ya, lad. Hopefully, between Áki and Merrick, you've learned these drills. But I won't yell at ya until tomorrow evening for gettin' 'em wrong." He lifted an eyebrow at Tran. "You look put together, Cathak." His eyes narrowed when Sonder cleared his throat. "Get in line. Both o' ya."

"Little messed up to laugh in front of the drillmaster," Tran complained as they fell in line.

"It was funny when he said it." Sonder covered his smile.

"How long'll you be here?" Tran twirled his sword and got into the first form.

Sonder grew somber as he followed suit with none of the flourishes. "I'm not sure," he whispered. Nearby eyes kept darting his way, and he blocked them out with a steadying breath.

"Well, I'll have to make quick work of beating ya, then," Tran said. Despite the lightness, Sonder could hear the disappointment, too. He felt the same way.

Sonder was happy to be getting out of his leathers by the end of drills. The color consumed the sunlight greedily, and he couldn't imagine sitting by a fire for a week. Each breath he took was filled with the smells of the castle that he had missed: horses, cooking food, and the sea breeze that ravenously devoured anything metal. As he and Tran returned their blunted swords to the armory shed, the smell of oil and rust mingled with the stale air, and he gladly took another deep inhale to slow his heart. The sun's angle through the back window told him it was nearly dinnertime.

"I'd ask you to run through more practice with me. I know you'd say yes, too. But by the way you've been watching the big ball in the sky, I'd feel bad if I did. I'll have to wail on you tomorrow when we do four-on-ones." Tran held out his hand for Sonder's sword.

"Why is that?" he asked as he relinquished the blade. It was a dumb question, but his excitement formed a timid ball in his chest.

"That might work on Merrick, but not me." Tran laughed. "C'mon. The girls should be getting back from the hospital." Their swords clattered against the others piled on the racks.

The other boys hung back until they walked out. Tran slapped hands with a few of them as they walked past. Sonder offered a tight smile to the ones who met his eye.

Tran had been right. Already it seemed most were getting over the spectacle. That made it tempting to take Tran up on extra sparring. There was camaraderie in hitting each other with wooden swords. It would have been an easy choice had it not been so long since Sonder had been home.

As they neared the central courtyard, there was a fair amount of activity as grooms took horses and maids returned with baskets full from errands. The bells outside the castle walls began to chime their evening song ushering in the night. They stayed out of the way, and Sonder let his eyes scan the faces trickling through the gate.

A laugh echoed down the stone tunnel and cut through the pleasant bluster of the yard. When she stepped out of the shadow, the sun caught the familiar warm brown hair. She wore the waves tied back with a simple ribbon. In one hand, she clutched some books to her chest, and with the other, her fingers twined loosely around Alessia's. Rhianwyn faced away from him, but when Alessia saw him, her face softened to match the smile that broke through his seriousness.

Rhianwyn tilted her head when she noticed, then followed her friend's gaze. Her voice didn't carry through the noise, but Sonder saw his name spoken on her lips.

"You ought to admit it already," Tran said at his elbow.

"It's not like that," Sonder said, not looking away from her. Instead, he began to walk with cadent steps and a neutral face. Rhianwyn tugged Alessia to meet him.

"You say that, but you turned your other best friend down. Actually, I lie. I knew you'd turn me down, so I didn't bother," Tran rattled on.

Sonder didn't have the chance to respond before they came together. Rhianwyn dropped Alessia's hand.

"Sonder," she said again.

They stood looking at each other forever until she threw her arm around him and hugged him tightly. He held himself back as he wrapped his arms around her.

"You stink," she muttered into his shirt.

"That's what I said!" Tran waved his hands to the sky.

"Shut up," Sonder moaned.

Rhianwyn stepped away with a laugh and let her hand fall into his.

He smiled tightly, then looked at Alessia. "Alessia." He squeezed Rhianwyn's hand before dropping it and offering his to the other girl.

She placed a hand on her chest and gave Rhianwyn a look charged with girlish giggles and flattery. She bit her smiling lip and took it with a curtsy. "Sonder," she lilted, "you flatter." She grinned, then boldly flipped her hand around and kissed his. "And you still blush like a boy, though you're hardly little anymore."

Rhianwyn rolled her eyes when Alessia looked back at her. "Stop it." She stepped up to Tran and placed her hand on his shoulder, stretching on tiptoes to kiss his cheek. "It's always lovely to see you, Tran."

Tran bowed and kissed Rhianwyn's hand. "You see me every day."

"Never gets old." She laughed, then turned to Alessia. They kissed each other's cheeks. "Thank you for walking with me, Aless. See you tomorrow?"

"You're asking me?" Alessia teased. When Rhianwyn gave her a look, she sighed. "I'm only joking. I'll meet you in the library after breakfast. We can go to Wilkin's together." She looked at Tran, who offered his arm, and she placed hers politely in the crook of his elbow. "Thank you for walking me home."

"I do it every day." Tran winked at Sonder, who was grinning again. The boy gave him a heavy thump on the shoulder. "Get ready. Tomorrow I finally beat you."

"I'll be there," Sonder said as the two walked toward the gate. Alessia waved with a more subdued smile, which he returned.

Rhianwyn pressed up against his side and wrapped her arm around his. "Let's go."

They walked steadily, even though Sonder could feel her thrumming with energy. Maybe he was, too. She had stepped away from him, but he'd feel her brush his side, or he'd touch hers on accident.

She smelled like roses and loam, and clean sweat. It made him wish he had taken a quick bath with the other boys. But his trunk in the barracks had clothes that were too small. He regretted it every time he caught a whiff of his musty clothes, which smelled like the road.

A few servants called out greetings to Rhianwyn, and she offered smiles and waves whenever they did. They muttered and bowed when they saw him. *Master Sonder*. The ones who had known him forever at least smiled politely.

It wasn't until they passed through the garden gates that he felt relaxed. The tension left his shoulders, and he realized he had been holding Rhianwyn away when she melted back against his side.

"I'm glad you're home," she said. She matched his slowed pace. They strolled through the greenery as the daylight nuzzled against the horizon. "Even if I know you're coming, I never know exactly. I heard the horns earlier. Nothing was harder than not sneaking off during the lecture and then my shift at the hospital."

He was still nervous that someone was watching or listening in. Plus, everything he wanted to say was jumbled. Listening to her talk as if it had just been a few days instead of nearly six months loosened the knot in his throat.

She inhaled the evening air with a smile. "Tran said you were training tomorrow. Are you excited? Did you train today?" She hardly paused to let him speak.

Sonder finally broke a smile. "It was alright. Tomorrow, Áki is going to lead a four-on-one exercise." Thoughts of Mikhail crossed his mind like a whisper, but he had no desire to tell her about it. It was a minor conflict, one Rhianwyn didn't need to know about.

She leaned into him to guide him off the main walkway. "That was that nonsense about beating you tomorrow. I don't see the appeal of getting whacked by swords. I get you have to train, but I swear it's sadistic how much you all enjoy it. I end up treating quite a few of them, you know. Was Sir Rodrick glad to see you?"

The stream of questions continued. She never seemed to mind his short answers. The whirl of her stream of thoughts filled most of the conversation, and Sonder welcomed the chance to let his racing mind slow down and listen. She led him with subtle tugs and pushes through the garden pathways, but he knew nothing she did was aimless.

When her chatter slowed, he asked about how things were for her. Unlike with him, one question was enough to get her going.

She was the best storyteller he knew. Even the mundane conversations with the guild masters or shopkeepers were full of color and detail. He could almost imagine what it was like to be normal.

When she finished explaining the candle-maker, Miss White, something dawned on her, and she looked at him. "What's it like for you? You've never told me."

The happiness inside of him slipped. "Lots of riding between towns and cities. Cleaning gear," he deflected.

She knew what he was trying to do, and her face lost some of its luster. "But, what do you do? In the cities? Constantly on trials?"

Sonder shrugged. "Mostly just watch, as I do here. It's not all that different. Sometimes we chase people or conduct investigations like they do here in the slums." He saw her face pale. She knew about the effects of the raids throughout the city by the Justices and Spiders. She knew because the Healers Guild tended the wounded left behind or the people forced from their homes. "I don't participate," he said quickly. "I usually stay with Merrick to watch the nobles." He didn't have the heart to tell her he sometimes pointed out suspicious people.

She looked forward and stood up taller. "Then tell me why there's a new scar on your hand."

It took Sonder a second to think about what she meant. Then he barked a laugh, earning him a scowl when it came to him. Rhianwyn knew most of his scars and injuries, and not just because they were friends. "Errant arrow." He held up his free hand to appease her. "I'm not laughing at that. It's just—you would notice." His voice softened, and he felt his heart do that thing again in his chest. "Your talent shows."

She was an incredibly talented healer, and he didn't need to be here daily to know.

They came to a spot where yew trees grew tightly together with a bench tucked beneath their branches. It was hard to see the sun setting because their leaves wove together.

Rhianwyn tugged him to a stop. For a wild moment, he was afraid. Despite all the times they had held hands as children or hidden under bedsheets, he was painfully aware of her closeness. It felt stupid, dangerous, and thrilling all at once. When she looked up at him, he almost hoped she would kiss him because he wasn't brave enough to kiss her. If she did, he wouldn't stop her.

They felt safest under the canopies where no eyes were likely to see them.

Rhianwyn's face softened, and she reached up to push his hair off his forehead. "You're finally taller than me."

The pounding of his heart slowed. Or he just came back into his body. "I missed you."

She always smiled like that when she was shy—rolling her lips over her teeth so they wouldn't show. She squeezed his hands. "How long are you home?"

Sonder's smile relaxed into a line. "I don't know. I don't think long."

Her grip loosened. "You're just here for the ceremony, aren't you?"

"That's what Merrick thinks. And tests."

Soon it was just her fingertips holding their hands together, but he wouldn't let her hands fall.

"When will you come back?"

The restraints in him broke, and he pulled her against him. He worried about how he smelled or if anyone would happen to see them until he felt her hand against his back. "I don't know. I'm so sorry, Wyn. But, if I'm back, I'll take you to the ball. I promised."

She laughed in the back of her throat. "That's not the only thing I'm worried about."

"I know." He held her tighter.

Her breath caught, and she looked at him. "You're nervous about the ceremony."

Sonder nodded and loosened his arms. "I'm afraid of what it means for me." He laughed darkly. "I'm afraid of everything that's in store for me. I hate the queen's tests." Then, letting his arms fall, he glanced down at the scar. It looked like a thin rope across the back of his hand, still angry and red.

Rhianwyn took his hand in hers, seeming transfixed by how their skin looked together. He was darker than her for once because of riding in the sun. "You're not doing it alone. You know?"

"I know," he said again. It was half-hearted. He didn't tell her nearly all of it.

He wasn't as tall as Tran, but she still had to stand on her toes for her lips to brush his cheek. The urge to kiss her gripped him once more, and he resented how afraid he was to do it. So instead, he kissed her forehead roughly. She closed her eyes.

His stomach clenched, then let out a loud protest that echoed off the trees. Her eyes went wide before she burst out laughing. "Have you not eaten?"

It wasn't as funny to him. "Not since breakfast before we got to the city. I was too busy studying and training to eat."

She balked. "It's past dinner!" A wave of thoughts crossed her face, and she said more quietly, "And you need to bathe." She shook her head as she picked up her book. "C'mon. We can talk more later. Let's get you taken care of."

She rolled her eyes, but he saw the little satisfied smile toying at the corners of her mouth.

The next day, Sonder stood beside Tran as Áki paced through the rows of boys. Rodrick stood nearby and watched like a hawk where the hulking man's eyes could not see.

"It's one thing to be a clever fighter in a duel," Áki said as his battle-axe swept at random faces. Although his voice grumbled and growled, it was hard for Sonder not to see the man stuffing pastries in his mouth while pestering Merrick. That changed when Áki confronted him. "It's something else entirely to stay alive on the battlefield." With the grizzly spike of the axe bearing down on him, Sonder could imagine the man taking on hordes of men. His body went cold.

A few of the nearby boys shifted. Áki wore black leathers, the same as him, and there was no hiding it. Everyone in the radius around him held their breath to see what the redhead would do. But a flicker of recognition entered that glare.

Áki moved on, and Sonder let his breath go. The other boys relaxed, too.

When it came time to draw sticks, the boys jostled each other in line while Rodrick held out his hand. The man barked at some clumps to break up depending on how well-matched the boys were. Sonder and Tran gravitated toward the middle of the line, but unsurprisingly Tran was one of those ordered to move. Sonder kept his face neutral. The order of combat wasn't why his heart hammered. He was nervous about making his mentors look bad.

As he stepped forward to draw his straw, Áki leaned down and spoke under his breath, "Remember what I said this morning. This is just training, not a test."

The thin piece of wood slid out of Rodrick's hand. A smear of green paint winked at him.

"Go stand over there," Rodrick ordered.

Áki's heavy hand pressed down on his shoulder. "Don't worry."

As he took his place in the group with green paint, he kept his eyes light and never let them settle on the others.

Of course he was worried. How could he not be? Merrick and Áki had indicated no hidden meaning in these drills, but everyone watched. If it weren't the boys wondering just how good a squire trained by the queen's elite was, it would be echoed through the staff and eventually whispered in a room where someone cared. Everything ultimately made it to the queen. At least, that was what Merrick harped on him about constantly.

Do not let her find cause to question you. Never show your weakness.

Those were the things Merrick said to his face. But Sonder overheard the conversations the adults had. They constantly forgot he was there. Merrick voiced concerns about what would happen if Sonder didn't meet the proverbial expectations—which felt as attainable as catching air. Drisil, meanwhile, was concerned that Merrick worked him too hard. Even Áki, with his jokes, watched him anxiously.

Sonder wasn't stupid. He knew they worried. So how could he not worry now when everyone was gauging him?

Rodrick rambled off four names and then called Sonder's, pulling him from his thoughts. "You'll go against them."

Tran wasn't one. Nor was Mikhail, thankfully.

Three arenas were roped off. Three groups ducked into their rings while the rules were declared. No blows to the head. Leaving the roped area was disqualifying. Like Sonder had as a boy, a page stood by, handing out helmets and additional armor. He hung back as the other boys jostled each other, deciding if they wanted shields or not. Most didn't.

Already, Sonder's position as a squire was forgotten. They expected him to take a shield and planned on overwhelming him with speed.

"I have my helmet," he said quietly. Rodrick appeared then and handed it to the page. It was a relief Áki hadn't done it. The boy handed it up to him. "I'll take a buckler as well, please." There were a few options of swords left, so he took his time testing their balance. When he found one he liked, he spun it to feel its limitations. "Thank you," he said with a tight smile before ducking in.

Sonder took a steadying breath. The dusty scent was familiar—not tinged with pine trees, soil, or foreign cities. It was the smell of the castle yard, somehow virgin, like a fresh barn, bright with hay and the scent of the sea. When he opened his eyes, four sets looked back at him in confusion.

Rodrick shouted for the ready. Three other masters paced the perimeters to watch for strikes or fouls. They would take notes for improvement. Anyone trained in the Royal Yard was an investment that wasn't entirely expendable. In that, Sonder wasn't unique.

"Fight!"

They came at him together. That was what would likely happen in a real battle. Numbers inflated their confidence, especially since he only had a buckler.

Sonder waited, then flung the buckler like a flying disc. All four threw their hands up to block. Sonder closed the distance in the span of hesitation and picked off the boy on the edge of their line who had chosen a rattan spear. It was a clean cleave to the side that bent him over. Sonder grabbed the weapon from his hands before he declared the hit.

Not knowing its weight, Sonder flipped it around clumsily, especially since the defeated boy's fingers held on too long. But it was still enough to block the nearest swing. Each movement felt slow and erratic in equal parts.

Sometimes you have to be bold. Áki's voice echoed. *You'll have to learn when those times are quick. You'll be dead otherwise.*

Sonder knew where his belt was. It was almost an unfair advantage. These boys didn't have fitted armor like him. The wooden sword slammed into place.

Use any advantage.

With his second hand freed, it fell on the spear's shaft, and he thrust it into a boy's chest. There was no time to enjoy the slack-jawed look. Sonder was already moving on to the next as the boy threw down his sword angrily.

The last two had regained their wits. It wasn't a silly game, nor would it be easy. They had unfortunately realized it too late.

 Now they dueled.

As they circled, there was time to formulate a plan, to watch any favoring or potential weaknesses. Sonder's awareness noted that one arena had fallen quiet already, and even though a few voices cheered at the crack of colliding swords, most were silent.

They were watching him.

You've got to see with everything, not just your eyes. Merrick. It was exhausting being conditioned to minute details. Yet Sonder was good at it—he had to be.

He dug the spear's tip into the dirt and kicked a cloud up toward the one he suspected to be a better fighter. The boy stepped out of the way but rolled his ankle on the discarded buckler. Again, Sonder rushed in and swept the boy's legs. He fell but still blocked the sloppy thrust of the spear. Sonder wasn't strong with the ranged weapon—his training was limited on the road. But he knew that and let a hand go to draw his sword once more. The boy brought his blade up to block in a panic. Sonder thrust downward and pinned his hand down.

He didn't complete the strike; he held himself back to prevent an injury. But it didn't matter. Not really. He would have met resistance reclaiming his blade if it were real. At least, that was what Merrick and Áki told him.

Too slow! Too slow! his mind bleated as he stumbled over the prone enemy to regain his field awareness.

Then Sonder was bent over by a wooden edge biting into his side. It wasn't hard. The last boy had held back, too. But it was a killing blow.

"Hit."

For all Sonder knew, the only sound was both of them panting. No other weapons punctuated the silence, and no voices rang out.

Sonder closed his eyes and cursed himself. Then, lowering his sword, he offered his hand to the winner. "Hit," he confirmed. The strike tingled as the skin began to bruise. The boy wore a stunned look as he accepted.

Sonder offered a hand to help the tripped boy up.

"That was incredible," the boy breathed as he got to his feet.

"I lost," Sonder said with a sad smile.

They turned to clear the arena for the next group. Áki stood like stone with his arms crossed. But instead of a look of disappointment, he wore a satisfied smile. The fear that had made Sonder tense up during the fight was released, and the relief almost overwhelmed him.

Chapter Fourteen
Ceremony of Names

The Queen's Tower, five years ago

"Where did you get these?" Aspera snatched the bundle of documents from Randal.

"Merrick found them in the last raid," he said.

Aspera peeled the leather thong off and unfolded the first one. Her fingers traced the lines on the pages. "Did we capture the person who had these?"

"No, Your Majesty. It appears they got word. However, we believe the home belonged to a relative of Bran's who maintained loyalty to the Lorists. No idea how he found them, but it seems his hunting around Tal Vyrens and the ruined keep led him to these."

Aspera scoffed as she finished the letter. "He wrote this to the witch to ask her to pray for him before he died. Seems it was never sent." She set it down and opened the second. Randal waited as her eyes scanned it. "This is what we've been looking for. There is some information here about the magic that runs through the boy's veins." Another sheet of paper flipped. "It appears incomplete, though. This isn't what I had imagined. Why did Bran protect this so fiercely if there's nothing about how it links him to the gods?"

Randal watched her flip through the pages more haphazardly. "As of yet, my queen, there is nothing else they've found."

Aspera huffed and replaced the pages she had gone through. "Well, it's a start. It looks like there is record of the Auza-Bendith. Hopefully, it will prove fruitful." She handed the papers back to him. "Study them. Send word to Merrick to continue searching." She looked out the window, and her eyes narrowed. "Something doesn't feel quite right."

Present, age fifteen

Áki watched Sonder's fight breathlessly. No doubt the lad had known he had lied about the importance of the exercise. Few secrets could be kept from him.

When Merrick turned his back, Áki was the one who saw that glimmer in the boy's eye. The thoughtful, hurt, curious, constantly whirring observation. Even if Áki subscribed to the lies on occasions, Sonder was no fool. He'd expected the boy would fight hard—the extent still surprised him.

The satisfied smile Áki wore was far from a lie, and Sonder mirrored his relief before turning back to his opponents, who chattered in his ear.

Roderick stood beside him with arms crossed. "You realize that was incredible, right?" The man wasn't stern like Merrick, but his tone edged toward solemn.

Áki smirked. "I warned you, didn't I?"

Roderick looked up at Áki from the corner of his eye. "Y'did." The man shook his head and sighed. "Merrick won't be as pleased as you."

"Let him grumble. The lad deserves some happiness. Besides, now the boys won't go so easy. It'll be fine." Áki kept his hawk-eye on Sonder.

Cathak had just reached him and was pounding him on the back while a few others stood by shyly.

"I forgot why he thinks ye a blockhead." Rodrick patted the man's shoulder as he left to call out the next group.

Áki ended up being right. Once they had made it through the first round, the boys were divided by who delivered the killing blows and how long they lasted. Sonder's next competitors were cautious, and the cheap tricks didn't work. The killing blow came from two boys. Sonder was good, but there was still room for growth, still time until perfection was demanded.

Still time to be a kid.

The month leading up to the Naming of Wards was spent training the boys in the yard. It was restorative. Even Merrick strolled out of his cave to watch and teach.

Áki would lean against the wall with a grin as the old man paced through his lessons. He caught Sonder's eye a few times, making the boy look away before he cracked his own smile. Áki would be cleaning his nails with his dagger or tossing it in the air before Merrick could turn his glare on him.

Watching Merrick was enjoyable. He was surprisingly nimble, moving as if he were dancing. Merrick taught the bold tricks like throwing concealed weapons or a buckler, claiming discarded weapons, and having an uncanny awareness of the battlefield.

He was the true master between them; Áki had no shame admitting it. Merrick couldn't turn down knighthood as he had. He would have been a true Black Knight if the stories were true about the order. Áki just battled like a bull. Bloodthirsty bellowing went a long way.

A few times, the two of them crossed swords for demonstration. It was a treat Áki rarely got. Merrick maintained his skill well for a man who rarely raised a weapon beyond parting heads from shoulders. While Roderick lectured on their technique, Áki felt a thrill at any blow he deflected.

Each night, the two men sat in Merrick's study, enjoying their camaraderie.

"I still don't get why you got Battle Master," Áki complained on a day he had fared well against the man. "I'm a better sword than you by far. I beat you."

Merrick blew on his tea. "You beat me today," he corrected. "You're a blundering nightmare. No foresight, just luck."

"You looked prim saying that while you blew on your little cup." Áki slapped his knee. "I swear your little finger was out."

Merrick glared over the rim. "Battle Master is too serious for you." He took a sip.

Áki grinned wolfishly and put his elbows on his knees. "I think I'd get better results making it fun."

"No blood. You'd get bored." Merrick set his cup down and lifted an eyebrow.

"So, you agree you're boring?"

"You'd also grow fat and out of shape because it requires foresight to keep your fitness up. I saw your surprise when I pushed you back. You know, because I calculate instead of blunder around." Merrick brought the cup up once more as he spoke.

"So you're fat and boring?" Áki said with no hesitation.

Liquid jumped as Merrick let out a huff of laughter. "Wrath's reign, you're insufferable."

Áki leaned back with a satisfied grin. "Liar. You adore me."

"Adore is pushing it." Merrick remained smiling.

Four years ago, the man had stopped drinking. They'd grown closer because of it. It wasn't duty that made Áki sit with him day and night, nor a promise or obligation. His morals and tenderness for Sonder wouldn't hold him here longer than necessary.

Merrick's blue eyes looked up and met his, and Áki grinned back.

"Your eyes sure glitter for someone who can't stand me. They're radiant."

"Do you need praise? You've done a fine job. You were right; I was overly worried. Is there anything else?" Merrick grabbed a slice of roasted venison that sat between them.

"I'm handsome?" Áki batted his eyes and stroked his unruly beard.

"Absolutely not. Even with a bath, you still stink, and that combed hair makes you no less hideous." Merrick tapped his nose, indicating the little jog Áki's took because it had been broken. "You don't protect your skull. Likely why you're dim."

Áki chuckled and took the piece of meat Merrick offered. He could have pushed it further. He could have cut the man deep like he used to, remarking on his preference for battle scars. But he knew better. Áki had grown fond enough of the man and valued the counsel they shared to not dig into wounds. If Drisil were there, she would have given him an approving look. Even praised him in her pretty bird-song voice in private after.

They were good for each other.

Áki changed the subject. "This has been good for Sonder."

The crust of bread Merrick bit into crackled so perfectly, Áki reached for a piece. Merrick spoke through a mouthful. "I think you're right. We needed the rest."

Áki lifted his slice as if he were toasting. "He needed to be just a boy." He chewed thoughtfully, then took a sip of warmed cider to wash it down. "Has the queen said how long we'll stay?"

"No. It is dependent on his scores. I suspect not long after the ceremony."

"When will it end?" Áki growled. He instantly regretted speaking the words.

Merrick's face darkened. "When she realizes there is nothing left to find out there. The books we found four years ago will be the last." He blinked slowly, challenging Áki to continue the conversation to the inevitable dead end.

It was futile, so Áki said nothing.

"I don't want to know how it ends. I'd rather it never did," Merrick sighed.

"That's dismal, even for you."

"Do you know what the boy said to me? That he doesn't want to be king."

The statement chilled Áki as much as it had Merrick. "All these years calling him ward. I've never thought of it that way."

"Because she would never." Merrick reached for another piece of the venison. "Yet since he said it, I'm haunted. I want it over, too. You're right. He needs to be here. If he is supposed to be a warrior, he should learn to stay alive. But the farther he is from Stellamar, the farther he is from her." The meat disappeared into his mouth.

Áki tilted his head. "You don't have to always eat like we're on the road, you know." He wondered if the man knew how to stay still.

"I prefer to avoid her. I only dine here when she requests me. I'm not like Drisil and Randal, raised in court."

Áki hiccupped. "I wasn't raised in court." A bubble of gas gurgled up, and he burped into the back of his hand.

"I still can't make my mind up about you. But I'm not like you, either." Merrick began with laughter in his voice. It faded as he rubbed his forehead like he had a headache.

"You can say it. I'm fearless." The chair protested beneath him as he sank further into it.

"Or dim-witted." Merrick took another sip of his tea.

Áki considered it. "No, fearless. There is no one scary enough to keep me from good food." He claimed the last of the roasted vegetables. "You know there are other places to eat than rubbing elbows with Aspera, right?" Áki brandished his mug at Merrick. "Don't insult me, by the way."

The afterthought made Merrick laugh. "I'm not ready to go to taverns. I don't trust myself." He grew serious again.

Áki heaved himself to his feet with as much noise as a kicked-in door. "I get it, lad." The look Merrick gave him in response never got old. His hand landed on the man's shoulder with an audible thump. "I don't envy you, but don't forget I'm here for you."

Merrick stood and looked up to meet the man's eye. For a moment, there was all the rage and darkness the man kept locked away, glaring up at Áki. He was terrifying—until who he was beneath the cloak broke through. Merrick's need for reassurance was as large as his self-assuredness. Áki grinned, and they embraced briefly.

"I want nothing to do with his test tomorrow," Merrick growled into Áki's shoulder.

"Drisil and I have already made arrangements. I'll tell you as much or as little as you want." Áki stepped away and pounded his back.

"Don't tell me any of it."

Áki let his hand linger on Merrick's shoulder. He let his mind open and seep into the other man's for a breath, and was met by one of the thickest walls he'd ever encountered. So much of Merrick was locked behind it. Áki's mind trailed down its roughness, testing for any cracks—as he always did when he used the Touch on the man.

There never were any.

It would be agonizing if Áki chipped away at the secrets guarded within, so instead, he let his goodwill breathe into the muscles clenched like angry tree roots, fighting under the strain.

Merrick's shoulders slumped. "I'm not ready to face the evil of what I've allowed her to do."

It was only enough to ease the headaches. There was no telling how Merrick would react if he found out about Áki. "She never harms the boy."

Áki couldn't stand how he had a good heart under all of that fear. He rarely ventured into Merrick's mind because it reminded him of the volatility that lurked there—volatility that could be exploited if Aspera figured it out.

Merrick laughed darkly. "Get out. You're giving me that look. I'm not thirsty tonight. I don't need you pestering me." So narrow-minded. Merrick's face softened. "I'd be half the man without you. Thank you."

Áki smiled and felt his frustration melt. "I know."

"I'll see you at the ceremony," Merrick said with a more confident nod.

•••———————◆✦◆———————•••

The day of the ceremony had come. Sonder sat on the window bench in his room, head resting against the frame as he watched the people move about the courtyard. They could have been anyone as their silhouettes winked across the glass. He could imagine being in a tavern watching townsfolk go about their day, or some city of old with a college. The people could be students walking to their lessons.

After years of being taught arithmetic, different schools of magical theory, and complex forms of language, Sonder had realized there was no college he wanted to be at. He sighed, letting his head rest heavy.

If he could be anywhere, he wanted to be somewhere quiet. A cottage in the forest with just enough to get through each year. He'd probably still have obligations—he couldn't imagine a life without having some demands placed on him. But serenity was all he wanted in return.

There was a knock at his door, and he peeled his bones away from the wall. "Come in." His voice rattled a bit from disuse.

Áki ducked into the room, and some of Sonder's anxiety faded. It was easier to talk to the man.

"You look washed up, lad."

"I'm glad it's you." Sonder slid off the sill to his feet.

Áki lowered his voice. "Merrick is just behind me." Sonder's eyes went wide, and Áki laughed. "I'm joking."

Sonder pushed him. "That isn't funny." Áki grabbed him to muss his hair. Sonder pushed him off and began to smooth it back down.

"Ah, he already knows he's a drag to be around. That's why he sent me. He could use his feelings being hurt occasionally." Áki winked. "He admitted he was boring and fat last night."

The dimple on one side of Sonder's face appeared. "You still laughed at my expense," Sonder complained. He swatted Áki's arm away before the man could use his head as an armrest.

"Well, it's not a very nice thing to say about your knight." Áki tugged at Sonder's tunic to smooth some wrinkles.

"He makes these tests more difficult," Sonder said seriously, letting the man scrutinize his appearance. "It's easier to do them alone." The sickness in his stomach returned, and he looked down. Under Aspera's gaze, he felt vulnerable, and he hated to continue to fail.

"Hey." Áki lifted Sonder's chin. "I'll be there. Same as Drisil. We'll not let you go alone. Makes no difference to us if you pass or not. We'll keep trying. And Merrick isn't disappointed in you, neither. He's just afraid."

Sonder felt a surge of hope. "Of what?"

"Magic," Áki said dismissively.

Sonder knew it was a lie, but he nodded. Not for the first time, he wished Bran were still there. The memory of the man was a strange ache. Not only had he been important to Merrick, but all of his mentors had been held in Bran's sway somehow. Sonder remembered the way the man had looked at him. Bran had felt vast and oddly like a home Sonder would never know.

Drisil knocked on the doorframe and stepped in. "You're on time," she teased Áki as she touched his arm and kissed his cheek. Her kohl-lined eyes turned on Sonder. "And you look handsome." Her tone was motherly. The sound of her hand sliding down Áki's arm sent a chill through Sonder's spine.

She also straightened his clothes. The sapphire silk of her under-dress shone at her collar, and the braided hems on her sleeves glowed with one strand of the color woven into the black cords.

As the smell of her perfume filled his mind, he remembered being a child and tugging at the colorful fibers.

So many memories were coming to him.

Aspera had appeared in his dreams last night and followed him like a specter through the images. Her presence had made him lock up like it always did when she came as he slept. It made Sonder feel frayed and pulled apart the following mornings.

Drisil's warm fingers brushed his cheek. "It'll be alright." She fixed his hair, stood up straighter, and guided him toward the door.

As Sonder walked past Áki, the man fell in step beside him and mussed his hair again. He inevitably smiled, knowing Áki did it to irk the sorceress.

Sonder ignored the nervous looks from the staff as he walked through the corridors flanked by the two of them. It gave him time to brace himself before they reached the heavy banded doors that led up to the Queen's Tower. Certain circles called it her Poisoner's Tower. Those doors were ominous despite the beautifully wrought work of blossoming flowers and shapes that reminded him of bounding deer.

Immediately through them was a small throne room. Nothing like the one where people gathered for court or ceremonies. It was intimate, with towering stained-glass windows that always seemed to have a different image glittering. A heavy carpet warmed the space.

Sonder had overheard Merrick complain once about hating the room. It was where they had met with the queen when their employ began. It was the room where he had been presented as a ward by Bran all those years ago.

The next floor led to the queen's private chambers, a dining room, studies, and private apartments. He knew because the breakfasts he and Rhianwyn took with Aspera over the years had been eaten here. Once, when Randal had escorted him to a test, the sorcerer had looked down that hallway and whispered how he'd spend lots of time up here once he was knighted.

Sonder didn't let his mind linger on that memory, and he looked away quickly before the illusion of the tapestries reaching out to him overwhelmed him.

The climb into the tower proper was oppressive. Sonder knew little about magic, but he could feel it here. His skin crawled as if the whispering walls brushed his skin. Glowing vials and pieces of dissected creatures filled the rooms lining the stairway. He was glad he hadn't eaten anything that morning. He felt nauseous.

Áki tugged him to a stop before they reached the top, spun him around, and held him by both shoulders as he knelt. Sonder had grown, so he was taller than the kneeling man. "Get outta yer head. I won't say what Merrick would; you know it. Don't be afraid."

"I'm not," he lied.

Áki tousled his hair. "Course you're not." The man used his shoulder to stand up, and Sonder felt his stomach stop churning.

Drisil and Áki stepped in front of him. Sonder saw their shared look, but he couldn't decipher it.

The doors opened. Black stones glittered in the morning light. After the first test years ago, the urge to run to the balconies and look out over the city had died. But that didn't make the glimpses of the world any less spectacular. After the ceremony later that day, he would get the freedom to explore the city without a chaperone. Then he could go and watch the sea if he wanted. Or see the markets. There was nothing like looking down at it, but he could still climb the roofs.

Sonder saw Randal first, standing by the table in the middle of the room. His back was toward them, but he looked over his shoulder as they walked into the cavernous chamber. "Master Sonder."

Aspera's sky-blue gown pulled away from one of the windows before he could respond. Sonder averted his gaze. "Ah, good morning." She brushed past him as if he didn't exist, going over to Drisil. The two women kissed each other's cheeks. "Drisil," the queen said warmly, then turned to Áki and sharply said, "Áki." She finally addressed Sonder, speaking as if he were still a small child. "You can go look out the windows if you'd like. The view is breathtaking."

Sonder kept his face downcast. "Good morning, Your Majesty. No thank you, Your Majesty. I'm afraid of heights."

"Have you never climbed a tree?" Aspera laughed as she folded her hands into her long sleeves. "Nor walls or rooftops?"

Sonder went numb. He always did when he felt caught in a lie by her. He had begun lessons with Drisil to ward against magic, which required him to remain calm. Merrick never let up about it, either. He swallowed and kept his face as impassive as he could. "Those are not so high, Your Majesty."

"Fair." She brought her hand up under her chin while her amber eyes swept over him. "You'll grow to love the view, I'm sure."

She walked toward the table, where a velvet satchel lay. Randal opened it as she approached, then stepped aside. She retrieved its contents. Sonder watched, his curiosity getting the better of him.

"Today will be short. After all, we've all got a ceremony to prepare for this evening." He wondered how her teeth were so white as she smiled.

The queen placed a delicate glass vial into Randal's hands. Áki made a noise that turned into him clearing his throat. Sonder fought the urge to look at the man.

"Come here, child." Her sleeve drooped as she held her hand out to him. Randal stood beside her.

Drisil urged him forward. "Go on," she whispered.

Sonder had to obey. His pulse hammered as each step brought him closer. Even though Aspera looked at him kindly, he saw something else there. Randal was a blank slate, holding the neck of the vial in one hand and cupping the bottom with the other as if it might shatter if he wasn't careful.

When he reached them, Sonder bowed. "Your Majesty."

Her cool fingers snaked under his chin. He fought not to pull back. Instead, he let her lift his face to look up at her. Despite her beauty, he found no comfort in the curved bow of her lips. "You look more like your father every year," she said.

His insides felt made of glass, spiderweb cracks lacing through him. The velvet cloth sat on the table, and the queen threw back the burgundy fabric to reveal the gleam of a dagger. The memory of her magic stabbing his heart seared through his chest. He flinched as the vice of her hand closed around his. He couldn't pull away even though he wanted to.

"This won't hurt," she purred.

Sonder's breaths came in deep gasps as he watched the paper-thin blade slice viciously through his palm. She was right—it didn't hurt much. But he hated when paper split his finger, and this was his palm, and metal. To his horror, she dug at the edges of the wound. Blood pooled and dripped down his hand into the vial that Randal held.

Something kept his jaw clamped around the scream, clawing for release. His lip trembled against it. The same thing held him on his feet when his knees began to feel weak. It was surreal watching the clear glass become coated by the droplets. Sonder had never observed how blood flowed thick before. It crept slowly up the sides.

Sonder winced as her nails continued to worry at the flesh, which grew angry. When his eyes darted to the slab of redwood behind her, an ember of solace sparked inside of him. It was a twin to the one in her throne room, the one he had traced since childhood.

"Almost done," she said.

Finally, with the vial filled, she turned his hand, so his palm faced upward. It trembled in hers as the pain began to radiate into his wrist.

"Such a brave boy," she soothed, pressing the sleeve of her dress into the wound. Red slowly seeped into the pale blue like blooming poppies.

The pain increased, and eventually, the burning felt as if he were holding his hand over a flame. And still, it grew. His face scrunched, and he bared his teeth until a groan escaped. Sonder barely heard her shush him as if he were a small child enduring an alcohol swab to a skinned knee. It dulled, but still, his hand quivered from the trauma. The ruined sleeve was removed, and he was alarmed to see that she had healed it.

Aspera's magic was different from Rhianwyn's. The girl's tingled and burned like an itchy scab. The queen's was agony. She forced his flesh together instead of coaxing it. His hand looked ugly, and it continued to weep.

He was still staring at it when she reappeared and took it once more to wrap a piece of linen around it, nearly the same color as his flesh.

"That's all we needed." Aspera patted his wounded hand. "You did well." She looked over his head to Áki and Drisil. "You may remove him."

The queen led him to them, and Áki's grip spurned him on.

"Mistress Drisil?" Aspera called after them. Drisil stopped, even as the two of them continued toward the sanctuary of the door. "I may require your skill. You will come when I summon you."

Áki didn't wait for the sorceress. Sonder also didn't need to hear her response to know that she agreed. It hadn't been a question. Drisil had no choice.

That didn't remove the feeling of betrayal at whatever she would do with his blood.

When they reached his room, Áki closed the door and immediately pulled Sonder's hand away from his chest. It still hurt, and he could see the line of blood in the fabric. The man scowled as he traced it with his thumb.

"I didn't know she'd do that." His blue eyes looked up from the wound. "Don't tell Merrick about this?" Sonder had never seen him look so pale.

The boy shook his head and pulled it back into his chest when Áki let it go. He didn't want to tell anyone about what had happened.

Áki nodded. When he opened the door, Drisil was about to knock. Sonder's red-rimmed eyes met hers. Áki stepped out, and Sonder heard the man angrily ask her what had happened.

"I don't know blood magic," was all Sonder heard Drisil say.

He was left alone until the sun began to set. Merrick was the one to retrieve him for the ceremony. Their formal suits were mirror images.

"You look like a man," Merrick said with a warm smile. Sonder said nothing. "Let's get this over with."

The overwhelming urge to wrap his arms around the man came over Sonder. But instead, he made the scent of his proximity be enough. He was sure to keep his fingers wrapped around his injured hand to hide the bandage as they walked side by side to the royal throne room. He hardly looked different, but now the servants gave him small nods of praise.

When they approached the closed doors, a handful of nobles were milling around with glasses of wine in hand. Instead of seeing them, however, all Sonder saw was Rhianwyn, her back to him as she conversed with Gwenyvir. She wore all black as well, with most of her hair braided and piled on top of her head except for a few pieces left to hang long. The woman glanced at them, and Rhianwyn's eyes followed.

"Ah! Sir Merrick!" one of the nobles called out. "This is quite the spectacle, wouldn't you say? Naming wards."

Rhianwyn's eyes smiled. Sonder ignored Merrick's response to go to her.

They stopped a modest distance from each other.

"You look dashing." She looked roguish, knowing they had to comport themselves.

He saw that the black was actually a deep purple. Rhianwyn looked like the young woman she was. "You're beautiful."

She blushed. "Are you nervous?"

"I want it to be over."

Her smile fell, but before she could say anything else, an usher opened the doors and made the announcement beginning the ceremony. Gwenyvir and Merrick closed around them as the stragglers disappeared into the throne room. Soon, it was just them.

It was brighter outside of the room, so all they could see was the impressions of the people gathered, and all they could hear was the echo of their voices.

A herald's voice cut through the noise. "Bring forth the wards!"

"Ready?" Merrick asked as if Sonder had a choice. He must have realized it because he laid a hand and rubbed the boy's shoulders reassuringly.

The gesture made Sonder miss the road. Merrick tended to be more forthcoming with his moods away from the watchful eyes of the court. Sonder's mind drifted to the feel of a horse beneath him. He imagined its withers warming his thighs and making him sweat, until he felt Rhianwyn's hand slip into his now that their mentors' backs were turned. The bandages tugged, and he winced.

Her face hardened in a shadow of a question. He shook his head, nearly imperceptibly, but it seemed enough for her.

They stepped through the doors, and she dropped his hand and folded hers as they walked. Áki and Drisil waited inside and fell in with them as they strode past the curious eyes.

They had been the queen's charity case until now. The ceremony when they were eight had been like a contract. The queen had opened her home to them in exchange for their service. They were tutored to serve the realm, orphans taken in out of kindness.

They had been able to keep it a secret from the other children, and only their masters with a need to be privy knew. This day was always intended to come. But as the mosaic of faces stared at them, the sliver of hope died inside Sonder.

There would be no quiet cottage in the mountains for him, dutifully repaying his debts. Now the city knew him for what he was. Mikhail's scowl caught his eye, and Sonder met it with a solemn regret that their fledgling friendship had gone up in flames. Undoubtedly, the smoke would deter many other boys unwilling to take on Lord Vardulf's ilk—but the other boy didn't scare Sonder.

The ceremony dragged on. There wasn't much different from the droning at executions. Praise for the queen and her kindness, the lists of feats qualifying their mentors. It was self-indulgent in Sonder's eyes.

Perhaps that was Merrick speaking. The man needed no preamble because he chose to let his actions speak for him.

"Mistress Gwenyvir," the herald's voice projection echoed through the room. "You present the orphan girl, Lady Rhianwyn."

Rhianwyn averted her gaze, as all well-behaved, demure ladies were supposed to. But she still knew how to turn just so to meet Sonder's eye without anyone being the wiser. Her nose scrunched as she blinked, and it was enough to bring warm memories before she stepped forward to follow her mentor.

Rhianwyn settled on her knees between Gwenyvir and Aspera, bowing her head while she was presented.

"Your Highness. As the counselor of Royal Medicants appointed to represent the Healers Guild, I present the Lady Rhianwyn. Since the inception of her tutelage, she outpaced your expectations placed upon her. She is more than worthy of your grace, which will give her the means to continue her studies and represent you amongst her peers and the kingdom."

"She was required to show great prowess in magic. Do you bring others who support your claim that she is worthy?" Aspera's voice rang out. It sounded cleaner than the herald's, as if she sat beside each person, with no echo.

Drisil stepped forward. "Your Grace, I, Drisil, Royal Justice and High Sorceress, vouch for the young lady." She swept her long black sleeves aside as she stood beside Gwen and bowed.

Randal's chin tilted upward, and he spoke. "Your Highness, I, Master Randal, Royal Overseer of Magic and Justices, speak on behalf of the girl."

This caused the gathered people to murmur. Sonder looked around to see what their faces held.

"Miss Rhianwyn," Aspera said with a smile, "do you swear fealty to your Queen and uphold your oath to protect the people of Sosten?"

"I do, Your Majesty." Rhianwyn's voice projected differently still. That also set people to talking.

Aspera looked impressed. "Then rise my ward, dear girl."

Soft applause filled the throne room. Rhianwyn rose gracefully to her feet despite the tangle of her skirts, and she curtsied. She fell in behind Gwenyvir once more and returned to Sonder's side. Before she could give him any more reassurance, the herald's voice pulled his attention away from her.

"Sir Merrick, you present the usurper's orphaned son, Master Sonder."

It felt like a cold knife plunged into his gut. He had no idea where the idea had come from, but no one was supposed to find out who he was. His feet followed behind Merrick out of sheer habit. He kept himself from falling to his knees under the weight of everyone's eyes bearing down on his back.

Compose yourself. Don't let your emotions show.

"Queen Aspera, I, Sir Merrick, Battle Master, High Justice, and Black Knight, present my squire, Master Sonder, to you. He has met your expectations of his tutelage." Sonder thought he heard a clip to his mentor's tone. His voice projected naturally, dying around the fringes of the room.

"Sir Merrick, I'm sure you are aware he was to show exceptional potential in warfare. Who else vouches for his talents in both blade and ability to utilize deceptive magics required by our justices?"

Sonder felt the burn in his palm once more.

"I do, Your Majesty." Áki's voice naturally carried, and Sonder heard his boot steps muffled by the carpet beneath his knees. "I speak for the boy."

"As do I, Your Majesty." Hearing Drisil's voice made tears spring to Sonder's eyes, which he blinked back as he kept his head bowed.

"Your Highness, I also vouch for the boy." Randal's voice was less confident than it had been for Rhianwyn. Sonder lifted his eyes to look at the man, and he couldn't mistake the look the queen gave him—as if she was annoyed he had spoken. He let his eyes fall before she could see him watching.

Merrick shifted his weight. "I am obligated by my oath to say that the boy has yet to show any promise in magic. However, with the counsel of your highest mages, he is versed as I am. He will bring you glory."

"Then I ask the boy. Do you swear fealty to me and vow to uphold your oath to protect the people of Sosten?"

Sonder's heart pounded, and his voice quivered with the shock of how things transpired. "I do, Your Majesty."

"Say the words."

Sonder felt Drisil's hand on his bowed shoulder, and the warmth of her magic steadied his mind, so the words came to him. "I swear my life for yours, Queen Aspera. Your will is mine."

"Rise absolved of your family's crimes as my ward."

There was restrained applause. As Sonder turned to follow Merrick, the herald gave a long-winded recap before he declared the festivities commenced.

It was a lie. He may have been absolved, but everyone now knew who he was. No one would forget that.

When they were out in the hallway once more, Merrick turned to Drisil. He might have kept his voice low, but he had a habit of forgetting that Sonder had ears. "I didn't expect him to stand up."

Áki was the one to respond. "Just be glad he did." Sonder didn't miss the look the man gave Drisil behind Merrick's back.

He and Rhianwyn attended the dinner, split to either side of Aspera. With their mentors as a buffer, they ended up at the table's edge, sitting on full display. At the dance, it was the same, as a line of well-wishers filtered through to offer praise.

It was the first time Sonder had seen a ball, and he watched the people twirling beneath them. Then, they were allowed to partake in the group dances, giving him and Rhianwyn only a handful of seconds to share small smiles.

The whole thing was only bearable because of the prospect of next year's Equinox Ball, where they would attend with no parading.

• • ———————— ◆◆◆◆ ———————— • •

It was past the turning of the torches when they were dismissed. Rhianwyn slipped through the servant's door and closed it with hardly a rattle within a half hour of him locking is door.

She had changed into a simple wool dress but had been too hurried to remove her makeup and take her hair down. She didn't mind that Sonder was already in his underclothes. Instead, she rushed to him, taking his injured hand and prying it open.

"What happened?" she breathed. The wound was swollen.

He winced, and her hazel eyes searched his face. "It was part of the magic test this morning."

She hated seeing his shame. "May I?" she asked.

He nodded, clearly knowing he couldn't deny her. She carefully removed the bandage. The sight of it made both of their breaths catch.

There were ugly strands of fresh skin that mimicked stitches pulling the wound together. It had the appearance of any new scar, shiny and red, even as parts still gaped and bled.

Rhianwyn groaned. "Who healed this?" She forced herself to look back at him. His eyes were wide with fear.

"The queen." Sonder didn't look at her. "Can you fix it?"

Rhianwyn bit her lip and examined it once more. She shook her head. "No. I don't know what she did. I've never seen anything like this. It's like she wanted it to scar." Even if she did know how to fix it, she knew that it would only expose her, which compromised her promise to Maeveen. It broke her heart, and she brushed her thumb along the inflamed skin. "Why would she do this?"

"I don't know."

She knew he was lying—he hadn't been open in a while about what he endured in private. But she didn't press him. Instead, she looked up at him with teary eyes. "I can make it hurt less?"

Even without his answer, she released the warmth of her magic into him. It tingled and itched them both as the wound began to heal properly. As she let herself fade into him, she could feel the void Aspera's magic had opened inside of him, clawing at her, too.

Sonder's lips quivered as he smiled, then curved up in response. She wanted him to close the distance.

He fell into the routine they had established. "She used a dagger from a velvet satchel," he explained. Hopefully the knowledge would let her magic work better. He hesitated but went on, the truth healing him too. "She collected the blood in a vial Randal held."

It looked far less angry when Rhianwyn was through, and the bleeding had stopped. She had drawn as much of the memory of Aspera's magic out as she dared to. Its darkness and bitterness coiled in her stomach.

Rhianwyn needed to get into the garden tonight to tell Maeveen what had transpired. The idea that Aspera was trying to use blood magic on him frightened her. She might already be too late.

Her lips brushed his cheek as she held his hands in hers. "Meet me at the gate tomorrow after lessons."

She turned to leave, but his grip tightened, and her heart broke. Rhianwyn would have stayed with him until he fell asleep if she could have. But she had to leave. They couldn't be caught together. She had been whipped the last time they were, and Sonder still harbored that guilt.

They had been eleven then.

Bracing herself, she turned back and smiled at him. "Happy fifteenth birthday."

"Thank you," he whispered.

Her fingers squeezed his, and he let her leave.

Chapter Fifteen
Jealousy's Dance

The Gilded Harpy, seven years ago (six months after Bran's death)

They sat around a table in the Gilded Harpy. Food was piled high in front of them, and a barmaid came up with a glowing smile. The mug she set in front of Áki overflowed with foam. Another woman with two cups brushed past her.

Her face fell. "You've got to be kidding me," she protested, setting the additional drinks down. "I waited so long she beat me?"

Áki wrapped his arm around her waist and scooped her into his lap. Some of the ale sloshed out on the table, and she yelped. Giggles consumed her, and he turned her face into his and laid a passionate kiss on her lips.

Merrick rolled his eyes and grabbed one of the drinks. "Can't you find a private place to do that?"

Áki turned blearily on the man while the woman covered his cheek in kisses. "Look, my boy, I can pay. It's alright to have the personality of a log. There's girls would happily pretend you're the life of the party. Maybe even make you feel like it." He poked Merrick's chest. "I know a few." The woman turned his face back to hers and shut him up with her mouth.

Drisil laughed into her glass, which made Merrick glare at her. "What?" she said. "I somewhat agree. Although, Áki, if I'm unable to charm the man, I doubt anyone could. You'd have to pay double the asking price just for enduring him, and the deed left undone."

The woman let Áki pull away, and she pushed her cheek against his with a laugh. "You two are terrible. I could take a crack at it." She smiled and offered her hand across the table. "I like prudes."

"I don't share," Áki said menacingly. He buried his bearded chin into her neck. She squealed, keeping her hand out.

"I am no prude," Merrick growled. His sharp blue eyes looked at her, and her hand dipped. "I just see no use without love, and I refuse to make the mistake of thinking Aspera won't exploit that again."

The woman looked confused, but Áki sobered. "Peace, Mayze. He's just drunk."

Jealousy's Dance

resent, age fifteen

The hallways echoed with the memory of the celebration, a buzz of laughter, tinkling crystal, and the whisk of silk gowns as their ladies spun and wove through the gaiety. The last of the party was sustained by a ragtag group of musicians and a handful of revelers likely desperate to forget whatever woes they left in their distant estates. Exhausted servants continued to extinguish the candles and torches gradually. Áki stood in the shadows, noticing their glances. As a man who regularly shut down bars, he knew those looks well.

It was a shame that they held no authority to kick everyone out. He knew many barmaids fearless enough to grab him and haul him out who could lend a hand.

He took a sip of his mead and lamented how he no longer attended the city's parties. Tonight, he was nearly sober. He always was for significant events like these, only starting to drink once the queen had left. She had long since departed, but this was only his second.

It unnerved him that she never danced, instead sitting on her throne to watch. Randal always perched beside her, and they would whisper to each other. They never stopped plotting and formulating, doing whatever scholars did when they lost the ability to revel. That was a touch unfair to Randal, though. None of them ever stopped working anymore. The twig of a man still occasionally danced.

Like tonight. He had stayed after Aspera left to share a few dances with Drisil before he bowed out himself.

Áki took another drink. A servant walked by carrying a tray nearly emptied, so he flagged the boy. "Excuse me. Do you have plans for those?" He pointed at slices of roasted meat and fish.

The servant narrowed his eyes. "Madame Cur told us not to let you take the scraps. She's tired of the strays yowling at the kitchen doors."

Áki flashed his most charming grin. "I've seen you leave some on your way to feed the pigs." When the servant reddened, he laughed. "These are for a special little guy. I'll not tell your secrets, and I'll feed thems on the street, hm?"

The boy glanced around. "Fine," he huffed.

"There's a good man," Áki said as he snagged several slices and stuffed them into his pocket. "Now get. You're blocking my view."

The boy glared and walked away. Absentmindedly Áki fished a piece of the meat from his pocket and put it into his mouth as he once again found Drisil on the dance floor.

She was resplendent in her fitted gown. Unlike most women, her curves were quite visible. There were no embellishments or excess layers, just a simple navy dress, heather silk woven into her hair, and natural beauty. The cabinet hopeful she danced with spun her around and pulled her in. Áki couldn't help but be drawn in by her smile from where he stood. Even her coral lips were subdued for her—a blushing innocence he rarely saw.

As he watched, Áki grew solemn and almost longing. Her magic was potent, and he wondered if it clouded his mind or if it was seeing the shimmer around her that made her beauty captivate him.

Poor fool, Áki thought as he finished the mead and set it on the stone lip beside him. He wondered if the man she danced with had any inkling of her talent.

The song ended, and the two breathlessly stepped apart, laughing. Whoever he was, he held on to her hand as if he could keep her for eternity. But, to her credit, Drisil beamed as if he were extraordinary.

Áki was too far away to hear their conversation, but he knew the man was begging for another dance while Drisil gave excuses not to stay. The next note struck a ballad, and he reluctantly released her. Her hand lingered in the air as if it pained her to go. A few more parting words, and finally, she turned to leave.

Áki leaned against the wall and waited for her to pass. For a large man, he had learned a thing or two from Merrick, and she didn't notice him until she was nearly on top of him and he grabbed her hand. Her face went from a mask of pleasant surprise to the dark look he was used to—her candid ferocity.

"You startled me," she said with admiration and annoyance.

"Thank you." Áki pulled her closer and lowered his voice. "How did you get Randal to throw his lot in with us?"

She went rigid beneath his grasp. "I don't know what you're talking about."

"You do," he said just above her ear. Her perfume was heady, and his voice grew husky, digging into their proximity. "I don't need to be a charlatan to know Aspera had no idea it was coming. What'd you say to him?"

Her dark eyes angled toward him, her lips forming a line. "Does it matter?"

"Not really. Not to me. But to Merrick, it will. What am I supposed to tell him if he asks?"

She pulled her hand out of his. "Tell him he must've had a change of heart."

The answer genuinely shocked him. "So tell him she's doing blood magic with Sonder?"

Drisil softened and hid her hands in the fabric. "No. Tell him because Randal remains hopeful they'll find something." She moved to leave but stopped. "That's what Randal is telling the queen."

Before she could walk away, he grabbed her elbow and pulled her back. "Humble me with a dance?"

Her eyebrow arched up over her smirk. "I thought you don't drink for these things?"

"I don't," he said. She gave him an intrigued smile. "I'm self-aware enough to know I'm an ass when I drink."

He coaxed her hand back into his.

Drisil let him. "Who is this man trying to charm me?" She laid a hand on her chest. "You know I've seen you charm many women, right?"

"You, I'd not ask drunk. I'm not brave enough." He grinned, and his eyebrow lifted suggestively. "You're terrifying."

She laughed. "Fine. One."

They led each other to the dance floor. Her hand was feather-light on his shoulder, and his rested politely on her waist. It was tenser than he had hoped. He should've expected nothing different. They were firmly rooted in friendship, and Áki knew better.

"You look disappointed," she teased. When he said nothing, she looked over his shoulder smugly. "We all get lonely sometimes." His grip tightened, and for an inadvertent moment, he felt her thoughts. She knew the brush of his Touch, and her eyes slid back to his face. "Don't you dare."

He would count grappling with her among his worst nightmares. It would be nothing for her to tear his sense of self to shreds. "You're thinking about Merrick."

"As are you," she said slowly.

Henaild went both ways for anyone privy to it. Like the ebb and flow of the tide, pushing and pulling. Of course she knew his essence. "You give a lot to him."

She looked away. "Did you ask me for a dance to interrogate me?"

Áki chuckled despite the heaviness between them. "Actually, no. For some ill-forsaken reason, I imagined I'd feel special. I lack foresight, not conniving. I mean what I say."

A shy, genuine smile softened her face. "You've been practicing your vocabulary." He mimed lifting a visor at the jab, and she shook her head. "Residual glamour, then."

"Don't do that," he said. "You're stunning always, but tonight even more so."

She searched his face then. Really looked at him. He knew her walls far better than Merrick's, and he didn't mind sitting with her as they opened. "I'm a beacon for the lonely," she said harshly. A double-edged comment, with Randal poised on one side and Merrick on the other. Before he could reassure her, she went on. "Don't patronize me. You and I both know I put my lot in with the aching souls. You're not tormented enough." Her shaped eyebrow arched over a playful look.

He could see right through her dark humor. "He loses more of himself every day. You know that."

She inhaled sharply. "We all do, Áki." The flash of anger dulled as quickly as it came. They both knew he lost very little of himself. She looked away as if ashamed.

"Have you ever thought about how you want this to end?" he asked.

He became acutely aware of their waltzing. The song was nearly over, and the look he had craved to see on her face finally appeared. A strange admiration, with her eyes fixed on his and her lips parted slightly. It wasn't at all what he had wanted. The desire to kiss her wasn't there, or the ire of desire. But she was still beautiful, and he loved her profoundly, no less. He couldn't help as his mouth tugged up in a lopsided grin. Finally, he understood why that stare intoxicated the lonely.

The look grew more beautiful as she saw only him. "Who knew," she whispered. The music ended. She placed her hand along his bristly jaw; his red beard was tamed for once, even if the lines weren't shaped to perfection. "I don't know if I ever told you how very sorry I was about Solena. She was luckier than I realized." The brush of her thumb along his cheek warmed his heart. "Now, if I may go?"

The mention of his once-lover was precisely the balm he craved.

The grief had long since subsided; he had gotten good at loss. But sometimes, he needed to feel the ache. As he looked down into Drisil's face, he imagined it was her. The woman who had captured his heart when he had been just fine casting it out like a net, only to release the women it snared. But Solena had been a mythical creature of old in a sea of fish. She'd hooked him right back.

Drisil smiled at him, and he saw the ghost of Lena reminding him of the joy they shared. "You honor me, Lady."

Drisil laughed and patted his cheek. "You too."

As her hand slipped from his cheek, he grasped it in both hands. She faced him once more. "For what it's worth, Sil, I don't know what end I want, either." He kissed her fingers. "What you choose matters little to me."

He saw the muscles around her eyes narrow just slightly as she undoubtedly wondered what he meant. But they both knew there was no hidden meaning. Randal had made his choice to cozy up to Aspera. Áki might jeer at the man, but ultimately, he didn't care. Drisil could do the same.

Perhaps it was because he knew both of them well enough to understand their motives. He knew what to expect from them, and maybe that was the insult she found.

Merrick, though, he wouldn't forgive. Again, the man filled his thoughts as Drisil's hand slid from his. Áki watched her walk away as he let the idea take shape.

He and Drisil were somewhat at odds about the man. But his conflict was not with her. Still, he pushed into the realization. He had waited for it to finally take a cohesive shape, and its discomfort was worth it.

They both loved Merrick. Admired him. Clung to the betterness of him. Thought highly of him and wished for him. Áki was suddenly fiercely jealous of the woman because she would be the one to pull the old man into the grasp of the queen, and Áki so desperately hoped he wouldn't go.

He saw so much of himself in Merrick, and desired to glimpse the self-assurance there. Áki would gladly sit beside the man if he chose Aspera with conviction. But he wouldn't. Áki knew very little about Merrick, but he knew he couldn't do that. Unless the demons he carried finally won.

He didn't want to see the man shelled.

An exasperated servant passed between them as Drisil rounded the corner and disappeared. His last thought was that he saw himself in all of them. Randal and Drisil understood the futile nature of stopping the queen, same as him. They loved Sonder but saw no way to save him. They enjoyed the comforts of being next to royalty. But Merrick was the best part of him. Áki didn't want to see that corrupted. He couldn't forgive Merrick if he let that fire to live and rebel extinguish because Áki didn't want it to die.

Another couple brushed past him, and he heaved a sigh. There had to be a tavern somewhere staying open into the wee hours of the morning. He took a step, and the hunt for a bitter beer and a drunken lass beside him in bed commenced. Indeed, both could still be found.

In the morning, they got word that they would leave the following day. It was disappointing but necessary. They had no say in the matter. Nine men joined them as they went, all wearing black and astride the kingdom's best destriers. As they mounted in the bailey, a flurry of ravens took to the sky. Their caws filled the air, and everyone paused to look as the sky pulsated with their blue wings.

"What is that?" Sonder asked.

A scroll fell to Áki's feet. He picked it up and read it. Concern and anger gripped his chest as he handed it up to Merrick.

Merrick read it, then crumpled it and dropped it to the ground. "It appears she's sending word to the other cities about us." His horse shifted as he looked at Sonder. "They'll know who you are."

Merrick turned his horse to ensure the other men were ready. Once he wasn't looking, Sonder bent down and retrieved the crumpled note. Áki squeezed his shoulders as he read:

I hereby name Sonder Uland-Baramore, son of usurper Lucrid Uland, my ward and heir to the Black Knights.

Bow to him.

"I'm sorry, lad. It'll be alright."

Chapter Sixteen
Innocence Taken

Merrick's study, ten years ago

"Bran?" Sonder asked tentatively.

He grunted to show he was listening. Silently, he cursed Merrick for putting him alone with the boy, even after telling him it was painful.

"Who are the Lorists?" Sonder whispered.

"Our enemies." He sent a prayer to the Goddess for silence.

"Why?"

Bran stopped walking. Only in the past year had he become sentimental to the old ways, but it felt like a moment's pause was given to him. A chill ran through him, reminding him that his life's purpose had become this child, and understanding why their order had fallen. To repeat Aspera's lies would be to forget that.

Bran kept his face downcast as he turned to Sonder, feeling the man he wanted to be fighting with Aspera's puppet. "They're the last link to the gods and their stories since the colleges have fallen, and our order is no more."

"But you're still here. They say you're the last Knight of old. You're helping rebuild it, aren't you?"

The shake of his head was merely a twitch. "That means nothing." Bran's heart began to ache as his role in the fall began to wake inside him.

Sonder was pensive, but then Bran watched thought dawn on that young face, and the pain was replaced by admiration.

"If the Lorists keep the gods' stories, wouldn't that mean they were friends of the Black Knights? With what you've said about them being a link."

Bran didn't miss how he said "them" instead of "us," but he let it go. He couldn't tell Sonder the whole truth. If only he had known sooner that Aspera would bind the boy to her so he couldn't escape.

Instead, he smiled sadly and laid a hand on the boy's shoulder. "Never stop observing, Sonder."

Innocence Taken

Present, age fifteen

Sonder looked up at the bright blue sky, untarnished by clouds. After months of riding, it felt as though they had gotten nowhere reasonable, with each day blending into another. He was surprised to see a plump half-moon even as the sun beat down his back. The heat made it feel like he was cooking inside his riding leathers. Sweat found opportunities to run down his skin before being trapped by the layers of fabric.

He had been in the kitchens once when the sea-beetles were cooking, screaming as they boiled. Now, he envied them as another drop trickled down the arch of his back, and he wiped a bead from his temple.

Sonder wished he could scream.

The face on the moon snarled down at him, gnashing at the clean white edges of its prison. At night it would be a crisp image. During the day, however, the shadows bled into the sky. He imagined celestial beasts making light-puppets against a sheet, as he had done with Rhianwyn as a child.

A dragon moon already? Or is it the wolf?

His brain leapt as it began working through the numbers. They were at least a month's ride from Stellamar. It was mid-summer. If they made fast time back, they could . . .

But they wouldn't; they never did. Not unless a blue raven summoned them back, and there was little chance in that. Merrick was no longer a prominent justice. The man's sole purpose was to see to his lessons, which somehow these expeditions were. There were no significant tests for him, which the ache in his hand was a reminder of.

They'd only get back by Equinox if Merrick just rode through the villages. No chance of that, either. Unfortunately, the man had a habit of lingering or extricating himself from the group for days, as he had a week ago.

Rhianwyn's letter burned in Sonder's chest pocket. Her neat scrawl asked if he would be back in time for the ball. Missing festivals had become normal when he was twelve. This year's was the one that mattered, though. They had both come of age last year.

The knuckle of his thumb came away from his temple damp.

It's cutting it short, but we can still—

"What are you daydreaming about, boy?" The gruff voice abruptly cut Sonder out of his thoughts.

"Not daydreaming, sir. I was judging the time." A half-lie. The boyish flush of getting caught felt at odds with the new deepness in his voice.

Sonder's horse shifted away from the second animal. He berated himself. It was impossible to mistake the sound of their harnesses, yet somehow, he had tuned out the noise.

He had grown accustomed to Merrick's absence and had forgotten that the man had returned two days ago. Sonder composed himself before peeking at him.

"What time would you say it is?" The man met Sonder's gaze, and there was a twinkle in his eye.

"I'd say around three post meridians, sir," he answered correctly. Gauging the sun's position was like breathing.

"Very good. You've gotten a handle on telling time quickly." Merrick's eyebrow arched. He didn't buy Sonder's explanation. "It will become convenient whenever you've arrived for an assize. I'd work on your lying face more than time telling." His lopsided smile softened the reprimand.

Sonder gave one firm nod of understanding. "Yes, sir."

The two sat atop the hill together. Sonder gazed at the village, still some miles out. Theirs was a strong economy. The steady stream of people coming and going was evidence of that. It was rare to see so many willing to travel outside the safety of the walls, especially in a town tucked into the countryside, several days from any large city, and without a substantial royal presence. The Stellamar dragon flew above the manor, but the banners hanging from the ramparts were of local house militia. Few towns were so welcoming as to freely open their gates.

As he watched, movement in the fields caught his eye. A shadow undulated through the grass until it rammed up against the artery of packed dirt. A group of children burst free and streaked across the road in front of a laden cart. The dray-beast threw its head and reared. Sonder didn't need to be any closer to hear the curses the cart master spewed. The band of troublemakers took no heed.

He remembered games like theirs from before he was squired. The memories tugged at his lips while he watched the kids disappear into a sea of green.

"What is this town useful for?" Merrick asked.

Sonder was roughly drawn out of his thoughts, and he quickly fished for the answer. The truth was, he hadn't looked at the maps in several days. He couldn't be bothered to remember all the names of the villages they passed through or what local lord oversaw them. All he knew was that Merrick left when they were near Teul to see an old friend, so he pitched the first thing that came to mind. "They raise horses for our messengers?"

Merrick looked at him with his eyebrow cocked again. "Is that an answer or a question?"

Sonder sat up straighter. "It's an answer. They raise horses."

The look of disappointment made Sonder's heart sink, and he broke eye contact with his mentor. He had gotten the answer wrong and would have to endure extra lessons when they returned to Stellamar.

"You're right," Merrick said.

Sonder perked up, but the older man just watched the ebb and flow of peaceful life below them. There was a wistful look in Merrick's eye he had never seen before.

"Be careful about letting your uncertainty creep into your answers. Own them. You may only be fifteen, but few match your success." He met Sonder's eye with earnest. "There is nothing more dangerous than answering the queen with uncertainty. You must remember that. Be confident with your information. Always."

These instances of Merrick being candid were growing more frequent. After years of being guided by a firm hand, it was hard to reconcile this gentler side.

"What if I'm wrong?"

"Better to be wrong with confidence than show your ignorance. Seek the counsel of those you trust when you don't know. Or give the last information you know is true and how you're seeking the answer."

Sonder's chin dipped gravely.

Silence stretched between them as they watched the village a while longer. They were afforded so few moments to sit together in comradery rather than duty.

"Tell me, what led you to conclude that this was land for horse stock?" Merrick asked.

Sonder's eyebrows furrowed. "Well, part of it was remembering where we were on the maps three days ago." They never spoke of Merrick's absences, so he said nothing about what he surmised. "Based on that, I guessed. We've been skirting the region of the herds for a few weeks now."

"Good. Another way is to look at the land. Notice the crops." Merrick pointed at the fields the children had run through. "That's alfalfa. Not many can afford to dedicate so much land to feed crops. We subsidize their food so that they can produce the best horses." Merrick's tone took on a bright quality whenever he was teaching.

He was watching something in the distance, so Sonder looked too. "I hadn't thought of that," the boy said as his mind wandered off once more. The children were enveloped in the welcoming arms of a woman.

"In a way, you did. You just needed help putting the information together."

Sonder acknowledged him, then found his eyes drawn once more to the scene. The smallest was lifted to a hip while the others took off toward the gate.

It was rare to see children playing. His mentor's look made sense. It was the same look Sonder had caught as Merrick watched him play all those years ago. Before he had been taken to the castle and everything changed. The only thing he didn't understand was why it felt so sad.

A crimson mop of hair appeared over the crest of the hill. His shout cut their conversation short. "Merrick, the informant is here."

"Thank you, Áki." Merrick nodded a greeting that was returned. Then, he turned back to Sonder. "About time, if you asked me. I think you've got the lesson. Let's go tend to our guest," he said, nudging his horse forward.

Once Merrick had passed, a grin spread across Áki's face, and he winked at Sonder. Before Sonder could stop it, a shy smile spread across his own. Áki's grin broadened as he fell in beside him, and the two shared in the joke behind Merrick's back.

It was a short distance to camp. The other soldiers of their party fanned out in a circle. All were veterans who had fought with Áki. It made them a cohesive unit, vital for hunting Lorists and rebels. Only he and Merrick were outliers, yet none of the men seemed to mind.

Merrick had worked primarily alone until he formally took Sonder on as a squire. He still had little idea what Merrick had done before, even after listening to him and Áki talk. It was mostly because of the redhead's trust that the other men were loyal to Merrick.

Inside of the circle stood a man flanked by two of the knights. Sonder saw that the informant's hands were soft, and there was nominal sun damage on his skin. Those details, coupled with the expensive green dye of his clothes, marked him as a wealthy man.

Most striking about him, however, was his hair. His forehead was growing more prominent, and what hair remained he styled in an attempt to hide his baldness. It looked awful, and revealed him as a vain man who refused to accept that he wouldn't have a full hairline until the end of his days.

"Ah, hello, sir. I hope I didn't keep you waiting long," he said as their three joined the circle. The man's voice was high-pitched and soft. He nervously spun a thick gold ring around a pudgy finger.

Merrick dismounted and gave his reins to Sonder. He entered the circle, and the hand he offered was shaken enthusiastically. "We welcomed the rest."

Sonder could hear Merrick's forced smile. He never ignored reports, but he held little respect for people who turned their neighbors in.

The man resumed fiddling with his ring. "As I said in my letter, I'm a shop owner in town. Name's Cedric Hebert. I carry most everything, with a specialization in herbs. Lots of different sorts come into my store."

Merrick twirled his finger.

The man licked his lips. "Right. Sorry, sir. Your time is precious. I believe a husband and wife are harboring fugitives from her Royal Highness, the Lady Aspera." Men like him always said her name that way, as if layering it with reverence would gain them more favor.

"What proof have you?" Merrick's hand came to rest on the pommel of his sword. The implied message was clear: lies had no place here.

The speed of the ring increased with another round of lip moistening. "They've come from one of them cities, just two years ago. Been asking after extra foods. More'n the usual amount people ask for. We need to make sure our town's supplies stay strong. Tierrion has always been known for abundance, and even we've had to start rationing with the war."

"Those are hardly reasons to accuse them of conspiring against the crown. Maybe they've moved to build a family and are expecting child?"

"I doubt that," Cedric began to argue. Sonder didn't need to see Merrick's face to know the look he wore. The other man's flush was enough. "Sorry, let me explain, sir! It's enough food for at least another adult. There's more, though. They've been asking after ingredients none have really asked for since the queen outlawed certain practices. Ones that fell out of fashion when she abolished the College of Herbology." The more he referenced the law, the more self-righteous he sounded. "Old recipes used to cure certain diseases that only befall those who escape the Hunters." The man's voice dropped to a conspiring pitch, and his eyes swept the twelve of them as if they were friends.

An intrusive voice slipped through before he could suppress it. *We're the Hunters*, Sonder thought. He struggled to understand the queen's justice sometimes, and today the years of lessons failed to silence his misgivings.

"They have lots of odd folk come through. I think they's practicing and helping rebels by hiding them in their cellar," Cedric finished. The look on his face was greedy, not fearful.

Merrick drew in a thoughtful breath. "You claim they're Lorist rebels?"

"I do, sir," the man said without hesitation.

Merrick's body shifted. It was enough for them to investigate. "A bold claim. Assuming these visitors aren't just friends and family, what do you hope to achieve?"

The man fought to hide his smile. "Ah, nothing much. Mayhap an opportunity for my herbs to be inspected to supply the crown. Maybe even become an advisor to the herbologists or the queen herself."

Sonder snorted back a laugh. Then, just as quickly, he coughed into his hand as critical eyes turned on him. A tingle rose against his cheeks when he caught Merrick's scathing glare. He recomposed himself, but it was too late.

Cedric saw the exchange and became dejected. "Money is always welcome, if not," he sulked.

Merrick turned on his full charm to undo the damage. "I can bring your request to the court and see what can be done." He tilted his head kindly. "Is there any other information you can give us before investigating your claims?" Merrick had a way with these people. For someone who had no knack for magic, his ability was uncanny.

The reassurance reanimated the man. "Oh, I nearly forgot! I've looked in their window a few times, and I swear I see books there."

Merrick stood up straighter and turned his full attention on the man, which only encouraged him further.

"Horses are dying off, too. Symptoms are the same as thems odd ingredients, only used as a poison." The man lived for gossip, the way the words tumbled out of him.

Merrick made a rough motion with his head, and the two men flanking Cedric stepped closer. "That's enough." One of the knights grabbed the man's arm. "Say nothing of our coming. We will follow you shortly. Stand by their home, so we know which one. After the assizes, we'll discuss your reward."

"Oh, thank you, sirs! Thank you!" The man bounced along as he was led away, trying to turn back around. The skin on his cheeks and jowls wiggled as he continued to praise them all.

Once it grew quiet, Merrick brought his hand up to his head and rubbed his temple. "If he would have started with the books and the horses, he wouldn't have had to explain the rest of it." He sighed. "As if we care she's expecting a child."

"Do you think that's the reason?" Áki asked.

Merrick grew serious. "No, I don't. I'd bet they are harboring fugitives. But, without the right information, that's all it was. I don't have the authority to initiate an investigation without a warrant anymore. We would have had to wait another week to exchange ravens." Merrick walked back to his horse. Before pulling himself up, he paused and gazed down the hill where the village lay. "There's no end to people reporting their neighbors for nothing." Merrick looked up at Sonder. "They'll fill your ear with uselessness, hoping they'll receive extra."

Sonder nodded his affirmation.

Merrick hauled himself into the saddle. "Suit up. We're expected in Tierrion for the assizes by evening. Sonder, help them."

The men became a well-oiled flurry. Armor was removed from bags. The traveling guards wore simplified plate with the symbols of justice hammered into the breasts. It was lighter and easier to don, allowing them to hunt unimpeded.

Sonder's assistance wasn't required, but the men humored him. Most of his time was spent breaking down tents and repacking gear. It took only fifteen minutes to have everything cleared and the men remounted.

Merrick smiled approvingly at Sonder from the saddle. Unlike the rest of the men, neither he nor Merrick would get into their full armor. They were Black Knights. Their plate was akin to that of the cavalry, with many layers and buckles. Each piece was a velvety pool to be worn in battle or ceremony. Instead, they'd remain in their leathers, just as recognizable and reinforced with plate in case of an attack.

Merrick tapped his helmet as an indication for Sonder to put on his. As the metal surrounded his head, a birdsong whistle sounded, and they were in motion.

Citizens never knew the assizes were coming. It made their reactions genuine. Most people gave them a wide berth as they passed through the portcullis, while some were so overwhelmed they'd fall to their knees and uttered praise for Her Royal Highness. The most zealous would reach up, touch their feet, and brush their horses' sides.

As they rode through Tierrion's market, however, it was evident that word had proceeded them. Parents pulled their children closer, and women with baskets balanced on their hips bent their heads together.

As Sonder's eyes swept the crowd, he thought he spied the four children he'd seen earlier. Then, for a brief moment, his heart caught as he saw a grass crown, similar to the ones Rhianwyn made, sitting atop a little girl's head. She must have been no older than five.

Motion caught Sonder's eye as people broke away through the alleys. Remembering himself, he tapped out a signal on his metal jaw. Merrick whistled a different tune, and two men at the rear dismounted and began the pursuit. The children had unsettled him in a way he couldn't place. Now that he was refocused, he saw the oldest woman he had ever seen being led away by a girl barely older than him.

This town was like no other they had been to before.

They made their way toward the lord's stone manor, rising above the rest of the buildings. Merrick and Sonder both noticed Cedric mulling outside of a wattle and daub home as they drew near. It wasn't unique from the others, except it boasted a chimney, which meant an indoor kitchen. Once the man was sure they had seen, he quickly disappeared. Two more soldiers dismounted. As they kicked in the door, a shout came from the back.

They reached the manor, modest compared to anything in Stellamar, as the viceroy burst through the large wooden doors. "My lords! What an honor to have the assize come to Tierrion."

Their big black horses halted, and the remaining six soldiers stopped behind them. Twenty-four horses in total made a formidable sight packed into the tiny paved courtyard. Faces peered out from every window and corner.

Merrick offered no greeting in return. Instead, he considered the thin man below him.

A boy who looked to be about seventeen came hustling down the steps with his arms full of books. His red cloak marked him as a court hopeful. Sonder couldn't help but stare. A second boy no older than eight trailed behind, wearing the white robes of a page.

When they reached the viceroy, the older stole a glance up at Sonder and Merrick. His face flushed, and he quickly averted his eyes and thrust the books at the man. "Sire, the records for the justice to consider." He lowered his voice. "I believe these are the Black Knights the queen's raven sent word of last winter."

The viceroy looked alarmed. "Master Sonder," he breathed. The books made it awkward for him to dip to a knee. The boys similarly inclined their heads. "An honor." He wobbled as he stood up.

Sonder hated it just as much as in the first city—it only wore on him.

Merrick's horse shifted, and he sat straighter in the saddle. He pitched his voice so it would carry and the gathered could hear him. "Viceroy Rankin, were you aware you're harboring fugitives and known conspirators against Her Royal Highness?"

As if on cue, a bone-chilling wail cut through his words. Murmurs rose from the crowd—they looked sad.

The viceroy took a cloth from his pocket he dabbed at his upper lip. "I-I-I don't know what you are talking about, m-m'lord. I assure you that if there've been reports, we knew nothing of it."

"That remains to be seen. Are there not stable hands to tend to our horses?"

Rankin bobbled the books as he tried to do many things all at once. "Yes, of course." Finally, he shoved the precarious pile back at the attendant and hissed, "Take these!" He began to shoo the two boys away. "Go. Go! Get the rooms ready."

The boys collided, and some of the books toppled. The recognizable sound of sobbing materialized in the commotion. The older boy froze and looked up. The color drained from his face, and he gasped in unmistakable fright.

Sonder was the only one to look back. Blue-tinged armor shone in the aging sun as two Hunters emerged from an alley. One dragged a young woman. Her face was streaked with tears, and her hair tumbled from its tie and stuck to her bloodied cheek. The other knight followed, leading a boy just shy of his manyear.

The attendant must have felt Sonder's curious gaze because their eyes met briefly. Then, the boy turned beet red and fled, leaving the confused page to collect the fallen books.

Merrick spoke over the noise, "We require a place for the detainees. Have your advisors bring us their documents."

The viceroy tore his wide, glassy eyes away from the girl. "Yes, m'lord," he stammered.

The rest of the day consisted of scouring documents produced for review until dinner. The meal was a formality to show solidarity and compliance. It was a welcome relief from tallies and manifests.

It was uneasy, though. The tension with the viceroy was palpable. The echoes of additional prisoners from the courtyard also punctuated the meal. Each attempt to start a conversation physically hurt, and Sonder wished Áki or Drisil were there. But they weren't.

Áki had been sent to manage the arrests. Drisil usually traveled with them, but she had been called away for another matter. She typically tested the food for poisons. Since she wasn't there to do so, Merrick insisted all dishes be served communal style, divvied out on the spot by the servers.

Sonder kept his face composed by focusing on the meal of local specialties. Three different preparations of horse were offered, along with leafy greens and tufts of mushroom found only in this region. A light, flaky fish was served as a fillet and mixed into a spread to top the bread. By the time the creamy, fermented mare's milk blended with fruit came out for dessert, Sonder couldn't wait to return to the census reports.

It was near the turning of the torches when they found themselves bathed and winding down. As usual, Sonder bunked with Merrick. The older man slowly paced the room while Sonder watched, sitting on the couch with his legs tucked underneath him. A pitcher of warm wine sat atop the table, yet Merrick sipped tea scented with mint and lavender.

His demeanor had altered now that they were alone. Where before he had been somewhat playful during lessons, now he seemed on edge. Sonder knew of Merrick's constant dissatisfaction with their traveling work; it made the man irritable. The more they traveled, the less inclined he was to perform well—he became less thorough, relying more on Sonder.

"Have we covered everything?" Merrick's voice cut through Sonder's reverie.

"Yes, sir. The taxes, legal documents, and goods manifest checked out except those discrepancies."

Merrick nodded, looking out the window. "Áki will give us a prisoner report soon." He took a sip of tea and savored the liquid, letting out a restrained sigh. The torches in the street began to sputter. "Is there anything else?"

Sonder hesitated, causing Merrick to look at him. This was his least favorite part of their debriefings. The things he reported resulted in people being punished. It was more complex this time. The feel of this town was different—like the people were a community. Seeing the child with a flower crown had made him think of Rhianwyn and the garden. He had never reported anyone, and this somehow felt like breaking that promise. But it was his duty to uphold the queen's will.

"I haven't reported my observations."

"Ah, yes." There was a funny look on Merrick's face as he considered his empty cup. Sonder thought it looked like regret. "Go on."

Sonder faltered. "The older attendant. When he saw the girl, he got a funny look about him. I think he knows her." A sick feeling twisted suddenly in his stomach. Saying it out loud made it dawn on him. The look on the boy's face was the same look he'd seen on that man's face while he and his lover were taken into custody—the hopeless realization he couldn't protect those he loved.

"We'll look into it. I noticed Rankin had a similar reaction. White as cleaned sheep's wool." He sucked his mustache. "What does your gut say?"

Sonder's body flushed, and the question brought a brief image of touches shared in private. One of the many changes he had begun experiencing on this evolution of travels. "Well, I—" He took a deep breath to steady himself. "I think the attendant and the girl are intimately involved. The viceroy must know her, too. Maybe because of the boy. But that would be my initial line of investigation."

Why did he keep thinking about Rhianwyn?

Merrick rested his arms on the back of the armchair as he listened. It always made Sonder's stomach knot when his mentor considered him completely. For the briefest moment, the man seemed to be searching him for something. Then, there was that odd, sad smile again. "You've a keen eye for this. You'll be a good servant, I think."

Sonder wanted to ask Merrick about his choice of the word servant, but there was a knock at the door, and Áki slipped into the room.

The large man let out an exhausted sigh. "All the prisoners have been seen to. Both those detained by us and those already locked up."

"Good. There's a manifest for the accused. In the morning, we'll hold trials, then rulings. How go the investigations?"

"More difficult than usual, but we're managing. There aren't many people wanting to come forward."

Sonder stopped listening. He was spent as far as enduring lectures and formal reports went. So instead, he drifted back to the grass crown and the elderly woman. It was easy to reconcile the Lorists as enemies because he had never seen them before, and the criteria were vague. But the nagging thought from that morning kept coming. The wrongness of their presence shuddered through his mind.

If children still played and the people grew old, surely there was no need for the assizes.

"Thank you, Áki. It has been a long day." Merrick sighed, signaling the end of it.

Áki's shoulders slumped. "Has it ever," he groaned. Enthusiastically he poured a glass and plopped down next to Sonder on the couch. No one else drank the wine, and his eyebrows shot up. "Are you not drinking, Sonder?"

Sonder glanced at Merrick.

Áki followed the look. "Oh, come now. Just because he's gone sober doesn't mean you have to be." He poured an oversized portion and thrust it toward the boy.

Sonder watched the red liquid kiss the rim. Then, nervously, he looked at Merrick and saw the smirk playing at his lips while he poured more tea. "Go ahead." He sat in the armchair.

Sonder took a tentative sip. He could physically feel the flavor, and his mouth went instantly dry. In response, his nose wrinkled.

Áki chuckled into his glass. "Go on. The first sip is always hardest."

The second sip was a bit smoother, and Sonder's face no longer displayed his disgust.

Áki raised his glass. "See? I wouldn't lead you astray, lad."

Merrick smiled into his cup. "The boy earned that wine."

"Did he, now?" Áki leaned back and put his arm behind Sonder.

"He did. He helped us root out additional leads, and he may have uncovered a conspiracy within the viceroy's house." Merrick paused for effect, and Áki's eyebrows lifted as he took another sip. "I'd like you to investigate the relationship between the older attendant and the young woman. There's some intimate relationship there, and I doubt it was unknown she's a Lorist sympathizer."

Áki considered Sonder with a soft whistle and an admiring chin dip. Sonder felt embarrassed by the praise from both men, whom he admired equally. It made the uneasiness he had felt all day loosen.

Áki raised his glass. "Then let's toast. To Sonder's sharp eye and budding career."

Merrick inclined his head and raised his cup. "To Sonder."

They managed only a few hours of sleep. Sonder stifled his yawns as he shadowed Merrick. Rankin looked like a chicken, head constantly dipping as he toured the preparations. A dais and podium had been erected overnight, and the pillories still smelled of fresh wood. The man spewed a constant stream of amicable nonsense while three knights with their hands on their swords trailed them.

"If there's anything else we can do to assist you, please let us know. It's truly an honor to have the queen's assizes." Rankin bowed again. He was completely oblivious as Áki stepped up behind him.

"There is one more thing we wanted to discuss with you," Merrick said, finally addressing the man directly.

"Yes, my lord. Anything." Rankin turned his head and noticed Áki. He jumped and clutched his chest. "You gave me a fright, m'lord."

Merrick clasped his hands behind his back. "My second has some questions. If you'd accompany him."

"I don't know anything, really," he protested. Áki grabbed his upper arm and began to steer him away, followed by one of the other knights. The nearby servants winced as he continued to plead. Whatever work they were doing suddenly had them all hurrying away.

One tried to slip past them, but Merrick flagged her. "May we have some breakfast, please, miss?" His voice was genuine and warm.

The woman's regret was evident. She closed her eyes and steeled herself before turning with a forced smile. "Pardon, m'lord. The master said you'd dine with him, and he doesn't eat till later."

"Whatever is available now is fine. There's no need for a spread."

She began to wipe her hands on her apron like a nervous tick. "You're going to take him away, aren't you?"

"Excuse me?" Merrick asked.

She blinked back angry tears. "I've been tellin' the master this day'd come." She dropped her apron and stood taller. "He's a good man, you should know. Heart too big." She sniffled, considering Merrick as if he may change his mind if she spoke of a good man. "Just like the people in this town. He couldn't throw 'em out."

Merrick leaned closer, though it was not a threatening gesture. "Would you be willing to tell my second more about it?"

"Course I wouldn't. But I've no choice, do I?" She looked between them both with tears still brimming her eyes. "I'll see to your breakfast and then your second." She curtsied and excused herself.

The afternoon came, and the trials began. The proceedings always followed the same pattern: minor infractions first, and when the shadows lengthened, treason. Everyone was required to attend for the traitors. Only nosy neighbors made it an all-day affair.

Yet today, the quad was full of solemn faces from the start. As the local judge rattled off the neighbors' complaints, levied fines for tax evasions, and sentenced some to labor, the crowd stood by as if in solidarity. It was as if the presence of their black armor had cleansed the typical pettiness.

An orange tint on the horizon meant the purpose of their visit had come, and Merrick stood up. The judge bowed ceremoniously and stepped aside.

Four people who had warned of their arrival were brought forward. Next came the husband and wife initially reported by Cedric. A second family followed. And between them, three refugees with bounties on their heads. Last was the bowed head of the viceroy, flanked by the young woman who turned out to be his daughter and the attendant who loved her.

Merrick carried his helmet under his arm so his voice could be heard and his eyes seen. "Before you stand those accused of treason and conspiring against Her Majesty, Queen Aspera."

Sonder watched the crowd while Merrick spoke. The speech was always the same. He would reference the deaths of King Drynard and Queen Abril, and the ongoing war. Sonder mouthed the punishment as Merrick said it: *Death.*

A slab of maggot-infested meat sailed through the air and hit the viceroy in the jaw. The man wretched, but he had been denied food and drink. Rotten tomatoes followed, which splattered across his daughter's chest and at their feet.

A woman clawed to the front of the crowd and spat. "Evil witch!"

The girl's lip trembled, but she looked forward, maintaining her pride.

Sonder watched with his mind somewhere else. He had written Rhianwyn that morning, hoping he'd make it back in time for the ball. He kept his focus moving lazily across the crowd, relying on repetition to alert him if something happened.

The execution guards stepped forward at an indication from Merrick, and the familiar words droned in the back of his mind.

First, the spies. As their punishment was declared, Sonder mouthed it too: *Death by asphyxiation so that they may feel the hellfire of their wasted breath.*

As the four were led to the gallows, one began to shriek, promising to tell them whatever they wanted. The rope tightening around his neck cut off his shouts.

It was a gruesome way to go. It wasn't a clean hanging. They would be lifted and dropped however many times Merrick deemed necessary before they'd be hoisted and left for display. Basing it off Merrick's mood, Sonder guessed it would be quick.

Three times. Merrick was moving at a clipped pace, even for himself.

"Next, two families and the Lorist traitors they sheltered. Books banned by Her Majesty were also found in their basements. . ." Merrick's voice continued.

It was a never-ending task, rooting out the underground network of books and the transport of traitors. In the years of his tutelage, Sonder had witnessed the knowledge base shrinking. They had burned many libraries and hauled texts back for review. Anything that condemned the queen, or contained information about magic or schools of thought that were outlawed, would be destroyed.

They are a blight on our great civilization. They will be locked underground, given nothing but the water, which symbolizes the tears Queen Aspera has shed. Left to rot like the things they hid. . .

Queen Aspera was a sovereign of grace and kindness, who only ruled with a heavy hand when she had to. Sonder was an example of that. He was the son of the Black Daemon, given a position of honor to mend the betrayal of his family. This was necessary somehow.

Guards stepped forward to lead both families away. One of the wives held her head high and spat at Merrick's feet as she passed him. It got her a cuff to the back of the head. Sonder's breath caught when he saw the little girl with the crown shuffling behind her, head bowed. Sonder saw Merrick's eyes flicker. A subtle hand gesture and the child was pulled aside. She wailed for her mother.

It was odd watching the scuffle as the woman managed to fight through two guards, trying to reach her daughter before she was overcome and dragged into the prison's black jaws. Sonder felt numb to the screams. His eyes cast around the crowd, and he saw the old woman clutching her heart.

Sonder watched the little girl get led away, and he kept his mind from wondering about all the other children they had taken. He had never seen any of them again.

All that was left was the mayor and his kin. The sky was painted.

"Lastly, Viceroy Rankin has been sheltering his daughter, and her lover, despite knowing they were among those sowing rebellion. He created a haven for the Lorists."

There were hisses from the crowd, but most were misty-eyed. The mayor's head still hung, and his face was streaked with rotten blood.

"The punishment for his daughter is death by fire."

The girl suddenly tried to run, but one of the knights was too close, and he grabbed her roughly. The guards dragged her, kicking and fighting.

The young man struggled against his captors. "No!"

The gathering began to murmur.

Merrick continued, stone-faced. "She shall feel the flames of the war she fed." There was an odd draw to Merrick's voice now, as if he were far away.

The girl kicked out viciously as the guards struggled to tie her to the post. Her heel connected with one of their chests, but the man barely flinched.

"The punishment for the attendant is to watch his lover burn, so he may know the grief of those who have sacrificed their loved ones for this kingdom. Then he is to be beheaded. Rankin will watch, so he knows the pain his betrayal has caused. He shall bear the grief of those who suffered because of his weakness. He shall be crucified and left to rot, so all among us today will know what awaits them if they commit treason." Merrick's eyes swept the crowd, and they were brought to a hush.

Tar was smeared on the girl's arms and face. She sagged against her bonds when it was done, exhausted, weeping silently.

Sonder was forced back into himself when Áki offered him a torch. Sonder looked up at the man but couldn't make out his expression under the shadow of his helmet. He sought Merrick, who just nodded with an indecipherable stare.

The heat quickly soaked into his black gloves, and the flickering light danced on his black armor, making it look alive. His heart hammered as he approached the girl. A glance at the crowd revealed all eyes were watching him.

They were afraid of him.

He stopped in front of Merrick.

"It is time for you to begin the end of your training. This is your honor to be had." The hand Merrick laid on his shoulder wasn't a comfort.

Sonder regarded the girl. She wasn't much older than him. While he closed the distance, he considered for a moment that they may have played together in another life. This was the first time he was to carry out the law. The sword he wore had always been for show or practice.

As he stood there, with the fire close enough to warm her face, she lifted her head and fixed him with her hazel eyes. Their fierceness gave him pause until they grew afraid, as if she couldn't believe a boy would carry out her execution. Her brown hair tumbled into her face in a knotted mess.

Before his courage fled, he lifted his chin and threw the torch at her feet. He clenched his fists to hide the tremble. They held each other's gazes, and he watched as her face quivered and her defiance began to break.

The accusation was undeniable.

Then she shattered, and her mouth opened as a horrible shriek cut through their shared stillness.

He turned away, unable to bear it.

The attendant's keening mingled with the haunting sound. The boy strained against the guards, calling her name over and over. Rankin squeezed his eyes shut as his shoulders shuddered.

Sonder stood next to Merrick, feeling like a child seeking reassurance. His eye caught the servant from that morning. She wept silently, rolling a string of beads through her fingers in prayer.

"Now you're a killer."

Sonder looked up. Of all the things he wished to hear, that was the last. He felt panic rising as he searched his mentor's face. Merrick didn't look back, as if he were suddenly unworthy. The lack of acknowledgment, even a simple nod of approval, made it feel final. As if that was all he was meant to be.

Merrick remained aloof, looking toward something only he could see. "You'll behead the young man."

Finally, Merrick looked at him.

Those eyes spoke of a deeper meaning. It had been five years since he had been caught kissing Rhianwyn, and Merrick never stopped reminding him to remain focused. There was a reason Sonder had been able to decipher a look only in passing. It was the look of lovers. Merrick was making it doubly clear: there was no place for love in his life. It would be their death.

If he had been able to find these two out with a look, then someone who was watching could find him and Rhianwyn out just as quickly.

Sonder needed no more clarifying. He simply nodded his understanding to both things Merrick said. He was a killer and the queen's servant; there was nothing else. He looked away and clenched his jaw. He could almost recall how his cheek had burned when Merrick struck him all those years ago.

He could also remember how Merrick looked at Bran as he buried his sword in the man's gut.

Angry tears burned the back of his eyes as the last of the girl's screams finally choked off. Sonder drew his sword as he walked to the attendant. The young man was forced to his knees, and he looked up at him with bloodshot eyes and snot strung across his lips. It was similar to the girl's. How could a boy who no doubt had developed a young love himself do this? This was a man's work.

The boy pressed his eyes shut and began to cry again as Sonder grasped the sword with both hands.

If only their duties didn't trap them, maybe he could have run away with her—the boy and himself.

Sonder's blade cut through the boy's neck far more easily than he had expected. The substance of someone should have fought back harder. Blood splattered his face, some landing on his lips. If he didn't feel so suddenly hollow, he'd have recoiled. But he felt nothing, drawn into a place of safety inside himself.

The body crumpled, and Rankin let out a choked sob. He had fallen to his knees. Sonder looked at the man with a blackness he'd never felt.

It was the old idiot's fault this had happened.

Sonder wiped his blade on the man's shoulder. The viceroy whimpered and shrank from the touch. *Let it be known to him that his weakness did this*, Sonder thought. Then, two guards lifted the man just as the pool of blood reached his knees and dragged him away to be crucified.

Sonder released his aching jaw. He hadn't realized he'd been clenching it. He began to snap out of his rage. The blood rushing to his head felt full of air, and he brought a hand up to be sure it wasn't floating away. The sensation formed a sick pit in his stomach, one he had to swallow back, and his sense of balance faltered. The murmuring from the crowd sounded like a raging torrent. The scream of the mayor as his hands were nailed was too much.

This was the beginning of his end.

The swords had just been a test of strength. The lessons were just information to be endured. All of it had been marked by an airy sense of innocence. Sonder could pretend there was some semblance of freedom that lurked behind it. But now, he saw their faces instead.

If this was what he was supposed to be, then every nook and cranny of his mind that he held safe would be crammed with faces.

A tickle on his lips brought his gloved hand up. They were wet, but the black leather hid whatever it was. Fearing he was crying, because now he felt the unmistakable burn, he licked it away. The metallic, salty taste of blood seared his tongue. He must have looked like a monster, licking another person's blood from his lips.

Sonder looked to Merrick. Those blue eyes were locked on him but lacked the reassurance the boy's lungs were gasping for. Tears blurred his vision. Sonder couldn't place the look on Merrick's face, and just then, he didn't care to. He never again wanted to read into his mentor's moods. He sheathed his sword and walked back to their room.

If he was to be a killer for the queen, so be it.

Chapter Seventeen
Return

Middle district, fourteen years ago

Two men sat by the window of Nightingales Hollow, a seedy tavern straddling the borders of the lower and middle districts. It was notorious for under-the-table dealings where everyone turned a blind eye, so the two paid no mind to their surroundings as they gazed at the castle.

One leaned toward his companion. "That light is always on," he said. "Why'd'ya suppose that is?"

"Word is our little princess hasn't returned to her quarters since that Verndari incident a year back." His companion grinned.

The first man's mouth formed an O. "That so?" He looked back up at the lit spire with wide eyes.

"Aye. But I don't think that's true. Theys call it her Poisoner's Tower, and I'd bet whatever she's working on up there keeps her up. Her and that mage, doing Goddess knows what. Probably doesn't even have to sleep anymore with that magic of hers," his companion responded. Before he could say more, he let out a wheezing cough.

The first man seemed oblivious to his companion's distress as he scrutinized the black spire. "Where'd you hear all that?" The second man crumpled forward, and the first turned toward him. "Are you alr—"

Merrick stood there, hood drawn and a bloody dagger in his hand. The first fell out of his chair. "Please! No!"

Merrick wiped his blade on the second man as he drowned and twitched. "It's a crime to speak blasphemy about the queen. But not to listen. I'd remember that if I were you." He glared at the first. "Get out."

The man fled, shrieking as he stumbled through the door and into the night. Merrick's eyes swept the empty tavern before he left.

"Odd sense of justice, mate." Áki was leaning against the doorframe—the reason why the man had cried out.

"She gave me liberty to enact justice on her behalf. I'm fine with the bare minimum," Merrick growled as he shouldered past and began to walk through the empty streets to start the hallowed raids.

Return

Present, age fifteen

errick watched Sonder walk away. The smell of burnt hair still filled his nostrils, and he noted Sonder's boot prints leading away from the pool of blood. The sickness in the pit of his stomach threatened him once more. He gripped the fabric of his cloak, and he heard the crackle of crushed parchment.

There were far more distraught cries than jeers as he tried to steady himself. Then, with a sharp look, he met Áki's eye. Nothing else needed to be said. The hulking man followed the boy. Merrick felt exposed with both of them gone, but he had to stay.

The entire town stood watching him. In the blackness of his mood, Merrick scanned their faces. He saw a few people slipping into the alleys, but his ire homed in on the familiar hairline of Cedric near the front of the gathering. There was a grin playing across his soft mouth, and Merrick strode to the staging center. The presence of a High Justice commanded the conversations to cease.

"Her Majesty rejoices you brought attention to the traitors in your midst." He addressed Cedric directly. "You will be rewarded for your loyalty and service. May the gods' will be done."

It was satisfying to see the man turn the color of the girl's ashes as the people surrounding him stepped away. Merrick had done this enough to know the merchant would be shunned. The disgusted glares made him hopeful the serpent would disappear before someone was released to drop the gold into his hand.

Merrick stalked away. Closing speech be damned. He overheard one of his men whisper the same sentiment about Cedric, and he was glad to have the thought spoken into existence by someone else. *May the gods' will be done.*

His men would not report him for invoking them.

The process of appointing another viceroy would take several days. He would oversee it all, and it would be constant until everything was settled and the mantle passed.

Before he was halfway to his rooms, a flushed attendant came huffing from behind—already, it began. Before anything could be said, Merrick waved him off. It could wait until the smell of flesh and blood had been scrubbed away, at least.

Without pause, he pushed the doors open and was surprised to see Áki standing there—until he realized Sonder had also sought their room for solitude.

The two men shared a look filled with a torrent of unspoken words, understood through years of friendship. Merrick glimpsed the balcony and saw

Sonder staring at the dusky sky, rigid as stone. Áki stepped up and cut his vision off.

Merrick grasped the man's arm to steady himself. "Stay with him." He felt like he was falling.

Áki acknowledged his turmoil and squeezed his shoulder. "Take my room. I'll come to you later."

Gratitude welled up in Merrick. He dipped his chin and then let his gaze linger on Sonder's back before the door separated them.

That feeling remained while he sat in Áki's room, sipping tea. Without the man, everything would have fallen apart long ago. His good-humored seriousness kept Sonder from being crushed under the expectations laid on his shoulders and held Merrick back from the currents that threatened to drag him away.

Merrick was deep in thought, rolling a crumpled parchment in his fingers. He didn't look up from the fire when Áki finally came, only listened to the door close softly and the sound of approaching boots.

"The look you gave me earlier, I was afraid I'd find you deep in your cups tonight," Áki said, only half teasing.

"By the amount I've pissed from this tea, I may as well have." Merrick sighed. "I've spent nearly every minute trying to convince myself one would be enough. Days like these, nothing quenches that thirst." He finished the last of his cup. "But one is never enough."

Áki stood over him and offered him a brimming mug. "I know."

The smell of cloves and cinnamon wafted off the steaming liquid, and Merrick took it tentatively.

The other man sat down heavily beside him. "I figured some warmed cider would help take some of the edge off better than that flavored water."

Merrick huffed a laugh, then took a small sip. The combination of company and flavor did help ease the itch. Then, with another heavy sigh, Merrick laid his head on the back of the sofa and searched the ceiling. "You know me too well. How's the boy?"

Áki sat facing Merrick with his arm draped over the back of the couch. "Not talking. I don't think he will for a while. It was unkind to call him a killer. That's the last thing he needed to hear."

Merrick's expression twisted. He lifted his hand from his knee and offered the crumpled parchment still between his fingers. Tears began to burn the bridge of his nose, and he pushed them back.

"The queen asked for it all," Merrick said when Áki finished reading it. "She wants his training stepped up. It's never enough for her. I don't know how much more I can push the boy and not lose my mind." The words came spilling out of him, and Áki listened. "I swear he gets a look every time I toe the line. Like he can see right through me. What I wouldn't give to confess everything to him. Tell him he's right. That I only do this to protect him." The thoughts kept coming, and Merrick swallowed the tears. "Tell him he's more than a killer."

Áki balled the note up more and rolled it between his own fingers. "No, I suppose you can't."

Merrick just held the pewter in his lap, letting the warmth seep into his hands. "He wrote to Rhianwyn this morning. I don't know how to get it through to him that there's no place for love in his life. It'll be nothing but trouble for him."

"You say that because you are too busy holding everyone at a distance, thinking you're protecting us," Áki said. "Relinquish some control already. They both know the dangers. You've seen to that." With the last sentence, he emphasized the remembrances of Merrick's heavy hand.

Merrick looked at him. The directness didn't make him angry. A crushing sadness settled in his chest instead, and a soft breeze blew through his memories, stirring the sands that buried them. Merrick brought his hand up to Áki's face as if he were waking from a dream and seeing him for the first time in years. Áki didn't flinch from the rasp of Merrick's thumb on his beard nor shy away from the way Merrick's eyes searched his. "I forget."

"That's why I am here. You aren't doing this alone," Áki spoke softly.

"What if I fail? What if I destroy the boy?" Merrick let his hand fall and looked back at the painted ceiling. "I'm unworthy of protecting his innocence."

"Bran didn't think so. Perhaps you say that because you think yourself unworthy of the loyalty those have for you? But he asked me to look after you so you wouldn't forget. You have Drisil and me." Áki looked down and shrugged. "We trust you."

"To what end? What kind of life are we living, hoping the boy will have a fruitful life? For him, that means serving the queen. What life is that?" Merrick grabbed his hair and hid his face behind his arm. "She takes everything and leaves nothing."

Áki reached across the space between them and squeezed his knee hard. "That's why he needs the girl, and Tran, and friends. We're going to stop traveling so much. Let him have the space to nurture those personal alliances. We are two old men, far removed from the turmoil of coming of age. Let Rhianwyn help him through this." Áki took the untouched cider from his hand and took a deep drink.

"Neither one of them can afford to fail in their studies. They have a duty to—"

Áki cut him off. "Rhianwyn is focused. She helps the boy more with his studies than I think you give her credit for." His brow furrowed as what Merrick said finally dawned. He looked confused. "I thought the goal was to stop her from getting her claws into him?" When Merrick didn't answer, Áki sighed and offered the mug back to him. "Drink already. Relax. There is no harm in laughter and joy. That's the easiest way to keep her darkness at bay."

Merrick gave him a side-eyed look but obliged. It helped, warming his chest and spreading to the muscles in his neck and back. He released a breath, letting the feeling continue to build. Looking into the honey-colored liquid, Merrick's brow darkened again. "She always finds out."

"She isn't all-powerful, Merrick. You know that. Her sights are set on her books, and her Spiders whisper in her ear. So keep focusing on building the good people around him. He's a good kid." Áki retook his shoulder and shook him gently, the cider precariously close to sloshing over. "You're a likable guy. If anyone can do it, it's you."

"That's assuming I'm not the reason she finds out," he whispered, his face growing distant. A memory from earlier came back. It had played over and over in his mind while he sat waiting. Their talk of Sonder had pushed it to the forefront again.

"That woman who spat at me earlier? The one rotting in prison right now?"

"Aye, I remember," Áki said slowly, as if reluctant to see where this was going.

"She called me a traitor." He looked at Áki and saw the man had grown grave, which was a rare sight. "She knew my name. Yet I have no idea who she was."

"Grace?" Merrick nodded, and Áki's disapproval grew. "She doesn't know who you really are, does she?"

Merrick shook his head. "I wonder what she'd think of me if she did know the truth."

Áki drew in a long breath, then let it out with his words. "It's not an easy task, what you do. You risk too much already whenever you go to see the woman. It's impossible to save them all. It's important to protect yourself, too."

"I can't take her daughter to Aspera." Merrick remembered her running through the fields just yesterday, how little fear she'd had as she watched them ride by, a flower crown atop her head. "Aspera mocks me by making me continue to bring her children. They get swallowed up and never seen again. The girl's mother may die cursing my name. Let the girl hate me as well. But I will not do it. Not this one." Merrick didn't know why he had to blink back tears suddenly. There was a dull headache building. "Is there somewhere to take her?"

Merrick didn't know he wore the look of determination that meant he would challenge death in a staring contest.

Áki's breaths deepened. "You're a fool, my friend. But that is why I love you. I will look into it." He reached for the cider once more and finished it. "Stay with me here. Let the boy have his space."

Three days of endless meetings ensued. Merrick sat with the town officials in constant discussions punctuated by Áki's appearance at his elbow with updates from outside his confines.

A new viceroy needed appointing, the local justices needed rebellion-suppression tactics, the spy network needed to be revamped, and an emergency plan established. It was an arduous task. Sonder was a silent shadow the entire time with a faraway look.

Merrick was well aware the process wore on the boy differently by his permanent scowl and how his hand rarely left the pommel of his sword. Merrick knew the desire to turn on mewling idiots, but each time he talked another person into submission, he braced for the blade to be drawn.

Merrick lamented to Áki about the greedy, power-hungry mongrels snapping at morsels of favor during a moment of quiet.

"It's nearly over, sir," Áki said with a grin hidden beneath the surface of formality.

"Any updates on the other people Sonder noticed?"

The boy stirred at the mention of his name.

"They're still being watched. Hopefully, they'll lead us to others. The local guard is aware of them, and another group of Hunters should be here tomorrow to take over."

"They won't get away?" Merrick asked.

"No, sir."

"Thank you." Holding his thoughts together was like grasping mist. Sleeping huddled on Áki's couch had given him a crick in his neck that made his head throb. "Let's review everything after dinner. We'll be available to the officials then." Merrick sighed. "I need another pair of eyes. Everything must be in order." His callused hand rasped against his cheek.

Áki's smile broke through. "I can do that, sir."

"Tell the men to be ready to ride tomorrow."

The other man bowed. "Yes, Sir Merrick." As he passed Sonder on his way out, he squeezed the boy's shoulder. It was the first time Merrick saw an inkling of Sonder's face softening. The redhead glanced at Merrick with a cocky smile.

I'd be lost without that bastard, he thought.

The sun rose the next day, and everyone was eager to go. Even the horses had grown restless. Their provisions overflowed despite the finest inns always being open to their needs. There would be no wanting for the month-long journey to Stellamar.

The path home would not be the most direct, however. That morning, Merrick had received orders to check in on towns along the way. The news didn't dampen anyone's mood, though, because it still meant home.

"Thank you again, my lord. Her Majesty has high hopes for your service." Merrick offered the honeyed words to the new viceroy.

Sweat beaded down the man's face, and his eyes continually shifted toward his daughter. She was being helped onto her horse. "Of course, Lord Merrick—"

"I am no lord," Merrick said with a tight smile. "Just a knight."

"Of course, sir. Her Majesty's will be done. But"—he glanced at his daughter once more—"is there no way my daughter can remain here, with my wife and I? Two of our three sons have died in the war. Have we not proven our loyalty?"

His wife clung to his arm and squeezed tighter. They were calm, though there was no hiding how worn they were.

"Your daughter will be well cared for, Lord Adolar. I'll see to it personally." Merrick didn't miss the flicker of misgivings. "The queen demands a child be taken as collateral in these situations. Where one town official commits treason, more follow."

"Our son still serves in the army," the lady said, her knuckles nearly white. "She's my only girl."

Merrick let them argue in hushed tones. If it had been any other justice, the husband would have been right in reprimanding her. The slightest defiance could be seen as treason in the wrong eyes. Some wouldn't hesitate to take mother and daughter. Perhaps that was what she hoped for in speaking up.

Merrick no longer had the energy to maintain his performance. "I admire your fire, my lady, and you have given much to the crown. But stay here with your husband. I will put in a petition so your daughter's stay may be short. I can promise nothing, but take it as consolation."

She stood up taller despite her tears. "Thank you, sir," she whispered.

They all bowed, then Merrick turned to join his men, who were already mounted and ready.

A crowd had gathered, but he spared no other glance. The noise they brought overwhelmed Merrick's senses. The spectacle was more manageable sometimes, but his reserves had been tapped days before.

He saw the same elderly woman Sonder had seen among the assembled, and he got swept away in the stories those wrinkles must hold.

Áki walked up to him and touched his elbow. "What's wrong?"

Merrick had frozen beside his horse. He blinked, then leaned in to keep his voice low so that no one would hear. "What do we know of the Lorists here?"

Áki straightened. "What do you mean to do?"

"Leave them to continue. They had no idea what Aspera was capable of. Now they do. I know not a damn one of us feels right tearing this town apart, whatever their reasons."

"The men are loyal. But I don't see what we can do."

Merrick leaned closer. "Leave one of our men behind. Have him set up a way for those in power to contact me directly, then ride hard to catch up. I'll find a way to get their daughter back so they know my word is good. Get Justices who are sympathizers here. Regardless of what stories they tell, gods they pray to, or magic they practice, hardly a soul wanted to see the brutality of what we did here. Even if all we accomplish is for them never to see the black ride through again, that's enough." He swallowed hard, then stepped back. "Tell whoever stays it's just a seed." Merrick looked out at the many faces still watching them. "Maybe we can create a place at peace."

The chiming of a harness cut through the commotion. Sonder was riding fast, throwing caution to the wind to get away.

He is too much like me, Merrick thought. Defiant and angry. He feared what would happen if the queen snuffed out the kindness before it could truly take hold. Merrick ordered the ride while Áki moved to do as he asked.

The crucified mayor pleaded for water as they rode through the gates. He had no idea that he was begging those responsible for his position by his looks. One of Sonder's hands dropped to finger the fletching of an arrow. It was evident he was tense with rage.

Merrick counted his breaths and waited for what he would do. He let himself be satisfied only when they were out of the boy's range. He and Áki rode behind Sonder for many miles, giving him the needed space.

The queen's herds grazed near the fences, their well-shaped heads perking up as they rode past. Off a ways, a small river flowed with lush trees marking its banks. It was a beautiful country. The untouched quality was hard to find near the kingdom's center and closer to Aspera's influence.

The morning air was heavy with cool moisture and low clouds obscuring the mountain tops, promising to hold the sun at bay and keep it from beating down on their black leathers. The beauty worked on Sonder's mood while Merrick gradually urged his horse closer.

There was a rebellious set to the boy's shoulders, but Sonder's mind was almost audible as it turned. He was ignoring Merrick, and the man wondered if he did so by imagining his horse had six legs.

There was a switch in his posture, and Merrick urged his animal to close the distance.

After three days of tense silence, it was nothing to ride beside him for a while. Sonder wasn't going to say anything, which left Merrick to start the conversation. But, after several restless nights thinking about it, Merrick still didn't know what to say.

The most straightforward approach was the only clear thought he had. "The first one is the hardest."

"How is it so easy for you?" It sounded like an accusation.

Merrick kept his eyes on the road. "What makes you think it's easy for me?"

Ever thoughtful, Sonder remained silent. They continued to ride together, which told Merrick he had been right—the boy no longer wanted to be alone. If he just waited, Sonder would confide in him.

He is nearly a man, Merrick realized as he took this time to really look at him. Little softness remained in that face.

"I wanted to kill him." Sonder's jaw was clenched again, and his body radiated anger. "They died because of his stupid selfishness. But putting an arrow through his heart would have been too great a kindness for what he deserves." His voice dropped so that Merrick had to strain to hear him, "I wanted to kill them all for gawking." Sonder looked at him. "Am I a monster, Merrick, like my father?" His look seemed to ask, *Like you*?

The humanity Sonder held on to was admirable, even if the monster the queen wished for glimmered beneath the surface. Merrick paused to consider his response.

Raising the boy under the queen's watchful eye had proven more difficult than expected. Now that their time was drawing near the end, he wanted to be candid. He knew, however, how much was at stake. Every night, he agonized over the position with Áki.

With a steadying sigh, he began to speak. "It's true you've been raised to be a warrior. War makes even the best men do ugly things." He looked at Sonder, who was still angry. "I didn't know your father. That was part of the reason Aspera let me mentor you. I believe you'll find a way to be a better man than him, and a better man than me." He nurtured the child who so desperately needed reassurance for a brief moment, but the queen's pull made his voice grow stern again. "I have to make you a soldier. If I teach you to be a killer, you may live long enough to be that man."

Sonder's mouth tightened.

The road gradually calmed him back down, and by that evening, he was using more than two words at a time.

A blue raven waited for them at their second stop. The city garrison handed the letter to Merrick, who broke the wax seal. It was the confirmation that he'd known was coming. They would stay in Stellamar upon their return, and Sonder was expected to prepare adequately for advanced training while they traveled.

He and Áki began running the boy through drills every night. Sonder had always picked up weapon-craft quickly. One night, Áki ran him through a complicated routine. The weapons' cries haunted Merrick as he watched. He wondered what would befall them if Aspera deemed the returns unworthy despite being trained by two of her best warriors.

The way Sonder swung his blade, there was no doubt the boy had felt that pressure long ago and taken it upon himself to be exceptional.

Each town offered provisions and fresh mounts that they didn't need. Merrick silently handed the surplus out to the beggars when they reached the cities. If an assize was requested, they deferred to the local officials to send requests to Stellamar. The boy should have been excited that they were making a straight line to the city, but somehow, he withdrew into himself further.

Only once did Merrick tarry.

It was a chilly day. The halfway point had been crossed, so the mood was light. One man was telling an animated story until the rear guard shouted a command to halt. The laughter immediately died.

Despite the warning, the woman continued to stumble through the waist-tall grass toward them.

The knight nocked an arrow. "I said halt!"

Still, she came, and the man drew back.

The grass parted, and she became fully visible, stained with dirt and dried blood. She stopped in the middle of the road, filthy hands clutching her abdomen.

"Please." The strength required to get her voice to carry visibly pained her.

The drawn arrow trembled by the guard's cheek.

"Stop," Merrick commanded.

He was dismounted, waving the men off who moved to follow without a thought. It was clear the woman was ravaged by fever and near death. He reached her just in time to catch her as she collapsed. Carefully, he eased her to the ground despite the smell of infection permeating her body.

Cradling her head, he offered a drink from his waterskin. The relief eased her twisted face.

"What happened?"

He had to hold his ear close to her lips to listen.

The men stood by faithfully, scanning the stands of trees and deserted road. They turned a blind eye to him, as was their way. It was a small grace they allowed.

When she finished, he took her hand in his and said Phyrias's prayer of guidance and reunion.

A tear rolled down her cheek. "My ma said those words over my nana when she died," she whispered. "They killed her for treason."

Merrick had known by her accent that she would recognize the words and find comfort in the Lorist death rite. Aspera had outlawed it after Dagda's college fell.

"Please," she rasped, "let Phyrias come for me."

His dagger found her heart with quick, uncanny accuracy. Merrick left her body curled up on the side of the road, her hand draped over her belly. He couldn't afford the time for a proper send-off.

The men watched as he walked back to his horse without belying anything.

"We ride to Aninarok."

Some of the men shifted uncomfortably. It was out of their way. By the time they arrived, it would be early evening. But, as with any of Merrick's odd requests, they obeyed. Áki shadowed him silently, and no one asked any questions.

Aninarok was a small city nestled near the skirt of the Mother's Range. The ore-rich hills made it a hub for both jewels and weapons, and the wool from the mountain sheep was warm.

The city garrison met them as they rode through the gates. Some of the finest warriors were raised here, and the ones who chose to serve their home regarded them now as Merrick walked straight into their midst.

"Áki, with me," Merrick commanded as he dismounted. "Who is in charge here?" Merrick called out.

A man grinning from ear to ear sauntered toward them. "That would be me. To what do we owe this pleasure? We had no word to expect a High Justice."

The officer extended a hand to Merrick but instead found a sword buried halfway to the hilt in his stomach. It was such a sudden, brutal gesture that everyone was dumbstruck for two beats while Merrick snarled in the man's face.

The stationed garrison readied their weapons all at once while the men left on their horses drew theirs. Áki took guard at his back while pole axes bristled around them. Merrick admired his men's reactions. It had been unkind to lead them into the city without mentioning what he planned, but they were fearless in the face of many times their number.

Merrick reclaimed his sword with a savage twist. Splatters of blood disappeared into his black leathers. "Stand down!" he barked. "Who is second here?" His blue eyes blazed as they swept everyone there.

A nondescript man lifted his hand for his men to hold. He returned Merrick's anger with scrutiny. "That would be me."

Merrick stuffed his free hand into his breast pocket as he began to walk toward him. The clatter of weapons should have frightened him. Black could only buy him so much. A woman stood between them, and he smelled the familiar twinge of war magic.

Bran. The memory nearly made him stumble, but he steadied himself.

Merrick pulled out a document bearing the queen's seal. The second touched the woman's shoulder, and she lowered her weapon. The man read the words scrawled across the page, which stated that Merrick could enact the law as he saw fit.

"This document doesn't give you the liberty to remove a standing officer without cause."

Áki inhaled sharply.

Merrick said nothing, putting all of his trust in his way with people instead, and let the loyalty of the small band at his command speak for him.

There was a tense moment where everything hung on what the man would decide. Then, finally, he raised his voice. "Stand down." The man was no idiot.

"What is your name?" Merrick asked.

"Sir Mathis Camden. I was lieutenant for Captain Urian Anistian."

"You are the commanding officer now," Merrick said. His eye was briefly drawn to the bastion as a woman lowered her crossbow.

"What is the reason for this, sir?" the man asked, handing the paperwork back.

"Some information that was brought to light warranted swift justice," Merrick said.

"Is there a risk of further investigation?"

"No. If you have any problems, you can send word to me in Stellamar." He looked around at the silent faces around him. "I don't suspect you'll have any issues."

The man sheathed his sword, and the rest followed suit. "No, sir, there should be no issues here."

With a curt nod, Merrick turned. Áki continued to watch his back and ensure no one made moves to avenge the dead man in the bloodied mud. Then, wordlessly, Merrick returned to the saddle and led them from the city.

Sonder, Áki, and Merrick rode silently together for a while. Eventually, Áki broke the tense stillness.

"Why?"

"The girl told me the commander promised her a future to bed her. When she told him she was with child, he invited her to travel with him to Cethre to meet his family. Instead, he forced a miscarriage and left her where we found her." He raised a hand to cut off Áki's argument. "I acted alone in this. What was not seen is unknown. Remind the men. I'll think of an explanation if Aspera asks." Merrick looked at the Lorist girl from Tierrion. "It's time you got her to safety. Take her to Teul."

Áki nodded grimly. "Steady home," he said, peeling off to do as asked.

Merrick met Sonder's gaze for a moment, and the look of admiration returned to the boy's face as they rode well into the night.

Chapter Eighteen
Spinning Silk

Middle-city square, ten months ago

Rhianwyn kept the hood of her cape tugged down to hide the side of her face. "She named him at the ceremony," she hissed. She had sent a jay the very night after she had left Sonder. "The court is in an uproar that she has taken him on. 'Cannot trust traitor's blood,' they're saying. Worse, she's doing blood magic. The wound was hideous, Mae. She's—" Rhianwyn's voice caught.

Maeveen's hand slipped through their cloaks and squeezed Rhianwyn's. "Hush, little."

Rhianwyn took a steadying breath. It wasn't the fact that other members of the court were talking. She had already decided how to handle that. It was the blood magic that sent a chill through her. She was terrified for Sonder and what was next for him. He had left the next day with little time to say goodbye. It was enough to make her heart ache and feel close to shattering.

"I'll tell Mother Eissie what you've told me. About the magic. She'll hopefully know what it means." Maeveen's words were hard to hear over a crackle of small fire-bursts rattling on the cobbles. The crowd gathered to watch the performers exclaimed in delight.

Rhianwyn pressed on, needing to speak her fears so they wouldn't overwhelm her. "He keeps secrets. It's harder to get him to talk."

"What is he hiding?"

"The lessons he learns about his family and what happens at the magic tests." A fleeting hope swelled in her heart. "Can we get him away from this?"

Mae's hand tightened. "Maybe. But, even before Mama was caught, we had to keep to the shadows. Now we can't afford Aspera's wrath outright."

Before Maeveen could go on, Rhianwyn sighed. "That's why you've asked me to spy," she whispered. She had grown to be great at it. "I already have a plan for the nobles. Just promise you won't give up on him." Rhianwyn's hazel eyes were imploring.

"You're the only one who can make that decision."

Spinning Silk

Present, age sixteen

The summer was sweltering. Rhianwyn kept her windows thrown open to the sea breeze. Her room was on the ground level of the castle, so the curtain walls and towers shredded it to a measly thing, but it helped cool her skin.

Since the ceremony, she'd been kept busy between her continued studies and her apprenticeship with the Healers Guild. Gwenyvir often took her into the city, where she trailed her mentor's skirts during house calls. She was well-liked amongst the nobles, but now she had become a household name.

It was challenging to maintain all of her obligations.

She pulled a soft linen dress dyed pink by fruit pits over her kirtle. From the corner of her eye, she could see the little orange breast in the branches outside her window. She had no answers to offer, and she dreaded the ones that await-ed her.

Mistress Olive knocked on the doorjamb. "Lady Rhianwyn, Mistress Gwenyvir is expecting you."

"Thank you, Olive." Rhianwyn tore her eyes away from her exhausted like-ness. She donned her smile as she threw a light-blue scarf over her hair. "How do I look?"

"Like a lady going to market," Olive said.

"Then let a new day begin," she said with more cheer than she felt.

The stalls were full of summer fruits. It was a good year for foreign ven-dors, too. Housekeepers lined up and shouted over each other to make offers on the rolls of silk. The festival season was quickly approaching, and seamsters sat under their awnings as they worked to entice new patrons.

Rhianwyn's heart pined as she wove her way through the bustle. She had spent years looking forward to this Equinox. The sights of the season were supposed to be joyous.

A familiar sign swaying on its rusting chains came into view. A delicate flower and mushroom were painted on the wood. Mulling across the street was a woman wearing a cloak the color of the forest. Their paths came together as the warbler flew off overhead.

"Good morning, lady," Maeveen said politely.

"Mind if I look as well?" Rhianwyn smiled.

Under her cloak, Maeveen wore a simple dress similarly woven with the magical thread. It was wrapped around her legs and belted for easy movement. Her curtsy was sloppy like a commoner's, even though Rhianwyn knew she could blend in with nobles, too.

"Did you see the spinners up the way?" Maeveen asked in code for spies.

"No, I didn't. What wears are they?" Rhianwyn asked.

Maeveen's voice dropped. "I've heard no word of their silks."

So there still was nothing from Mother Eissie about the blood magic or getting Sonder away.

Rhianwyn slid in beside her sister and fingered a bolt of linen. "Mae, I'm worried about him," she whispered. It was an endlessly complicated dance they wove, pretending to browse as if their spare coin would tell them what to buy. They were outside Gwenyvir's shop, a small project permitted by Aspera.

"Why?" Maeveen asked, standing by as if waiting for Rhianwyn to finish so she could look as well.

Rhianwyn clutched her scarf tighter, then turned so her sister could stand closer. She examined a bundle of dried herbs hanging from a beam. "His letters have stopped. He always writes."

"Silence still speaks." They could only stand together like this for so long. Maeveen didn't need to say what came next: *What does his say?*

"She's winning." *He believes what the queen says*. Sonder needed her, but if Sonder fell too deeply into Aspera's ploy, he could become a monster. If only she could—

"You can't tell him."

They had argued about this before—or discussed to be more accurate, because Rhianwyn trusted Maeveen and never pushed back.

The rattle of a patrol echoed down the street, and Rhianwyn looked toward the sound. She saw Maeveen tug her scarf tighter to hide her hair before grabbing a canister of crushed herbs and placing it into her basket.

"I still have faith," Rhianwyn said quickly. *I still believe he is good.*

"What about your endeavor? Have you found anything out about the noble families denouncing him?"

"Not yet, but I'm cultivating it." The guards grew closer, and she dropped the subject entirely. "I hear jays like peanuts. I saw a vendor a few lanes over that had some."

Maeveen dipped her head and dropped a few coins into a jar for the items in her basket. "Thank you, lady."

Her sister's cloak faded into the crowd, and the guards passed without looking in their direction. As the sound of their metal boots receded, Rhianwyn let out a sigh of relief. That was too close.

There were no posters of Maeveen hung on the notice boards, but a glimpse could spur interest. Questions were too great a risk.

To steady the hammer of her heart, she continued to examine the other wares on display. The linen was imbued with calendula flowers to stave off infections. The magic thrummed beneath her touch because she had made it.

She had asked Maeveen to get them out of Sosten, yet this was her home. Every month that passed, she became more firmly rooted.

When she felt ready, she turned and pushed the door open to Gwenyvir's shop. The smell of herbs and earth filled her lungs, cleansing her remaining tension.

Her mentor's poof of gray hair rose from her notes. "Ah, there you are. I have no work today. A member asked me to transcribe her notes."

"I can help," Rhianwyn offered.

Mistress Gwenyvir waved her off. "Nonsense. Take the supplies to the castle, and then the day is yours." She straightened and hobbled to a package wrapped in cloth. "Mum is the word. I'll tell no one."

Rhianwyn held her arms out, and her mentor set a basket and piled goods into it.

"What am I supposed to do with a whole day?" she complained, even though she was tired.

"Knowing you, you'll sort these, then the whole hospital." Gwenyvir placed her hands on her wide hips. "If you must find something, see if Master Wilkin needs help. Or, just enjoy the markets." She wore a kind smile.

"I'll see to it, Mistress Gwen." Rhianwyn had surpassed the woman in height two years ago.

"Good girl. Go on, then. Tomorrow we'll visit the master healer from Cethre. He's come asking the guild for help with the disease plaguing their crops. I'll need your keen eye."

Rhianwyn nodded, then turned to leave. She was thrilled at the idea of the work. She had already set herself on investigating the blighted crops. A servant had mentioned overhearing Cethre's lords bringing the issue to court. Further rumors revealed that the estates suffering the worst had fallen from favor. While not directly linked to the questions posed by the Lorists, it felt relevant. It mattered.

She cared for the kingdom as much as her people. Maeveen warned that her position was at risk of being compromised, but she wouldn't abandon Sosten. Not while she had hope.

These thoughts carried her through the people mulling around the goods on display. Their faces blurred into the mosaic of Stellamar she so loved. She wasn't prepared for the searing fear that bolted through her when her arm was seized. Filled with traitorous thoughts, she feared the guards were detaining her.

Rhianwyn nearly dropped the basket as she whirled around.

"Mikhail," she gasped. "You shouldn't sneak up on girls in the market!"

"I called your name several times," he said. His face was apologetic, and he let his hand fall away from her elbow.

She hadn't heard. "You did?"

"Let me help you with that." He indicated the neatly wrapped supplies in her arms.

She began to protest, but with a crooked smile, he took it anyway. The weight lifted, and she became acutely aware of the ache suffusing her arms and hands.

"I insist," he said warmly. "So long as you don't mind my company along the way. Where are you taking these?"

"To the main hospital," Rhianwyn said, grateful.

"Let's be on our way, then." He held the basket against his side and offered his elbow. With a shy smile, she placed her hand on his arm.

Rhianwyn had always held Mikhail at a sociable distance. She knew the older boy disliked Sonder for his position as Merrick's squire. And when the queen had revealed that Sonder was Lucrid's son, Mikhail had mirrored his father's disdain.

Lord Vardulf was known for opposing the old order of Black Knights. He was vehement about soldiers never holding such power again. It had taken some digging, but King Drynard had stripped the Vardulf estate at the guidance of the Auza-Verndari. The second Aspera had asked for assistance against the Baramore-Uland's, he had been the first to send his men.

Now, Mikhail's father had turned his campaign on Sonder. She knew her friend didn't need to see the court's quarreling to know the scrutiny on his back.

"I hear Sir Merrick and his men have been called back," Mikhail said with a guarded tone.

"Have they?" she asked with a veil over her excitement.

He grunted, and she looked at him. The boy's dark curls obscured his face, but Rhianwyn could see his frustration in his clenched jaw.

Unperturbed, she plowed ahead. "Was it said when?"

His eyebrow arched as he turned his bright hazel eyes on her. "Does anyone hold the head Justice accountable to time?" He looked away. "How can you still look forward to his return?"

She knew he was speaking of Sonder now. "He's my friend," she said smoothly, dancing with his criticism.

"He's traitor's spawn," Mikhail said incredulously.

The words that had whispered through the court since the ceremony. Although they hurt, she held her head high. "Are you saying we're all doomed to repeat the mistakes of our parents?"

"Perhaps." His jaw jutted stubbornly.

"I don't know my parents. What of me?"

Rhianwyn met his eye with a defiant smile playing on her lips. She hoped that Mikhail was not like his father—that he could be swayed. But, at the very least, she was nudging into the confidence of nobles circling like vultures, waiting for Sonder to slip up so they could condemn him to his sire's disposition.

"There is no way someone as regal and giving as you could be from traitors' ilk."

"You're sure it's not a ruse?" Flirtation slipped into her words.

"You'd be the best actress," he said, taking the bait.

Her smile deepened, and she squeezed his arm. Then her eyes swept ahead, and she saw the castle gates fast approaching. "Would you appreciate someone distilling you down to a copy of your father?" she probed more carefully.

Mikhail tensed beneath her. On occasion, he had confided in her about his father's firm hand. Lord Vardulf had been cruel when Merrick had chosen Sonder over Mikhail. It was a knife's edge she walked, but drawing the similarities between the two boys could serve her well.

"I suppose not." She took his sigh as a resignation to defeat.

The shadow of the tunnel engulfed them. Cut off from prying eyes, Rhianwyn let the side of her body press against him. "Good. Because you aren't." She stepped away from him like nothing had happened as the mid-afternoon sun bathed them once more. "I'll have you not do the same to my friend."

The tilted smile lifted the side of his face once more. "As you wish, my lady."

They reached the hospital, and she peeled away from him to open the door. "I'll thank you for your kindness and help." She tried not to touch him as she went to take the box, but he stepped into her.

"Join me for the afternoon." His gaze held her, and he did not ask.

"Mistress Gwenyvir asked me to put these things away, then clean the hospital," she lied.

"Let me help you, then," he insisted.

"I couldn't possibly take up any more of your time." It was an attempt to return them to normalcy by being polite and guarded.

"I planned my afternoon around your company. If I can't pry you from work, let me lessen your burden."

The box had ended up in her arms, but Mikhail's hands now held hers. Rhianwyn's heart fluttered. Despite the dangers of the game she played, the corners of her mouth softened.

"Okay," she breathed.

The chore was spent easily. Mikhail was nothing but polite. He placed vials, herbs, and clean linens in their places with her direction. Where he had been forward earlier, anytime their hands came close to touching, he pulled away with a shy smile. It was endearing.

For the most part, they were alone. Occasionally, other apprentices came in to retrieve books or notes. Rhianwyn hardly noticed their grins and sly glances. It was nice to have company and someone to ease her loneliness.

As Mikhail placed the last bundle of herbs into her hands, her eyes twinkled. Still, he didn't touch her.

"Thank you for your help."

His dark eyebrow arched over his confident smirk. "Just like that, you're sending me away?"

She laughed, though she felt a nervous knot in her stomach. "Don't dare imply I used you. You offered!"

"Walk with me in the garden to thank me." Mikhail held his hand out to her.

"The royal ward and a lord's son. We would make a striking sight." Even though she smiled, Rhianwyn was deflecting, knotting her hands in her apron to hide her unease.

"I ask as a friend, not a suitor." Mikhail's face darkened with what she thought was hurt. "You do it with Sonder all the time. Do you think less of me?"

His frankness was both refreshing and frightening. The smile fell from her face, and she placed a hand in his. "That's not what I meant."

His fingers closed around hers, and he tugged gently. "Then it's decided."

The ferocity in his eyes surpassed a suggestion, and her protest fled as she followed.

Despite her qualms, Mikhail's company remained genial, and the fresh air was soothing. Gwenyvir had been right about her needing a break. But, unbidden, her thoughts also drifted to how unlike Sonder this boy was.

The path he chose kept them to the manicured flower beds, with no reservations about being seen or heard. He was unafraid to speak his desires, and his hands were less an offer and more demanding. It was exhilarating.

"Would you like to join me for dinner?" Mikhail asked as they made their way back to the hospital.

Rhianwyn giggled. "You've been wonderful, and right, all day. But I have a few things left to do. Tomorrow, Mistress Gwenyvir asked me to help her interview a master from Cethre." They stopped at the threshold of the little building, and she turned to him. Looking up into his handsome face, she took both his hands and smiled. "I hope you feel properly appreciated. Your company was unmatched."

His lopsided smile looked vulnerable, out of place on his confident features. "If I can't convince you, then I'll concede. It will have to be enough for now." He pressed a soft kiss on the back of her hand.

Rhianwyn's laughter was genuine this time. "Oh, stop, Mikhail. Don't be ridiculous. We're friends. You can have as much of me as you want."

He stared at her through his lashes with that hungry look again. "Don't tempt me."

That made her blush. Reluctantly, she pulled her hand free. "If you're so inclined, I can keep you plenty busy here."

The grin was wolfish, as if he knew of the heat that flushed her body. "So long as I can be with you."

She laughed and put a hand on his shoulder. "There's no winning with you. Thank you, Mikhail. I'll see you later."

His hand covered hers until she brushed passed him. Then, as she stepped inside, he called out a farewell, and she waved.

It was a relief when the door separated them. Rhianwyn let out a heavy sigh to help still the fluttering of her heart. Her emotions were a mess.

A voice startled her. "What in the world are you doing?"

Rhianwyn spun. "Alessia." She placed her hand over her chest.

Alessia stood with a hand on her hip. "Well?"

She waved her hand dismissively. "He was just helping me with my chores, and we went for a walk. It was nothing."

"Sure looked a little more than nothing." Her friend's concern was impossible to miss. "What're you thinking? You know Mikhail dislikes Sonder."

Rhianwyn's good mood soured. "It's not like that. I can have other friends."

Alessia wasn't convinced. "Mikhail isn't known for doing just friends."

Rhianwyn rolled her eyes and pushed away from the door. "Well, that's all he's getting." She busied herself collecting books that needed returning to the shelves.

Alessia caught her hand. "What about Sonder?"

Rhianwyn bit the inside of her lip. "He's coming home."

The other girl knew she was desperately hoping Sonder would make it in time for the festivals. Alessia knew just about everything, including her fears, even if it was only the surface of them. She offered a well of tenderness that Rhianwyn's sister lacked.

"He finally wrote?" Alessia's joy stung.

Tears pricked Rhianwyn's eyes. "No," she said flatly. "Mikhail told me."

Her friend pulled her into a brief hug. "It's probably that grim-faced mentor of his. At least he'll be home."

Rhianwyn breathed in the warm cinnamon of Alessia's hair. "He's never not written before, though."

"I'm sure it's nothing. You'll see. He always snaps out of his moods." Her warm eyes met Rhianwyn's as she pushed her hair back. "But I mean it about Mikhail. Be careful. He's charming at first. I know because he tried it on me once when we were little. Told him to shove right off."

Rhianwyn laughed and rolled her eyes again. "As I said, he's just a friend. I've got it under control, alright?" She couldn't mention her plan to use Mikhail to influence the lords.

"I'm sure you do. You're a smart girl. Regardless, Wyn, please be careful. Okay?"

Rhianwyn kissed Alessia's cheeks and smiled. "I promise. Come," she said, lacing their arms together, "let's go eat. You're the only dinner date I want."

Chapter Nineteen
Dancing with the Deceiver

And when the time came for the champion to fulfill his oath to the Lady Serafina Aurbornet, he turned his back, swayed by the counsel of Aaren the Deceiver. The resulting war took one hundred thousand lives and tore Diaga Realta into the three jewels—Sosten with Stellamar, Göttinberg with Grüinstern, and Setareh with Jân'aab. Stricken with grief, the Goddess of Stars fell at the feet of Lir of Taliesin and begged she use the Auza-Bendith to return reason to the warring tribes.

As a result, one jewel rose above them all, bestowed to the Lady of Silver Branches, and the power further shifted into the hands of the people, and the gods trembled.

Rise of Sosten, recordings of Gwyn'Teilwyr Iufias

Present, age seventeen

Late summer saw the group's return to the capital. The crops were dressed in full splendor, vying for harvest. Thin grape skins threatened to split on the vines, ripe apples glistened, and the green fields turned into seas of gold.

Merrick led the way as they wove through the crowded East Road. It was packed with merchants hurrying before the seasons changed. Hardly anyone looked up, but everyone slowed and shuffled aside to make way.

Sonder thought they looked like wights. After hearing the queen's horses for a score of years, it was white noise. The distinct chime of the harnesses had conditioned everyone, even if they denied it.

Sonder hung back as they crested the final hill. The vantage looked over the rooftops to the docks, which were so full that tall ships rocked at anchor out in the bay. A stream of dinghies skimmed the water like bugs, carrying seafarers awaiting their berths to shore. Hulls were being readied for the final expeditions before the seas became too treacherous for all but the most desperate to brave.

Greedy transporters were no doubt already taking advantage of the need. Sonder had watched many a soul shuffled away into slavery for their debts.

The gate dumped them into Middle Market Square. Usually, the sights of the season filled Sonder with excitement. He loved when the sailors and mercenaries for hire migrated into the affluent districts while the rhythmic symphony of tools shaped decorations lain across laps. Practicing tumblers put on shows for the shoppers while musicians played and women and men in skirts danced. People forgot their stations, and the resulting energy was intoxicating. But not today. The approach from the east meant the castle reared into view far too quickly.

The snapping banners and rising towers made his pulse hammer, and his stomach filled with dread as if the butterflies he usually felt had begun to fester. He could still taste smoke and blood.

A unique horn blast announced Merrick. Chains rattled, and the heavy outer gate wrapped in metal bands opened. Instead of it stirring awe, Sonder cursed it. He would have been happy if the battlements were deserted, and they could never return.

His horse crowded the beast in front, knowing there was grain waiting at the end. The metal-shod hooves sang against the tunnel lined with murder holes. The inner gate stood open, and Sonder imagined tugging the reins and galloping away.

The sun was blinding as they emerged into the vibrant courtyard. Sonder knew that head of hair running across the yard to see them, peeking around the gathered footmen. As his palfrey walked past, he saw Rhianwyn wave from the corner of his eye. But even as he dismounted and followed Merrick like an obedient hound, he didn't spare her a glance.

Rhianwyn's face fell, her fingers reclaiming her excitement as she watched.

That first week, it was easy to avoid her. It wasn't uncommon for him to spend hours with Merrick as his routines resumed. Rhianwyn knew he hated the tests he endured after being on the road. No doubt she worried after their reception, but she would trust him to seek her out when he came out of his melancholy.

Sonder took full advantage of her good faith. She didn't even risk sneaking into his quarters. It was the only place he could truly be alone, and that was what he needed most. Besides, they had wordlessly agreed it was a forbidden space for them—she had only braved it to heal his hand on the night of the ceremony.

Still, every night, he feared the servant's latch would turn. The bundle of unsent letters wrapped in oilskin shoved under his bed gnawed his nerves as he lay awake, waiting for sleep to take him. It grew more tempting to throw them into the fire that laughed at him. Its crackling sounded like the switch licking Rhianwyn's skin when she was beaten because of him—the whisper of his sheets as he tossed like her tears. In the space before respite, his hand would ache.

The nightmares filled with shrieks, and the smell of burnt flesh that had plagued him for months worsened. Now that he was back in Stellamar, the girl's face morphed into Rhianwyn's. He would be ripped from sleep, clawing at his throat as if he were choking on blood and smoke. The panic was made worse when his mouth tasted like iron and ash. Once he regained his bearings, he would flop back down, dripping sweat and embarrassed by his shouts.

Sleep rarely returned afterward. Instead of lying restless in bed, Sonder began attending the early-morning drills. Being on the road for nearly a year meant he could use them. It became the only time he truly got out of his head, if only for a handful of hours.

The praise for his efforts was welcomed, but after a few days, he realized he could continue to avoid Rhianwyn. The exercises left narrow windows for meals, and he took on extra chores in his free time. Soon, the masters supported him however they could, even letting him rearrange his schedule. His time was so erratic that he became hidden in plain sight within two weeks.

It got back to him that Rhianwyn was asking after him, yet not even Tran could tell her where Sonder would be. Under normal circumstances, he had little energy to dedicate to alleviating the tensions with the other boys. Between his traveling with Merrick and the aftermath of the Ward Ceremony, they largely left him, the orphan of a traitor, alone. Now, he used it as a blessing.

It was a week before the Equinox Festival when Rhianwyn finally cornered him on his way to the library during lunch. The lack of meals and sleep had worn him down. He hadn't seen her at all; his mind had been so addled.

She stepped into his path and fixed him with a fierce glare. "So, you're just going to avoid me?"

Sonder avoided looking at her as he tried to step around. "No. I've just been busy."

She stepped in front of him. "Too busy to write? Too busy to come find me? Even too busy to deny that you've been avoiding me?"

The seething anger inside of him loomed large with sleep deprivation, and it terrified him. Just that morning, he had been startled awake from the dream where he had his hands around Rhianwyn's throat as she questioned him, pushing him as she did now.

He stood up to his full height and looked down at her. His body had filled out, which he tried to use to intimidate her. "So, what, you're stalking me now?"

Rhianwyn didn't back down. "No. I'm tired of constantly missing you, so I asked Tran where you were. Luckily, he was right today. Neither one of your best friends knows anything about you anymore."

He scoffed. "Since when do you talk to Tran?" It was a stupid thing to say, but his brain was too foggy to do better.

She crossed her arms. "Yes, Sonder, I talk to people other than you. Including Tran. If you were the only one, I'd be struck dumb by now. My whole vocabulary sent off with my unanswered letters. Maybe if you, I don't know, *talked to me,* you'd know more about my life." She opened her arms, challenging him.

He tried to muscle past her this time. "I don't have time for this. I'm busy, Wyn."

She grabbed his arm and used her shoulder to stop him. "Then let me not waste your time." She held him out at arm's length. Looking at her, Sonder became trapped in her gaze. "Are you going to ask me?"

He feigned ignorance. "Ask you what?"

It wasn't hard to miss the hurt that flitted across her face like a breeze through grass. It didn't cool her anger but rather fed it, like air and fire. Her annoyance turned into more. "To the ball, Sonder. To the Equinox Ball."

"I don't know. I might not make it." To openly deny her was egregious. He wrested his arm free and took a step down the corridor.

He had been worried he wouldn't be home in time just two months ago. Yet here he was, standing in front of her, acting as if he hadn't been promising her for years that they would go together.

"Someone else asked." Rhianwyn's voice was soft, but she held her head high beside him.

Sonder stopped but didn't look at her. A split second saw jealousy, betrayal, and loneliness crash over his psyche and cast him further into turmoil. But to her, there was no hesitation as he said flatly, "Then go with them."

Maybe she gasped. Maybe she cried. Perhaps she hated him then and would never speak to him again. Sonder didn't look back to see. His choice to scorn her felt like it was frozen in time, with both ambiguity and finality experienced only by youth. He was severed from himself.

Now that he had been outed, he made himself more present, hoping that Rhianwyn would confront him again. But anytime he saw her, it was always in passing. Her smiles were endless with everybody, and she appeared enthralled with every conversation.

The weather was still warm, so she treated people on the porch of the hospital. As he passed, he would slow down to watch how she tended to them and offered comfort. He had been too close to her to realize how beautiful she looked, being present with whoever she was with.

It was a long week of watching her gossip and giggle with Alessia, or enduring the attention of other squires with demure grins. The distractions earned him many bruises during drills.

Rhianwyn was the only person who could have recognized how sick he had become; notice the weight he was losing. But she no longer spared him a glance.

It was late afternoon with two days until the ball, and wooden swords echoed through the yard. Sonder had convinced Tran once again to exercise with him. They had graduated to blunted weapons, but they still liked to play with wooden weapons in their free time. The swords still had heft and hurt like hell, but the difference was enough to hone their reflexes. They were the only two at that hour exchanging blows.

Tran bluffed high, and Sonder brought his sword up clumsily. For whatever reason, he shut his eyes. Instead of the wood swords rattling together, Tran swung low and caught him in the hip. Sonder's eyes shot open as he faltered and dropped his hand. Taking the opening, Tran swept down on his opposite shoulder, forcing him to drop his knee to catch himself. Two blows, back-to-back.

"You're distracted." Tran stepped back and twirled his sword with a cocky grin.

Sonder rolled to sit, knees falling open, and leaned on his elbow. "I am not." He rubbed his smarting shoulder.

"You flatter me, implying that I've gotten better. But you are." Despite admitting he was the lesser swordsman, the boy enjoyed the win. "You're never that slow."

A girl crossing the yard caught Sonder's eye, and he glanced at her. It wasn't Rhianwyn.

Tran followed the look and then laughed. "Oh, I see. So, it's Wyn then?"

"No," Sonder snapped.

Tran leaned on his sword and grinned down at him. "Is so. Look, you're blushing."

Sonder kicked out and caught Tran's blade with his heel. "Is not."

Tran was able to recover, and he hopped back. "If you say so, lover boy. So, you're going to the ball with her then? Have you decided what you'll wear? Wait, don't tell me. Black, right?"

Sonder knew he was joking, but it irked him anyway. He grunted and began to stand up. "I'm not taking her. Someone else is."

Tran was incredulous. "What? But she asked you. What do you mean she's going with someone else?"

Sonder paused, resting on one knee with his arm braced against his leg. "Exactly that. She's going with someone else. I told her to."

Tran's jaw dropped, and his eyebrows threatened to crawl into his hairline. "You're coldhearted, my friend. A girl like that waits for you to ask her, and you tell her to find another partner?" He considered it for a moment, then shook his head. "Cold," he repeated. "Who're you taking instead?"

Sonder tested his bruised leg. "I'm not going."

Tran relaxed and laughed. "You almost had me there. You're too good at that moody stuff." Sonder fixed him with a look, and Tran's shock returned, his eyebrows somehow getting higher. "You're serious?" He let his sword lean against his body, bringing both hands to the side of his head. "What is wrong with you?"

Sonder stood there, sword hanging at his side. "Nothing is wrong."

Tran sighed and let his hands slide down his face. "Oh, man." He looked at the sky, then the ground, rubbing his forehead. Then, puffing out his cheeks, he tentatively looked at Sonder. "Look, I know you feel like you're a loner, but you don't have to be. It's a self-inflicted wound."

Sonder ignored him. "Do you know who she's going with?"

There was no hesitation. "Someone smarter than you."

Tran let out a yelp as Sonder came at him unfettered. After the first blow, which he clumsily got his sword up in time to block, it was a heated battle. Seven minutes went by, and they were both panting and covered in sweat when they finally conceded. They both had extra bruises, but Tran had his own dark welts indicating a significant loss.

"Well, see, you're already perking up." Tran held his ribs where Sonder had got him, grinning. "Girl trouble suits you. You fight harder." Sonder fixed him with a scowl, and Tran laughed. "Alright, have it your way. But, look, my date is a merchant's daughter. I'm sure she has a friend who would be delighted to go with you."

"I don't want to go." Sonder rolled his shoulder, feeling it tightening up.

"Yes, you do. You can't lie to me. I've had to listen to you talk about going since we were children. You'll thank me when you're older." Tran clapped him on his bad shoulder. "Having a date is to help distract you when you see the lucky man walk in with Rhianwyn on his arm." He whacked him again.

Sonder faked a strike with the pommel of his sword, which got Tran to flinch away. "Fine, if it'll make you feel better." He wasn't in the mood to laugh, but he took Tran's sword from him, seeing how he favored one side.

"Trust me, it's not for me. Let's get washed up, eh? I'm hungry." Tran draped his arm over Sonder's shoulders and used him for support as they headed toward the barracks.

Their conversation moved to safer territory. With the Hallowed Tournaments coming, there was plenty to keep them from more serious topics.

Tran let out a satisfied sigh as he slipped into the communal baths. "By the way, I'm not training next week. You'll have to find someone else to weasel into your Rhianwyn Avoidance Scheme. Better yet, take a break. You look awful."

Sonder's brow furrowed. "What are you going to do for a week?"

Tran reclined against the wall. "I have a lady to woo."

The night before the Equinox, the dark scent of smoked meats began to waft through the castle, the oily tones promising the tenderest cuts. Dawn brought fresh loaves and the acidity of sugary fruit sauces, creating the perfect balance. Overnight, the regalia had come out.

The sun illuminated dazzling banners hung from the castle walls, each embroidered with autumn's images. Fresh flowers imbued with magic lined the walkways strung with paper lanterns, while candles shaped into celestial beasts drifted in the fountains, waiting for sundown.

It was the perfect day. Music drifted up from the city on the sea breeze, which only hinted that colder weather was approaching, while performers already in costume waltzed through the gates.

Merrick knocked on his door before Sonder could even decide if he wanted to let himself enjoy the day. Their trek to the Queen's Tower was reminiscent of the year prior, gutting any chance of reprieve.

"I'd like you to compete in the Hallowed Tournament this year, Master Sonder," Aspera said, haloed by the rising light. "Now that your duties are here, it's time you start wooing the people, as every good champion should." Sonder didn't miss the look she cast toward Merrick. He knew it had to do with Bran. "You have a reputation to uphold," she finished.

Sonder bowed, still too numb to read into hidden meanings, though he knew they were there. "Your will is mine, Your Majesty."

She smiled and inclined her head to dismiss them. "Enjoy this day. You've earned it."

This was the first time Sonder didn't go roaming the castle with Rhianwyn to find food trays. Instead, competing in the celebration of death gave him an excuse to drill. It was his first Hallowed Tournament appearance. He needed the extra training, and by midday, he was the only one who remained.

The series ended, and Sonder asked for another round.

Roderick was exasperated. "Come now, boy! Don't you think you've trained enough? I'm calling it. Take a break. Go celebrate." He yanked the dull sword from Sonder's hands. "If Merrick put you up to this, I swear . . . Go on, get!"

Sonder continued to put off getting ready. But the entire castle crawled with activity, and the noise was inescapable. Finally, Tran cornered him on his way to the kitchens.

"You're still in training leathers?" he chided. He was already formally dressed, and his hair was freshly trimmed. "We'll be late!" Tran began to steer him toward his room. "You're not going to make me look bad."

Sonder tried to shrug him off. "I have plenty of time." Tran didn't relent, and he sighed. "Fine, I'll go."

"Nope. I don't trust you." Tran followed him to make sure of it. At the end of the corridor, the boy excused himself with another stern warning.

For whatever reason, it struck Sonder standing at his door how unused this room had become. He had been traveling and now usually crawled into bed well past midnight and left before dawn. He had even taken to cleaning up and spending his free time in the barracks.

A servant carrying a tray came hurrying by, and Sonder snagged a glass of watered wine and a slice of bread spread with soft cheese and jammed peppers. It was all he had eaten besides an apple that morning.

Gently, he ran his thumbnail over the notches in the frame that marked his growth. It was something Merriweather had insisted on doing. A glimpse at the nearby tapestry brought the memory of Rhianwyn and himself ducked behind it, laughing as they drew on the wall.

The burning girl from Tierrion flashed in his mind, and a knot formed in his throat. He took a sip of the wine to loosen it.

Merriweather looked up when he opened the door. She was aging, with dignified streaks of gray in her hair. Her wrinkles spoke of more years spent smiling than scowling. The warmth she radiated when she saw him conveyed her tendency to kindness. His request for her years ago remained cherished.

"You've grown taller since last I saw you, dear." She pushed out of the chair with a groan. "Took your time, you did. Now we're pressed to have you ready."

She was no longer his caregiver. He had outgrown that position, but she kept his chambers and finery in good repair.

A bath was brought, and Sonder washed. The soap had a pleasant woody smell with hints of warm spices. An oil was offered of a similar scent to mask any odors that would creep up from a night of dancing. His hair was trimmed, his face shaved since he lacked the ability to grow a proper beard still, and with lots of fussing, the dirt was cleaned from his nails and buffed to a shine.

Merriweather pulled out a suit with a plum-red silk shirt. The black jacket had long tails and gold details. Sonder preferred the ease of riding leathers, but he was impressed by the costume.

"I matched it to Lady Rhianwyn's gown. Missus Olive gave me a swatch. You two will be positively handsome together."

Sonder's face fell, and the lingering dread surrounding the event came back. "I'm not going with Rhianwyn."

Merriweather blanched. "You aren't?"

Sonder fought to remain straight-faced. "No. I'm going with a merchant's daughter from town. Her seamstress should have sent a swatch." He hid his disappointment to spare her feelings.

Merriweather put her hand to her cheek. "Oh, that poor girl. I thought she was just a hopeful suitor. Oh, now, where did I put it?" She rushed around the room, opening draws and shifting piles of books and clothes needing mending. When she found it, she gave a triumphant nod and moved to compare it to his outfit. She became distraught. "Oh, they don't match. The poor lass!"

The girl was going in saffron and purple. The colors would clash, knowledge he had thanks to Drisil.

Merriweather chewed on her nails while she looked at his outfit. Finally, she sighed and looked at him. "I'm so sorry. I think the only solution we have is to send you in all black. We can use the swatch as a pocket square and get some flowers to tie you two together. We can reasonably say it was short notice, right?"

Sonder considered it a moment. "No. Keep it. We can remove the gold. Use the saffron for an accent. I'm sure some flowers can bridge the difference." He reached out and ran the jacket between his fingers. "I have a lifetime of black ahead of me. I'd like to keep the colors." He tried to give her a reassuring smile but wondered if it fell short.

Merriweather nodded, then hurried off to flag down a chambermaid to get the flower arrangements. While she was gone, he dressed in the underclothes. She helped him with the rest when she returned. Finally, the flowers arrived, and she pinned them to his chest.

The woman stepped back and admired him a moment, then stood on her toes to push a rogue lock of hair into place. "How you've grown."

Sonder took her hand and kissed it. "Thanks to you."

She swatted him, failing to stifle her giggle. "Oh, off with you. You'll be late. Go charm that young girl of yours, not me."

Sonder grinned as he gathered his coin purse.

The plan was to meet at Tran's family estate, just a few rows from the castle. Tran's family had arranged for everything; all he had to do was show up.

Sonder walked through the gate fifteen minutes later than planned. Tran and his family milled in the courtyard, and as he approached, he was given an irritated scowl by his friend. As a formality, he was introduced to Tran's parents. They instantly knew who he was, and Sonder bowed, uneasy that his station had preceded him. It was a relief that Tran made it an abridged affair and ushered Sonder into the waiting carriage.

They collected Tran's date first. She was a pretty blonde with brown eyes. They had chosen a rich navy with sunset orange, which was stunning on her. It was fun for Sonder to watch Tran, usually confident and smooth, stumble over his words. When Tran saw his grin, he reminded him that he was next, which reopened the pit in his stomach.

Sonder's date lived farther still from the castle. She was dark-haired with clear blue eyes and an almond tone in her skin. The color choice made sense the second he laid eyes on her. The saffron complemented her complexion, and the purple made her eyes look like the ocean. Everything was forced as he introduced himself, going through the formalities. The girl's father nodded approvingly, yet Sonder couldn't help feeling like a fraud as she placed her hand in his, and he helped her into the carriage.

With the four of them all crammed in, they struggled to keep from brushing elbows, and the mix of different perfumes could only be remedied by cracking the window. The girls' chaperones rode beside the driver and continued to peer back at them to ensure nothing unsuitable took place.

With time to kill, they went to the markets. They bought sweet cakes and smoked meats while the girls admired the fall charms, masks, ribbons, and lace dyed in the season's jewel tones that hung from awnings. Tran bought a delicate rose-gold necklace with a small leaf charm for his courtly love.

Feeling obligated, Sonder turned to his date. "Would you like one?"

He had never been more relieved when she answered, "No, thank you."

Tran and his girl whispered together and laughed as they strolled through the stalls and watched the performers. Unfortunately, Sonder couldn't recall his date's name. They spent most of their time in awkward silence or exchanging superficial pleasantries until Tran made them hurry to catch the gates opening.

The sunset painted the castle rose-gold as their carriage clattered through the entrances in the long line of guests. Lanterns flared just as they passed beneath them, lit by people dressed as Fae. The girls swooned, and the blonde placed her hand in Tran's, who finally relaxed, realizing it had all gone as planned.

Pages opened their doors, and the boys led the girls through the arched entryway with stained-glass windows that reached the ceiling. The sunset's glorious display pooled into the grand lobby. The presentation was a testament to the magical abilities of the queen. A chill rolled in on the dusky air, yet her magic kept the room comfortable despite the open windows. The waver of magic was like floor-length drapes and always gave Sonder a sense of wonder.

They milled with the other guests, and the girls fawned over their friends or offered tight-lipped smiles to those they did not like. Sonder and Tran introduced them to the other squires.

The night was going well, and Sonder began to think Tran was right in convincing him to go. With one glass of wine working through his system, he felt his nervous energy dissipating. He was engaging with his date's story about her summer when the crowd parted and he saw her.

Sonder thought he could recognize Rhianwyn anywhere, but her appearance shocked him. Her plum dress made the red in her hair stand out, tamed in a royal maiden's style, with tendrils of her natural curls falling softly. The gold reflected the light, making her radiant. His eyes locked on her as she curtsied to someone. Sonder couldn't see who she had come with because the crowd refused to cooperate.

"Are you listening?" His date sounded genuinely disappointed; they had just started to connect.

"Of course, forgive me. The beaches sound like they were lovely this year." Sonder smiled at her and saw he had missed too much of the conversation to salvage it. "Excuse me a minute?"

He didn't wait for her response as he dodged around her to look for Rhianwyn. But the crowd had swallowed her again. Sonder grabbed Tran's arm more roughly than he intended as he passed.

"Ow!"

Sonder whispered to him, "Rhianwyn is here."

"She is?" Tran looked around. "Who is she with?"

"I didn't see. She—" He was cut off by the bell that rang for the feast, and they were swept up.

Due to his station, Sonder and his girl didn't sit with Tran. Instead, they sat closer to the queen. It wasn't quite an honorary position, but it still put them in the limelight, which seemed to please the girl. Usually, Rhianwyn sat with him, but she would be placed with whoever she'd come with.

What station would he hold? Sonder wondered. *Where would he be sat?*

Purple was the fashion, and many other women wore plum. Sonder searched the crowd as everyone took their seats. As fewer people were left hunting for their chairs, he worried he had missed her. She sat with her back to him, but his eyes instantly knew her profile when she turned to somebody beside her. He craned and fought to catch a glimpse of the person. Finally, the screen of milling revelers parted, and he saw the man.

Mikhail. Arrogant and entitled Mikhail. Sonder hadn't considered it, but now that he knew who it was, it felt like the one person he couldn't tolerate.

Mikhail had become outright cruel in the way he bullied the other boys. He was the reason most wouldn't talk to Sonder, fearing he'd make their lives miserable too. At seventeen, he was old to be left unsquired. The recent talk was that his father was trying to convince Elio to mentor him since Merrick continued to refuse. They were desperate to avoid him being knighted in the standard army until he proved himself.

To Mikhail, it was all Sonder's fault.

That was why it was the most grievous individual for Rhianwyn to be pining after. Not because Sonder hated Mikhail, but because Mikhail hated him. He didn't trust it at all.

Through the entire meal, Sonder watched them. Rhianwyn's table was animated with laughter, while his was an awkward hodgepodge of individuals muddling without guidance. At one point, Sonder heard someone ask how he and his date had met. By then, she was irritated enough that she cut the idea off and said it was an arrangement to please their mutual friends.

The friendly touches on Mikhail's arm and the returned smiles were tolerable. But as the desserts were delivered, Sonder saw Mikhail place his hand on Rhianwyn's leg. Finally, he stood to excuse himself.

When the meal was done, Tran cornered him and pulled him close. "Sonder, I beg you, please. You're making me look bad, and I want to impress Mila."

"She's here with Mikhail," Sonder said, his face expressionless.

"I know, I saw. He's a rotten lot. But try to give Katrina a good time. At least dance with her. Please?"

Sonder nodded. "For you." Tran was visibly relieved.

Sonder moved as though they were in a class, stiff and at a prudent distance. When the song ended, he pled a cramp. The tension between them was a miasma, the look of annoyance plain as day on Katrina's face. Another dance came and went. A gentleman approached nervously to ask permission, but before he had finished his request, she offered her hand and was whisked away.

It was nearing midnight when Sonder saw Rhianwyn dancing a slow ballad. The way they held each other's gazes and pushed the limit of what was acceptably close held him in a perverse captivation.

In the end, Mikhail took her hand and kissed her fingers, then placed another on the back of her hand. No doubt he would have kept going had Rhianwyn not half-heartedly told him to stop.

Sonder left, the limit of his tolerance met. He spent the rest of the night sitting on the wall walk, looking out over the city as it celebrated, feeling isolated as he rewatched the young lovers from Tierrion die by his hand. He hoped Rhianwyn would find him, and he could explain everything, but she didn't come.

Chapter Twenty
Hallowed Be His Name

Hallowed Tournament, eight years ago

Merrick watched Bran's brown eyes fade. Every muscle in his body trembled as the wound across his back threatened his consciousness. Bran had fought hard. For a terrifying moment, Merrick had thought the man had changed his mind, until he saw the opening, so masterfully set it would never be questioned that his death could have been staged.

Blood leaked around the blade in gushes, and Bran's punctured lung gurgled, trying to draw air into his starving heart.

Merrick's body still burned with battle lust. The musk of gore made him wild. Blood loss made him romantic. His muscles screamed to reach out to the man in his final moments. All it would take to feel those lips one last time was inches.

So close he could taste the smell of them.

Instead, he trembled with the effort. The onlookers were too far away to read their faces, but Merrick willed himself across the distance so Bran wasn't alone in death.

Merrick whispered something inaudible to his own ears "I love you."

Bran gripped Merrick's wrist, his palm slick. An awful clicking sound came from deep in his chest as he choked on blood. His teeth were stained with it as his tongue tried to form words with air that wasn't there.

Even if he knew it was coming, how terrifying it would be to feel the life slip from him.

It was a croak. Maybe even closer to a throat finally contracting to give air to words. "Do it."

Merrick's neck writhed against the tears as he brutally wrenched the blade to end Bran's suffering. Then he pulled his sword free, and they fell together, one heaving in air while the other would never taste the sea breeze again.

Bran's body lay on top of him, and Merrick let his forehead rest against his shoulder, taking deep breaths of his scent. It was hard to smell through the tang of salty iron, but the spring grass was still there.

"The gods saw this fight and have deemed Bran a traitor of the crown! Sir Merrick is victorious!"

A knight lifted Merrick to his feet and raised his arm to the roar of the crowd.

Aspera stood and lifted her chin. "Sir Merrick, you have defended the crown and proven yourself this day. May you be my sword."

He stumbled, delirious from blood loss. The knight struggled to hold him up when he bowed too low, nearly toppling them both. When he looked back at Aspera, his eyes shone in their bloodshot sockets. "My life for yours, Your Majesty."

A woman working on her embroidery caught his eye, and he nearly lost control of the suppressed sobs wracking his body.

Present, age seventeen

After the Equinox, gourds adorned entryways, and animal skeletons of every shape hung outside of shops. Performers dressed as beasts donned ghoulish masks while the City Guard patrolled in regalia for the Hallowed season.

In the lower districts, long-burning candles which would last all month were lit at alters to guide the deceased. People concealed their faces to pray and leave offerings. The stories spoke of demons stealing the souls of those who aided the dead, yet the spirits became the demons if left to wander. The tradition wasn't practiced up the hill, but that didn't stop the superstitious from slipping out of their homes with baskets of excess wealth. Money and position didn't make monsters less scary.

The traditions had fascinated Sonder as a child. The ghouls delighted him when they came to the castle, and the flickering alters through the fog made his imagination run wild.

Unfortunately, the magic had died when he learned how the queen exploited the rituals to send spies disguised as pilgrims into the city. Crime spiked, with the chief complaint being kidnappings, the rates of which were higher in the poorer districts.

He knew the Justices were the demons who stole children from condemned families, or urchins caught stealing the offerings. It was odd to Sonder that they were punished for desecrating religious practices, even while Aspera did the same. The remembrance of her magic occasionally flared, reminding him not to question it, even in his private thoughts.

Sonder's mental state deteriorated. He took to climbing the walls every night until he dozed off and woke chilled and was forced to brave the stillness of his room. Images of Mikhail and Rhianwyn crept into his dreams, and Mikhail was the one who sneered at him as he watched Rhianwyn burn.

Everyone but Sonder had suspected the courtship. He had just missed the signs because he had been a recluse. He still was, but now it did him no good since the two had dropped all discretion and seemed to be everywhere he was. Like when they strolled through the yard, Mikhail placing kisses on Rhianwyn's cheek and lingering. The distraction had earned Sonder a bruise that remained tender long after the discoloration healed.

Sonder spent his free time with Tran for some respite, which he got when the boy wasn't talking about Mila. With the tournament coming, they trained often.

Now, Tran watched one of Sonder's arrows errantly arch toward the wrong dummy. He had never been good with a bow, but his aim worsened. Sonder shouted a frustrated curse.

"I know that bruise didn't ruin your aim. You're lucky I'm the only one who saw that. What's eating you?" Tran asked.

"I swear Mikhail is suddenly making himself more visible and rubbing it in my face," Sonder glowered.

Tran shook his head. "No, he has always been around. You're just hyperaware and letting him get under your skin." Sonder shot him a glare, and he shrugged. "If it bothers you so much, why didn't you take her?"

Tran had asked him already.

Sonder grabbed another arrow to focus his annoyance. "We're supposed to focus on our studies. I didn't expect her to be gallivanting around so carelessly." He released the arrow. It went wide. "It's complicated."

"It's complicated," Tran mocked. "You say that every time you don't want to tell me something. I get you're the queen's ward and Merrick's squire. That's a lot of pressure. But what could be so complicated you can't try and explain? I'm no ward, but I can manage my duties and make time to not be an ass to those I care about."

Sonder was about to release another arrow but paused. Merrick's words echoed in his head. He spoke them aloud in the same tone. "I have a duty, and there's no room for anything else." The arrow whizzed across the yard and buried into the dummy's torso.

Tran sat up with raised eyebrows. "Well, that's one way to be dramatic."

On their way to the baths, Tran did most of the talking, idle nonsense to fill the void. They passed a group of boys, and a thread of words caught their attention. Tran trailed off.

"I'd wager any day now I'll have her naked in bed."

Sonder slowed as the rest of the group sniggered. He glanced over and saw Mikhail wearing a wicked smile.

The boy looked him dead in the eye. "Or maybe I'll try to take her in the garden, or a cleaning closet. It would be all the same to me."

Sonder's temper flared, and he abruptly turned toward the group. "Don't you dare talk about Rhianwyn that way."

When Tran heard Sonder's voice, it clicked, and he turned around with a curse. "Shit!"

Mikhail continued to leer. "How do you know I'm talking about Rhianwyn?"

Tran snagged Sonder's arm. "No, no, no!"

The boy laughed along with his companions. "He's angry," he said in a childish lilt. "I would be too if I was the idiot who turned down such a woman."

Tran anticipated Sonder's lunge and placed himself between the two. He used Sonder's momentum to throw him off. "Ignore him, Sonder. It's not worth it. You can't afford the scrutiny a fight would bring."

"Say, how goes the training, O Noble Squire? I hear you're competing this year in the tournament. By Queen Aspera's request. Is that right? You've seemed off, though. Worried about losing? I could help you train. Or, if you're disappointed you blew it with Rhianwyn, I can introduce you to some other girls. It helps, you know." Mikhail mimed a thrusting motion with his hips. He grinned when his companions burst out laughing.

"I hate him." Sonder let Tran push him back. "Someone should put him in line," he said darkly. Tran looked confused, as if wondering if he'd heard him right. They turned to leave.

Mikhail called at their backs disappointedly. "It's probably for the better, you know. Your traitor's blood would only bring her misery."

They walked the rest of the way to the baths in a tense silence. "I told you he was doing it to bait me," Sonder growled, finally breaking it.

Tran opened the door. "Well, don't make it so easy next time. You know he thrives on confrontation. You, however, do not. You also have a lot more to lose."

Sonder pulled his shirt off angrily. "Of all people, how could she possibly choose him?"

"Well, he can be a mite more charming than you. He at least took her to a dance he told her he would. And danced with her." When Sonder scowled at him, he shrugged. "What? I'm still listening to Mila complain on Katrina's behalf. You're zero for two with the ladies, mate."

Sonder just grunted, then slipped into the warm pool. He continued to say nothing as Tran explained how eventually Rhianwyn would come around, or at least see through Mikhail. He didn't endure it long before he stood up and excused himself, using his lessons as a reason. Tran sighed and waved him off.

Sonder knew where to find Mikhail. He was waiting for Rhianwyn to return from the city. The boy was alone, and as Sonder stalked up to him, he stood from tying his boot and looked down at him with a smirk. "Come to ask for help after all?"

Sonder stopped a pace away. "I challenge you. In the tournament. For her honor."

Mikhail barked a laugh. "Really? We're fighting for her honor, are we? What good will that do? Even if you win, she's already let me stick my tongue down her throat and get my fingers wet between her legs. You think she'll come back to you because you beat me?"

Sonder hoped he was lying. "It won't matter. I know she'll never bed a piece of shit like you. I challenge you so no matter what happens, at least you'll know you can't use her without me bloodying your nose."

Mikhail's smile spread. "So you think? Fine, I accept. I guess the humiliation of me taking your girl isn't enough. It'll be a pleasure to embarrass you in combat, too."

"You didn't take her," Sonder said through his teeth. "I turned her down."

Mikhail sucked air in through his teeth as if he were hurt. "Some sound advice, man," he said, laying a hand on Sonder's shoulder. "I wouldn't go around telling people that. It doesn't sound as intimidating as you think." He left Sonder standing there as he walked off.

Sonder heard Rhianwyn's voice, and it twisted his heart. He walked off with his anger as his only companion. Mikhail didn't understand the connotation, and he didn't care. He had cut Rhianwyn off for her own good. Even if he were a killer and monster, unable to give her everything she deserved, he could at least protect her from a scumbag.

The next day, he removed his armor after a duel with Tran. He had lost again, and he tore the grieves off his leg and threw them down.

"You can't still be upset about last night, can you? I thought I told you not to let Mikhail get under your skin."

"I challenged him in the tournament," Sonder snapped. He knelt and began to tear the buckles open on the other leg. "I challenged him for Rhianwyn's honor."

"What?" Tran exclaimed. "Tell me you're lying?"

"I'm not."

"You mean to tell me you left the bath to look for him? After I told you not to let him get to you. You sought him out? Are you an idiot?"

"He's using Rhianwyn to get at me, and that's not fair to her," Sonder said, tossing the other aside.

"That doesn't matter. You know he has been competing in the tournaments since he could, right? He's been around more because he's putting in extra time! You make it so easy." He pulled off his sweaty gloves and threw them in Sonder's face. "Why would you challenge him like that? Rhianwyn is going to be pissed." Tran punched him on the welt he had given him earlier.

Sonder grabbed the awakened bruise. His anger was still hot, and he looked at Tran with determination. "Help me train, then."

Tran groaned. "What have I been doing? At this point, you'd do better to ask me to start performing magic. That's what you need now." He gave him a side-eyed glare. "Honestly, ask Rhianwyn if she can," he said unkindly. "That would do you better. I should stop helping you, so you make a fool of yourself."

"You like me too much." Sonder stood, and grew serious. He couldn't bring himself to tell Tran that he was right. A loss would be worse than Mikhail getting bragging rights, or wounding his pride over what boiled down to a girl.

"Not with your dour mood lately. I can't remember why I liked you in the first place at this point," Tran protested.

"Because you're kind and took pity on me. And I brought you pastries as thanks. Then you found I was better company than Mikhail and his ilk."

"That's debatable at this point." Tran knew the consequences, too. He sighed. "You better start bringing me pastries again."

Sonder drilled hard until Tran and Merrick insisted he rest.

The day of the tournament dawned cold and wet like most days that autumn. Winter had claimed the sun early and not let up since. In an attempt to keep the tournament grounds from turning into a muddy pit, straw was laid out. However, if the people were asked on the street, they all would agree that the added hazard would make the games more fun to watch.

"Let a man or horse fall in the pursuit of victory," they slurred.

The first half was dedicated to knights fighting for qualifiers. Sonder watched these games alone, pressing his face to the bars of the squire barracks. Watching two men fighting still gave him the mix of trepidation he had felt the first time as a child. Since then, he had learned the difference between the refined skill of dueling and striking people down on the battlefield. Sonder knew the calculation and rage it took to win in both. Despite being haunted by the convicts from Tierrion, it still excited him. Even if he couldn't kill Mikhail today, he dared to believe he'd enjoy it if he could.

As always, the men who traveled and trained with Merrick won and went on to the finals, including Áki, who was given an exception to fight despite never taking a title. Merrick no longer competed, instead sitting under the queen's tent, sipping tea and whispering to Drisil. Whenever he was announced as the queen's champion, he would stand slowly and wave.

Sonder never understood the ceremony of Aspera giving him a glass of clear wine, but the man always obediently downed it all at once before returning to his tea. In theory, he could be challenged, but no one ever came forward, not even Sir Elio, who never left the queen's side.

Between the preliminary fights and the finals, the squires would compete in their version of the games. It was a popular spectacle. People turned up in droves to watch the hopefuls try their arms against each other. It was a high gambling affair. People placed bets on whose squire would be crowned the winner.

Not only was it fun for the viewers, but trainees not yet squired, like Mikhail, hoped to be discovered and apprenticed.

Qualifiers ended, and they began calling for the boys in ascending order by age. Sonder didn't stay to watch, instead putting on his black leather armor. It was worn from traveling and smelled foul. Instead of his sword, he would use a standard-issued blunted blade, not as well balanced but still usable. The sound of clashing swords and spears and the crowd's reaction was all he gathered of the battles while he let his mind wander.

"Next up in our seventeen-year-old age range is Mikhail, son of Ealdric Vardulf, yet to be apprenticed." The herald was just a drone in his ear. "His challenger is Sonder, ward of the crown and apprentice to the Royal Battle Master, Queen's Champion, and High Justice, Sir Merrick!" The name finally drew his attention. "To witness such an honored squire debut, pitted against a crowd favorite, will be quite the treat!" The sing-song voice drew out several of the words, making the crowd roar louder.

Sonder stood and walked out to the gate. Mikhail was already there, waving through the iron bars.

Mikhail saw him and grinned. "Ah, there you are. Haven't decided to forfeit? It isn't too late, you know. Spare my nose, you see. I've already won her."

Sonder chose to ignore him, and stepped out confidently as the gates opened. Trinkets and flowers fell on them, mixing with the rain. Sonder was like a black blight in the center of the field while Mikhail peacocked around the ring in his custom armor dyed with his family's colors. He knew how to perform for the crowd, waving at them while they shouted back at him.

The other boy stopped in front of a girl. Sonder saw Rhianwyn, and his stomach knotted. Mikhail drew out a token from under his armor that matched his family's colors, which he presented to her. The crowd grew still while Sonder's heart hammered in his ears. With the prettiest blush, she accepted, and the roar of the spectators was deafening. It looked like she glanced at him when Mikhail turned to preen some more, but it was hard to tell.

The announcer used magic to project his voice over the noise. "Our very own Lady Rhianwyn, ward of her royal highness and apprentice to Mistress Gwenyvir, would appear to have a suitor." The announcer cooed the words, turning this display into the newest gossip. "This fight is dedicated to you, our sweet girl!"

Watching the crowd's response, it wasn't just the nobles who took delight in this, but also the commoners present. With a sinking feeling, it dawned on Sonder just how well-loved Rhianwyn had become throughout the city and how much he had taken her for granted.

A sparse group of people in the crowd chanted Sonder's name, and he raised his hand to acknowledge them. However, the overwhelming support remained for Mikhail and Rhianwyn.

The announcer raised his arm to indicate the match start. The noise died down in anticipation while the boys took their places.

Mikhail twirled his sword before he crouched into a power stance. It was hard not to laugh at how stupid he looked. Sonder chose to hold his blade in front without flourish. There were only two rules: don't kill the other, and don't go for the head. In the event of a draw, it would come down to how many strikes the other took. Otherwise, it was a fight "to the death" or until it reached the fifteen-minute time limit.

A bell tolled, and they launched at each other.

Sonder was good—and fast. He had begun training a few years before most, being preordained to follow in his father's footsteps. He had to be good if he was to give the queen an acceptable return on her investment. So many different techniques and styles had been drilled into him, and he moved with the fluidity of battle. Quick and clever, like Merrick's squire should be.

Mikhail was good, too—strong and confident. Where Sonder beat him with agility, he made up for in brute strength. They were built similarly, but the other boy held a better command over his center of gravity. Each block he made, or strike, he pushed Sonder just enough to keep him on the edge of balance. It wasn't unknown that Sonder was a clever fighter, so Mikhail started strong.

Bets would be placed as the two clashed swords. Those in favor of Mikhail believed Sonder wasn't strong enough to overtake the other boy. Those going for Sonder knew that Mikhail had a tendency to go too hard too early, and word had gotten out about his ability to hold out.

Four minutes in, they had settled into their rhythms. The sense in the crowd was that Sonder would prevail because his strikes were consistent, whereas Mikhail appeared to be wavering. The gamblers yelled in a schism of excitement and dismay.

They clashed once more, and Mikhail used Sonder's momentum to push him back, and they paused, both heaving from the exertion, blades held ready. "Give up, orphan. You heard the crowd. I have her."

Sonder came at him with a yell, a quick strike low, and an attempt to swing around to catch him high, but Mikhail was fast enough to stop both.

The force of the blow forced Mikhail to take a step to the side to balance. "You gave her up," Mikhail continued to taunt.

Sonder panted. "Not knowing she chose a snake like you."

Mikhail coughed out a laugh. "The symbol of desire. Exactly what she'll do when I slip my hands up her—" He was cut short as Sonder came at him in a fury. It took all of his skill to ward Sonder off.

The crowd gasped as this happened. None could have heard them speaking, but this appeared to be the end. No doubt they believed Sonder was opening up after tiring out his opponent to make his final strike. Mikhail moved backward on the defensive.

Sonder made to strike, baiting Mikhail to block. The other boy brought his sword up. With a show of all his strength, Sonder swiped his blade around.

Sonder had been too blind by his anger to see it until he heard the crowd's exclamation, but it was too late by then. His blade came down on nothing. Mikhail called the bluff. He had stepped into the space left open and swung where Sonder's defenses were down. It was a bold, reckless move on Mikhail's part.

Pain blossomed through Sonder's dominant arm as Mikhail's blade moved with all his strength, breaking the bone. Stunned, Sonder staggered and lowered his weapon. He couldn't recover in time as Mikhail swept his feet from under him. Sonder fell into the mud with a thud so loud the crowd likely his teeth clack in the hush that had fallen.

As he lay on the ground, trying to catch his bearings, the dulled point of Mikhail's sword pressed against his throat so hard he couldn't swallow. Sonder looked up at the other boy and fought his panic by gritting his teeth.

"Such a fool to try and fight for her honor," he whispered. Then he raised his voice so that all could hear, his voice echoing in the cold air. "You shame your station!"

Sonder's face flushed a deep red. The crowd hesitated, but Mikhail thrust his blade into the air, and the frenzy retook them.

A young page sprinted over and knelt next to Sonder. "Do you need help, Master Sonder?"

Sonder growled and tried to shoo him away, but his foot slipped when he tried to stand. He hissed in pain as it jarred his limp arm. The boy hoisted him up, then beckoned for him to follow the medics.

Sonder held his arm tightly against his body to help keep it steady. There was a slight hitch in his step, but that was a minor injury. For a second, Sonder looked up to where Rhianwyn had been watching. Their eyes met.

It was the first time they'd looked at each other since they last spoke. The look of concern on her face held no grudge, which wrenched his gut. He watched her turn as Mikhail approached. The man lifted her from the stand and spun her around.

It was early evening when she came to see him. Sonder was still in the makeshift medic's tent, sitting on the edge of a bed, enjoying the warmth from the little stove inside. It was just a broken bone, which they had set and then placed in a sling. A young woman in her twenties offered him a cup of tea. The tea would help with the pain.

When Rhianwyn walked in, he looked up, and his heart skipped a beat.

"Oh, Mistress Rhianwyn, hello." The young woman smiled.

"Hello, Marzia." Rhianwyn walked toward them. "Would you mind excusing us a moment?"

"Not at all." The girl began to walk away, but she touched Rhianwyn's arm and smiled slyly. "Congratulations on the win earlier. That was something," she whispered.

Rhianwyn blushed and tucked her chin against her shoulder. "Thank you."

The girl shimmied her shoulders and giggled as she went to tend to some other minor casualties from the tournament.

Rhianwyn looked at him. She bit her lip to stifle her smile, but she couldn't hide her mirth completely. She wore a dusky-purple dress and a heavy wool cloak—ready for an evening out for the festival.

"How are you?" she asked, talking out of the side of her mouth.

Sonder sighed. "I think my pride is the most bruised part of me."

Her eyes grew heavy as she scrutinized him. "That's a bit dramatic, don't you think?"

He shrugged, but hissed as his arm flared.

"May I sit?" she asked, indicating the edge of the bed next to him.

"Sure," he said. As she sat, he felt his weight shift toward her, and he could smell rose oil in her hair.

"I know how to help the bone heal faster. I can try if you like?" She hesitated. He waited for her to say what she usually did. Offer to make it hurt less. For a moment, he saw it poised on her lips until she seemed to decide against it. "It will help with the swelling."

He nodded, and she set to work. Her hands were cool through his tunic. It took a few seconds, but then he began to feel the tingling in his arm.

The truth was, magic was intimate. He could feel how quickly it worked, which spoke to how well she knew him. It made his pulse race, and his head light with the proximity. "You're wonderful, Wyn."

She gave him a tight smile. "The head Master says I have a natural talent. Says I'll amount to quite a lot in life." She softened. "I just think the human body is so fascinating. It's a lovely machine, with everything working together in harmony. That's beautiful." Her eyes began to sparkle as she talked, and he saw the telltale glimmer of magic around her.

She was beautiful.

For a while, he stayed quiet, looking at her while she concentrated. It had been so long since he had seen her like this. There were so many things he wanted to say to her, but he settled on the easiest. "How have you been?" It sounded unnatural.

There was that rose kiss on the apples of her cheeks again. "I've been wonderful."

The blush made him angry. "I can see that," he said, the edge in his voice making her look up and her smile fall.

"Are you upset about that?" Her tone was low, and her eyes narrowed.

"I am, yes. Mikhail isn't a good match for you."

The magic faded from his arm as her hands dropped to her lap. "You're the one who scorned me. You do realize that?"

"I didn't know that meant you would stop talking to me," he said.

Her jaw fell for just a second. "You're joking, right? I gave you space because you obviously needed it. Now you're mad at me? For what, courting someone else?" She stood up.

Sonder scoffed at her choice of words, and her anger grew. "It's not that. It's the way he acts with you. It's not proper, and he doesn't respect you. I challenged him for your honor today."

She snorted. "He told me. A lot of good that did you. Look, Sonder, it's none of your business how he and I are together." Rhianwyn lifted her skirts and began to rise away, but then she turned back on him. "Anytime you needed a friend, I was always there. In all that time, did you ever for one second think about whether or not I needed one? You might not like Mikhail and me, but he was there when I needed someone. You weren't. Maybe he is a little too brash, and it's improper. But he cares for me. I wonder if you ever did."

She left him alone. There was no denying that he cared for her. He wondered how she could even question it. It forced him to recount each of their interactions.

Hours passed, and it wasn't until Merrick walked into the tent looking for him that he realized the sun had set. In his good hand, there was still the tea, untouched. The tournament grounds had long since emptied, and most of the injured men had left.

"What are you still doing here? I've been looking all over. You've been cleared, haven't you?" Merrick sounded concerned.

"Yes, sir, he has." The nurse from earlier was folding linens nearby. "Mistress Rhianwyn came by earlier, is all." She looked Sonder up and down with a smug look before taking the linens to be put away. "She tended his arm, so it should be just fine for him to leave."

Merrick sighed. "Come on, boy. Let us leave so she can finish cleaning up."

The distance muffled her voice, but her sarcasm was unmistakable. "Please."

Sonder set the teacup down and stood. He limped behind Merrick, who thanked the nurse.

Once they were out of earshot, Sonder spoke up. "I know I've failed you, sir. I've forgotten my lessons, and I lost."

Merrick waved him off. "Sonder, there is no shame in this." He glanced at the boy as they walked. "I am proud of you."

Sonder looked up. "Sir?"

Merrick stopped, looking around briefly to ensure that no one was close enough to overhear them. Then, he placed his hand on Sonder's shoulder. "Listen to me. There is no shame in caring for the girl." Sonder was alarmed. "Of course I know. It's no small secret. Therein lies the problem, though, you see?

"It's not that you forget your lessons. You excel at them. What you haven't managed to figure out is how to be cunning. Your soft heart will make you well-loved among your men, which you will need to survive on the battlefield and in court. But you cannot wear your heart where all can see."

"You drink tea with Drisil where all can see," he said without thinking.

Merrick said nothing.

Sonder's brow furrowed, not entirely understanding. Merrick indicated they should continue walking, so he fell in line with his mentor. "Are you telling me to keep my emotions under control?"

Merrick spoke firmly. "No. I'm telling you to separate yourself from your outrage and dishonor. I try to teach you mindfulness. You let your enemies know your weak points. Why do you think Mikhail could undermine you so easily using Rhianwyn? His father has begged me to take on his son as my second squire for the past two years. Now he's leading a campaign against you."

Sonder couldn't help but let his curiosity show. "Why don't you? He's a better swordsman than I am."

Merrick's nose wrinkled in distaste. "It wouldn't be a good fit." He looked at Sonder out of his eye to iterate his point. "You're a worthy squire."

This was the first time Merrick had talked to him so openly. It gave Sonder a sense of relief he hadn't felt in a long time. "So, I shouldn't keep Rhianwyn's company?"

They were getting closer to the castle walls, so Merrick stopped them again. "No. A woman's friendship is a needed thing, as much as I hate to admit it. Tran's too. But you must find your discretion, boy. The time is fast approaching that you will not have me by your side to guide you—or mitigate your mistakes." Merrick's eyes implored him to understand. "Abide less by the literal meaning of your lessons, and be cunning. In all things." Understanding began to dawn on him, and Merrick looked satisfied. "Think about it. Come, you're probably hungry and need rest."

After only a few steps, something that had worried Sonder's thoughts for years returned to him. Emboldened, Sonder blurted it out, letting it take its form. "Why did you kill Bran?"

Merrick froze. The man just stood there, and Sonder watched his shoulders rise and fall.

"How do you know that?"

Sonder was confused. "I was there."

Merrick looked at him, and it almost looked like he didn't recognize him. "You knew him?"

"Of course." He sounded insane, but Sonder didn't dare say it. Instead, he took a safer approach. "He mentored me when you were away or too drunk." He looked down at his bruised fingers. "He was Drisil's lover." Sonder felt Merrick's shock. He couldn't help feeling smug. Finally, Merrick would understand that Sonder had been aware of everything. But the thought still filled most of him, leaking out. "He was your friend, wasn't he?" He met Merrick's gaze, tentative. "You loved him, didn't you? So why did you kill him?"

The poison left him. The wound that had festered and spread when he killed the two in Tierrion was finally realized. Merrick's lashing out whenever it involved Sonder's wayward heart was brought to light. Looking into his mentor's eyes now, he understood it, at least a little more.

Merrick swallowed the tears that clearly threatened. "I did." The words were heavy with acknowledgment. "He asked me to because it was my duty." The man looked down to compose himself.

A wordless apology.

He could offer no solution, and his pain conveyed that. They needed their friends, even if the queen, or anyone, could use them against them. Sonder understood, and when Merrick put his hand on his back and steered him, he resigned himself to finding a way, so he could have both worlds if he was meant to be caged.

Chapter Twenty-One
Songs of Magic

***On the road, seventeen years ago
(days after stealing Sonder)***

Randal and Áki had ridden ahead to town for fresh mounts while Merrick and Drisil stayed behind with the infant to set up camp. The work was second nature to Merrick, so he built a fire and cooked. That left a reluctant Drisil to care for the child. They played while Merrick split wood, and he saw the way it renewed her wonder.

Merrick refused to acknowledge his memories. He had stepped in the previous day because if the wailing continued, it would have raised too many questions. He had no desire to burn another village while it slept.

But the way the two laughed as Drisil tickled the baby's nose with seeding grass was hard not to appreciate. They were beautiful. Even kidnapped and orphaned for some war-hungry queen, the innocence was still infectious. He let his memory of simpler times have that much.

In the fading light, Drisil leaned against a tree, bound by the sleeping child curled in her lap. Merrick offered her a steaming bowl of stew.

She seemed surprised, but took it. "Thank you."

He sat across from her, and they ate in silence for several minutes.

Merrick broke the silence. "What you did back there was impressive."

Drisil tucked her hair behind her ear, looking uncomfortable. It astounded him, because she had been abrasive ever since they'd received the same offer of pardon. "Thank you."

"Are you ashamed?" Merrick asked.

It wasn't the first time she became awkward after using her ability to glamour a group of people to cover their trail. But it was the first time he had seen her look shy.

Drisil's eyes narrowed as she looked into the fire. She wasn't often candid, but he had begun to tell when her guard came down. "No. I've just never been praised for it. It's terrifying to most. They don't want to realize how easily they can be manipulated. How fragile our illusion of self-righteousness is." Her dark eyes met his.

Merrick grunted thoughtfully. "It is terrifying." He paused. "You're terrifying."

A smile pulled at her lips. "So are you."
Present, age seventeen

Winter in Stellamar was usually mild, with it being so close to the ocean. However, most mornings dawned with the cobbled streets slick with frost and the roofs dusted with snow. The wind blew in from the sea, keeping all but the bravest huddled inside. It left everyone with little else to do but gossip around a hearth after the tournament. It made Drisil's job easy, and her bones ache for arid places.

The castle buzzed. It was the season for wintering nobles to marry off their children to strengthen their houses. The talk should have centered around the suitors after the celebratory meal to honor the winners—the winter parties always followed. But the whole debacle of the fight between Sonder and Mikhail dominated. The rumored courtship between Mikhail and Rhianwyn meant speculations were exploding.

The rivalry, born between two young men at odds, was reduced to jealous boys fighting over a girl.

Merrick stood behind a sullen Sonder as two servants walked by with baskets of dirty linens chirping away about it. The boy's shoulders slumped further, and Merrick patted him on the shoulder. Drisil watched this, perched beside the man's elbow. She at least let her smile show.

Master Sowa, the Royal Practitioner, removed his spectacles, which shrank his saucer eyes to normal. The man sighed. "I am inclined to decline your request to have the boy return to drills until the prescribed duration of six weeks, Sir Merrick."

"The girl tended to it." Merrick's tone was measured. She knew he hated that there were more capable healers, including Rhianwyn, yet Sowa still held sway over the royal squires.

"I am well aware of that. However, I cannot tell what she did. Thus, I can't declare the injury sound. Unless you can convince her to come here and tell me what she's done, I can't in good faith clear him." He tapped his folded spectacles on his chin as he spoke, then brandished them. "You know, sir, she and Gwenyvir are very secretive about her lessons. As the appointed practitioner and overseer of medical studies, I've spoken to them about it. They've refused to share her talents. Master Randal, too, has been little help. Perhaps you could convince them to divulge? You being the official voice for the children and all."

"I'll see what I can do," Merrick said, voice thick with perfunctory courtesy. "C'mon, boy. Good day, Master Sowa." Merrick bowed.

"To you as well." He inclined his head toward Drisil. "Lady. Sonder." His smile was tight as he returned to his work.

"Pompous ass," Merrick muttered once they were well out of earshot and on their way back to his study. He turned to Drisil. "I've little to offer him while he's forbidden to train."

Sonder walked a few paces ahead of them, no doubt listening.

"I'll see to it. Use the time to focus on yourself," Drisil said. She touched his elbow and smiled. She was happy to heckle him about his exhaustion.

The old grouch was still struggling to find a good rhythm to his priorities now that he was stationed in the capital. His workload included overseeing most of the Justices. Not only was he managing the multitude of investigations, but he was also teaching the next generation of Black Knights how to interact with the population to ferret out dissenters. If it weren't for Áki shouldering most of the younglings' training, the general army wouldn't be as thoroughly tended to.

Throughout each day, Drisil let her path cross Sonder's so she could watch him. She asked the other masters about his performance. The change of pace was invigorating. She sat with Merrick beside the fire to round out her evenings and recounted anything of note.

One day she had discovered that Sonder had found a clever way to keep himself fit by strapping bags of grain to himself. Merrick had laughed when she told him.

During this time, Drisil fell in love with mentoring alongside him. Being in Stellamar had done him well. Sonder's excellence meant there was no higher voice hounding them. It made it easy to descend into the peace they found as the days went by.

Sonder was doing so well, they decided that Drisil should take him into the city.

"Take him. Show him the power of disguise and suggestion like only you can." Merrick's tone and face were kind, but there was never any denying the distrust that lurked like a caged animal behind his eyes. "Besides," he said, the glimpse disappearing entirely, "if you can save one of us from these chittering fools, save him."

"So noble of you, Sir Merrick." She dipped her chin with a smile. "I shall save him from the rumormongers while you hold them off."

"Her dress was red, Drisil. Have you heard? Just like her lips, which I suspect she gets from you." His face and voice were dramatically animated, which played into him being at his wits' end.

A laugh burst out of her, and Drisil covered her smile, surprised by it and by him. "Blessed grace and all that's good." She composed herself and settled her face into mock agony. "Your sacrifice will not be naught." She placed one hand delicately over her breast, and the other reached out to him as she slowly turned to leave.

"Leave me to my fate." His voice returned to normal, but the twinkle in his eye lingered before he returned to his desk.

She walked beside Sonder as they strolled the markets. They both wore black cloaks, lined and trimmed with fur against the cold. People parted around them without a glance, much like they would have had they worn harness bells as anklets. They might as well have been specters traversing the gathered. This was the first time he saw her magic on full display, and his awe as the people passed without touching them made her smirk.

"This is what I've been trying to teach you. It's an invaluable skill to travel without being recognized. Some of the work we do requires that we not be seen." Drisil extricated a hand from her sleeves and raised it at a man to make a point. There was no acknowledgment from him.

"Isn't that the new baron of magic?" Sonder asked, transfixed as the man stepped around them.

Drisil tucked her hand back into her sleeves. "Indeed it is. It appears you were paying attention at dinner. Merrick was worried you weren't."

He was unmoved by her attempts to poke fun at his stern mentor. "Shouldn't he be able to see you if he's the baron?" Sonder's face showed his skepticism.

She relished his surprise. It was a power move to display how incompetent the man was. "He should. So, take that to demonstrate what glamouring looks like."

His brow furrowed as he looked away. "You know I can't do magic." He said it as if the words tasted bitter.

Drisil wondered if he resented her role in his tests. "You don't have to be a proclaimed magician to do it. It's all about knowing people. That's where all magic starts. Understanding then grows from there. Everyone can technically do it. It's knowledge and talent as much as a desire for it."

He didn't seem convinced, but he remained attentive as they spent the rest of the day discussing and watching the bundled citizens shuffle by.

They ambled through the posh markets and dined at a ritzy inn packed with vacationing patricians. Their grumbling about the extreme cold kept them so busy she hardly had to use her magic to hide them. Afterward, they went down the hill through the middle markets and farther still to the wharves and slums. The wind picked up as they ended their day outside a rundown bakery. They sipped warm chocolate and ate buns sprinkled with cinnamon sugar as hunched hirelings passed.

"What do you notice?" she asked.

Sonder didn't look at her, instead continuing to study the individuals going by. She had listened to Merrick gush about the way the boy's mind worked, but it hadn't prepared her for the proud swell as she watched it for herself.

Sonder was engrossed. "Many of these people don't notice much. They're caught up in their apprehensions. But they notice the guards. Or anyone who has wealth, for that matter. It would be difficult to move here because everyone seems to know each other or tend toward distrust. But—" He paused as a middle-aged woman passed by them, her lips moving silently. "It was different in the moneyed part of town. They noticed more and less, somehow. They compared each other and scrutinized people. Yet they probably wouldn't notice much out of the ordinary unless it was glaring." His brow furrowed in thought.

"Good. You're thinking and noticing. Understanding the movement of people under different circumstances and surroundings is important to this magic. Knowing what people want to see in you. How you carry yourself. Whether you meet someone's eye or not. You must have a sense of them just by looking at them. Understand it well enough, and you could even find yourself able to convince a tavern to forget they ever saw you or look like someone else entirely."

Drisil's skin prickled. The magic thrummed through her body as she let herself get swept up into it. She took in a steadying breath and realized he was watching her. Her blood ran cold, but she kept herself taught and smiled. "That's all it takes."

Sonder's eyebrow arched. "What? A costume and a bribe?"

Drisil laughed. "That only goes so far if you can't wear it well and offer the right price." She would have imagined he was putting on a front if she didn't feel his honest energy.

Sonder finished the last of his cocoa and gazed thoughtfully at the destitute streets. "What do they see now?"

She knew the context of what he asked. "We look like well-to-do trade makers. A mother and her teenage son come to a small bakery to support those only slightly less fortunate than ourselves, though society would have us believe we're better."

She plucked the mug from his hands and walked their dishes inside. The owner smiled gratefully, and the two women shared encouragements and wished for warmer weather.

* * *

Sonder watched them for a minute, but he soon grew bored and slouched with a sigh, resigned to wait. Then, a song thread drew his attention to a courtyard with a roaring fire and a group of men. By their weathered look and the number of empty tankards collected at their feet, he guessed they were sailors just paid handsomely for a winter crossing.

Ladies scantily dressed for the weather sat in their laps and draped on their necks while one sailor sang a catchy tune about the women he had slept with. Then, with a smile full of rotting teeth, he leaned toward a woman and sang louder:

I've got a wench in Stellamar
Her name is Lucy Rose.

The men and women hollered and raised their glasses. The woman in question stood up with a look of defiance.

"You wanna sing o' me, do ya? Add me to that shanty o' yours?" With a wicked grin, she began to stomp her foot, and immediately everyone began to taunt the man with hearty *Ooooohs*. The ladies started to clap, and once they did, Lucy hiked her skirts up and began to dance.

You speak of taking us ladies as if we ain't hearin' thee.
A made-up girl in e'ery port and e'ery shore you go.

You think you're made o' gold and believe e'erything thing we've told.
But you haven't got a clue what we say o' you.

We girls aren't fools; we've taken men from every crew.
We've ranked all o' thee, and ye've come in last.

She finished by placing her hands on his legs and leaning into him. They all roared with laughter except him, and she leered triumphantly.

"Oi! Now that wasn't very kind," the sailor complained.

Another man elbowed him, spilling his drink. "She got you, she did!"

"Sur'Tuli, you idiot, you spilled on me!" There were some additional shoving and jaunty shouts. "Alright, you've proved yar point, Lucy." The man pulled her into his lap and kissed her. The woman said something Sonder couldn't hear from the bakery, but he couldn't help but feel flushed by the way she bit her lip, and the man looked back at her. "Sing us a song of the Goddess of Weather and Sea, you saucy thing."

The men and women began to hum while Lucy smiled first at the sailor, then at all of them.

•◦————————◦◦◦◦————————◦•

Drisil stepped back into the cold and pulled her cloak tighter as the first bar rose. The descending sun offered no warmth beside the colors it painted over the docks. The look Sonder wore was distant and sad.

"What do you see there?" she asked. Sonder startled, and she followed his gaze.

He stood and straightened his clothes. "Nothing. I was just—" His face creased, and he looked away before continuing. "I was thinking."

"About?" The song continued to drift up to them, fading into the background.

"Merrick has no ability with magic, does he?" Sonder looked back at her.

The question caught her off guard. "That's correct. Not a magical bone in his body. He has some awareness of it, but only in limited situations. Why do you ask?"

"He can talk to people just like you did just now." He chewed his dry lips. "How does he do it?"

Drisil sighed. She wanted to be careful not to say too much, not knowing what Sonder knew about Merrick's position. "I've wondered the same, if I'm honest. My guess is it has something to do with his authenticity. He hides everything but the heart he wears on his sleeve, and he fears nothing and everything." She saw that he understood what she was saying, even if her answer was whimsical. "Come." She beckoned him to walk next to her. "We should head back."

He hesitated, looking at the sailors once more. "Drisil?"

She folded her hands into her sleeves. "Yes?" There was so much troubling him, and she hadn't the faintest idea what.

"Those sailors. One of them used a curse, Sur'Tuli. That's the south wind, isn't it?"

"The fabled wind the weather sends to drive sailors into the frigid north, yes."

"Now they're singing about the Goddess of Weather and Sea." He looked at her as the string of notes and lyrics came clear before slipping away again. "Why do we punish some for those things and not them?"

Drisil laughed through her nose. She didn't mean to be insensitive, but she had a fondness for the creatures of wooden islands on the water. "Sailors are a superstitious lot. Keep all manners of charms and stick their skin with ink images for good luck. They won't even whistle for fear of angering a jealous wind." She rolled her eyes with a smirk. "Most people believe them to be half-mad. They have to be to spend so much time away from the world and choose the poisoned waters." She looked at the gathered group and watched the woman twirling her wool skirts as they transitioned into another song. "We let them pray because they're at the mercy of many things. They need something to hold on to. But," she said with a lift of her eyebrow, "I've talked to a sailor before, and they're not nearly as mad as they seem."

Sonder's smile returned, softening the corners of his eyes. Finally, the sun slipped below the horizon, and the street plunged into torchlight.

She smiled back and tilted her head so he would know she sympathized. "You ready?"

He nodded.

Drisil drew him close, and he fell in beside her. "Now, let's see what you've learned today. We can start by understanding the movements of a crowd. While we walk, make us invisible."

He failed miserably, and she was a terrible teacher.

As they sat with Merrick in his study for dinner, he asked after their lesson. She sighed her disappointment, and Sonder made a self-disparaging comment about his lack of magical ability.

Merrick stoically looked at Sonder. "Don't worry about it. The knowledge will still serve you. You'll blend in with crowds, inspire those around you, and gain people's trust."

Drisil watched him with the boy, his callused thumb rubbing against the hair beneath his lip. She realized that he was happy. They both were. She knew it was true when Merrick felt her eyes on him, and he glanced at her.

Later that evening, after Sonder left, they were alone in Merrick's study. The fire crackled cheerily, which chased the cold out of the stone and warmed her. Over the kettle's whistle, she heard the scrape of flipping papers as Merrick continued to work despite the late hour.

He let out a frustrated sigh. "At least one of us got out of this forsaken place today. Did I tell you that her dress was red? If I hear one more thing about Rhianwyn's courtship, I may lose my mind, Drisil." Merrick shuffled a letter to the bottom of the pile.

Drisil chuckled and set his cup of tea in front of him. She slid down onto the couch beside him. Then, she swiveled her hips and placed her legs across his lap, so he was forced to put his work down.

"We only hear so much because they're our students," she said, adjusting her fur-lined robe and taking a sip of wine.

Merrick rolled his eyes. "Lose my mind. I may have already."

"Take a break then." She sat up and took the pages from him, tossing them onto the table. Some slid too far and fluttered to the floor.

Paying no mind, she cozied herself deeper into the plush armrest.

Her look was infectious. A smile blossomed on Merrick's face. It had been a long time since their friendship wasn't fraught with some type of disagreement.

"The two are doing well in their studies, thanks to you. But how are you? How are you holding up having to teach these kids knowledge and how to behave?" Merrick asked, leaning over her legs to grab his tea.

"Much better than you. I've enjoyed it, especially with Sonder. The injury helped to refocus him. Which reminds me, have you had any success getting Rhianwyn to talk to Sowa?" Drisil took a sip to let him speak.

Merrick rested his arms on her legs, and the warm cup brushed her bare ankle. "No."

A grin spread across her face, which she hid behind the rim of her glass, knowing Merrick wouldn't take kindly to it. "And she refuses?"

Merrick groaned and leaned back, letting his head fall back. "Yes. Gwen and Wilkin still refuse to make her. It stopped being worth it a week ago."

"Well, it would appear the distance you pushed for has—"

Merrick cut Drisil off. "I told the boy he needs the girl."

Drisil laid the tips of her fingers on his shoulder. "You did?" He had said nothing to her about it, and it was a shocking turn of events.

Merrick blinked slowly. "I did. Tran, too. But I also told him he needed to focus on your classes and become more cunning and not take things so literally."

She preened while he spoke, but he turned his bright blue eyes on her once he finished, and she grew more serious. "Well, I did mention he has been doing well with me. I could—"

Merrick spoke over her again, no doubt seeing her eyebrow arched in frustration as she sucked her teeth. "I'm more worried about the girl, actually." He took her hand from her lap. "Sorry to cut you off. But you've not heard Randal taking a sudden interest in her, have you? I'm worried about what Sowa has said about this fiasco."

Drisil let her face soften, his interruptions forgiven. But she didn't hide the edge that crept into her voice. "No, Merrick. There has been no indication of that. He and the queen are still very much focused on their current endeavor. Which, let me remind you, means you ought to do your best to mitigate the conflict and manage your responsibilities. Perish the thought you lose a modicum of control."

Merrick kissed the back of her hand, a rare smile becoming visible through the hairs that tickled her skin. "Not today. It is an endless argument of ours. You alleviated my worries. The only thing stopping me from my duties now is that you threw my things."

Drisil pulled her hand away with a laugh. "You say that, but you can hardly blame me." She took a sip of her wine. It had been a while since she had enjoyed his company so much.

Drisil had long ago accepted the nature of their friendship and how Merrick was, but a wave of grief came over her, and she retook his hand. "I've missed you, Mer." She realized this was the first time since Bran's death they had sat like this together.

He tapped his teacup against her glass. "That's why we need friends, right?" Nothing about his tone or body language felt convinced. The laughter had left his eyes.

Reading his thoughts was easy. "Your boy will be fine. He has been gone for so long from his studies. It's probably alright that he's applying himself to keep his mind occupied. Like someone I know." She nudged his hand with her knee and smirked, laying on all the sexual charm she knew would fall flat. "Come, what would it take for you to finally relax, hm? Seventeen years and I don't think I've ever seen it. I have a few tricks that would help."

Merrick stood up, which forced her legs off of his lap. "A walk?" he asked, offering his hand to her. She balked, and the grin on his face was self-satisfied. "I'll loan you my coat, even though your misery would make me feel better."

Her eyes narrowed, but she still laughed; they both needed it. Suffering the cold was a small price to pay. Her hand slid into his, and he pulled her to her feet.

The bailey was nearly deserted at night, and the garden had hardly any torches lit. One of the few places within the city that allowed their eyes to adjust to the darkness to see the sky. Drisil happily watched the stars winking between the bare branches. She hugged Merrick's arm as much for warmth as to enjoy the experience.

"You made a good call," she said.

"You love everything about the outdoors except the outside part." He kept his gaze forward, and the gray in his beard and temples shone in the dim light.

"How very astute of you. Wisely put." She shook her head. The memory of Sonder during their lesson in the city came back to her. "Which I think your boy is, as well." There was no mirth in her voice.

He looked down at her. "Oh?"

"He can see people's magic." Her deep brown eyes met his.

"I thought there was no indication he has magical abilities? The tests haven't shown anything, have they?" Merrick's body turned toward her while they walked.

"He doesn't, and they haven't." She looked away.

He stopped her and placed a hand on her shoulder. "How do you know? Why haven't they?"

"I don't know. I doubt he was being deceptive. Between Aspera and me, he would have to be a master, and he's far from that. But it was how he looked at me when I explained it to him. At that moment, between being swept up in the magic and harnessing it, he saw it."

His hand fell away. "I can see that, and I have no magic ability. Just an awareness."

Drisil tilted her head. "You know me," she said flatly. He began to understand. "Besides," she continued, "it was different somehow." The spot where his hand had been was growing cold again.

"Who else knows?" He sounded afraid.

Her anger flickered. "Only you, Merrick. I'd not tell anyone else."

He sighed. "Of course." Then he visibly relaxed and began to lead her once more.

The only sound was their footsteps on the mix of dirt and stone for a while. They were both lost in their thoughts. Merrick was likely considering what the news meant, and Drisil was drifting through the mix of emotions. Her renewed grief had brought her face-to-face with things she hadn't confronted in years.

"You know, your boy is getting philosophical," she said, breaking the silence.

"I know," he responded gruffly.

The man was full of surprises tonight. "Do you?"

"He asked me about Bran on Hallowed night." Her heart skipped a beat at hearing the name on Merrick's lips. A chill ran through her when his blue eyes met hers. "What made you realize it?"

It took her a second to collect her thoughts. "He saw some sailors singing about the gods, and he asked me about it."

Merrick nodded. "Sounds about right."

"What are you going to do about it?" she asked, surprised by how calm he seemed.

"Same as I always have: keep him alive."

It was nearly the turn of the torches when she laid a kiss on his warm cheek and bade him goodnight. His cloak still hung from her shoulders, and she enjoyed the oversized weight. "You're letting me keep this as payment. I still have to walk back to my estate." Drisil burrowed deeper into it.

"It's yours as long as you need," he said with a laugh. Then he grew serious as he looked into her eyes. "You're sure you don't want me to walk with you?"

The way he looked at her ignited the memories of Bran in her skin. She wanted to ask him. But she also knew herself. She wanted more for the sake of having it. She would ask him to stay, and her needs ran deeper than desire. She didn't want to put him in a place where she asked him to oblige her. He deserved better.

Though her heart pooled with loneliness, she smiled. "I was once a woman of the night, Mer. I'm not afraid of the dark."

The brush of his thumb against her cheek left a blazing trail in its wake. The cold betrayed her sharp exhale. "Goodnight, Sil," he whispered. His rough beard tickled her forehead, snapping her out of it.

She closed her parted lips. "Until tomorrow," she said.

His cloak offered more comfort than keeping the cold at bay. The temperature made her sense of smell acute, and the sharp, peppery smell of him remained with her as she walked alone through the castle gates. It held memories of their first years together on the road before Aspera had their reward posters taken down, and every inn suddenly became open to them. Fireside memories. Merrick was always more himself as he tended to a campsite, ensuring they were kept fed and warm.

In the stillness after all the tasks, he almost opened up.

A shadow stood on her doorstep, and frustration washed the remnants away. She was a beacon to the lonely.

"To what do I owe this pleasure?" She let her voice drip with sarcasm.

"You're home late," Randal said, pushing away from the wall.

"I don't remember making plans with you, so I don't see why my whereabouts matter." She stood defiantly in front of him, her chin tilted up.

"I didn't come to argue," he said softly. He reached out and took the pendant at her throat in his fingertips. Drisil held still, not letting herself react to his touch.

"Then why did you come?" she asked. She was afraid he had somehow overheard her and Merrick in the garden. There were secrets about the boy she was resigned to keep, but she wondered if voicing them to Merrick had somehow betrayed them.

"I just haven't seen you in a year," Randal said, still toying with her necklace.

"Since Sonder's trial, you mean. When you took his blood."

She met his look unwavering, and his face showed a flicker of anger. "Which I made amends for by standing up for him in front of the queen. May I remind you I lied for you." He tugged on her necklace before letting it fall back to her skin.

Drisil sucked in a shocked breath. The metal radiated heat into her winter-weary bones. He smiled again as if there were some grand conspiracy. It was unnerving how quickly he was making advancements with his magic, even if they were as small as making her necklace warm.

"We've been looking at how different materials can be used to transfer energy. It's a little trick I learned this morning. It's worn off, though, hasn't it?" He sounded dejected. Already his confidence had slipped. Her displeasure with him remained a tender spot.

Drisil wrapped her fingers around the pendant, and it was indeed cooled. "Why are you here?" She knew the answer.

"Aspera has asked for your services. She wants you to join her in the morning for breakfast to give you your assignment."

"And for you? A blue raven would have sufficed."

Randal took her hand and stepped closer to her. He leaned in and whispered in her ear, "I know Merrick doesn't tell you how beautiful you are when you're in the presence of magic."

"He also doesn't desire me, so it doesn't matter," she snapped. His thumb brushed the corner of her tight smile, and she faltered.

Drisil remembered how Sonder had looked at her earlier when he saw her henaild. Merrick was right in that it wasn't a big secret. But the way Randal was looking at her now made her desires twist into an ugly mess. A mix of her grief, longing, and the underlying need to protect Sonder, even if Randal had no idea about his ability.

The primal need to be seen and touched overtook her, and she pressed her lips against his.

Chapter Twenty-Two
Northern Refuge

Merrick's lost journal, six months after bending the knee

Present, age seventeen

The weather remained overcast and cold for the next month. Since Merrick's duties had shifted to Stellamar, there was less need for Sonder to oil armor and care for horses. Coupled with Drisil being sent away on another mission, his classes were shortened, and he was unaccustomed to the lack of structure. There was a foreboding sense that his tutelage was nearing its end.

Sonder had started exploring the city while his arm healed. Initially, he stayed close to the castle. However, after he realized Rhianwyn's magic had expedited the mending, he ventured further. Despite having little money, he enjoyed walking the streets.

After the lesson with Drisil and the additional free time her absence represented, it became an opportunity to practice what she had taught him. Using body language and clothes, he became unrecognizable and could enjoy being unnoticed. He had missed watching people, and he did so for hours. Each day, he explored a different district, some no more than small clusters of blocks marked by decorative flags.

After months of doing this, he happened across a corner along the northern wall that was nearly abandoned. There, he found a house that squatted precariously on a sheer, jagged drop. Its roof was mostly caved in except for a section held up by a doorway, forming a cavity protected from the cold wind blowing off the Caelum Sea.

Sonder speculated that a ground-shake had collapsed the cliffs, and the house had narrowly avoided the clutches of the churning salt water below. Many roads dead-ended at cliffs for that reason.

It didn't matter, as this little nook, nestled at the world's edge, became his haunt.

Some days, Sonder stayed to watch the sunset. Small boats would drift by lazily, going out to sea or upriver toward homes or other ports. The view back was magnificent as well. The castle rose, with the rest of the city splayed at its feet. The sun would glint off the grass reclaiming the other crumbling buildings and roads along the wall.

Across the channel stood the lighthouse, tended by an older man. The building reminded Sonder of the cloaked giants from Rhianwyn's stories, holding lights to guide Rebirth through winter. Their limbs were stone, their magic kept by moss that glowed like stardust, which tricked the og'luan to nest in their lanterns until morning.

That was much like how the man living by himself tended the lantern that winked in circles endlessly, guiding ships along the coast. Only the light-tenders understood the elaborate mechanical system driven by mysterious magic. The massive lenses magnified and focused the fires so they reached the horizon, and royal guards brought oil each morning and night to keep the flames lit.

Sonder had read about it in a book. Those same pages said that lighthouses were the only genuinely altruistic thing in the world. The author claimed there was nothing for the lighthouse to gain from guiding sailors out at sea.

The crumbling house was the type of place Rhianwyn would love. The irony didn't escape him that he came to this place to avoid her, yet here he thought of her anyway. His exploring began as wanting to give her space, and it had garnered a place for peace instead.

The ritual of him sneaking continued even after the old doctor declared him fit to spar again.

It was the enduring gossip that drove him away. The rivalry between him and Mikhail had been reduced to him being a sulking loser incapable of winning the girl. It was no secret the new song the bards sang was based on him. It would've been impressive how too much free time could create such an elaborate story if he weren't the victim.

Sonder's duties had been relaxed with his injury. This continued after his clearance until the masters started talking to each other and discovered he had skirted his work for an extra month. They reeled him back in soon after, which meant he had to actively ignore the whispers and sidelong looks.

There was the chance to get some solitude still, but Sonder realized how much Tran had picked up in his absence. A handful of boys picked up the rest. When he returned, they gladly relinquished the tasks with no complaint. He also bribed the others to get assigned with Tran, promising to help with weaponry or take their errands.

"You didn't tell them?" Sonder asked while they worked.

"No. You only took advantage of it for an extra week, right?" Tran shrugged with a grin. "No use making your life more miserable."

A month, Sonder thought. It made him feel guilty, so he took on a bulk of Tran's chores, too.

Two weeks later was the Solstice, where anyone of note dressed in colors of the sun and danced and drank with abandon. Sonder didn't go, but he still heard about Mikhail and Rhianwyn. The boy had given her a rose-gold necklace dusted with so many gems it sparkled like captured stars, and their waltzing was like the ethereal dance of the sun and moon. They were the envy of the ball.

It was all anyone could talk about the following day, and it had worn on Sonder. As he turned down the hay for the cavalry horses, he sighed and looked up at his friend over one of the chargers. "If I hear one more person talk about how lovely Mikhail and Rhianwyn looked at the ball, I will do something stupid. Maybe challenge him to a duel or something."

Tran couldn't help but laugh. "No, you won't." Sonder shrugged as a way of agreement, and Tran continued. "Just give it time. It will be old news soon."

"Of course. Then they'll go on to the next lavish gift she's adorned with. Like the chocolates she couldn't possibly eat on her own." Sonder scooped more hay. In frustration, he stabbed his pitchfork into the dirt, causing the beast to lift its head in surprise. "I know you're tired of hearing about it, but I miss her, Tran. He's only doing it to get at me. She deserves better."

Tran continued to rake away. "Well, in fairness, she deserves better than what you gave her, too."

Sonder ran his fingers through his overgrown hair. "I know that. That's what makes it worse. I can't even tell her that. She ignored my letter and won't even look at me."

"Well, you're just going to have to wait for her to accept your apology. In the meantime, I'll continue to offer my sage advice. That way, if she does come around, you'll not be so dense the next time."

Once they finished putting away their tools, they headed toward the baths to wash for dinner. The sun had nearly set, giving the yard a dusty-violet quality through the overcast. Guards were making their way around to light the torches, creating pockets of shadows where the night grew eager.

As the boys passed a storage building, a familiar voice solidified. "I'm so tired of her accepting my gifts and getting no return. What else could she possibly need? Haven't I done enough for her?"

Sonder's mind tried to convince him it wasn't Mikhail. But when he looked into the shadows between buildings, he saw him and two other boys. Mikhail looked up as they came into view. A wicked grimace crossed Mikhail's face, realizing he'd been overheard.

"Well, look who it is. Finally done licking your injuries, Traitor's Ilk? Maybe you can help me. What's the secret to getting Wyn to undress? Any tips?"

"I wouldn't know." Sonder kept his voice measured.

"Really? I heard you got her beaten for getting caught in your bed. Couldn't even make it worth her time? How very like the Black Daemon's heir. Unworthy of everything you've been given, and willing to let everyone fall with you."

Sonder took a step forward, but Tran's hand on his chest stayed him.

"Sonder, don't."

"Neither of us deserves her." Sonder breathed heavily but didn't make another move, letting Tran's hands ground him.

"What's the matter? Lost your zeal to fight for her? Wasn't the Black Daemon known for raping women before he burned them? Realized you don't want a repeat of Tierrion?" Mikhail elbowed one of his companions.

Tran wrapped his arms around Sonder's waist before he could take more than two stumbling steps. Sonder imagined squeezing the life out of Mikhail's laugh.

Tran shoved Sonder away with a grunt. "Go!" he hissed.

Sonder turned, and Tran held him by the back of his shirt to keep him from going back.

The boy yelled after them, "I'll let you know what it's like when I finally have my way with her. Go find a different girl to help with that energy, so you won't feel bad when you get her killed!"

Sonder fumed as Tran held on to him. When they were out of sight, Tran jerked him back to face him. Sonder immediately tried to push him off, but his friend grabbed his arms. "Would you stop it!" Tran's energy matched his. "If you'd stop acting like a wounded animal and use your brain for one second, man. He's saying those things to get to you. It's all smoke."

"I'll kill him," Sonder whispered, still shaking from his rage. "I've killed for less."

Tran let go of him and sucked in a pained breath. He rolled up his sleeve to look at his arm, beginning to bruise and swell.

"What happened?" Sonder asked, alarmed.

"You were using my arm like it was Mikhail's neck," Tran said lightly, rubbing at the angry marks.

"I'm sorry." He felt suddenly unclean. The memory of his rage back at Tierrion flooded back, and he remembered the taste of blood. His appetite soured.

Tran grinned sheepishly and roughly thumped his shoulder. "Better my arm than Mikhail's throat." He began to push him along again. "Let's go. I could go for a big bowl of comforting soup."

Sonder appreciated Tran's attempt to lighten the mood, but he was shaken, and there was no undoing it. He still hadn't told anyone about his nightmares, or why he had pushed Rhianwyn away in the first place, but Mikhail had found out.

As they ate dinner, everything that had happened since Tierrion played over in his head. Anytime Tran bumped his arm and hissed, Sonder felt his shame like a hot iron—he had begun to lose control.

He hardly took two bites, and bless Tran, because when Sonder begged to be excused, the other boy didn't question it.

Sonder's thoughts swarmed as he walked along the barely lit paths of the garden. As the cold gnawed through his cloak, memories of the first time he and Rhianwyn had fought about their friendship came back. Instead of telling her the truth, he'd made the mistake a second time. Instead of giving her the option to decide his worthiness or if he was a monster, he had made himself one.

In the aftermath of his outburst tonight, he realized how badly he missed her now. The weather forced him inside, and his heart still beat in his ears as he paced his room. Weeks of introspection, and he had finally driven himself mad.

The letter he had written after the tournament had lacked all of this self-reflection. It had merely said sorry. Of course she didn't forgive him—it was an empty apology. He couldn't even tell her about the monster she was courting, because he had destroyed his own merit.

Although he told Tran that he would give Rhianwyn space and wait for her to see the truth, his skin wouldn't stop crawling with the urge to find her. Finally, after an hour of pacing, he grabbed his cloak and left. He knew where to find her.

As he was rounding the corner to the library, she walked out. They nearly collided, and she jumped, almost dropping her books.

"Lords," she breathed. When she saw him, her face darkened. "Oh, it's you. What are you doing here, Sonder?" She clutched the books tightly to her chest as if to create a protective barrier between them.

"Wyn, I know you're angry. But I have to tell you. Tonight, I overheard Mikhail and— "

Mikhail turned into the hallway, and the sight of the other boy made Sonder stop.

"What did you overhear?" Mikhail asked. Rhianwyn had her back to him, so she couldn't see the triumphant smile he wore. Instead, he put a protective arm around her, letting his face morph to concern.

Stunned, Sonder couldn't speak. His pulse beat wildly. Her presence had put him off-guard. Seeing Mikhail under these circumstances made it difficult to find his voice or anger.

Mikhail lifted his chin. "He obviously didn't expect this. Can't tell you what he overheard with me here to defend myself." He pulled her closer, and she crumpled into him. "Trying to tell lies to spoil us."

Sonder began to protest, but Rhianwyn cut him off. "Sonder, please." She looked tense in Mikhail's embrace, and she didn't radiate how he remembered.

Sonder's anger began to awaken. He wondered what Mikhail had done to make her believe he would sabotage her out of spite. Then he remembered he had been a right ass all on his own.

Before he could come up with any response, Mikhail said, "Come on, my love." He began to lead her away, and she followed. As they walked, his hand slid to rest on her hip.

Sonder was left alone in the hallway. He felt like a fool, and as he saw Mikhail's hand drop, he flushed with anger and shame. When Sonder later told Tran about what had happened, his friend only sighed and told him what he already knew: he had made a mistake.

Chapter Twenty-Three
The Gods Call

Mother Eissie,

I've heard rumors of your capacity to welcome those of us who brought ruin to the old ways. I know you would tell me there is nothing to forgive, because what's done is done. I beg forgiveness anyway.

The Goddess continues her silence, and I'm a damned man desperate for absolution.

I am afraid of meeting death not knowing if the Star Mother thinks I'm worthy enough to meet Phyrias and be ferried across the stars to sit with my people again.

Will you pray for me as if there is still time? There is majick in prayer, even across distances, is there not?

I've spent more time reflecting on all that I have done. I suspect I'll carry my remorse for killing Aoife, and Lucrid, and all our people for the rest of eternity, regardless of if I'm forgiven or cast into the River Graniöch.

I found a letter written by Lucrid to his wife, saying he had found Astraía. Is it true? Did he find peace before I killed him? You're the last Gwyn'Teilwyr I know of.

I ask as if you'll be able to respond before my time, which is impossible. It's my last stream of thought, however. Did he make his wish? Did he use his Auza-Bendith?

Before she died, Aoife told me to keep faith. You Lorists and your trust in us Knights. You've always known us, haven't you?

I wish I knew why we failed, yet you've remained true to what the Goddess asked.

I pray my actions have reached your ears and speak for themselves.

I've taken measures to keep Rhianwyn safe for as long as she remains among us. I may have destroyed many threads in your network, but I left the strongest in place, and they are thriving. Above everything, the children must be kept safe. I pray my efforts were enough. Of all the letters I've written to you and burned, I am finally willing to die for the truth.

I bow before the Goddess.
Bran

A letter to the Lorist Mother Eissie, a week before Bran's death
Present, age seventeen

Rhianwyn wandered through Stellamar's streets with a muted-maroon cloak wrapped around her for warmth. The hem of her dress was muddy from the puddles in the seams of the cobbles. Stone buildings hung over her with deep, weather-stained beams and drawn shutters. Most had stores on the ground level with signs swaying overhead and apartments above. Many guild members resided in this district, serving their neighbors instead of wringing them of coin like the nobles' merchants who lived up the hill.

A woman scrubbing the muck from her entryway looked up and waved at the girl with a warm smile. Rhianwyn lifted a hand in greeting as she continued.

Before long, she recognized the carved sign she was looking for. Deep grooves formed the shape of a burning candle. The bright white and warm reds and yellows stood out against the blue background, even if the paint had begun to wear away, revealing the dull, splintered wood beneath.

She realized she couldn't remember the path she had taken, her brain was so addled with exhaustion. Silently she prayed it hadn't been one borne from habit—she couldn't afford to be so careless.

The homely aroma of oils seeped through the closed door, and Rhianwyn felt a sense of comfort. The door had a beautiful stained-glass window gifted to the shop owner, depicting blazing suns and moons with rainbows streaking down from their warm rays.

Small bells chimed to announce when she pushed the door open. The inside glowed brilliantly. It was as if the sun were setting within the little shop. Drawers of candles lined the walls, a neat scrawl marking each one.

Candles of varying lifespans and wax of every color overflowed their bins. Some of them had medicinal qualities, aiding healing and relieving stress.

Hanging from the ceiling was a massive fixture. So many shards of perfectly shaped glass spun slowly, each drop catching the light differently, casting tiny fragments of color around the room.

"Is that who I think it is?" an older woman called from the back, where many lenses could be seen with a steaming pot of wax over a low-heat fire.

"Depends if that's a good thing," Rhianwyn called back, tugging off her gloves.

"You, my dear, are always a good thing." A bent woman shuffled through the doorway, leaning against a gnarled staff. Her wrinkled face was radiant, surrounded by a bob of dark silver hair.

Rhianwyn pocketed her gloves and met the woman by the fireplace, where a rickety table and chairs sat. "How are you today, Missus White? How are your eyes?"

"I am terrible. This weather makes my joints ache. This light is horrible to work in. I'm a delicate flower, and these wretched clouds keep me away from my beloved."

Rhianwyn pulled a chair out for the woman. "You are like a flower. You wilt more every day without the sun. You're a child of Harina, aren't you?"

"Who wants to be a child of Bors?" White asked incredulously.

Rhianwyn set a kettle to boil and pulled a pouch of herbs from her satchel. "Mistress Olive called me a summer child when I got in trouble," Rhianwyn remembered. "Seemed an insult to me."

"A compliment. I'd rather be innocent forever than grow crotchety. Far more fun to see life through shades of spring than icicles. Although, I've seen snow kicked up on a wind so gentle that it glittered like diamonds in the sky as the sun shone."

Rhianwyn's smile remained painted on her face as she sat down and began to work a balm into Missus White's swollen hands. She loved listening to the woman speak about the play of light in the world.

White was so gifted in her control over the substance that her body shimmered as if her skin were made of rainbow. "How are the non-flickering candles coming along?"

The woman sighed. "Terribly." When Rhianwyn glanced up, she waved her off. "Alright, I'm dramatic. Just not nearly as fast as I'd like. You healers deserve to have a candle that doesn't waver for those long nights. You grace us commoners with your talent. The least we could do is give you reliable light. But, no! I seem to be the only one of us candlemakers who give any measure of concern to the task. So, it's slow, is what I'm trying to say."

"What of your eyes?" Rhianwyn asked, switching to the other hand. Already the swelling had gone down in the one she'd just finished.

"You pester."

"I worry. You've been warned about staring through those lenses and at the sun. You damage them."

"The spots still go away," the woman harrumphed. "I don't need to see very far. The sun is quite obvious with how bright it glows. I know people's voices to know who comes in. Patrons who don't know to holler a greeting aren't ones I need to bother remembering."

Rhianwyn chuckled at the woman's spunk. "Well, if you aren't careful, you know what will happen. I'm looking for a solution to protect your eyesight, but I haven't come across anything yet. Maybe the secret libraries will bring something new."

"I have faith you'll figure it out." Missus White patted her hand dismissively. "You're the most talented girl I know."

Rhianwyn finished rubbing the ointment in as the kettle began to whistle. She got up, made them both tea, then returned to her chair. The woman held the cup in her hands greedily and seemed to thaw out as the steam curled around her nose.

"What news from the guilds?" Rhianwyn asked. "How have you all fared with the queen's new laws about teaching?"

"Not well, but we manage. Apprentices grow ever harder to find. People are so focused on surviving they can't afford to take time away from their farms or businesses to learn. Anyone who shows any talent leaves and takes our secrets to the queen. Rumor is she wants to use our knowledge for war, or weed us out of the market altogether. It's an ongoing battle. You know this. Truly it hasn't changed. But our majicks are slowly dying. What's left is a sliver of what it once was."

Rhianwyn sipped the hot liquid carefully. "Have any more tried to flee?"

"Thankfully, there haven't been many raids lately. No word of any, either. The queen seems quite content to stay busy with whatever project she's working on."

Rhianwyn still had yet to discover anyone who knew what that was. Anyone close to the queen was inaccessible to her. "That's a relief."

"I avoid scrutiny, just like Gwen. We're too valuable. For how long that will last, who knows. That's why the constant flow of apprentices to the crown is so worrying. It's only a matter of time before she finds a way to replace us. Then who knows what'll happen?" Missus White shrugged. "We survive, right?"

The bells rang once more. Miss White looked up, although her eyes did not focus. Rhianwyn turned, and a flood of relief filled her.

"My guess is that's the other one, no?" Missus White grumbled before Rhianwyn could say anything.

Rhianwyn rose from her chair, and the two girls met, embracing tightly. It had been about nine months, but it felt like longer. Her heart grew heavier as she inhaled the frozen summery smell of Maeveen's cloak.

"I've work to attend to," Missus White said as she hauled herself to her feet using her cane. "You girls enjoy the fire."

The clunk of the wood faded to the back room, and they finally released each other.

"I was worried you might not make it," Rhianwyn said as Maeveen adjusted her rope braid.

"It wasn't so hard today. The weather helps conceal, as much as I hate it. It's still warmer than the mountains." Maeveen smiled, then looked to the fire. "But I could use some tea to warm me."

They settled themselves in the chairs. Miss White hollered from the back that she had put together a plate for them, which Rhianwyn retrieved. The backroom was also a kitchen, common to most shops nearby. There were sliced apples, which were a touch mealy, and cured meats to put on cracker-bread with soft cheese to smear. She was shooed when she thanked the woman.

"I've already slipped in on some of the other guilds, so there's no need to tell me. I already know their state and how Aspera keeps stealing talent," Maeveen said, snagging an apple slice and wrapping it in the meat. "I'm more concerned about you. Tell me how you're faring. How is the spying going?"

Rhianwyn would have rather basked in the joy of having her sister here before immediately going to the topic she dreaded. "Well enough." How was she supposed to explain how entangled she had become?

The clouds inside her returned—telling Sonder off the way she had still wore on her. But Mikhail was growing pushier by the day to be more intimate and solidify their courtship—which included denouncing Sonder. When he found her in the library, she had just been arguing with Mikhail, and she didn't want Sonder to do anything reckless to tarnish his name further.

Maeveen sipped her tea. "I've heard rumors you're being courted, and it sounds like you've had quite the season. I've enjoyed hearing about how lovely you've been at all the dances and parties."

Rhianwyn smiled shyly and began to pick at the hem of her sleeve. "Well, it's spying first and foremost, but I suppose he is. It's been lovely. A little overwhelming, but a nice change of pace."

Her sister smiled. "You're of the age you should start living a little. It sounds extravagant. Although, what's his name? The one you've been getting on with?"

"Mikhail." She should have felt happier telling her older sister about the man courting her.

"That's it. He treats you well?"

"Well enough, yes. He lavishes me with more gifts than I know what to do with. Some of my lessons have begun to slip, though, because he always wants to be with me. But I suppose it makes me feel special." She took a sip of her tea.

"What about Sonder? Have you spoken to him? He has returned, hasn't he?"

The directness of the question hit hard. It felt just like getting punched in the gut. She swallowed and took a moment to steady herself. "I haven't really, no."

"What happened?" Maeveen asked. Rhianwyn suspected she was pretending ignorance if she knew about the parties.

"He refused to talk to me when he got back." Rhianwyn sighed, letting the words closer to the truth come out. "That's why I invested more time with Mikhail; he has always been taken with me. Part of me hoped it would make Sonder jealous, but he didn't care." She rolled her eyes angrily. "Then he went and challenged Mikhail in a duel for my honor, of all things. As if I haven't fought his battles for him before. I'm fully capable of deciding who I spend my time with."

"You're very angry about this," Maeveen said, eyebrows rising in surprise.

"Well, of course! Should I not be?"

"You have every right to be. I just wonder if it's worth it? You're not typically so passionate. I don't see what it has to do with your spying."

Rhianwyn's brow furrowed. Maeveen hadn't seen many sides of her. "Well, I'm angry at him. Disappointed and angry."

It felt good to say it for the first time. Even Alessia seemed to marvel at Mikhail's charm. The girls hadn't gotten into much else, though Alessia had asked her how long she would remain angry at Sonder just that morning.

The pull of her emotions was exhausting.

"Do I dare ask what you know I'm going to?" Maeveen looked at her gently.

"I don't need it right now," Rhianwyn snapped. She didn't trust herself to commit to the finality of damning Sonder.

Ashamed of herself, she looked at the hanging fixture of glass. There was a magical component to it, where it drifted slowly and continuously in a circle, just like the lighthouse. A small, slow-burn candle lit in its center created all the colors.

Miss White had been the one to perfect the candles. That, and find a way to make them burn like daylight, dim, or even glow red to protect night vision.

Sadness returned to Rhianwyn, and she took a shaky breath. This city, in so many ways, was her home. She had grown to love the populace as much as the people who shared her blood, even though she had never met the latter.

"I'm not ready to make that decision, Mae. I've told you that." She looked into her sister's bright blue eyes.

Maeveen's red curls were in a messy bun, so unlike Rhianwyn's darker hair, neatly twisted into a courtly rope braid, though it too sometimes shone red. Maeveen always said she looked like their mother, darker in everything—even her hazel eyes, which glistened with tears now.

"I know you want me to come home. But this place is home, too. I have a man courting me, and friends, and I enjoy what I do here to keep our gredwyr strong. We'd be nothing without them; you've said so yourself. Plus, I want to see the hidden libraries once they're put together."

"Wyn, our networks don't need you. Like I said when I walked in, I've already heard about the guilds. You don't have to be the one who tells me. There are other ways."

"Right, but what if she finds out you all are sneaking into the city and finds a way to bar you? She has done it before. People, might I remind you, get caught and executed. You don't tell me about those things, but I hear about them. I witness them." Rhianwyn could be a master of arguing when she put her mind to it. She took her sister's hand. "I don't want something to happen to you. If she bars you, then what? It might fall apart, and then we'd know nothing about what's happening here."

"You build a clever case. But you forget that your presence here lies solely on the assumption that Sonder can yet be helped." Maeveen paused a beat. "So can he?"

Rhianwyn's heart quickened, and her silence spoke for her.

"Do you love this Mikhail enough to truly forget everything? Where do his loyalties lie? Have you even asked him?"

Maeveen's words cut to the quick. The glossy idea that he loved her enough to either abandon his namesake or accept her as she was felt flimsy. "I haven't, no. It didn't feel important since I need to keep my cover." She doubted Mikhail would ever bring her enough happiness to leave her identity behind.

"Mother Eissie would tell you she accepts whatever you choose. But I struggle to have that same acceptance. If you don't want to come home, and you've given up, I'll be forced to take your memories, Wyn. You know that, right?"

"I haven't made up my mind," she fired back. "I'll talk to Sonder, alright? I'll figure out what's going on inside his head."

Maeveen took her hand. "I do not ask these things to make you angry. When I heard how lovely you looked at the Solstice Ball, dressed like the night sky dancing with the sun, I could see it. You deserve that sort of happiness. But you can find it elsewhere. Your portal of escape shrinks every day. I'd rather you did it now if there's no hope for him than stay and become ensnared by her spells."

"Why can't we take Sonder, though?"

Maeveen sighed. "She would hunt him to the ends of the known earth. So long as she knows he lives, she won't stop. He is the last living heir to Astraía's magic that anyone knows about. His legacy is too valuable to her, even as a ruthless killer. There's power in that."

"What magic, though? He has none. They've taken his blood. Who knows what they've done with it?"

"Exactly," Maeveen said. She made Rhianwyn look at her. "Mother Eissie hasn't told me. Even if she had, it's too dangerous for you to know. But Aspera is doing blood magic. She is no idiot. If he ran, she would know where he was."

Always the same conversation. All Rhianwyn wanted was peace with him.

She reclaimed her hand and folded her arms in her lap. "I understand."

Maeveen sighed and looked at their tea. It had gone cold, and the plate left scarcely touched. "Look, our network isn't as expansive as it once was. Bran saw to that in the queen's name. But he tried to rebuild what he could in the end. You know some of them, like Miss White and Gwen. But there are many you don't because it's still being reborn in the people who just want peace, and to see their neighbors given true justice." Maeveen hesitated, obviously struggling to decide if she should tell her more or not. "There's a woman named Grace, who is instrumental in helping people trying to escape the kingdom. She sheltered Merrick and the others when they stole Sonder, and she has remained close to Merrick since. If you need to escape, she is the safest way."

Memories of helping Merrick when he had nearly died jarred Rhianwyn. He had always been kind to her, even if he'd only spoken to her a handful of times.

Maeveen raised her eyebrows at Rhianwyn's silence, so she nodded. "Alright." Her curiosity was piqued. "Can we trust Merrick and the others, then?"

"Absolutely not. They may have been close to Bran, but the man is gone, and they've been under the queen's influence without him a long time. Don't let their friendliness with some of our people make you forget who they are and what they've done."

"Okay."

Rhianwyn had asked the question in order to gauge her sister, not to let it sway her. She also wondered in what circumstances she would need to escape. She couldn't imagine being desperate enough—surely Maeveen knew that.

"Good," Maeveen said with finality. "I know you say you love this Mikhail boy, but don't let him cloud your judgment. You're as strong and smart as you are beautiful. You'll find greatness wherever you go."

She hadn't said she loved Mikhail. "I know."

"Don't wait too long to speak to Sonder, either. There's talk of the queen being restless. I'm sure you've heard them, too."

Rhianwyn nodded.

"Good." Maeveen stood up. "I have to go. I've stayed longer than I should have." She snagged another bit of everything from the plate and took a bite of the little tower they formed. "Be sure to eat something. You look tired." She kissed the top of Rhianwyn's head and hugged her. "I love you, sister. Trust your gut. It won't lead you astray."

Except it had. As she made her way back to the castle, Rhianwyn thought about everything. She regretted admitting to her sister that she had used Mikhail to get back at Sonder, even if Maeveen hadn't focused much on it.

She was terrified for her friend. Since the tournament, Mikhail had kept her too busy to talk to him. She had read the letters Sonder had sent in apology, but still fumed about the ball and his challenging Mikhail like an idiot. A return note wouldn't do her ire justice. It was no way to rage at him properly. She hadn't even been alone long enough to decide what she wanted to say to him.

It had been so long since they'd last spoken that she didn't know how to broach the rift between them.

As Rhianwyn entered the courtyard, Mikhail appeared at her side so quickly she nearly jumped out of her skin. "Goodness, you scared me!"

He took her hands and turned her from her path, forcing her to stop. "I didn't mean to. I've just waited so long the guards let me sit inside out of the cold."

He kissed her fingers and then went to kiss her on the lips, but she turned her head, so it planted at the corner of her mouth.

"Wyn, I'm sorry about this morning. That's why I waited. I even skipped drills to ensure I didn't miss you," he pleaded.

"It was unfair how upset you got, Mikhail. You hurt my feelings."

He pulled her into his chest. "I know. It wasn't fair. You have to tend to your duties to the guilds, too, I know. I just feel like I never see you anymore." He began to plant little kisses on her cheeks.

Despite herself, she giggled, even as she tried to push him off. "Mikhail," she gasped, "alright! Alright, I hear you. Stop." She forced a smile. "You see me all the time."

"It's not nearly enough," he retorted, then kissed her hand. She gave him a stern look. "But I understand. I'm sorry. I've been stressed lately."

She thought a moment, then nodded. "I forgive you. Have you heard anything from your father? Has anyone agreed to take you on as squire?"

He squeezed her hands and grinned at her. "Not yet. But it sounds as though Sir Elio may!"

It took all her self-control to feign surprise instead of horror. "That's wonderful news! That's what you wanted, right?"

"It's the next best thing from what I wanted!"

Rhianwyn didn't let her smile falter. From the corner of her eye, she saw Sonder and Tran walking away from the stables. She didn't let her gaze linger for fear Mikhail would notice. Instead, she stood on her toes and gave him a lingering kiss on the cheek to appease him, even as her mind raced.

"I can take the evening off to spend time with you. Let's toast to the great news, hm? Dinner is on me," she joked, knowing full well a palace dinner would be free.

Rhianwyn finally found herself blessedly alone after managing to usher Mikhail out of the training hospital. Her body thrummed with the need for silence.

Trembled, in fact.

Her laughter had become more forced. Now, neglected tasks nagged her while she tried to slog through the day's events.

What am I doing? she thought to herself bitterly. The task of turning Mikhail against his father was hopeless. Nor was she willing to relinquish her identity. Who would she be if she deemed Sonder a lost cause? Maeveen had said only Rhianwyn could, and she hated that responsibility.

She returned to the way Sonder had looked when she turned him away at the library. So stern and distant.

A knock on the door frame followed by a wash of cold air on the back of her exposed neck silenced her thoughts.

A tentative male voice called out, "Wyn?"

She turned. The mop of unruly brown curls and warm brown eyes was a relief. "Tran," she breathed.

"Do you mind?" The boy hovered on the threshold, waiting for her permission.

"Of course."

Her relief turned itself into a smile. As he stepped inside and closed the door, she crossed the room. When he turned, she crushed him in her arms.

Tran stumbled back. "Whoa," he laughed.

He patted her back nervously. But she didn't care. The chill on his cloak brushed her cheek, and she breathed the smell of him. Thickly sweet and woody, like raw honey.

"I've missed you." She continued to hold him tight so he couldn't see the threatening tears.

Tran relaxed and wrapped an arm around her. "I'm always here," he said, laughter still tinging his voice, though she could hear the concern.

Rhianwyn took in another deep breath to steady herself before she pushed away. "I know. I've just been so busy; I haven't seen much of you." She did her best to smile up at him, hoping he couldn't see her watery eyes.

His lopsided smile revealed he wasn't fooled. "That's why I'm here, actually." He ran a hand through his hair. "I wanted to check on you without Mikhail around."

Rhianwyn kept her face collected. "I'm good as ever. Master Sowa has the matron keeping me busy. Running me through all manner of tests." Yet another thing to nag at her mind—Aspera never stopped hunting her abilities.

"I'm asking about you, Wyn, not your chores." He let laughter seep into his words as often as she did. She knew the cut of his seriousness despite it.

It made her heartache rattle the confines it was stuffed into.

Friendship. Genuine, unyielding friendship stood in front of her. Held her captive in that gaze obscured by those fluffy curls of his. Only a handful of people could pin her so and make her feel safe. All of them she had kept at a distance while she weathered the task she had set upon herself—one of them stricken from her by anger.

"Tired," she relented. "Tired and angry."

"As you should be. I've been sure to wheedle Sonder endlessly, so he'll know he's an idiot."

A snort of laughter escaped her. "You're a good friend."

Some of the tension left him, and his grin broadened. "The best," he said. The turn of his lips faltered. "But, he's a caring idiot." Her brow darkened, and he held up his hands. "I'm not here to defend him, or tell you otherwise. He deserved it. But that's why I'm here. You don't have to listen to him, but I hope you'll listen to me."

Rhianwyn's flash of frustration faded. "About what?"

"Mikhail is saying things about what he wants to do with you. If I weren't busy stopping Sonder from fighting him, *I* would have wrung his neck." Tran's irritation tore his boyishness to shreds. "Lies about the things he has done already." Tran's anger was as still and calm as the rest of his character

She felt her face drain. "That's what Sonder came to tell me." Tran nodded slowly. "Does he believe them?" It felt stupid that, of all things, that was her first concern.

Tran shook his head. "I don't think so."

"Have you seen him?" Rhianwyn reached out and took his hand, squeezing it tightly.

Another head shake. "Very little." He clenched his jaw; whether from the pain or his frustration, she couldn't tell.

She loosened her grip, though her fingers caught and twined in his. "If you see him, tell him I'm sorry. Mikhail was there, and it was easier to send Sonder away to avoid conflict. I didn't want to, though."

Tran's fingers tightened on hers before they let each other go. "So, you believe me?"

Guilt marred her smile. "It's easier to believe you than him." She knew her self-deprecation wasn't missed.

"What about Mikhail?"

She ground her teeth. This news confirmed what she had feared—trying to forge Mikhail into an ally was impossible. Her self-imposed mission had failed. The energy she spent gleaning useful information was eclipsed by what it took to hold his slavering affections at bay. "I can deal with him. He's a gentleman with me."

"Are you sure?" Concern furrowed Tran's brow.

"Of course. I'm not helpless." She rolled her eyes. It hid the trepidation she felt. Already, her mind was calculating how careless she was to get herself so entangled.

Reassurances continued to fall from her lips as they made to part ways. Finally, she asked him again to tell Sonder she was sorry if he found their friend.

Tran's hand fell on the door handle and stilled. "Wyn?" His gravelly voice stilled her. "If you're in trouble, you'd tell us, right?"

His gaze swept over her, and only then did she realize her words of warmth and gratitude had rolled off his tense shoulders.

"Of course." The lie came too quickly. How could she admit what she had done? Still, he eyed her, and her façade cracked. "I will."

Seeming satisfied, he left.

Chapter Twenty-Four
And the Fist Fell

In the garden, age nine

"I don't need you to always stand up for me." Sonder's shoulder's slumped as he prodded his split lip.

"Yes, you do." Rhianwyn knelt in front of him and dabbed at it with her sleeve. "I don't mind keeping you out of trouble when I can."

"You'll just get in trouble, then. I don't want you to suffer because of me."

"They won't say anything. They'd have to admit they got beat by a girl if they did. Stupid highborn thugs. It's not your fault you're Merrick's squire." She lifted his chin and smiled at him. "Besides, I know you'd do the same for me if you could."

Present, age seventeen

On an especially gloomy day on the cusp of spring, Sonder woke with his thoughts blissfully calm. The sun dawned bright through the clouds, teasing that it may successfully burn them off.

Sonder had no obligations. Drisil was still gone, Merrick was busy, and Master Fallen was ill. When he had tried to report for drills, Roderick turned him away because of the weather. To top it off, Tran was taking the day to gallivant around town with Mila.

The sensation of being trapped made him restless, so he asked the kitchen to pack him a lunch, and he rode through the drizzle to the house on the crumbling shore.

Come midday, the clouds redoubled, blocking the weak light, and the drizzle turned into a steady rain.

He watched the day pass in the form of sailboats and large seabirds with wobbly throats gliding upon the blistery wind. He never grew tired of admiring the bright greens of the shore against the dark stormy blues and grays of the water and sky. Fog obscured the castle and the markets. To the north, he caught glimpses of the Mother's Range dressed in snow as white as death, even as life broke free of winter's clutches.

There was contentment in his solitude, with no other company but the light-house. Even the cold seeping into his bones was a welcome companion. His horse stood beneath a nearby tree like a shadow, head bowed and dozing.

The day grew old. The setting sun brought the city guard to deliver the oil. As the group approached, the old man walked out to meet them. Instead of the typical exchange, the men surrounded him. Another figure peeled away and walked into the building, flanked by two guards carrying the fuel. After a few minutes, the two rejoined the group, and the tender was led away. Their lamps bobbed along the peninsula until they disappeared behind the deserted buildings against the north gate.

Curious, Sonder stayed longer than usual, waiting to see if they would return. He sat until well after sunset, when the road became an inky void, like the sea, with no sign of life.

Finally, Sonder's stomach gave its fifth grumble, ending his vigil. Picking their way carefully through the darkness, he and the horse came to a lit road and rode back slowly.

The guards gave him a hard time for being out late. Apparently, Merrick had been looking for him. Resigned to his scolding, when the page came to take his horse, Sonder saw it was Tran's brother, and insisted on putting the beast up himself. He felt no pull to hurry.

"Is everything alright, Master Sonder?" The boy stayed glued to his side as he directed the creature inside.

"Why do you ask, Gialan?" Sonder turned the horse and pushed it to make room inside the stall.

"You take on extra chores when you're upset." Gialan was matter-of-fact as he took the horse's lead and stared at him.

"Where in the kingdom did you get that?" Sonder asked with a laugh. "I do no such thing. I've just kept you late waiting for me. Go on to the barrack. I'm no knight yet."

Gialan pulled the reins away as Sonder reached for them. "If you insist on doing it, at least let me help. You took my chores when our da was sick. I've never repaid you."

Sonder softened. He remembered now. He hadn't thought twice about it. Their father was the blacksmith who made armor for the elites of the queen's army. Someday, Master Cathak would make Sonder's armor. "If you insist."

"I do," Gialan said with a nod. He immediately pushed Sonder out of the way to unbuckle the saddle. "'Sides, it looks like you took the animal for a swim. A Battle Master's squire should know better," Gialan scolded before flashing a lopsided grin. "Poor beast. I thought you were kind."

Sonder helped lift the saddle so the boy wouldn't need a stool. "Only a short swim," he said, earning him a giggle. He flung it onto the saddle stand. "Is that not good?" He removed the bridle. The horse nudged him gratefully, and he scratched where the leather had sat. "See? He forgives me." He took a handful of oats from a sack, and the horse's velvety nose began to snuffle them up.

"Because you have food," Gialan said as he started rubbing the horse down. "And you talk nice to them."

Sonder wiped his hand on his trousers and smiled. Rhianwyn had deemed him worthy of friendship because he talked to the animals. But he had botched that.

He didn't feel as kind as Tran's brother made him out to be, but he enjoyed the boy's company while they worked. There was a lull in their conversation, and soon Sonder's stomach redoubled its protest. The two looked at each other with wide eyes before they both laughed.

"Go on, Master Sonder. All that's left is to feed him. Don't bother insisting. I'm saving you from eating yourself." Gialan pushed him out.

The torches sputtered in the rain. The smile remained on Sonder's face as he made his way through the yard until a flickering light in the auxiliary hospital caught his eye. It was unusual for it to still be occupied this late. The boy strained to see inside as he passed.

His heart fluttered. Rhianwyn was alone, organizing the bookshelf. Her dark hair was falling loose, and she looked tired. Sonder willed her to look at him, but she didn't. Water dripped from his hair into his face, and he was reminded of how long he had been in the cold.

He reached the little kitchen garden, and his stomach let out another protest. Movement caught Sonder's eye again. A figure was slinking across the parade grounds. Whoever it was kept to the shadows, constantly checking over their shoulder. Sonder squinted to see through the glare. It wasn't common to see someone dressed in head-to-toe black. The person felt familiar, but he knew none of the Black Knights moved like that.

The person looked in his direction, and Sonder ducked into the doorway. The torches illuminated their face, and Sonder's chest tightened.

It was Mikhail.

Sonder counted his breaths before he peered around the frame to see if Mikhail had seen him. Instead, the boy rounded a corner and disappeared.

There was no denying he was heading toward Rhianwyn. Sonder leaned against the wood frame, letting the rain drum on his face, breathing deeply.

"Duty help me," he whispered. "Leave it be, you idiot."

There was no one to scold him as he tromped through the kitchen with his muddy boots and sodden clothes to rummage for food. All he found was a stale loaf of bread, but there were other places to look.

Try as he might to ignore what he had just seen, it chafed him. Part of him was scolding himself for being a jealous pervert for wanting to see what they were doing. Another was telling him that something was off. He took a bite of the loaf and chewed slowly, his mind racing.

In frustration, he tore the loaf in half and left the uneaten part on the table. "You're an idiot," he growled, shouldering back through the door.

It slammed behind him, but he was already gone, jogging after Mikhail, the mud sucking at his boots. He slipped around the cross paths he came to in case the other boy was there. When the small hospital came into view, Sonder kept to the palls.

As he approached, sure enough, he spied Mikhail standing inside with his back to him and the window. There was nothing good he could be up to alone and isolated by the rain with Rhianwyn.

Sonder ducked around to the back so he could get a better vantage. It was the training hospital, so there were few beds inside to limit distractions during lessons. Water ran down the window, so the view wavered, but he could see them profiled.

It was impossible to hear what was being said, and he had no way to make out their expressions. The excitement of the chase quickly washed away with the deluge as another slew of emotions took over.

Mikhail closed the distance between them and grabbed Rhianwyn's hands, pulling her closer to him. They exchanged a few more words.

Perhaps they were proclaiming their love for each other, because their lips came together. Sonder flushed with embarrassment, but he couldn't pull himself away from watching. He kept wanting Rhianwyn to push away, but then there was a flicker of movement as Mikhail's hand began to wander. Rhianwyn felt a world away.

Sonder spun around.

He was soaked to the bone, yet his body burned. Most of all, he felt ashamed. *You knew you were going to regret this.*

He took a step.

A thump sounded from inside.

Sonder held his breath to listen. Another. Slowly, he turned to look back at the window. He was again transfixed as Mikhail drove Rhianwyn back onto a bed. The longer he watched, the more it looked like Rhianwyn was trying to keep Mikhail back. But he persisted anyway, leaning into her. Mikhail tugged at her dress.

The patter of rain chose then to slow. The distorted image cleared. Mikhail's delight was actually teeth bared in frustration. Sonder could finally hear Rhianwyn's muffled voice, and he heard panic.

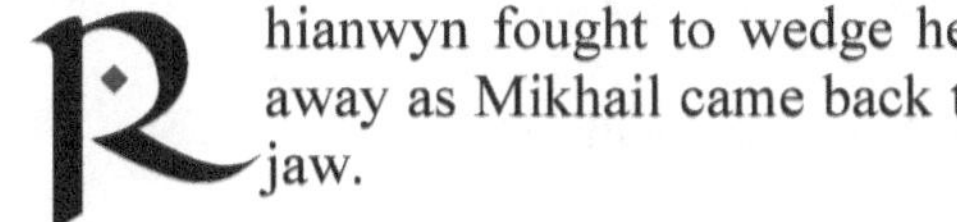

Rhianwyn fought to wedge her arms between them, turning her face away as Mikhail came back toward her. His lips knocked against her jaw.

"Stop it, Mikhail! I said no." Tears were beginning to fill her eyes, and her heart hammered wildly against her chest.

"Stop pretending you don't want this. No one will see," he panted into her ear.

His mouth hunted hers once more. She twisted her face the other way. Her head collided with his nose painfully. The rage lurking just beneath the surface erupted. He swept her hands as if they were no more than fallen leaves. With one hand, he held her, and with the other, he grabbed the laces of her dress and violently yanked them. The fabric gave, and he pulled once more. The sound of the seams ripping horrified her.

"Please stop," she sobbed before his mouth finally found hers and covered it.

Rhianwyn wanted him off of her. She probably could have gotten out of his grasp if she clawed or kicked, but she didn't want to hurt him. She hadn't had time to formulate a plan. So instead, she kept her jaw locked against his kiss.

It was a misunderstanding. If she could just get him off of her and catch her breath, she could reason with him.

The cold of his hands seeped into her skin as he pawed at her breasts and she was violently ripped from her thoughts. Her chemise may as well not have been there. Suddenly he sprouted eight hands, because he was pulling up her skirt, undoing his trousers, all while somehow fighting off her two hands trying to push the hem back down. Panic gripped her anew, and she latched on to the reserve of energy that surged inside of her.

Frantically, she forced her knee between them and began to wiggle out from under him. Her arms tangled with his weight.

With a frustrated shout, he struck everything away: her hands, anything between them, and her fight. His arm caught her on the side of the head, knocking her back. He pinned her, and his hot breath huffed in her face.

"You fucking owe me," he snarled.

Still, Rhianwyn writhed until she realized there was no moving him. Her legs trembled against his wrenching, then gave way, and his cold fingers ground toward his prize. Utterly defeated, she fixated on a spot on the ceiling, and tears spilled down her face.

In that knot where the beams met above her, she could stay safe from what she knew was coming.

Mikhail's weight lifted off of her.

A loud crash cleared the blanket of numbness. Rhianwyn's hands could move. She sat up deliriously and saw Sonder standing beside her, staring at Mikhail, twisted in a collapsed bookshelf.

Rhianwyn felt a different kind of panic and pulled her torn dress together. "Sonder," she gasped. He didn't hear her—or else chose not to face her.

What must he have thought about what was happening?

Mikhail rolled over with a groan. Sonder stalked across the room as he regained his bearings. Mikhail let out an undignified yelp, throwing his hands up to ward off his attacker. Sonder gathered the boy's shirt in both hands and lifted him to his feet with a yell she couldn't understand.

"She wanted it!" Mikhail bellowed back.

He hadn't gotten the chance to gain his feet before he stumbled as Sonder drove him. Mikhail twisted in his grasp as he yelped out protests. However, the words fell on deaf ears as the two barreled toward the door, thrown open and swaying in the breeze.

It dawned on Rhianwyn what Sonder meant to do. "Sonder, stop it!" she screamed. She could see everything from where she lay tangled in the torn fabrics.

With the strength of two men, Sonder lifted Mikhail and threw him into the rain. Mikhail fell backward into the mud. He used his momentum to roll up to his feet, raising his fists to meet Sonder, who strode toward him.

"Why can't you mind your own damn business?" Mikhail screamed as he threw a punch.

Sonder ducked it and made his own swing. Mikhail put his arm up just in time to block. The hook that followed caught Sonder in the side, doubling him over. Mikhail grinned and relaxed into a fighting stance, clearly thinking he had gained a moment.

Instead, Sonder lunged and wrapped his arms around Mikhail's waist in a vice. Another undignified yelp escaped Mikhail. A roar tore from Sonder as he lifted Mikhail off his feet and fell to the ground with him. There was a tangle of limbs and punches as Mikhail scrambled for purchase.

Rhianwyn fell out of bed and tripped on the mess of skirts. She threw herself at the doorway as the two fell to the mud.

Sonder straddled Mikhail and began to punch blindly.

"Sonder, no!" she wailed into the night as a strike connected with Mikhail's face. She couldn't see beyond the little dome of light from behind her.

He couldn't get caught like this.

She forgot the torn pieces of her garments, gathered the fabric, and ran across the yard. Mikhail's head fell back with a sickening crack, and his hands fell limp.

Before Sonder could throw another blow, she wrapped her arms around his. Her eyes fell on Mikhail's bloody face, and she felt sick. "Stop it," she sobbed.

But Sonder was seeing red. With a yell, he grabbed her by the collar. She felt weightless as he threw her down, knocking the air from her lungs as she struck the ground. Her head lay next to his knee. For a frightening moment, she feared he'd move to attack her. Instead, another fist arched through the air, and she screwed her eyes shut.

The sickening sound of breaking bones caused bile to rise in her throat. Air refused to fill her lungs, but she rolled to her knees and covered Mikhail with her body, even as she recoiled from what he'd done.

"Sonder, stop," she croaked. Her outstretched hand wrapped around his balled fist.

Sonder stopped. She watched his face splinter. "Rhianwyn?" he whispered, trembling.

His breath curled hot and heavy around his face, but he stared into her eyes, wide as plates. She felt close to bursting into tears.

The damage was done. Armor rattled, and guards surrounded them, drawn by the noise. She was too shaken to count how many came. They hauled Sonder to his feet. So many commands and responses flew as someone reached down and helped her to her feet.

The whole while, they held each other in their gazes. She knew him well enough to know how deeply her fear of and for him wounded him. They both felt the same agony. He had condemned himself.

An officer stepped between them. "What is the meaning of this?" He addressed Sonder.

Sonder clenched his jaw shut as his anger returned.

"It's not what it looks like, sir—" Rhianwyn stammered, stepping aside as two guards shouldered by to help Mikhail.

The officer glared at her. His eyes moved up and down the image of her state of undress, and she clutched herself tighter as her skin crawled.

"He attacked us," Mikhail moaned.

"Looks like a jealous boy to me." A glance down at Mikhail revealed his undone trousers. The guard's face flushed red as he turned his attention back to Sonder. "You're a real piece of work, you know that?"

Rhianwyn was slow to realize the mistake that had been made. She started to protest, but the guard shouted at her for silence, and she recoiled. Then she saw the officer was one of Vardulf's men, and she froze.

"Take him to Merrick. Have him deal with this," the officer ordered.

Sonder was shoved roughly from behind.

The guard turned on Rhianwyn then and pointed at her chest. "Get yourself dressed," he said with venom. "A wardess should be tending to her duties, not distracting royal squires from theirs." He turned away from her and shouted for the men to get Mikhail to the hospital.

A hand touched Rhianwyn's, and she started.

"Sorry, miss, I didn't mean to frighten you. Let's get you inside," a young chambermaid said.

A warm fur cloak fell around her shoulders. A sob escaped her, and Rhianwyn covered her mouth, trying to hold the emotions in. She retreated into herself to find safety again.

Chapter Twenty-Five
The Wall Was Deaf

Aspera's private chambers, nine years ago

"My lady, why let the boy continue to associate with the girl?" Merrick asked.

Aspera twirled her wrist, wine glass swaying. "Perhaps he'll fall in love."

"Why allow it? I've been trying to train such weakness from him. It could very well be his downfall, or yours, Your Grace," Merrick said.

She fixed him with a knowing stare. "I suppose you'd know." She said it both as a question and a statement. He must not have given her the reaction she wanted, because she sighed and went on, "You've said yourself the boy isn't particularly drawn to violence. Maybe the girl will be the motivation he needs. It would be good for him. Give him a reason to do well." She narrowed her eyes.

Merrick bowed. "As you wish." When he straightened, he met her gaze. "If I may be frank?"

The queen took a sip of wine, then lifted her glass toward him. "You're the only one dumb enough to be."

"It may not turn out how you intend it to."

"Then make sure you train him to be a loyal servant as well as a ruthless killer, so it does."

Present, age seventeen

The guards surrounded Sonder as they marched through the castle corridors. They tried to drag him several times, but he shrugged them off with a scowl. He could walk on his own. Their boots left a muddy mess in their wake, the rattle of armor disturbing the peace. Many perturbed eyes watched them pass, but Sonder chose to keep his anger focused.

The officer in charge of the watch hauled him around despite his cooperation when they reached Merrick's door. Sonder threw him off, too, only to feel the point of a blade at his back.

"Keep it up, boy. Give me a reason to gut you. All I'd have to say is you fought arrest, and there'd be no repercussions," the man rasped in his ear.

Sonder gritted his teeth but relaxed. The metal at his back was salt in the wound.

The officer pounded on the door. Then, without waiting for a response, he swung the door open and shoved Sonder forward. "Wait here," he ordered his men.

The door slammed behind them.

A fire crackled merrily, and the room smelled of spices. Seeing Merrick's contentment melt away hurt. "What is the meaning of this?"

"We caught this one in the yard. Fighting." The officer gave Sonder another push from behind.

Merrick's eyes briefly flicked to Sonder's face, then back at the officer. "Fighting? Fighting whom?" Sonder saw the man's mind was already made up.

That hurt worse.

"Mikhail. Sir Elio's squire. This one was spying on that healer girl, by the looks of it. Saw they were in the act. Got jealous and lost his temper."

Sonder kept his jaw clamped, the muscles working as he glared at the floor. His body betrayed him as cold water dripped down his back, and he shivered. He couldn't look at Merrick. There was no point arguing with the guard still there.

"Thank you, Officer. Leave us. I'll attend to my squire." He stood in front of his desk.

"See that you do. The queen will want to hear about this." He pushed Sonder again, baiting him to lash out. It took all his self-control not to throw an arm up to get the man off of him. "Either you can tell her, or I will."

The officer gave Merrick an unspoken challenge, which Merrick refused to answer. For a tense moment, Sonder thought he wouldn't leave, but then he turned and heard the door slam shut.

The room was so quiet they could hear each other's ragged, angry breaths. Sonder couldn't tear his gaze from the floor. He kept his fists clenched at his side.

Finally, Merrick broke the silence. "What have you done?"

Sonder looked up and yelled at the man, "It's not true!"

Merrick drove away from his desk and stood to his full height. "Don't you yell at me, boy! Do *you* know what you've done?" Sonder began to protest, but Merrick raised his voice even louder. "I don't want to hear it!"

Sonder clamped his mouth shut, glaring at the floor while Merrick began to pace.

"It doesn't matter what you have to say, Sonder. I've told you the consequences of fighting another squire. The squire you chose, of all people, is Elio's." There was a wild look in Merrick's eye as he stopped in front of him. "What have you done, Sonder?"

Sonder looked up. "He deserved it."

Merrick searched Sonder's face, his anger turning to distress. "I can't save you from this. Do you not understand? Since I brought you here, I've done nothing but try to protect you from the queen. Nothing else! All of the trouble you've caused, I was able to shelter you from. But not this." His fury flared again. "All because you can't keep your desires in check!"

Sonder raged back, "It's not like you're letting me explain anything."

"Because there is nothing you can say to fix this situation," Merrick roared, fists clenched. "You are a traitor's son living on borrowed time! You do not have the luxury."

Sonder looked away and took a ragged breath. "Fine. Have me punished, then." The back of his eyes burned.

Merrick made to deliver on the boy's request, taking a step toward him and lifting his arm. The movement caused Sonder to look back. When he realized that Merrick meant to strike him, his look became a challenge. A lifetime of accusations seething back at Merrick, willing him to do it again.

Merrick opened his clenched hand and held it out as if making to grab Sonder and shake him. A frustrated groan tore from him, and he took a handful of his own hair instead.

He began to pace, crossing his arms and tugging at his beard. He slashed his hand through the air like a knife when he spoke. "You have no idea what you have done." His eyes searched the room as if he could find the answers on the walls. "Go to your room. Stay there, and talk to no one. Under no circumstances are you to leave. I need to be the one to speak with Queen Aspera first." Merrick walked up to Sonder and rapped him on the chest. "Pray I can talk her down."

"You haven't even let me tell you what happened," Sonder growled.

A knock interrupted them. The door opened, and Áki slipped through without being invited in.

Merrick looked relieved. "Your timing is always impeccable, Áki." He went to his desk and put the papers away. "See Sonder to his room, and inform Merriweather he is to have no visitors or leave."

Áki had never looked graver. "Come on, Sonder."

Merrick gathered his black cloak and shrugged it on. Sonder turned, but he grabbed the boy and pulled him back to stand in front of Áki. "What have you heard?"

Áki chewed his mustache as he shook his head. "I'm here, and you didn't summon me, right?" The implication was heavy. Word was spreading in front of them.

Merrick glanced at Sonder before he stepped closer as if Sonder wouldn't be able to overhear them. "Keep him under guard until I've spoken with Aspera. Let's hope she hasn't heard anything yet. Vardulf and his supporters will try to control this narrative."

Áki clapped Merrick on the arm. "Speak well, my friend."

Of course she had heard.

The two men clasped arms. Merrick gave Sonder a final look before pulling his hood up and leaving. There was no way to hide the fact that both men looked doubtful. Merrick was casting his hope into a pit of the Queen's Spiders. Áki opened his arm, indicating for Sonder to lead the way.

The hallways were empty, aside from the servants scrubbing the muddy footprints from the carpets. Their eyes lingered a little too long as the two of them passed. To conserve resources, every other sconce had been dimmed.

"You don't have to take me. I can go on my own. I'm not going to try and run away," Sonder said, dejected.

Áki was grim in his response. "It is not so much to ensure you do as you're told, but to protect you." He paused as if for effect. "You chose an awful day to start a fight with him." Áki sighed. "He was named Elio's squire this afternoon."

A glimmer of gravity struck him now that his anger had burned down. "I didn't hear anything of it."

Áki looked away with a raised eyebrow. He had always struggled with sounding stern for long. A dark-humored edge crept into his voice. "Probably because you were missing all day." Sonder didn't respond. Áki had a much easier time managing high tensions. "Good, I got you listening. My advice, lad, is to listen to Merrick. Lay low until you've heard from him. There may be a way to salvage this."

"It's not what it looks like," Sonder moaned, suddenly feeling closer to tears. "He wouldn't even let me talk."

Snippets were returning as he gradually calmed down, and he remembered the horror on Rhianwyn's face, covered in mud, hair plastered against her cheeks as she gasped for air. Maybe he had misunderstood.

"There's no time, but he'll listen. Right now, it's more important for him to look like he has everything under control. Aspera doesn't care about specifics, just obedience." Áki heaved a sigh. "Even if you were just another squire, it's forbidden to fight. Which you aren't."

"Merrick called me a traitor's son," Sonder whispered.

Áki appeared taken aback, but then he recovered. "He loves you, Sonder. He'll listen. It's just, right now, he's afraid."

They arrived at the corridor to his room. As they turned the corner, Merriweather rushed at them. "There you are. Where have you been?" She clasped his hands briefly and looked him up and down, tutting. One of her hands came up and thumbed his cheek.

Áki placed a hand on her back. "Thank you for responding so quickly to my summons, Melody. He's to stay in his room until Merrick says otherwise. Under no circumstances is there to be any visitors unless Merrick approves."

She nodded gravely, giving Sonder a good nudge toward the door. "I'll do what I can. Just make sure you men do the same."

Áki inclined his head, turned, and left.

The latch slid shut, separating Sonder from the rest of the world. He stood unmoving in the doorway. This child's bedroom had become his prison. With the last adrenaline leaving his blood, he began to shiver, feeling weak.

Merriweather fretted over him. "Look at you. You're filthy." She touched his exposed arm and sucked a breath. "And you're freezing. Come, let's get you cleaned up." She peeked into the washroom.

"Melody?" Sonder said quietly, watching her. He couldn't recall if he had ever heard her first name before.

She busied herself, pulling out clean clothes. "What? You thought my parents named me a surname? You must be dense," she said dismissively. The clothes made a soothing thump as she threw them onto the bed. She turned to face him with her hands on her hips. "Well, are you going to stand there all night? The water is probably chilled now."

Sonder felt small and vulnerable. "I'm hungry." Another shiver racked his body.

Merriweather knew him well, and her demeanor softened. "Oh, Sonder. I'll ring for food, but you've got to get out those clothes. You're going to catch ill."

The water was still hot. That, or he was indeed that cold. After pulling off his shirt, he looked at his reflection in the mirror. It was a fearsome sight that made him hesitate.

Mud caked his hair and smeared his face. It had begun to dry and flake. There was a bruise where Merriweather had thumbed. Sonder's side blossomed with color. He couldn't recall getting hit. As he put his hands into the basin, the water turned rusty, and he saw that his knuckles were split and swollen. The cuts smarted as he scrubbed, the sight of the bloody water haunting him.

The blood in Tierrion hadn't been so much.

He stood frozen for so long that he jumped when Merriweather poked her head in to check on him.

"How goes it, dear?"

Sonder just opened his hands to indicate the murky water in the bowl. He hadn't even started washing, and his torn trousers still clung to his hips.

"Do what you can. I'll have another bath in the morning when the lads are awake."

Sonder averted his gaze and asked quietly, "Will you help me comb my hair?"

Merriweather smiled, close to tears. "Of course. Finish washing, then come eat."

The soak did little to calm his nerves. No matter how hard he tried, he wasn't sure he got all the muck out of his dark waves. When he emerged, he wrapped the fluffy towel around his waist to retrieve the clothes she had forgotten to set in the washroom for him.

The dinner tray on the table contained a light broth, hard cheese, stale bread, and some apple preserve.

Merriweather sat in a chair, and Sonder sat at her feet like he used to as a child. He had grown, but he didn't feel that way with his knees drawn to his chest. The slow strokes of the comb soothed him.

"How come you never told me your name was Melody?" he said through a mouthful of apple-smeared bread.

"You never asked," she said, the comb gliding through his hair. "Don't talk with your mouth full."

He smiled briefly, appreciating her wit. However, it quickly fell away again, and he sighed. "I'm sorry I've been nothing but trouble, Merriweather."

She placed her hands on his shoulders. "Don't you begin to talk like that. I wouldn't have stayed your primary had you been nothing but trouble." She resumed combing. "If you ask me, Mikhail's been asking for it for years, terrorizing his staff and parading around like his father. It's just a shame he chose you as a target."

They stayed quiet for a while, Sonder nibbling the food, and Merriweather taking comfort in the repetitive task as much as him. He wanted to ask her if she knew what would happen or when Merrick might be back, but he didn't.

If he was honest, he didn't want to see the man. Despite what Áki said, there was no satisfaction in imagining explaining what had happened, because he knew Merrick wouldn't even let him begin.

All he could really remember was seeing red and the deep satisfaction of his fists meeting Mikhail's face. Maybe he had been wrong about what he saw.

So Sonder resigned himself to whatever punishment was deemed appropriate. It had been worth it to beat Mikhail senseless. His only regret was that Rhianwyn probably wouldn't forgive him. Although knowing the queen, her punishment could test that.

Merriweather stifled a yawn. "Goodness, excuse me." She set him off too and laughed when he yawned larger. "Sounds like we're both tired. Get some rest. I don't think we'll be seein' Merrick tonight."

She patted his shoulder, then stood up with a groan. Sonder realized how old she was getting as she arched her back, then hobbled to turn down his bed.

He stood. His joints ached from the cold and fight. After giving his pillows a final fluff, she moved to add more logs to the fire.

Sonder shook his head. "It's fine, Merriweather. You've done enough tonight." He smiled as she straightened and looked at him.

She pursed her lips and tried not to look troubled. "It's an old habit, I suppose." She regarded him. There was no doubt he looked in a sorry state. "You're sure you'll be alright?"

"Yes. I can take care of myself; you know that. It's nearly midnight. Go rest."

The woman nodded, then made to leave, pausing to brush nonexistent lint from the bed and tug the blankets smooth. Her path brought her past him, and she did the same to Sonder, straightening his shirt and brushing him off. Her brown eyes, marred with purple bags, turned up to look at him. "Is there anything else you'll need? I can send for someone else."

Sonder couldn't help but smile at how she was fussing over him, even though his mood remained dark. "I'll be fine. Really. Thank you for staying with me and combing my hair." He felt vulnerable again, like the youngling he still was.

Her eyes grew warm and misty as she brought her hand to his cheek. "Oh, my love, thank you for asking." There was a heart-wrenching sadness in her eyes as she considered her young charge. "You've been asked to grow up so fast, and I fear you'll be asked to do so again." She sighed, then brushed his shoulder off once more. She sniffled softly. "Right then, I'll leave you to get some rest."

Merriweather patted his chest before she left.

⁘⸻⸻⸻⸻❧⸻⸻⸻⸻⁘

Rhianwyn hid in the shadows outside Sonder's room in the servants' corridor, hood drawn low over her face. Even fewer sconces were lit here. She hadn't stopped trembling since she slipped out of her room, and her tears hadn't stopped threatening. New aches continued to form, and she hid her bloodied, broken nails in the soft fabric of her cloak. Every little shuffle and creak made her jump, and she prayed for Merriweather to hurry.

Finally, the caregiver emerged, the door closing softly behind her.

Rhianwyn stepped out too eagerly, and as Merriweather turned to leave, she gasped, seeing the hooded figure standing outside Sonder's door.

Rhianwyn lifted her sore hands to placate her. "It's alright, Melody, it's me." She pitched her voice in a whisper.

Merriweather glared, holding her hand to her chest. "Miss Rhianwyn! You shouldn't be here," she hissed. "And it's Missus Merriweather to you."

Rhianwyn pulled her hood back, giving up on being unnoticed so the dim light could light her pleading face. "I wanted to check on him—"

The woman cut her off, taking a menacing step forward, which immediately caused Rhianwyn to step back. "You should not be here, miss. Sir Merrick has prohibited all visitors. Especially you."

"I just. . . Could you tell him I'm sorry? That I didn't want this?" Rhianwyn winced as she picked nervously at her nails.

"I'll do no such thing," Melody shot back. "Now, get out of here with you before someone sees. You've caused enough trouble in the boy's life."

The words stung Rhianwyn's already raw spirit. The caregiver couldn't see the details on her face as she complied. It was too dim to see her lip quivering and too easy to misinterpret the way she clutched her cloak to herself and flinched at every noise and movement.

As Rhianwyn left, she worried Sonder thought she wanted Mikhail to come. If Sonder knew exactly what had been happening or if he'd acted purely on jealousy. She had no idea how to tell anyone the truth, not even herself.

That night, she sat huddled in the corner of her room, wrapped in a thick blanket, crying until she fell asleep. Sonder similarly lay awake, watching the fire die out as his thoughts ran rampant.

Chapter Twenty-Six
A Letter to Die For

Fringe forests far to the northeast, seventeen years ago

"What are you doing?" Merrick asked.

Bran had spent several minutes scrawling out notes to be wrapped around a bird's leg, only to throw each one into the fire.

"Writing for help and then burning them."

"Why?" Merrick scoffed.

"It's something I saw Lucrid do once," Bran responded, as if that answered everything.

"Why?" Merrick asked again, his voice tarnished by his frustration.

Bran's jaw clenched as the third to last fluttered down like a moth flown too close to the fire, its edges bursting into flame.

"Because every time he requested help, he knew no one else would be sent to help him. He was always on his own, fighting the queen's battles."

The remaining two he closed in his hand, then stood.

"And what are those?" Merrick asked.

The man was supposed to have the answers for them. He was supposed to know why they'd been sent into the wilderness, to be attacked by whatever it was that stalked them through the forest.

Bran's dark gaze met his. "One is the request I know can be answered. The other I'd be willing to die for." He sent a bird off into the night. "There will be horses waiting for us when we return to Vyrens Fell, and hopefully soldiers."

"And the other?" Merrick asked, not letting Bran's deflection go unnoticed.

Bran sighed, clutching the note he claimed to be ready to die for. "To an old friend, who may be dead or as corrupt as I." Bran looked at him. "I need to know why I never knew about a keep our order kept hidden in the mountains between Sosten and Lorist lands."

Present, age seventeen

Merrick went straight to Aspera's Tower. The way she looked at him made his skin crawl like no amount of magic in the walls could. He felt each heartbeat in his chest as he stood before her. But, as he had endlessly instructed Sonder to do, he kept his face passive and answered only what he knew.

"There has been an incident, Your Highness. I felt it my duty to tell you first." He licked his dry lips.

She looked at him with a tight-lipped expression. "What happened?"

"Sonder and Mikhail were caught fighting." Saying it out loud made his disappointment return, and it took all his self-control to keep it hidden.

Her eyes narrowed. "Why?"

"A disagreement."

"Are there any witnesses?"

"Only the girl. The guards who responded showed up after."

Her tone darkened. "Where are they now?"

"In their quarters, Your Majesty." He had no idea where Rhianwyn was. She was the last of his concerns right now.

"And Mikhail?"

"Alive." It could have been worse had no one responded. She had wanted this to some degree, pushing Sonder.

"Well, how bad is he injured?" His response had annoyed her, and she did little to hide it.

"I don't know, Your Highness. My priority was to you first. I will find out."

"Was the girl harmed?"

"Nothing was said to make me believe so."

"Have you spoken to her?"

"I have not."

"Why?"

Merrick dropped to his knee and bowed his head. "Forgive me, my queen. I wanted to be the first to tell you."

To hell if she perceived his subordination as groveling. She couldn't hear the prayers he said in his head to gods whose names had begun to drift toward being forgotten. Prayers that she would give the grace they all spoke of for once. He even prayed for a distraction to remove the scrutiny from him. Merrick didn't want her to punish the boy for his own shortcomings.

Enduring the smirk on Randal's face was a small price to pay.

Elio spoke. "Did you know your squire had disputes with mine?"

It was known.

Merrick hid his trembling, wishing and cursing Sonder—of all days to lose control. "I thought it finished," he lied.

Euldric stormed in. "Where is my son?" He looked at Merrick, who still sat on his knees. "You! You've sworn to us that your *boy* would not turn out to be like his traitorous, bloodthirsty father!" Spittle flew from his mouth. "Your Highness, I demand you address this! And swiftly! *He tried to kill my son!*" he shrilled.

It was proof that the gods had a sick sense of assistance, but Merrick sent his sliver of thanks for their distraction as he rose slowly to his feet.

He argued on Sonder's behalf—that he was a worthy servant. Ealdric became nearly rabid when Merrick suggested the attack may have been provoked.

Randal even offered words in the boy's favor, but the deep distrust of the man's intentions made it difficult for Merrick to appreciate the help.

They were dismissed with no verdict made—a small victory in Sonder's favor. It would have been hasty and swift had Aspera decided on the spot. Thought offered a chance to temper the bite of her displeasure.

After the room cleared, Randal remained silent as he watched Aspera pace. Her jaw continued to work, and her body was taut.

This was the first time he felt true terror. He had defied her a second time in defense of Sonder. Merrick had been too busy distrusting him to see the flash of magic that stilled his jaw. Her silence now was directed at him.

Randal swallowed and closed his eyes, silently praying he wasn't making a mistake.

"Aspera?" he ventured.

She released a guttural shriek with her whole body, which he endured with little more than a flinch. In one powerful motion, she swept the table in front of them, sending books tumbling and vials shattering to the floor.

She whirled on him and slapped him across the face. "How dare you?"

Randal fell to his knees in front of her, holding his face. "My lady," he begged, "I do it not to rile or undermine you. Forgive me."

"I've lost control of those entrusted with my vision, and you dare encourage him?"

"I do it to preserve your vision, my queen," Randal calmly shot back.

For an agonizing minute, he endured her hatred. The boy's outburst had thrust seventeen years of building rapport violently to the forefront, and Randal realized how flimsy it was. It shook and shuddered. All he could do was hold on to it and hope it held.

Aspera whipped around and walked to the window. "Even my most trusted advisor turns against me."

"I do not!"

"Find Drisil. If you are so determined to preserve my vision, return to Knownth and An-Dagda college."

She was sending him away. "Drisil returned just last night, m'lady—"

"Find what you were unable to find before."

Randal paled. "We destroyed it, as you asked." A cold sweat broke over his body, remembering the place. In seventeen years, none of them had returned besides Bran, who had recovered them from their fight with the archmage.

Her look was knowing. "Perhaps you missed something. I want the boy's magic, whether through him or other means. I will have control returned to me."

Randal pressed his forehead to the floor. "As you wish." Shaking, he lifted his head. No matter how hard he tried, he couldn't stop himself. "What of the boy?"

"He will be reminded that he's alive by my grace. All of you, now, get out!" Aspera threw a glass against the wall.

Indignity chased Randal as he ran from her tower.

<hr>

Drisil was waiting when Merrick returned to his study. Merrick looked through her as he walked to the chair behind his desk.

The woman met him halfway. The hand she laid on his chest steadied the tremble in his own hands. He blinked and returned to himself.

"Witnesses are saying—"

"There were none," Merrick said more harshly than he meant to. "When did you get back?"

Drisil gazed back at him steadily. "They say Sonder lost his temper when he happened upon Mikhail and Rhianwyn being intimate."

Merrick closed his eyes and clenched his jaw. Then, after a shaky breath, he spoke. "What of Mikhail?"

"Mikhail is stable, but only barely." She lowered her voice to a whisper. "Sonder could've killed him had no one intervened." She stepped back and let her hand fall. "What are Elio and Vardulf calling for? What did she decide?"

"I refuse to speak it further into existence and give it more strength," Merrick said.

Drisil raised an eyebrow and tilted her head. "So, you've chosen superstition tonight?"

His mind was far away, behind the barrier of his memories, keeping his mind empty. He took her jaw in his hand gently. There was no doubt the touch spoke to her. Each breath came heavy and jagged for him. "Do not speak my secrets. Not tonight."

The steady beat of her pulse fluttered beneath his fingertips. The tangible feeling of holding life in his hands drew some of his fractured sanity together. He brought his forehead to hers and inhaled the warm spice of her skin.

"Your heart is showing," she breathed. Everything was a dark joke to her.

"Take it tonight. Keep it safe. It has always been a liability to me." Merrick was attentive as he pushed her away and stepped around.

There was no telling what she thought as she lingered. They hadn't spoken in confidence since she was sent away. The rift between them grew whenever Drisil met with the queen in private, and they hadn't mended it yet after years of letting it grow. This moment now reminded him of that. Not even a handful of winter months spent together could repair that.

The rasp of his pen filled the space where their words should have gone. He busied himself writing requests. Eventually, she left, and the pieces of paper began to flutter into the fire one by one.

As the horizon lightened, Áki slipped in through the servant's door.

He took the only two slips that were spared. The men's ghosts sat on the couch and watched them, the conversation a year ago about building a protective barrier of people around Sonder poised between them. "Give these to Merriweather. Let us see how deep our friendships go."

"Aye."

"And talk to Drisil. See if there's any way her Birds can find a way to head off Vardulf's men from instigating any more fires."

"She's already gone," Áki said slowly.

Merrick's heart dropped. "What?" He didn't know how they could manage to mitigate the damage without her. "When?"

Áki laid a hand on Merrick's shoulder. "It's alright. We'll get through this." The redhead thumped him on the back. "Get some rest if you can. You'll need it." He hesitated. "And, Merrick? Talk to the lad, alright?"

Merrick just grunted, knowing he wouldn't find rest.

If the situation took a turn for the worse, he didn't want anyone put out on their behalf, chief among them Merriweather. His note instructed her to say nothing about what he was doing. Instead, she was to arrange for her obligations to be tended to by other staff members. Those she asked would understand the gravity of their need. Sonder's foresight when he had requested her as his caretaker had long brought peace for them, proving invaluable.

Sonder remained locked in his room, and the only people permitted to enter were masked servants with only their eyes visible. Hopefully the seriousness of the situation would dawn on the boy.

Sonder had seen the practice throughout the city to some degree, but certainly while they traveled farther from the capital. The lower class did it to hide their alliances or to offer prayers in times of need. Plenty of people would be happy to put an end to the Black Knights, foremost among them Lord Vardulf—and Sir Elio.

In the castle, it had a different connotation. Only the queen's elite spies wore veils. Birds and Spiders alike protected their identities for the integrity of the filaments of their webs.

The second note had simply informed Merriweather that there was no update on the queen's decision.

By early evening, she and Sonder were still confined to his room, waiting just like him. Merrick gripped the wooden console as if he meant to wring the spilled liquor from years past out. Instead, growing tired of his own prison, he decided to go to them to alleviate his despair.

He arrived at the servants' door just before it closed. The latch kissed the frame as he caught it, so no one realized it hadn't shut.

Merrick listened through the crack, hidden behind the curtain to catch a glimpse of what he was walking into. He was afraid of not having answers.

"Thank the crown dinner is here. All your pacing was distracting me," Merriweather scolded.

"Sorry," Sonder sighed. "It has been a while since I've been confined to my room. I wish they would just make their decision already."

Merrick could tell by his voice that Sonder looked out the window. It was the first time the sun had mustered the energy to show its face in months. It would be a tragedy for him to have been kept inside all day. It always was, ever since he was a boy.

"Be glad you're confined here and not a cell," Merriweather retorted. "You also be careful what you ask for, you hear? The longer it takes, the more likely things will go in your favor."

Merrick's brow softened, the closest he could manage to a smile. He had scrawled those very words to her.

Sonder's voice still cast toward the window. "I know."

The masked servant made to leave.

Merrick carefully timed opening the door so none of them would know he'd been listening. He comprehended no magic, but he'd learned to trust his body. He knew the tingle in his fingertips as he held his breath and counted the beats of movement hidden from view. His timing was confirmed by the resistance in the handle.

The curtain parted, and he looked into a set of surprised eyes shadowed by a mask.

The meal was a simple, hearty stew. "Bring me a bowl, please," he asked the mysterious person.

The servant bowed and then slipped past him.

Sonder and Merriweather watched as he stepped into the tension and barred the door. He glanced at his reflection in the looking-glass.

Merrick was a disheveled mess. His beard was unkempt. His ordinarily neat bun hastily pulled back. There appeared to be new wrinkles on his face, and the shadows under his eyes gave them a sharp, crazed look. Finally, he looked away and closed the curtains, cutting off the warm glow from the setting sun.

"Has there been any trouble?" he asked, his voice breathy.

Merriweather laid her embroidery in her lap and turned her full attention to him. "No, sir, none at all. It's been quiet."

"Good. That is good news," he said. He pulled off his cloak, slung it over a chair, and then turned toward Sonder. "You are alright?"

A note of confusion bled into his answer, "Yes . . . sir. I'm alright."

Merrick nodded. "Good," he muttered to himself, over and over, casting his eyes around the room briefly. He wiped his hands on his trousers and took a deep breath. "Could you brew some tea, please, Melody?"

"Of course, sir." She stood up and readied the kettle hung over the fire.

As she did so, Merrick pulled the curtains back and looked outside. To hide his shaking, he ran his thumb incessantly over his knuckles.

"Is there any word, sir?" Merriweather asked, breaking the awkward silence.

Merrick raised his hand to silence her. "Once the tea is done." He took one look at them and realized he was unnerving them. "Both of you, sit, eat."

He was close enough to Sonder to place his hand on the boy's back and show him to the couch. He could feel Sonder's anger tense beneath his hand. The table was not nearly big enough to eat around, so they were forced to balance their bowls on their laps.

When the tea kettle began to sing, Merrick stood to get it. He pulled a small satchel from a breast pocket and dropped a silk tea bag into the water. Warm steam wafted up, and immediately, his shoulders melted down. He reminded himself to breathe.

A soft knock came at the servant's door. It parted just enough for Merrick to accept his tray with a curt thank you.

They ate in anxious silence, hunched over their bowls and leaning forward to retrieve slices of warm bread or the soft cheese from the low table.

Sonder's eyes continued to look between him and the caretaker. The three of them had never taken a meal together like this. Merrick hoped the reality of it made an impression. If only it were a fond moment and not a dark omen.

Merrick made another cup of tea after they had stacked their dishes, wiped clean with cheese-smeared bread to form a brothy treat. He sat for a while with his hands enveloping the cup, his dirty nails standing out against the pure porcelain. He felt their prying eyes boring into him. His mind drifted to the ritual of family dinners from all those years ago. He missed them.

Merriweather's patience cracked. "Oh, get on with it already. It's not going to go away. And knock off the worrying."

Merrick suddenly tasted blood and stopped chewing his cracked lips, tugging at his beard instead. "The queen still hasn't decided what she wants as retribution. It has become significantly more complicated. Mikhail's father is making demands, as is Elio, for the course of punishment." His lip curled slightly. "Wretched men, those two."

"Well, what is the usual punishment for two boys fighting?" Merriweather pressed.

"For a first offense? Five lashes and probation of sorts," Merrick said, gazing into his tea.

There was a soft sigh of relief. Sonder relaxed. Five lashes wasn't so bad; he had dealt with similar. Depending on who did them, it would be bearable. Merriweather seemed to relax similarly, giving the boy a slight glance over her cup.

"The issue is, they say he isn't a boy." Merrick fixed Sonder with a dark look. "And they're saying it's not your first offense."

Merriweather scoffed. "What do you mean, not a first offense?"

Merrick continued to hold Sonder's eye. The woman may as well have stopped existing now that the words were being spoken. "They're saying he has a history of insubordination, which I was hard-pressed to argue. The chief example is how you couldn't be found for Mikhail's ceremony. Worse still, they're saying it wasn't a simple fight. They claim he was aiming to kill Mikhail."

Sonder grew pale.

"How bad is the boy?" Merriweather butted again.

The mood briefly broke when Merrick rolled his eyes. "He's going to be fine. A concussion and a broken nose. His father is fishing for sympathy." He refocused on Sonder's grim face. "But you're lucky the guards responded as quickly as they did. Am I right?" Merrick took a sip of his tea when the boy remained silent. Then, with an air of nonchalance, he said, "They're saying he meant to harm the girl as well."

"That's a lie!" Sonder placed his hands on the couch as if about to stand up.

Merrick had anticipated Sonder's response, and his voice rose. "The men who responded saw you throw Rhianwyn to the ground when she tried to break you two up." His tone and look demanded that Sonder find his composure.

"I did, but I didn't mean to hurt her," Sonder stuttered. "I lost control."

Merriweather remained blessedly quiet, finally realizing this was a teaching moment.

Merrick softened and spoke normally. "Do you understand my agitation yet?" Sonder just nodded, and Merrick continued, "So, the claims are you tried to kill another man, aimed to hurt the intended royal healer, and you're a repeat offender." Merrick had to take a second to prepare himself to say the next part. He swallowed more tea. "They are pushing for execution."

Merriweather gasped, covering her mouth. Sonder's color drained further. Merrick had to hold himself together.

The words hung in the air before he pressed on. "Count yourself lucky, because the queen doesn't want that. She has spent resources on your training. They then suggested expulsion and slavery until you've repaid the crown's invested in you." He spoke slowly to ensure each word carried weight. "It would be a lifetime to repay it all. But the queen isn't satisfied by that solution, either. She doesn't want to be repaid for her benevolence. She has a specific vision for you, and she's unwilling to give up."

Yet.

Sonder ran his index finger over his thumb knuckle with a faraway look. "What does that mean?" He looked at Merrick, eyes wide.

Merrick sighed heavily. "If you mean what your punishment will be, I still don't know. The queen is deciding what it is she wants." Merrick leaned forward and rested his elbows on his knees. "These men would see you dead, and you could've killed a royal squire and Vardulf's last heir."

Sonder looked down, and Merrick looked at his own hands.

"I failed to teach you that we're all just here by the queen's grace." He finished the rest of the tea in one swallow, and his face screwed up. He felt resigned now that it was said. "You're to remain here until we receive word," he commanded. "There are some angry enough that you're best left out of sight until the queen has spoken. You're not to have any visitors. Especially not Rhianwyn. You're always watched, and we don't need to give them reason to push harder against us."

Sonder scoffed. "I don't think you'll have to worry about her coming."

Merrick stood up and put his hand on Sonder's shoulder. Now that their anger had cooled, it was a comforting gesture. Merrick wished he could say more to his young squire.

Merriweather sipped her tea, stone-faced. "When will we know?"

He looked at her, then back at Sonder. "Elio is pushing the punishment to be delivered after Mikhail is well enough. So that he can see the justice. It may be a few days still."

Sonder shook his head. "I wish they'd just get it over with."

"Be careful what you ask for," Merriweather hissed.

Merrick squeezed Sonder's shoulder hard. "One lesson you are about to learn is how the queen uses time against those who have displeased her. Part of your punishment will be the psychological strain of not knowing." Merrick's hand dropped, and he looked between them. "I should return to my study. There may be something I can do in the meantime that may yet help us. Wait for my word. And, please, by whatever gods remain in this world, stay out of trouble."

Sonder nodded grimly. He never showed any emotion that he could smell the alcohol on Merrick's breath.

Chapter Twenty-Seven
Punished

Two women in the market had their heads bent together, filtering through a selection of herbs placed in the sun to dry. The man running the stall ignored them. Instead, he chatted with a male patron about the last tournament winners.

"You'd think there would be more support for us women after what happened to the queen," the older woman ranted. "Husbands beating their wives and demanding we bear children. One look from that knight of hers to shut up any accusations that she asked for it. I wish we had our own Sir Elio!" The woman who spoke grew concerned and fingered her friend's bruised eye. "You don't deserve this."

The young woman smiled with watery eyes. "Thank you for buying the herbs for me."

"I'm long widowed by this war. No one will be any the wiser. Here, let's touch that up." She removed a pouch from her bag and patted some poorly matched makeup on the woman's eye.

Merrick and Drisil sat nearby, overhearing all of it. Drisil sat with her legs crossed, a slight smirk pulling at her painted lips. Her smoked eyes turned toward Merrick beside her. "Your anger hums so beautifully when you're feeling noble."

"It isn't noble. It's duty," Merrick growled. "Aspera may not care how women are treated, but I am her Justice. We've killed innocent people. Why not include some actual human filth on occasion?"

Drisil made a satisfied noise but said nothing. No one was going bat an eye if a wife-beater disappeared in the night.

Present, age seventeen

The entire castle buzzed. Somehow everyone knew before Rhianwyn's hair had dried. It should not have surprised her as it did. Talk of hers and Mikhail's relationship had proceeded since the Equinox Ball. But she had hoped the severity of the situation would have curtailed it. Instead, she felt like a carcass swarmed and picked apart by their whispers.

The imagery was fitting, since no matter how hard she scrubbed her skin, it still felt like it was crawling.

To make matters worse, when she reported for class the following afternoon, she overheard the head of medical staff talking to another student.

"Did you hear what happened? Mikhail is in the hospital. I hear he may not make it."

Gossip had always irked her, but she was too brittle to correct the woman. Instead, she held herself tighter.

When Rhianwyn stepped up to grab her supplies, the head of the hospital glanced at her and gasped. "What are you doing here? You must be shaken after something so violent happened." She turned her gaze back to the older student. "All because that Justice boy was jealous." She turned back to her. "I hear you're the one who stopped the fight. Truly awful!"

The woman misread everything about Rhianwyn's body language. She flinched away from the kindly pat, and her body began to shake. The look of misplaced sympathy was worst of all.

"Go and rest. Take as much time as you need. We'll manage," the woman said with a smile she didn't realize was condescending. "I hear Mikhail is doing well. You've done enough."

Rhianwyn instantly retreated to her room and built herself into a cocoon tucked behind her bed. Nobody came except the servants' shuffling in to leave trays of food. The curtains remained drawn. She curled up and slept. If she wasn't sleeping, she nibbled the bread on the trays like a mouse.

She had no idea how long it had been when there was a knock on her door. Rhianwyn ignored it. There was nobody she wanted to see.

The knock came again, and a muffled voice carried through the wood and iron. "Wyn? Are you in there?"

Rhianwyn wiped the tears from her cheeks. Her voice shook as she called back, "Come in."

Alessia slipped in, hardly opening the door. It was so dark she couldn't see. "Where are you?"

The blankets wrapped around her muffled her voice. "Over here."

Alessia cast about the room in the direction of the sound. She stubbed her toe on the unfamiliar furniture and caught herself on the bed. Her hands searched around the mattress before she realized it was empty.

"Where?" she asked again.

"Here," Rhianwyn said, letting the blankets fall away. The tears were starting to flow again, and even the single word was strained.

Alessia's face fell. "Oh, Wyn. I knew there was something wrong." She dropped to her knees in front of her.

"It's awful, Aless." Rhianwyn's voice cracked.

Alessia held her while she cried. She cried harder than she had yet, the weight of the loneliness crushing. When the tears began to slow, replaced by sniffles, Alessia held her at arm's length.

"Do you want to talk about it?"

Rhianwyn wiped her face with the heel of her hand, then wiped snot off her lips with her sleeve. "I don't know."

Alessia smiled warmly. "Then let's get you cleaned up, then something to eat, alright? After that, you can tell me if you want."

Rhianwyn nodded, and the other girl took over from there. A bath was brought, and the plates removed with dinner on its way.

Rhianwyn sat in the tub until the water grew cold. When she stepped out of the washroom, she saw that Alessia had laid out a simple blue dress made of cashmere. The fabric was soft and warm, and should have been cozy, but the way it clung to her body made her feel exposed.

Stepping out from behind the screen, she crossed her arms to hide her exposed shoulders. Alessia had tidied the room. The blankets and pillows were back on the bed. Her friend was picking up the dirty clothes on the floor when she came across the crumpled dress that was still damp, ripped, and torn. Her brow furrowed angrily, but when she saw Rhianwyn, she smiled tightly and set it aside in the hamper to be mended.

"I've always loved blue on you." Alessia beckoned her to sit. "I'll help you brush your hair. My mother brushes mine when I have bad days. It always helps."

Her friend gently worked the matted mess. It was a rhythmic motion. The comb was dipped in rose water and run through her hair, over and over. Finally, a food tray was delivered, but Alessia didn't push her to eat, and said nothing about how Rhianwyn continued holding herself.

It was as if each knot was tied to her tangled fear and grief. As each one was teased out, she felt the tension leave. The act allowed her to dissociate with her friend's safety tethering her.

Rhianwyn was so relaxed it meant nothing to her when Alessia set down the comb and rubbed aromatic oils between her hands to release the scent. It still meant nothing as Alessia gathered her hair to work the oils into her curls to make them soft. But when she heard Alessia gasp and touch the angry scabs on her exposed shoulders, she remembered trying to keep them hidden.

Rhianwyn flinched away and tugged in vain at the dress to hide the sores.

The response startled Alessia. "Rhianwyn, what happened?" The girl clasped her hand to her chest, dropping the comb.

Rhianwyn hugged herself. "Nothing."

Alessia saw Rhianwyn's hands. "Look, your hands are bloody too." She looked close to tears, but then her concern turned to anger. "Did Sonder do this to you?"

She shook her head. "No."

Alessia grew serious. "Mikhail," she said with shock. Rhianwyn began to excuse him, but Alessia took her hand and carefully squeezed it, a gesture that cut her off. "What happened?"

The story was halting at first. She had been suppressing the memory, which made the words hard to form. But it got easier as she described how Mikhail had come, wanting to celebrate, and how he had gotten angry when she had told him another time. Her lip quivered as she spoke, and Alessia was patient each moment she paused.

"He accused me of leading him on. Claimed I only wanted gifts. Said I didn't spend enough time with him."

Alessia scoffed. "You're always with him."

"I know. I told him how ridiculous that was. But he kept on. Then. . ." Rhianwyn tried to swallow the emotions weakening her voice. Her heart began to hammer again, and she felt sick. Hot tears fell down her cheeks. "Then I confronted him about things I was told he was saying. Then everything changed."

The shame of getting herself so caught up in her lies mingled with the terror and guilt again.

"He got furious. I tried to calm him down—told him no. But he came at me. Ripped my dress." Rhianwyn choked on the words. She covered her mouth and curled into herself. Speaking the words made it real again, but she couldn't finish.

"Did he . . ." Alessia gasped. Rhianwyn nodded, and her friend wiped the tears from her face. "My love, no." Alessia hugged her. "I can't believe he raped you."

"What?" Rhianwyn pulled away and wiped her eyes. "No, he just . . ."

Alessia looked at her firmly. "Honey," she whispered, and shook her head.

"It wasn't like that!" Rhianwyn snapped. She didn't know why she was protecting Mikhail as if she could still undo everything. "It was a misunderstanding."

Alessia sighed, but pushed a curl behind Rhianwyn's ear. "Okay," she whispered. They sat quietly, Alessia's thumbs whispering across Rhianwyn's knuckles.

"How did Sonder end up involved?" the girl finally asked to break the silence.

"I honestly don't know. He was missing all day. I guess he just happened to be walking by. Maybe? All I know is I hate to think about if he hadn't shown up. But I wish he hadn't."

"So, these are from Mikhail?" Alessia gently touched Rhianwyn's shoulders again. "And your hands?" She looked at the broken and raw nail beds.

Rhianwyn managed a laugh even though her voice was watery. "No. I tried to wash the smell of him off. I scrubbed until I bled. I couldn't wash the feeling of his hands off."

Alessia gathered her up again. "You know, my aunty helps women whose husbands force them to have more children, even if they don't want more. They usually hit them, too. They claim they love their wives. But that's not love, and it doesn't make it right." Her fingers combed through her hair soothingly.

Rhianwyn's shoulders shuddered with her tears, and Alessia repeatedly whispered that she was safe.

As her emotions became spent, Alessia said, "I hate that Sonder is being blamed while Mikhail is doted on."

Rhianwyn felt numb. "It's my fault."

Alessia shook her gently. "Don't you dare blame yourself for this."

"No, Sonder tried to warn me. I didn't listen. I just wanted to get back at him." Rhianwyn looked at her hands in her lap.

"To be fair, he did deserve it," Alessia said, trying to lighten the mood.

"But he doesn't deserve this. I tried talking to him and explaining myself to Merrick, but Merriweather turned me away. Said all of this was my fault." Her voice cracked. "That I'm nothing but trouble for him." It sounded truer than it ever had.

Alessia held her at arm's length. "No. Don't blame yourself. This happened because Mikhail thought he had a right to you. Disgusting pig. You have to tell someone what happened."

"They would never believe me. Not with the way I acted in public with him." She picked at her bruised nails. "If Sonder doesn't say anything, he must think I wanted it, which makes it so much worse. I'm so stupid." Rhianwyn looked up and blinked back another wave of tears.

"It's not stupid. Stop. You tried to move on with a proper courtship. That man turned out to be a bucket of night soil. The person you actually love treated you poorly, is the only witness, and is being punished for it. That makes it worse. Especially for you," Alessia said the last sentence with a look of understanding.

Rhianwyn smiled sadly. "Thanks for believing me, Aless."

Alessia's face showed utter disbelief. "What a silly thing to thank me for." Her face softened. "Let me finish with your hair." Rhianwyn settled back into the chair, and Alessia sectioned out the braid. "I know you said you tried to talk to Sonder, but I know things will turn out alright. I know him nearly as well as I know you, and if he hasn't said anything, he's most likely resigned to the punishment. Once it blows over, you'll see. But I don't want you dwelling on it. What Mikhail did to you was awful, but that's not your shame to bear. It's his. Men thinking they can just take what they want as they please." She huffed, tying off the braid. "Look, I know you want to hide, but I think coming to work will help. You've always coped with keeping busy."

Rhianwyn ran her hands over the neat plait. "I don't think I could manage to hear any more of the hearsay."

Alessia held up her hand to stop her and shook her head. "I'll tell the others that it's a sensitive topic. They all miss you. You're the best healer by far that we've got."

"It'll be a good day when I graduate and join the guild to start my own practice." Rhianwyn rolled her eyes with a bit of a smile. Then, steeling herself, she sighed. "Alright. If they say anything, though, I'm going to have to leave." She looked down at her hands. "I still feel like an absolute mess."

Alessia took Rhianwyn's hand in hers and squeezed it carefully. "The strongest, most beautiful mess I ever did know." The comment elicited a smile of gratitude from Rhianwyn. "Hopefully, they're investigating, and they'll ask you questions tomorrow. There's no way they won't, right?"

The thought terrified her. Rhianwyn didn't know what story she would tell. "I hope so," she whispered.

Alessia spent the rest of the afternoon with Rhianwyn, offering her a sliver of solitude. That night Rhianwyn blessedly slept so hard she didn't wake from the nightmares that plagued her.

The feeling of well-being went into the next day as the people around her heeded Alessia's warning. It annoyed her, but she accepted it, letting the work act as a balm for her heart. It quickly ended when a delirious patient grabbed her arm while her back was turned in the throes of his fever.

Instantly, Rhianwyn was thrust back to the attack. She pulled her arm away in a panic and crashed through the door into the bright sun. She fell to her knees and clutched her chest, gulping the cool air. Alessia rushed after and dropped to the damp ground in front of her.

The words she was saying made no sense, but eventually, Alessia coaxed her to sit. Then, the warm piece of fur between her fingers snapped Rhianwyn out of it. Her friend's face welcomed her back, where she was safe.

Rhianwyn's breath still came in deep gasps. "How did you do that?"

Alessia smiled. "My uncle has the Touch. I lack the talent, but he taught me a few things." She stroked her cheek. "Take the rest of the afternoon to help Master Wilkin in the garden. He doesn't care about gossip, and you can just wander around, and he'd still appreciate your help. I'll finish your work here."

Master Wilkin took one look at her and ordered her to make sure the plants were happy. Most of the plants were still dormant for winter. The older man mainly relied on intuition to assign tasks, and this one told her she was useless in the gentlest way.

A wave of gratitude washed over her. She knew of no other teacher so willing to accept the ups and downs of his pupils' lives, and she owed a lot of her skills to his unmatched teachings in herbology.

Both he and Alessia had known precisely what her heart had needed. She counted herself blessed, even in this situation, for having them.

The next day dawned cold and wet. The complaints of how the winter had been grueling had become a constant backdrop for the season. Spring was taking so long to come that people were beginning to worry if the crops would do well.

The gray weather was perfect for how Rhianwyn felt. She had been up late wondering about Sonder. The thought of speaking to Merrick for him had begun to take shape. She spent hours worrying about it, only for the nightmares to return.

People were giving her a wide berth. By the end of breakfast, she wondered if her expression had deterred them.

Alessia was a constant companion through the morning until they walked into the hospital to report for work. Immediately upon entering, the head healer gave her a task that sent her away. When Rhianwyn was given her assignment, everyone wore uneasy looks and fidgeted. No one talked to her or looked at her.

As she went about the small housekeeping tasks, she wrote the behavior off as their discomfort at what had happened the day before. They didn't know how to approach her without Alessia as a buffer.

A healer many years her senior nervously came up to her. "Excuse me? Wyn? Could you help me? My patient fell from his horse and splintered his arm."

"Sure," Rhianwyn said with a forced smile.

Injuries like these tripped many of the others up, yet for her, they were routine. Her typical annoyance was replaced by gratitude. It was nice to have real work to do and not feel coddled.

Rhianwyn was finishing the splint when Alessia burst through the door and startled everyone. Her friend nearly tripped as she rushed over.

"Wyn." She was out of breath and flushed from cold and exertion.

"What's happened?" Rhianwyn set the man's arm down and stood.

"It's Sonder." Alessia gasped and held her side. "They've decided his punishment." She sent a scathing look around at all the other healers watching them.

Rhianwyn blanched. "So soon?" It had only been a few days.

It dawned on her then why everyone had left her alone. They had known. No one had even asked her—there was no investigation.

Her anger grew. "What is it?"

"Twenty lashes."

Rhianwyn gathered her skirts and began to walk out. Her soul felt sharp as steel.

Alessia stepped aside. "Mikhail is there, alive and well," she said to her back.

Rhianwyn didn't heed the downpour as she hiked her skirts up further and ran headlong into the icy rain. She knew where to go, and it was too far. Even if it had been just outside the hospital, it was too far. She had no idea how long it had taken Alessia to get back to her.

She was too late to stop it.

As the mud grabbed at her boots, she had no idea what she would do. Her heart hammered in her chest as the throng of people came into view.

Every inch of her was soaked through. Nobles and servants alike complained as she shoved her way through their tight bodies. There wasn't time to be angry as they looked down and whispered her name, and began to make room for her.

A loud snap echoed through the quad, and she felt as though she would be sick. She cursed how many people had gathered to be nosy. She hated them fiercely. They only believed Sonder deserved this because the accuser was a Vardulf golden boy to them, and she a beloved lady reduced to a gilded pet.

These were not her people.

Another loud crack, and she felt her heart split like tender skin.

Finally, she pushed to the front. Breathlessly, she took everything in. Sonder knelt in the mud, and his exposed back wept. She cast around for any familiar face, and thanked Astraía that Merrick was close and the dais empty. She took off toward him with no regard for the people she clipped along the way, sending a silent prayer to the Star Mother that he would listen.

"Sir Merrick, what are you doing?" She stumbled on a foot and fell toward him, catching his hand to keep from falling.

"Rhianwyn?" Merrick's shock disappeared, and he turned his body to block her from the crowd around them. "What is the meaning of this?"

"Did he not tell you?" She felt frantic, but she had the mental capacity to keep her voice low. Another crack made her flinch and grab him tighter.

"Tell me what?" he asked.

Rhianwyn thought she could hear the same desperation she felt in his voice. "Mikhail attacked me. Sonder stopped him." She pled to Astraía with all her might for him to believe her.

"Is this true?" he asked, searching her face.

She nodded, then glanced quickly at the crowd around them.

Just as the masked man wielding the whip brought it up once more, Merrick raised his arm into the air. "Stop!"

Chaos rumbled. All eyes turned on them, questioning, which meant she couldn't stay hidden. Their scrutiny made her shame flare. Her own eyes darted at their gawking faces until she found Mikhail's angry glare. It took all her strength to meet his hatred with defiance.

Merrick made her look at him once more. "You are sure of this, Lady Rhianwyn?"

She didn't shrink away. "I swear it on my life." The memory of Sonder throwing her flashed through her mind, and she shivered.

She hadn't seen Merrick do anything, but suddenly Áki was on top of Mikhail with two other guards. The castle-dwellers grew louder, and Lord Vardulf materialized and converged on them as Mikhail was taken into custody.

The man shouted at them as he stalked across the yard. "What is the meaning of this? Why are you detaining my son?"

Sympathetic court members took up the protest.

Merrick leaned close to her ear. "Tend to him."

Rhianwyn rose to face the crowd, hauling her skirts up once more. Merrick fell in beside Áki, and she ran into the circle toward Sonder, in full view of everyone.

"Stop."

It became eerily still as the calm voice cut through the noise.

Rhianwyn's body froze on its own, held by magic, and she saw that Merrick had halted as well. She looked in the direction the sound had come from. A fear she had never known gripped her. She hadn't seen the queen mount the dais, but now she couldn't look away.

Nobody moved except, finally, for Merrick. All eyes were on him as he crossed to speak with Queen Aspera.

The cold air carried his voice, though he kept it low. "My lady, new information was brought I would discuss with you."

Sir Elio's armor rattled ominously as he shifted. It was a marvel that Merrick ignored him.

Aspera looked annoyed, but she stood up, causing the servant holding her parasol to adjust. Her long hair was hidden beneath a scarf topped by a crown. "I'll hear your case. Sir Elio, if you would see to finishing Sonder's punishment?" She lifted the hem of her deep red dress and began to return to the castle.

Rhianwyn sucked in a breath.

Merrick grabbed Aspera's arm. The crowd made a haunting sound.

"Sonder was protecting her!" His voice was angry and afraid, kept low, seemingly held together only by his will.

Elio's hand went to his sword, menacing.

The queen's voice dripped acid. "Remove your hand from me, Sir Merrick, or so help me."

He released her and stood taller. Rhianwyn was fixated by the tension in his neck and shoulders.

The queen addressed the crowd. "The punishment still stands." She turned her scorning back toward Merrick. "He violated the law. He is mine to command as I see fit. My will be done." Each word was articulate. She looked at Rhianwyn, and the heat of the queen's anger was a fire that consumed the warmth from her body. Aspera glanced at Áki, who still held Mikhail. "Bring him," she ordered. She inclined her head toward Elio. "My other ward may tend to Sonder after his punishment." She said it with an air of afterthought as she led the way toward the castle.

The silence of the onlookers was tangible.

Rhianwyn looked to Merrick once more, begging for a way to stop it. The look of hopelessness he gave her ran like poison.

Elio clattered past, and she remained held in place, removed from the crowd, on display to be gawked at.

The first five lashes were nothing compared to Elio's brutality for the final fifteen. The first lick of the whip caused Sonder to cry out so loudly he went hoarse. The second caused him to lose consciousness.

It felt perverse that she was grateful.

She counted them. *Eight*. Tears warmed her cheeks. *Nine*. She kept her eyes closed. *Ten*. She forgot how to go any higher. It went on forever. It wasn't until the rhythm stopped that she opened her eyes. The usual glee had been sucked out of the gathering. They stood silent.

Elio appeared in front of her. She jumped. He thrust the bloody flay into her hands, reeking of sulfur and iron, and she immediately dropped it and fell to the ground to throw up.

Chapter Twenty-Eight
Fall from Grace

"Gods help us all when she decides she has grown tired of us."
Condemned advisor, date unknown

Present, age seventeen

Queen Aspera flew through the doors before they had swung all the way open, her skirts hiked up. The irate clicks of her shoes echoed throughout the throne room. Then, mounting the dais, she tore the silk wimple from her head and whipped around to face the entourage of Merrick and the guards leading Mikhail. Her red dress blended with the giant slab of wood that hung behind her.

"What is the meaning of this, *sir*?" she asked.

Merrick dropped to a knee. "My lady, Sonder was wrongly accused." He stood and grabbed Mikhail, hauling him forward so hard the boy tripped and fell. "This boy was attacking Mistress Rhianwyn. Sonder stopped him."

Mikhail yelled at Merrick vehemently. "You're going to believe a traitor's whore?" Then, he turned to the queen. "Queen Aspera, it's not true. She's a sympathizer. She set me up."

Aspera lifted a hand, and the boy was silenced. Her eyes bored into Merrick. "How much are you willing to stake on the girl's claim?"

Merrick swallowed. The only indication he allowed to show of his mood was a tremble in his neck muscles. "My life."

Aspera folded her hands neatly in front of her and began to pace the dais. "It's an egregious act to attack my ward, Mikhail."

"You're going to believe him? He's as tarnished as all the rotting Black Knights!" His voice cracked, making him sound like a petulant child.

The queen faced Mikhail. "Do not presume to question what you do not understand. There is nothing you can say that could con me into believing you against my justice, trying as he might be." Her eyes flashed at Merrick briefly before she regarded Mikhail again. "It's a pity you were caught. Guards, take him away."

"No! It's a lie! She wanted it! My father will have something to say about this." Mikhail's yells echoed off the walls and into the rafters as he thrashed.

Merrick stood with his hands behind his back. Then, as the room grew quiet, he spoke. "What's to become of Mikhail?"

The queen had begun to pace again, and she looked at Merrick with a smirk, batting her eyelashes. "He is to be re-stationed and receive different training. It's a shame Elio lost out on a squire, but he will be useful elsewhere."

Merrick stood up taller. "Is that wise?"

Her anger reappeared. "Do not dare question me, Sir Merrick. What would be wise is for you to remember your place, for I see your station has clouded your mind. You've grown to believe you and I are familiar. We are not. I may take your life anyway." Her eyes regarded him head to toe with contempt. She hiked her skirts up again and descended the set of stairs. "I want Sonder ready to be knighted within the year. You also withheld the girl's prowess. She'll train with Randal when he returns. She is no longer under the direction of Gwenyvir, nor you. She is *my* healer." Aspera stopped beside him and spoke without looking at him. "And you will never openly defy me in public again. Do I make myself clear?"

Merrick licked his lips to moisten them, his mouth gone dry. "Your will be done."

"Good." She walked out of the throne room, taking her entourage with her.

The doors closed heavily, leaving him standing there, alone.

Merrick's trembling breath was loud in the stillness. The only other sound was the drumming of raindrops on the stained-glass windows high above. Nothing else moved. The carpets on the floor enraptured him, the floral designs offering him a way to keep his mind empty.

"You proud of yourself?" Áki asked.

Merrick nearly jumped. How had he forgotten the man was there?

"What?" he breathed. He looked at the redhead and saw his anger.

"You've chosen a side then, eh? This it?" Áki spoke through his teeth.

Merrick closed his eyes. "Not here." He opened them again, expecting to leave, but then he saw the glow of magic around Aki that kept their words hidden. His heart clenched. "You have the touch." Anger took hold then. "You better not've—"

"Fuck off with your pansy shit. We're talking about what I want for once. Here and now you're gonna tell me. Ain't no one going to hear, don't you worry. Is this the side you've chosen? Got cold feet cause some Lorist bitch knew your name? That's all it took?"

"This was bound to happen. There wasn't anything I could do."

"Bullshit," Áki spat. "You can't keep blaming her for all the shit things you do. All you had to do was listen. You're so quick to undermine her with peasants, yet somehow, with him, you can't even let him speak? Instead, you left him to the very men who want him dead. The men who framed his uncle. The ones who constantly push against the queen's vendetta to use him for her purpose. Threw him to the wolves who want to see the Black Knights gone!" Áki's voice gradually rose. "All you had to fucking do was let him speak!"

"It's not that easy!" Merrick's temper exploded in the face of Áki's. "What would you have me do?"

"Not think so low of him. You're so hell-bent on keeping him from having a heart. Go on, then!" Aki swung his arms. "Turn him into the man she wants. Fuck, you could've asked the girl. Yet, you're terrified of her because she's the only one of us who has seen you truly vulnerable. God forbid any of us know you."

"It's not like that." Merrick shook his head. His voice had come down, but his anger still boiled.

"I think it is," Áki sneered, taking a step closer and pointing his finger at Merrick's chest. "We've been telling you for years to pick a side. Can you really not see why? A man you claimed to love asked you to kill him because he thought this was worth it. Because he thought *Sonder* was worth it. You convinced us to listen to Bran."

Áki closed the distance more, his face beginning to match his hair while Merrick ground his teeth.

"You're the one who made us fall in love with the boy. We looked to you first! Yet when it came time for you to do something that mattered, you turned tail." Spittle flew from Áki's lips, and he swiped the air with his fists. "You claim to love the boy, yet you condemned him because of your own sick, twisted head." Áki ground his finger into Merrick's temple.

Both men were heaving.

"I look up to you! You were our leader, and you couldn't even let him speak!" He yelled into Merrick's face, the wires of muscles in his neck bulging.

Merrick launched himself at the larger man. But despite being a master of his center of gravity and knowing how to use leverage to his advantage, he was like a rag doll to Áki, who threw him off.

The other man had fought in the pits. Hand-to-hand combat was nothing for him, and once his blood got hot, it was like hitting a wall.

Merrick stumbled but regained his balance. He turned to see Áki stalking toward him with balled fists. Merrick's anger had helped burn off some of the alcohol that was making his head light. He was able to throw a decent punch that split Áki's cheek. But it wasn't enough to stagger him in his rage.

Merrick ducked a fist and landed a second shot to Áki's side before being lifted off the ground and thrown down, knocking the wind from his chest. For whatever reason, Merrick reached for his dagger.

The sole of Áki's boot pressed down on Merrick's hand, and he cried out as his grasp was wrenched between foot and stone and metal.

"The hell you grabbing that for?" Áki asked, leaning over.

When Merrick didn't respond, Áki lifted his foot, then kicked the blade away. Merrick cradled his hand and glared up at the man above him.

The room began to swim again, and the taste of his dry mouth reminded him that he was indeed drunk. But the pain from being thrown to the ground made him realize just how twisted it was.

"And you show up drunk to his fucking beatin'." Áki's eyes brimmed with hot, angry tears, and his lip trembled. "I'll tend to the boy for you like I always do. Come find me when you're sober."

Merrick just stared at the gloom bleeding through the windows. His bitterness still burned, but it had entirely turned in on himself. He was too ashamed to meet his friend's eyes.

Áki wiped the blood from his cheek and scoffed. His heavy footfalls and the rattle of his armor receded. The shuddering crack of the door slamming made Merrick wince, and it broke open the floodgates inside.

Gasping sobs shook his body, and he hid his face as he cried on the floor, their blood and sweat staining the carpet.

Chapter Twenty-Nine
To Mend

Teul, seventeen years ago

Grace's face grew stern, and Merrick was again reminded of her strength of will. "The way you thank me is to do right by that boy. Now, I'll have you know I'm loyal to the queen, but do right by him for our countrymen. I'll say it again, but folk ought to do what any good citizen should do, and our values run deeper than loyalties. The only thing we've got is each other, and that'll do more against the darkness that plagues this land than that sword on your hip will."

Present, age seventeen

Once Elio walked away with the rest of the guards, Alessia pushed through the crowd's edge. A warm oil skin fell around Rhianwyn's shoulders, and Alessia encouraged her to stand up. "Come on, Wyn. We need to get him to the hospital."

The words meant nothing. Everything was spinning, and she heaved again.

The crowd parted as Áki reappeared. Alessia groaned and uttered a curse as she left her side to help him cut Sonder free. Sonder may as well have weighed nothing the way the man threw him over his shoulder. His face matched his hair, and his breath formed hot billows around him.

Alessia reappeared and slung Rhianwyn's arm over her shoulders. "Come on, Wyn. Sonder needs you." Her knees sank into the mud as she struggled to stand.

Tran appeared then. "I've got you." His soft voice counted, and together, her friends got her to her feet.

Áki's gray eyes blazed as he shouted at the people in their way.

They tried to make a path, but they piled up as they stumbled on the gawkers behind them. Rhianwyn's vision spun with their judgmental leering as Áki was forced to shoulder through.

They were taking her to the auxiliary hospital where she had been attacked. It would give them privacy, which was so desperately needed, but Rhianwyn tried to pull away. The sickening sounds of fists pulverizing bone and the feeling of being trapped made her pull back.

"Please, no."

Áki kicked the door open so hard it bounced back, and he had to shield Sonder from getting hit.

"Get out," he barked at the two girls inside.

They stood up so fast that their chairs fell away from beneath them. The room was too small to run. They remained frozen until one grew brave enough to bolt past Áki's hulking form. The second whimpered and followed. Both girls covered their heads as they ducked into the rain and ran past them.

"Help him, Tran. I've got her."

Tran nodded grimly, then jogged inside.

Alessia turned Rhianwyn to face her. "You've got to breathe. No one will hurt you here."

Rhianwyn screwed her eyes shut to get her head to clear. Tran and Áki's whispers were loud in her ears. It grated her that she couldn't gather her wits.

She opened her eyes. "Let me see him." She gripped Alessia's arm for balance.

Rhianwyn stumbled as they passed the threshold. Sonder looked awful. His skin was pale and clammy, and his breathing was shallow. Worst of all, he seemed fragile. Her eyes assessed every inch of him. Áki had wrapped him in a gray cloak dyed with giant poppies. However, as Rhianwyn watched, the poppies kept changing shape.

Finally, the realization dawned on her it was his blood. Seeing him so injured made her body flush, and her vision narrowed to a point. She collapsed through Alessia's grasping hands. Everything in her stomach had already been emptied, so all she could do was dry heave.

"Uncle, do something," Alessia begged, pulling Rhianwyn's braid to the side.

The wood creaked under Áki's boots. Strong hands gripped her and pulled her to her feet. Her heart rate spiked, and she panicked anew. She looked up and saw the big man's face looming over her.

"Steady, Rhianwyn. Breathe. You're safe." He spoke softly, ending each sentence with an intentional breath.

Warmth spread from his hands. At his encouragement, she took a deep breath, letting it go when he released his. They took several more together until the room stilled.

"There you are. Steady, yeah?" A soft smile broke the tension on his face. "He needs you. From what I hear, you're the best, right?" With each word, more of her tension left her.

Her breathing evened. "Right," she said, nodding nervously.

"There you go. You've not experienced the queen's magic before, have you?" She shook her head, another sharp movement. "Go have your look. I'll stand guard. No one will disturb you."

It was frightening to need a guard, but she was glad for it.

"I'll stay, too," Tran said. His eyes were red.

"No." Áki's sternness returned.

"I want to stay!" The boy's fists balled. "I want to help," he said, less assured.

"You want to help, Cathak?" Áki waited until Tran nodded. "Go find the other boys who are sympathetic to Sonder. I know he's got friends. Tell them to say nothing if people come askin' about him."

Tran paled. "Why?"

Rhianwyn knew she should be tending to Sonder, but she and Alessia stood watching silently, her friend's hand comforting on her back.

"Mikhail has been banished. His father's men will try and incite a challenge, just as they did following the Betrayal."

Alessia gasped. "They'll not kill boys, will they?"

"They won't kill anyone. Aspera doesn't want another pile of bodies so soon after killing half the army because they liked Sonder's da. But that's not to say these men won't take note of who is sympathetic to the son for future use." Áki looked back at Tran. "Do you understand?"

Tran nodded.

"Reassure Sonder's friends. That's what he needs most from you."

"Yes, sir," Tran said. He jogged out into the rain.

"I'm no knight!" Áki hollered at Tran before he eyed Rhianwyn. "You're safe." He looked at Sonder. "Fix him."

The tenderness on his face made her want to reach out to him. Instead, she watched him step outside and take up his vigil in the pouring rain.

They were alone. Rhianwyn looked at Alessia. Her emotions threatened to overwhelm her again. "Stay with me?" she asked softly.

"Of course," her friend said with a sad smile.

They held hands at Sonder's bedside. Alessia squeezed her hand tightly to stay her before Rhianwyn could pull back the cloak.

"You should know, Wyn, it's challenging to see."

Rhianwyn prepared herself for what would come next. When she was ready, she began to roll the fabric back carefully. Every time it tugged, she winced as if it were her own skin. She knew Áki had done it to protect Sonder from the rain, but she cursed him all the same.

The first angry wound became visible. She choked, but she continued with the painstaking task. Tears spilled when it finally came away. She covered her mouth, and his blood smeared her cheeks.

She couldn't do this. "Gods," she gasped.

Alessia took her hands once more. "Wyn, I know what you do is magic."

Would the fear not end?

Alessia pressed on, "I know you're afraid. But you can do this. I'm not as good of a stitch, but I'll do it. All you have to do is stabilize him in the meantime. Once I'm done, you can use your magic while you apply the poultice. Let me carry some of the burdens."

Rhianwyn nodded once, then again with more affirmation. Alessia set to work, and Rhianwyn sat on the floor and held Sonder's hand, pouring herself into him.

It was difficult at first. As her henaild brushed his, it was like a wall of pain. It took all her resilience not to get ripped to shreds by it. It was one thing to touch a stranger's pain, because it wasn't her own. With Sonder, she felt it all. It lived inside of her even without binding herself to him. The two met in a violent storm. She had to take small measures. But as time went on, she felt his heart grow steady and his breathing ease.

Hours later, Alessia gathered up the bloodstained rags while Rhianwyn laid the last of the bandages. She gazed down at him. They were all utterly spent. There was no stopping the scarring, but at least they'd heal cleanly. Alessia stepped up beside her and laced their fingers together.

"How did you know?" Rhianwyn asked.

Alessia rested her head against her shoulder. "You know that uncle I told you about? The one with the touch? You met him today." Her smile was tired.

"Who? Áki?" Rhianwyn was shocked. The words had passed her by in the earlier chaos.

"The very one. He's not really an uncle. He was good friends with my actual uncle. The one married to my aunty who helps the women in town. It's an honorary term, but he might as well be." Rhianwyn's heartbeat quickened, but she let her friend finish. "I don't have a knack for it, but everything I know he taught me. That's why I knew about you. You pour yourself into people the same way he does."

Rhianwyn crossed her arms. "I don't know if I'd call it magic, so much as just a desire to help people."

"It's alright, Wyn. Your secret is safe with me. Do we really know how magic works, anyway? Fickle thing that it is. You're constantly studying, and there're countless ways to do the same thing. Maybe you *are* just book smart," she said. Both of them knew how ridiculous that was. "Whatever you call it, there's no doubt that he was in the best possible hands, and he's going to benefit from the level of care you gave him." She pointed with her chin at Sonder.

Rhianwyn smiled tightly, then looked back down at Sonder's peaceful face. While the compliment was well received, there was a dark foreboding. Maeveen had told her to keep her talents under wraps, but it was something she sensed, too. Now, being the leading healer had a more sinister feel, and she wondered if it had all been a test to find out her mastery of magic. The years of working and studying had made her complacent. She felt like a fool thinking she had been so clever.

Looking at Sonder, however, she wouldn't take back an ounce of the energy she had imbued into him. If this act confirmed her secret, it was worth it. She owed it to him for bearing the brunt of their combined mistakes. But then, something else dawned on her, and it took her a moment to find the bravery to speak it. "You're gredwyr," she whispered so softly she barely heard it.

"Your secrets are safe, Wyn."

Heavy footsteps creaked behind them. Both of them looked over their shoulders to see Áki crossing the room.

"How is he?" he asked solemnly.

Rhianwyn tried to smile. She looked at Sonder again. "He'll be okay."

A thick arm wrapped around her, and she was crushed against his body. "You did well, little one." He kissed the top of her head. She curled into him and heard the anger reverberate through his chest. "I've not seen war magic in a long time, the bastard." He wiped tears from his eyes.

Alessia suddenly yawned loudly, breaking her reverie. "I need to go to sleep. You should, too. That was too much."

"I'm going to stay with him," Rhianwyn said without looking away from Sonder's face. She loved her friend dearly, but she had never confided how precarious hers and Sonder's situation was, and she feared what would happen if either of them left the protective bubble. She envied him his innocence.

"I thought so. I love you," she said, hugging her tightly.

"I'll walk you home, lass." Áki knelt in front of Rhianwyn and met her eye. "My relief is here, but you can trust him." He squeezed her arms. "You'll be alright?"

She nodded.

"Alright," he said. He stood up once more and patted her shoulder. "Watch over him."

Alessia hugged her again. "Make sure you get some rest, alright?"

Rhianwyn wrapped her arms around her friend and held on. "I will."

It was a lie. She was far too restless.

Rhianwyn walked with them to the door. Áki introduced the other guard, whose name she immediately forgot. She trusted him because Áki did, but there wasn't an inkling of guilt as she bolted the door behind her.

She took to tidying. Once everything was in its place, she grabbed a book and sat on the floor beside Sonder's bed. It was a struggle to settle down. But the soft whisk of the turning pages and rasp of her fingers tracing words eventually lulled her. The warmth of the blanket and glowing stove chased the last traces of cold from her bones. She almost felt content.

The words on the page entranced her, so she didn't notice the change in Sonder's breathing. But then the covers rustled. His eyes moved behind his eyelids. She was gripped with worry, and pressed her hand to his forehead. His eyes fluttered open when she touched his cheek, and she felt her heart flip.

It took a moment for him to get oriented. She would never forget how his hazel eyes cleared and filled with gratitude at that moment. Wonder and adoration softened his face.

"Rhianwyn?" His voice sounded like the breeze through a broken window, catching on jagged edges.

"It's me." Tears pricked her eyes.

He reached for her clumsily. Fear gripped her as his fingers brushed her neck. She pulled away. His face played through confusion and hurt. "Wyn?"

Her nerves were frayed from her emotions and exhaustion. All she could do was let out a harsh laugh. "Sorry." The way she patted his hand was like a swat. "How are you feeling?"

He looked disappointed, but he didn't press. "Thirsty," he croaked.

"I have soup. It'll help settle your stomach." She stood eagerly—anything to avoid the awkwardness between them.

Rhianwyn had prepared a light broth with crushed herbs. She added wood to the stove and set the water to boil. The tea leaves floating on its surface would help with his pain.

She returned to his bedside. In an air of caution, she focused only on the dip of the spoon into the broth and then tilting it to his chapped lips. Acting as a caretaker meant she had an excuse not to address everything that needed to be said.

Dip, tilt, repeat kept her safe.

The kettle whistled.

"Excuse me." She sounded terse and formal, even to herself.

The tea was her concoction. It still needed perfecting, but it had been successful already. She turned her back while grinding a mixture of roots and birch bark into a milky paste. Honey to cut the bitterness, and poppy to help him sleep. She was putting the finishing touches on it when she heard the bed creak and Sonder's sharp breath and groan. She looked and saw that he was trying to sit up.

"No! Don't!" The spoon clattered to the floor as she rushed over to him.

He looked at her hopelessly. "I need to relieve myself."

"I can bring a pan," she offered.

His hopelessness fled, and he gritted his teeth. "Don't bedrid me."

"Let me help you, then."

It hurt her when he let out a cry as his stitches pulled. But he pushed through it with her encouragement. Then, once he sat, he waved her off.

There was no rush.

When he was ready, his sweaty fingers retook her hand. It was slow going to the pan in the corner. The sound of him relieving himself made her blush and look away. She had helped people like this hundreds of times, but this was personal.

By the time they made it back to his bed, Sonder was taking ragged breaths. He squeezed her hand so tightly his whole body trembled, and he made it half-way to sitting before his strength failed and he fell back. His face twisted, and he held her hand through the spasms.

"Queen's wrath, this is embarrassing," he panted.

"Don't be embarrassed," she cooed. "You're not the first person." She didn't know what else to say as he continued to settle. Finally, she had to break the silence when he didn't say anything. "Do you want to lie down? I want to check your stitches to make sure nothing tore."

He was still sucking in breaths. "Can I sit?"

"Of course. I can look this way." She extricated her hand from his and flexed it with relief.

Everything about the way she was treating him felt strange. She didn't push the sweaty hair off his forehead. Her fingers were stiff and clumsy as she gently pressed the bandages she knew would be prone to bleeding. There was no stream of conversation to help distract him. So it startled her when he said something she couldn't hear.

"Did you say something?"

He cleared his throat, which sounded painful. "I'm sorry," he said again, practically yelling to get his voice above a whisper.

She swallowed and smoothed his bandages. "I've already told you it's okay. This is my job."

"No. I'm sorry for all of this," he moaned. He reached for a small cup she had forgotten beside his bed.

"Wait!" She grabbed his hand and wrapped hers around it, holding it to her chest. "That's medicine. If you take too much at once, it'll make you sick. Let me help you," she begged.

Sonder stared at her, then relented with a nod. She dropped his hand and brought the cup to his lips.

He sipped enough to wet his throat. He held her in his gaze, but she refused to look at him.

She was deflecting, and it was clear that he knew it. When she lowered the cup, he took it from her hands, careful not to touch her, and set it back down on the table.

"I'm sorry, Wyn." His eyes didn't leave her face.

"I already told you, you don't—"

"Had I been a better friend, none of this would have happened."

He went straight to the root. There were no spoons, medicine, or bandages to distract her.

Rhianwyn finally met his eyes. The tears she had been keeping at bay pressed against the dam she had built. But she remained silent, transfixed by what he would decide to say next.

"I was a miserable ass. You told me not to make decisions about our friendship for you, and I did. You deserve better."

Despite herself, she let out a little laugh. "You know that's not for you to decide, right?"

A smile turned up the corners of his mouth. Then he grimaced. "Can I lie down now?"

"Of course," she said.

Together they maneuvered his limbs. When they had finally managed it, he flopped his head down on the pillow. This time, she pushed his dark hair away from his face, and Sonder smiled gratefully. The silence was less uncomfortable as he rested his vocal cords. She sat back down on the floor, and her face was nearly level with his.

"You don't hate me, do you?" he asked, sounding unsure.

"Why would I hate you?" She was only letting him speak through a hole in the wall around her heart.

"For losing my temper." Sonder licked his lips. He didn't seem to hear her dismissal. "Those scratches on your shoulder. . . they aren't from me, are they?"

She exhaled a little "oh" as she covered a shoulder. "No, you didn't. These are nothing."

He closed his eyes and made an odd gurgling noise as he tried to clear his throat. "Good," he sighed. A shiver ran through his body.

"You should rest," she said, reaching up and pulling the covers over him sloppily. He didn't say anything, so she touched his forehead again to check for a fever.

Rhianwyn felt his cheek. His hand wiggled out from under his hip, and he grabbed hers deliriously. Her stomach churned. His eyes opened, and when he saw her face, he let it go again.

"Don't worry about me. Are you okay?" There was an odd clip to the way he said it.

She arched her eyebrow at the absurdity of him asking. "You aren't really in a position to be worrying about me." The sharp look on his face cut away her attempts at playfulness. "I'm a little tired, but I'm okay."

"No, how are you really?" His voice was beginning to fail.

She realized what he was getting at, and the dam breached. Then, in a last-ditch effort to keep herself from crying, she said, "It's nothing."

"No, Wyn. You keep looking at me like a monster, but I can tell you're not seeing me."

The tears began. "Nothing happened." Why was she still protecting Mikhail?

"Wyn, I saw him raping you."

"No, you stopped him." Her voice quivered.

"I don't care if you hate me because I beat your lover or happened to be there, and I don't care if it was just in time. It still happened."

"Why didn't you tell anyone?" Her voice broke. The relief that he knew the truth was overwhelming.

"Merrick wouldn't listen. And then I thought maybe I had been wrong because I was so angry, I couldn't remember. So, I just accepted it." He looked at her. "Then you came and stopped it, and I knew." He cleared his throat again. "I don't regret it for a second. I'd endure it all again. I would have killed him if not for you. I still would if it meant you were safe." His voice was so weak now, but it didn't diminish the ferocity he spoke with. "I will if you let me."

"Then what? We'd have to run away." She hugged her knees to her chest. "I was so scared."

Rhianwyn broke down, and silently, he opened his arm. Every touch felt like a threat to her, but when she searched his face for any malice, all she saw was tenderness. She crawled to him and tucked into his embrace, awkward as it was with him lying on his stomach. He pulled her into his armpit, and she hugged his arm and cried. It was the balm her heart needed, and in the safety of their friendship he let her.

"I'm sorry I didn't believe you about his character," she said after her tears had run their course.

He must have started to fall asleep. "I didn't deserve to be believed," his voice rasped close to her ear, and she shivered.

"He managed to isolate me from everyone, even Alessia." She hugged his arm tighter. "I wanted to talk to you when you came to me, but he was always there. Always arguing. He especially hated that you and I were friends."

"Wyn, it's not your fault."

She turned her head so that she could see his face. "Would you let me hold on to some of the blame?"

His face softened.

It hurt her neck to look at him, so she rested her face against his arm again. "I only got on with him to get back at you. I was so angry, and I knew you two didn't get along. It started so lovely." She paused, and her voice darkened. "And then it wasn't. I feel so stupid."

There was a gravelly rasp deep in his chest, and she thought he was coughing until she realized it was a laugh. He pulled her into him and kissed her temple. His lips were warm and dry, and her heart fluttered. It was just a kiss, but it was everything she wanted, wrapped in a papery brush against her skin.

He spoke into her hair. "Fine, keep your blame." He loosened his grip. "I hope you let it go soon, though, because it's not your fault," he repeated, "and you shouldn't be ashamed. But you should know, I have been thoroughly chastised."

She tried to bite back her smile, but she failed, and she let out a dark laugh. "I guess you have been." She grew serious again. "I missed you."

"I hate what I did to you," he sighed. He pressed his head against hers.

"Why did you?" she whispered.

He told her everything. About how he had seen them in the attendant and his lover but killed them anyway. About how the pair's love had ultimately been their downfall. He hadn't confided in her much about the actuality of his training, but he did now. How he endured the endless scolding from Merrick, hammering at how anything outside of his duties was a liability. The constant nightmares plaguing him, where she stared back at him because he had failed her. Every detail seemed to pain him, yet he didn't cry.

Already, so much of him had been hardened.

"All I saw was red when you put yourself between him and me. When I realized I'd hurt you, I wanted to die. I guess that was part of why I said nothing. I wanted to be punished. Physical pain is easier to deal with than the internal agony. Then Merrick said they—" He stopped, and Rhianwyn looked at him curiously. "Merrick reminded me that I'm a killer's son. I'm a killer, and I was afraid you'd hate me."

The irony that she was a healer and he was a killer didn't escape her.

His last sentence repeated over and over in her head.

She found the right words to express herself. "Sonder, I've always known you were to become a knight. Being a knight means you're going to kill people. But I also know you're kind." The next part was hard to say, but she did it anyway. "I also understand why you hesitate to tell me things and why you can't be in a courtship."

"So you don't hate me or think me a monster?" Talking hurt him.

"Sonder, you're my best friend." She let her head fall against his shoulder. "I asked you to be my friend. You don't have to do this alone. Just don't ever cut me off like that, okay? I don't know if I could forgive you again."

His arm shifted, and he held her tighter. "I won't. I'll write, and be there for you, and let you be there for me." He buried his face in her hair. "I missed you, Wyn. More than I can ever say."

She couldn't help but smile, even though her heart hurt. She tucked her chin into the nook his arm formed around her neck. Her knuckles tickled her cheeks as she clung to him. She wanted so badly to let her lips brush his arm. But she let it be enough that he was there. He almost hadn't been. "How are you feeling?"

"It hurts, but I'll live." She could hear him struggle to swallow. "Do you mind if I don't talk for a while?"

"Not at all. Here," Rhianwyn said as she pushed away, "let me go get some medicine." She realized she had forgotten the tea. No doubt it had gone cold.

Sonder pulled her back against him. When she turned to look, he only shook his head. His eyes were closed. Rhianwyn exhaled a little laugh through her nose, then settled back against him. It was the first time since Mikhail attacked her that she felt unburdened. She felt safe and warm against him. She let herself enjoy it.

"I'm glad we talked," he whispered. His voice was heavy with exhaustion.

"Me too." The candles had gone out, and the curtains were drawn, so she couldn't tell what time it was.

"We should use codes." The randomness of the statement and his breathing told her he was nearly asleep.

"We can figure that out," Rhianwyn giggled.

"Merrick gave me the idea," he continued.

She let her thoughts wander while she listened to his breathing. Then, before he drifted off, she finally asked, "Will you hold me tonight?"

"If you don't mind if I fall asleep," Sonder mumbled.

She loved the way he sounded as slumber took him. She stayed there, half awake, letting herself appreciate the moment for a while. After a time, she slipped out of his grasp and curled up on the floor beside the bed. Eventually, someone would barge in on them, and this way would be less damning. Instead, it would look like she fell asleep tending to her vigil.

As she dozed off, she knew the protective bubble they enjoyed was gone. Merrick no long held sway over them—the queen wanted her debts paid. She watched these thoughts from afar, and they weren't crippling to observe. They didn't keep her awake, which was a blessing because she needed the rest, and she slept beside Sonder at last.

Epilogue
Stay

One year later

Rhianwyn walked into the northern forest with a blue jay perched on her finger. Tucked against the bird's chest was a rolled-up piece of parchment. When she felt far enough away from the city, she stopped and listened to the woods. She waited until the bugs started whirring again, and the birds singing. Reassured that no one had followed her, she planted a kiss on the bird's head and sent it off into the canopy.

Dearest Mae, Despite your begging, I have decided to stay. I have faith in our Black Knight, and I cannot leave him alone to the queen's cruelty. My talents are best used here, where I may act as an anchor point until we know how to stop her. Our gredwyr is strong. I will not abandon them. Astraía's blessing.

Acknowledgments

Wow. Here we are, at the end.

Words cannot describe how gratifying it is to be here, with you. I'm awestruck by the realization that this has come. I'm an author at the end of my own book.

It's tough to know what to say now that I'm here. I could go into why I wrote this book. But, just like you'll find in this series as it goes on, there's no way you can pack a lifetime into a condensed paragraph, or afterward. So, if you're here, know I'm glad you are, and I cannot wait to meet you in each subsequent afterward.

The real reason I want to write this, however, is to say thank you. Yep! I am a published author now, and darnit, I love reading the people responsible for bringing a project together, so I am going to indulge!

First, I want to thank my son. It was while I was pregnant with him that this idea came back to life. This book is dedicated to him. He was a beginning, just like this is the beginning of many threads of my life. I nearly named him Sonder, but gave him the dedication instead. At the time of writing this, he was three and a half, and the joy of watching him grow translated into the story. Young Sonder's was him. Without you, son, I wouldn't have known how to temper all that darkness with tenderness. So, thank you my sweet Dilly Bug. I did this for you, and because of you. I hope when you're old enough to read this you don't think it's garbage. Love you to the moon and back. "It's a nice day because the sun is out." No, it's a nice day because YOU are here.

Next, I want to thank my very dear friend Savanna Uland. She is also a writer and author, and her writing voice is gorgeous and fresh. Our coming together is fraught with pain, yet she opened her arms to me at my very lowest and has been a shining light ever since. It was because of her I even formed a five-year plan. Not only was she the external force that drove me to this point, but she was instrumental in making this story happen. She took it, read it, and marked it up so many ways that the world building part of it became fun. It's because of her keen eye and kind heart that this story is something I am proud of. She cared enough to demand it be better. Plus, she endured countless messages back and forth of me gushing about my love affair with each detail. So, Savanna, my soul sister, thank you so much for being a shining light in my life. Let's meet in the comment bar again.

She currently has two short stories available: **Monster in Her Garden** and **Mr. S's House Guest**.

Next on the list is Charles Allen! Also a writer, an author, a parent, and a got-dang Treasure Lad. He mentioned me in his own book, for goodness sakes! Sir, you were one of the first to hop on the band wagon of my social media, and by golly, you became a genuine friend. You've listened to me complain, celebrated with me, and made me laugh so hard. This talented man also laid hands on this piece as a beta reader. Between him and Savanna, this book ought to basically have their names as collaborators. Not really, but damn close. He similarly ripped it to shreds, because he knew what it meant to me to put out an amazing product. But the kindness and care he put into it was an honor. His talent, wisdom, and insight, are an *honour*. Thank you, thank you, thank you.

Please, look up his work. **Blood and Biscuits** and **Martini's at Midnight**. His story is a far better than mine.

I'd be remiss if I didn't also mention my longtime friend and one time classmate Daniel. Sir, you were the very first to reach out and offer to read the garbage pile in its infancy. I have no idea if you've ever read it straight through, but boy, do I hope you gave this revision (version epsilon, maybe?) a shot and enjoyed it. This man asked hard questions about the characters. Scoffed at their weak back stories. I'd even wager he helped me come up with some of the names. I won't go so far as to say he built the world, but he certainly gave me the bones to hang flesh on. His kindness and enthusiasm gave me the confidence to push on. I had never shared my work before. I'm so glad he was willing, even if it ended up on a Did Not Finish list. Plus, he's the one who told me my writing was like a mountain of Parmesan on spaghetti. He basically retaught me how to write. Thank you, from the very bottom of my heart, Chin. Cheers.

Next, Dylan, my fantastic editor. You saved the day taking on this project. More important than your guidance (and letting me argue about idioms and the spelling of towards), was how quickly you turned this thing around. Honestly, you're a machine, and never once did I feel like my momentum was tripped up. Your professionalism, attentiveness, and creative eye were invaluable.

Last, but not least, Stephanie. You're a beautiful human. You don't even like fantasy that much, and you hyped me. You're a wonderful friend, mother, wife, sister, and daughter, and I am so thankful to have had you along for my life's journey. The best Pegasus to do this life with. Sorry I stress you out so much, and always miss your birthday. Thanks for being proud of me.

Now for the quick bits.

Thank you to my fellow author friends:

Ian Conrey (**Haelend's Ballad**) who also had hands in early reading. Sorry you got that version friend; I hope you enjoy this one!

R.K. Brainerd (**Jagged Emerald City**), an advance reader, and just a beautiful human whose insights inspire me. She is absolutely an author to keep an eye on.

C. D. McKenna (**The Vorelian Saga** and more). Thank you for asking me when I felt like an author. That's probably my favorite question. Plus, you lifted me up when I fell so hard, and shared your talent and research with me. Again, so lucky to have connected with you. May the wind fill both our sails.

Danielle Paquette-Harvey (**The Prophecy** and many others). Girl, you're in everyone's corner rooting for them! You're so wonderful, thank you!

Rebeka Porter (**Adopted Saga** and others) another author, another gorgeous soul. The talent she puts into her books is amazing.

There's so many of you, honestly, from Twitter, TikTok, and Wattpad I've connected with. If any of you are reading this: Thank you. Seriously. I know what it takes to manage life on top of writing, and here you are reading this. I'm terrible at names. I not only misspelled many of my own character's, I also got their names switched, double used them, and even spelled my title wrong. I only remember my birthday a week out, for goodness sakes! So, truly, thank you so much for your support, even if I haven't named you.

Honorable mentions from personal life:

Victoria. You read the earliest iterations. How? Thank you. I've always admired you, and you liked it. I'm so honored. I hope you liked this version so much more. Your belief and support kept me going to make it. Here's to you.

Patrick. Another person who helped me world build. He's busy. I have no idea if he'll read this. But that guy is a champ. Also an old classmate who knows Daniel. So cool.

James Allen King. I only slap his whole name in here because he is an incredibly talented artist! Check him out. Get you a James. Just probably not him; I can't imagine he'd like being solicited. Again, you're a gem. Thanks for your support, and letting me keep Aki's name as is. I hope I did him justice.

Olivia. Your creativity gives me heart. Thank you for pouring so much of yourself into your art community. Seriously, Beaumont is better because of you, and this story began anew in your neighborhood.

Ciana. Your kindness to everyone is beautiful. Plus you're funny, and let me send you memes. Dilly and I love you guys. If you're reading this, thank you! A kick ass wife and mom, busy taking care of everyone, and you read this. Even if you didn't, your support meant something. I'm making them read your name.

Devin. You possess a brain I admire. Thanks for suffering me nerding out for many years now. I'll make it up to you by asking about off-roading soon. Let you have a turn!

Aditi and Dylan. Not because you're one person, but because I'd basically say the same, and this typing stuff is exhausting. Thank you. Your openness to the world, and more specifically, the Better Dylan and I, is the best. Also, cheers Aditi, for being one of the two original surviving playable characters from our campaign. I absolutely butchered yours, Dylan, and I'm not sorry. Merrick was by far better. Love you both loads!

All of my coworkers who were stuck in the middle of the ocean and had no choice but to listen to me. Real MVP's. I also daydreamed a lot. Sorry. Hope you enjoyed reading what I craft while I'm working. Promise I'm not crazy! None of these characters are remotely based on a single one of you. That's another book ;)

There's obviously so many more. But, I'm a wordy girl, so I'll stop myself here.

But, as many authors before me have said, the biggest thank you is to you, The Reader. We mean it. I know it sounds silly, but we do. We take these pretty shiny things from our heads, we craft them, then share them with you. And you read them. If you're reading this, that means you enjoyed it at least enough to get here. This story means so much to me, and you read it.

Thank you.

Fair winds and following seas.

About the Author

Michelle Piper was born and raised in Denver, Colorado, but has called all three coasts home. She still moonlights as a Merchant Marine, or as she fondly calls herself, a real-life bilge rat, though she finds herself crawling around the duct work of Denver International Airport most days. You can follow her yearly eclectic creative hyper-fixations and travels with her growing son on social media.

The best way to support her writing love journey is to consider leaving a review on Amazon and Goodreads.

https://linktr.ee/MichelleAshleigh

https://www.writerpiper.com

www.ingramcontent.com/pod-product-compliance
Lightning Source LLC
Chambersburg PA
CBHW020238010826
48973CB00006B/1558